THE LOST END OF NOWHERE:

THE COMPLETE TALES OF

KINGI BWANA, VOLUME I

THE LOST END OF NOWHERE:
THE COMPLETE TALES OF
KINGI BWANA
VOLUME 1

GORDON MacCREAGH

INTRODUCTION BY
SAI SHANKAR

ALTUS PRESS • 2014

TABLE OF CONTENTS

GORDON MacCREAGH was born on 8 August, 1886 in Perth, Clay County, Indiana. He was the son of Scottish parents; his father was a naturalist and historian who had come to America to study the American Indians. Gordon did his initial schooling in Perth and was sent to his grandfather in Scotland, who was a deacon. He attended school at Aldenham and Glenalmond, and went to study at Heidelberg University.

While at the university, in 1905, he got into a sabre duel with a German student, which he won. Believing the German to have died, he fled to India. (Later he learned that the German student had survived.)

He had been in correspondence with a man in Calcutta who offered him a job at a salary of 200 rupees per month. He took the job, but was not paid and left at the end of a month. Another more romantic version of the story has it that one day he woke up to find that the barge was deserted except for seven dead crew members, who had died of the bubonic plague. He jumped over the side and got in touch with his firm, who advised him to go back to the barge and await fumigation. As this was a virtual death sentence, he left Calcutta. Either way, he landed in Darjeeling, where he got a job on a tea plantation as a coolie overseer.

He started collecting Himalayan butterflies and insects for a museum collector. This led to his collecting bigger animals as well, and he went into this business, selling animals to Jamrach's Menagerie and Hagenbeck's Circus. He claimed to have covered India, hunting leopards and tigers. Given the road conditions then prevailing, he drove his car from Bombay to Calcutta over the rail route, straddling the rails. He had a removable grille across the back of the front seat, and covered many miles with a tiger in the back seat. He also collected animals in the Malay islands and Borneo. His specialty was big snakes and orang-utans.

He got restless and decided to go to Africa, still doing the same job. He collected more animals than the circus could buy, and spent all his money taking care of the animals. Broke again, he went back to India, this time to work for British Intelligence, then part of the Post Office. He held this job for five years. It was here that he first started writing. His first effort was a play, with Indian actors as princes and princesses. It had local success, and was seen by a New York producer, Mike Leavitt, who encouraged him to bring the show to New York. It opened on the Amsterdam theater in New York, but was shut down by the authorities on the grounds of offending public morality with excessive nudity.

MacCreagh was stranded in New York. He was a roommate of Captain A.E. Dingle, who was also trying to break into the fiction business at this time. At this time, he joined a music band as a bagpiper, to make some money. He was successful breaking into the fiction market, making his first sale to *Adventure,* the short story "The Brass Idol" in 1913. By 1914, he was selling his fiction to a variety of markets from newspapers to magazines.

He did serve in World War I. His autobiographical sketch in *Argosy* mentions the Navy, but is contradicted by his entry in *Who's Who* that talks about his joining the Air Force.

Two years after the war, MacCreagh, who by then had gained a reputation as an Oriental scholar, joined the Mulford Expedition on a trip to the Amazon. The expedition was led by Dr.

Henry H. Rusby, dean of pharmacy at Columbia University, and was trying to find new medicines for tropical diseases and collect specimens, among other goals. The expedition was poorly planned, and within a short time most of the members were bickering among themselves.

In 1922, MacCreagh was the last member of the expedition to return. All other members had returned earlier due to sickness and other reasons. He wrote a hilarious travel book, *White Waters and Black,* about his experiences on this expedition. This book is a classic of Amazon exploration.

The most interesting experience on this expedition was his participation in the Caapi ritual dance. The Caapi dance is a ritual dance to frighten devils away, and as part of this, the Indians consume a certain drug, caapi, which is the juice of a boiled vine. MacCreagh had no intention of joining in the dance, but he took a drink of caapi, and then proceeded to dance for a day before the effect of the drug wore off.

Returning to New York, he met Helen Komlosy, who was herself a traveler and expert rifle shot. They married sometime in June, 1923.

In 1927, the MacCreaghs set off on a trip to Abyssinia to find the lost Ark of the Covenant. This trip was funded by *Adventure Magazine,* in which periodic articles about the expedition appeared. Other aims of the trip included capturing specimens of the local fauna (lions included) and track down the Falashas, a legendary lost African tribe of Jewish descent.

The MacCreaghs were travelling in Abyssinia in 1927 and for the most part of 1928, encountering a herd of man-eating hippopotami on the way. They met the Emperor, Haile Selassie, and Gordon MacCreagh was created a Knight of the Golden Star of Ethiopia.

He published his experiences in his book, *The Last of Free Africa,* which was a bestseller and ran into multiple editions and printings. The book was highly critical of the attempts by the European powers to colonize Abyssinia, which was the last remaining free country in Africa.

The MacCreaghs returned to New York, and went back to Abyssinia for a return trip. They followed this up with return trips in the 1930s, going deeper into Africa. Gordon must have been busy going around on the lecture circuit, because he wasn't writing much at this time. On one of their trips, they came back via Japan, and from there to Seattle. From Seattle, they drove across the States in a used car, covering the tourist spots.

In 1933, he won a Chevrolet for his essay on why he liked his new Chevrolet. He related an anecdote of his Abyssinian trip on this occasion. A crazy Arab driver, just graduated from camels, smacked into a native and killed him. The Abyssinian law hanged him in public as a warning to other drivers. "And a damn good law it is too," he concluded.

When World War II came around, he went to work for Douglas Aircraft, and was sent to Africa as a translator and interpreter for the American and British armies there. On one of his flights, he was shot down. Luckily, he escaped with just one bullet wound.

After the war, the MacCreaghs lived in St. Petersburg, Florida, where they were local celebrities. He gave talks and lectures on his travels, and she hosted parties where she talked with the local women about her travels.

He died on August 30, 1953, of abdominal cancer. Helen passed away in 1962.

THE SLAVE RUNNER

"THE NEWS is that Kingi *Bwana* is dead."

The speaker burst into the Williams Hotel in Nairobi and exploded his news like a bomb, and with all the wide spreading and diversified effects of which a bomb is capable.

The Williams is the hangout in Nairobi during the off season of all the *safari* conductors of East Africa. Sun browned, heat withered old-timers, whose reminiscences are of the good old days before licenses, when ivory was lucrative spoil of any man who had cold steel nerve and a vast double barreled rifle that fired about ten grains of black powder and a bullet weighing a quarter of a pound.

Younger men in their forties, equally sun scorched and wiry, who helped the old-timers swear at the effete modernism that imposed a license upon each individual *bok* and *beeste* and allowed but a paltry couple or so of each per season. A few youngsters as brown, though not as yet so hard drawn, who envied the older ones their experience and dreamed still the dream that all of them had known of finding, perhaps, by some stroke of improbable fortune, some hidden stretch of new ground where the best heads had not been picked over by past *safaris*.

Men of many ages and many nationalities; but every one of them marked with the indelible stamp that distinguishes all their kind—the narrow eyes with the deep corner puckers that

reflect long days of gazing
into shimmery distances,
dancing yellow *veld* and
blue haze under the sun.

And all in the same
business. A business which
they called—strictly among
themselves—lamb herding.
Which meant that, since
East Africa had become a
fashionable picnic ground
for wealthy sportsmen
from Europe and America,
these hard bitten Africanders put their experience to
the practical purpose of
conducting these tender-
feet out on *safari,* and
showing them how to
shoot.

Among the gathering in
the hotel when the bomb
fell were a few officials of the colonial government, whose duties
took them into the outlying borders, and who therefore found
something in common with these men of the wide *veld.*

The bomb's diversified effect was not apparent till after the
first shock.

"Kingi *Bwana* dead? How? Where? Who's got the news?"

"Couple of his boys are in. A lion got him, they say, up along
the Abyssinian border."

"A lion at last! Good gosh! Well, he always took the most
awful chances."

Klein, a small wiry man, who was known throughout East
Africa to have killed some hundred and fifty lions or so—he

didn't know exactly how many, he had lost count—shook his head and announced in his querulous voice:

"I'll have to see those boys an' get an awful lot more evidence before I can swallow all o' that. Kingi *Bwana* got by a lion? That don't hold water."

"And he didn't take chances, either," another grizzled hunter put in. "You're wrong there, Jacobs. He gave the impression he took chances 'cause he'd smoke a pipe an' hold his fire till his game was right on top of him. But that was 'cause he knew jest 'bout exactly what his beast was goin' to do. Why, Kingi *Bwana* knows how a lion *thinks*."

"And he can shoot, boys, and don't let anybody forget it. Could shoot, perhaps I should say, if this yarn is anyway true.

Let's hope it's all just another of those nigger rumors. What are these two boys? Kavirondo? They'll surely have it balled up."

The other side of the bomb's effect came from Sanford, a deputy district commissioner, who seemed to harbor a grievance.

"Well, all I can say is—" he laid down the law thickly—"if this fellow King is dead, it's a very good thing for the border district, and for a lot of other poor devils besides."

Immediate indignation was loudly in evidence; but the loudest voice was Klein's, and Sanford's official standing was no check to the tough little hunter's anger.

"You shut right up, Mr. District Commissioner Sanford. I know what you're driving at, an' I say you've got no proof."

Sanford flushed. He was a big man and powerful, though running a little bit to flesh. His heavy eyebrows meeting above a strong nose denoted temper and wilfulness; and the dignity of his position sat heavily upon him. He might have resented Klein's peremptoriness more definitely; but he had been looking upon more whisky pegs than he could very well carry. So he contented himself with words.

"I know I have no proof. He's always been too bally sly. If I had had evidence on the half of my convictions he'd have been doing his time on the Breakwater two years ago. But nothing will ever persuade me that he's anything but a damned Yankee slave runner; and if he weren't dead, as I sincerely trust for the sake of his wretched cargoes, he is, I'd catch him red handed at it sooner or later."

A laugh came from the corner.

"You're a damned liar, Sanford," drawled the voice behind the laugh. "And if you weren't, you'd never catch Kingi *Bwana* at anything."

"Who says I'm a liar?"

The commissioner pushed himself not oversteadily to his feet, while the veins in his temples swelled purple against the flushed red of his face—with the effort, as much as with his

Jove-like anger—and he made as though to plunge at the insulting corner.

"We all do!" came an immediate chorus of a dozen voices.

The black eyebrows scowled their rage about the room. But hesitantly. Where, in the face of such universal opposition, could one begin?

"Well, I can't thrash twenty of you," the outnumbered man muttered, and slowly sank to his seat again.

The drawling voice from the corner took up the tale again.

"There's an example of the official mind. Somebody runs slaves along the Abyssinian border. He's too smart to be caught. King is the only white man operating around there. King's a smart man; moreover, he goes his own way and gets things done without either official help or permission, which is blasphemy and *lèse-majesté*. Therefore King's the culprit."

There was a general laugh. The lazy-voice had neatly hit off just about what most of these free men of the *veld* thought about most of those whose duty it was to impose official restrictions upon them. Sanford, fuzzy headed as he was, saw that sentiment was overwhelmingly against him. He heaved himself up and strode with heavy, unsteady dignity from the room, leaving only the Parthian shot:

"Some of you smart gentlemen will perhaps remember our little conversation when next you come before me for overshooting your licenses. Come along, Peterson; let's get out of this den of know-it-alls."

A youngster whose fresh English complexion denoted his newness to the country got up and followed him, and a voice followed them both—

"You'll have to have evidence of half your convictions, old man; don't forget that."

Various murmurs of approbation, of belated indignation, and calls for pegs swelled in the room. Above them Klein's nervous voice—

"And now I've got to get hold o' those two Kavirondo boys

and see how much truth I can beat out of them about poor old Kingi *Bwana*.

DEPUTY COMMISSIONER SANFORD and young Peterson were *en route* across the trackless *veld*. As a matter of fact, Sanford had come down to Nairobi to meet Peterson and to take him up and install him in his job, which was the rather ghastly one of British consul at Moyale, on the Abyssinian border, where the caravan trail came through to Kenya Colony. Peterson's predecessor had died of dysentery with the appalling suddenness of Africa, and Sanford, between gasps for breath and grunts as the Ford car bounded from hollow to grass clump where the road was no more than a general direction, was laying down the law of conduct.

"There are just two rules, young man; and they are absolute, without exception. Never step outside of your door without your solar topee on your head. That one is easy. The other one sounds easy, but it isn't. Always boil everything you drink. It isn't easy because you've got to see to it yourself. Leave it to your house boys just once, and they'll dip you up the nearest filth to save themselves trouble and will all swear themselves blind dumb that it boiled for half an hour.

"That's what happened to young Smith. He got careless. You watch those two rules and you'll pull through all right. Your job won't trouble you much. It's a loaf up there, really. All you've got to do is to hold up the caravans, which are few nowadays, and collect customs on them. Not more than a day's work in the week; and you'll get some of the best shooting that's left in Africa."

Peterson was immediately interested. Sport, of course, appealed to him much more than work. He fell to asking innumerable questions about hunting and about the beasts he might meet and about their ways. And Sanford supplied him with the usual miscellany of fact and misinformation with which colonial officials are so copiously supplied.

Sanford was doing all of his necessary talking now, in spite of the discomfort of the jolting car, because presently they would come to where deep gullies intersected the plain and the car would have to be abandoned for *safari*. *Safari* meant foot slogging over Africa; for the *tsetse* fly pest killed off all horses, and even mules, in three days. And on *safari* the bulky assistant commissioner needed all his breath for the deadly business of putting one foot before the other.

There was one important matter to be settled before that trial arrived. More important even than sport. Peterson introduced it.

"What about this slave business?"

Sanford's thick brows came together in immediate anger and weariness. The slave business was the particular cross that he had to bear, and he swore at the very mention of it.

"That's my blasted *shauri*. You don't have to worry much about that; except, of course, to help me with any information that you may get hold of. Though, at that, it'll trouble you enough. But your job is simple. It is British law that as soon as a slave sets foot on British territory he is a free man. You'll be having slaves skip across the border to escape from bestial treatment; and then a host of Abyssinian officials will come yelping to bluff you into giving them back what they call their property. They're the most insolent people on earth—nigger men boss in their own country. They think they're as good, or better, than a white man, and they'll shout and stamp and scream in front of you with no more respect than if you were a *shenzi;* and they'll try to bulldoze you into giving up their runaways. Your job is to tell them all to get to hell out of British territory unless they have passports—which they never have—and give up nothing; not even a dog or a stray cow."

Sanford was voicing no more than the universal opinion of every border official in Kenya Colony; and, while there was a good deal of truth in what he said, his statement was not free from official inaccuracy. He went on to furnish further misstatement according to the best of his light.

"My end of it will hardly affect you as far west as Moyale. The game farther east is to raid the runaway slaves and run them out of the country for sale elsewhere."

So startling a statement sounded like the horrors of fifty years ago. Slaves were bad enough; but traffic, organized business, in slaves, was incredible. Where could one buy or sell slaves in this modern day of grace? Peterson required enlightenment. Sanford supplied it with weary disgust; and this time his information was true.

"This is how it happens. Slaves escape across the border all the time. There exists one or two gangs of raiders, Arabs mostly, who round them up; either bluff them, lie to them, pretend they are British officials sent to protect them—the slaves are animal fools, anyhow—or they just recapture them by plain force. Then they jockey them along the border line. If we get after them, they skip into Abyssinia. If some Abyssinian chief thinks he'd like to grab up a good collection of slaves for himself, they slip over to our side. So they jockey them along eastward and finally run them across the corner of Italian Somaliland to the coast from where they ship them in native *dhows* to southern Arabia. And if anybody tells you you can't sell slaves in Hadramaut today, you can just have a good laugh at him. The Sultan of Es Shehr will snap them up as fast as you can deliver them, and the Sultan of Chishin will outbid him."

Young Peterson gasped at the recital.

"But, good Lord, that's frightful, don't you know! That sort of thing ought to be jolly well stopped."

Sanford grunted with grim disgust.

"That's my *shauri* to stop it. If the damned Abyssinian officials would cooperate we could do something. But they're useless. We have treaties with their central government about mutual help; but these border gorillas are too far away to care. Each little monkey chief is a law unto himself, and our complaints get nowhere."

"But—but hang it all then, sir, can't the Italians stop them going through their end of Somaliland?"

Sanford barked a harsh laugh.

"Pah! The Italians! *Imprimis*, they don't care. *Secundo*, it would cost a lot of money and men to keep up a constant patrol of their desert. And finally, if a patrol did attempt to interfere with a slave runner, it would get a good licking and the cargo would go through anyhow. We know perfectly well where they get through. Just north of Illigh there's a maze of little rivers and creeks called Baia del Negro, where, as its very name implies, they've shipped slaves through for hundreds of years. If we had that territory we'd stop the business in a week. But those damned dagos either don't care, or they're afraid to tackle the slave gangs, who are a pretty hard and cunning and desperate crew, let me assure you; and I know because I've dealt with them for two years."

Sanford was that type of stanch Englishman to whom every foreigner was a person inherently inferior by the automatic reason of his alien birth. Such a person might, if he conformed with religious strictness to the conventions of the Sanfords and their ilk, be accepted upon terms of gracious familiarity. But if he did not so conform, he was to be anathema, utterly without the pale, and was to be mentioned only with a properly qualifying epithet. Sanford's favorite epithet which adequately, to his mind, expressed the noxious foreigner, was "damned."

"That's pretty dashed thick," was all that Peterson could say.

Sanford continued with gusto. It was seldom that he got a chance to air his pet grievance.

"The worst of them and the best organized is a scoundrelly Arab-Italian halfbreed called Matteo bin Ibrahim. He is—he was—in partnership with this damned Yankee, this King fellow, and they were as cunning as they were conscienceless. But I'll trip him up now, by Jove; King was the brains of the combination."

"Was, you say, sir? Is that true about the lion then? And he seemed to have a lot of defenders of his character."

The stanch defense of the hunters in the Williams Hotel had evidently had its effect upon young Peterson. But the older man grunted forth his creed; and it was, without doubt, based upon his personal experience; though just whose was the fault for such experience it would not be quite easy to say. Pompous officialdom clashing with independent spirits might have explained much. However, Deputy Commissioner Sanford's opinion was his opinion; and, as such, he was ineradicably convinced it was right; and he voiced it accordingly.

"Hm! Those fellows will always side with anybody against a government official; and you may as well remember that in your future dealings with them. And the lion story is true, thank heaven. I had those boys brought before me and questioned them. It's a providential deliverance for the whole district; and I feel that now I shall be able to break up this horrible traffic."

All of which, as the drawling voice of the Williams Hotel would have said, was typical vaporings of the official mind; and of all officials, typically Sanfordian.

YOUNG PETERSON was out for sport. Intently and eagerly out. For two reasons. One was that a native had come in and reported a pair of roan antelope in the neighborhood, and had sworn that he could lead the consul *bwana* directly to them.

Roan antelope was a prize extraordinary; one for which many rich sportsmen would make a *safari* especially to get. One of the curious habits of this splendid beast is that it appears in a district suddenly from nowhere, and then disappears as suddenly without trace into nowhere. So no time was to be lost.

Another reason was that Peterson's servant had announced enigmatically—

"One *bwana* coming from Abesha side."

"Huh! A white man from Abyssinia?" This was unusual.

Native caravans came through; but white men at this farthest extremity of Abyssinia were as few and far between as roan antelope.

"From where do you know this news, M'boko?"

"One *shenzi* tells. One *bwana m'kubwa* comes; he got plenty men, plenty tent, plenty gun; he got even horse. One *bwana Amlikani*. Two days' time he get here."

Peterson had already given up trying to find out how the natives got their news. He had spent fruitless hours in questioning, just as had hundreds of other white men, who had also given up and accepted the thing as a mystery which they named "bush telegraph," the surpassing mystery of which was its so often astounding accuracy.

An *Amlikani*—an American—Peterson could believe. Any crazy thing was to be expected from them. One had come through last year. Peterson had heard a great deal about that one. An enormous fellow, traveling for some museum or other; loud mouthed and braggart, who tried to convey the impression that he alone, on account of his size and vast experience in organization and expedition equipment, could make such a trip. The hunters in Nairobi still laughed over his pretensions. The more so since an indigent family of Czecho-Slovakians, including a woman and a child, had made the same trek from Abyssinia to Nairobi with nothing more than they carried on their own backs. Yes, anything was to be expected of Americans. But a horse—and in that *tsetse* infested country? The old futile question shot from Peterson's lips—

"How do you know?"

The servant retired behind his mask of African obtuseness.

"One *shenzi* tells. Two days' time he gets here. You wait see."

Peterson had heard too many stories about bush telegraph to disregard this information in its entirety. Another American might well be collecting for another museum. Museums in America were insatiable, he knew, and were positively choked with money for expeditions into Africa. Roan antelope would be an achievement for such a museum to hurrah about. So

Peterson silently consigned all bally Americans to perdition—
he was young enough to follow in Sanford's school of scorn for
foreigners—and he girded himself swiftly to go out and get
those roan antelope for himself.

Of course, they were not where the little Kavirondo had said
they were. That is one of the peculiarities of roan. A long day
was spent in vain tramping over a burning *veld*, trudging up to
the tops of the low rolling hills and blinking at the far heat haze
through the field glasses, wondering fretfully whether the game
might not be lying down in the long grass just round the shoulder of the next hump of ground.

Impalla were to be picked out here and there in the open
plain, of course. *Impalla* are always to be seen sporting and
leaping in the middle of no shelter, relying, apparently, upon
their knowledge of their phenomenal speed to save themselves
from prowling enemies.

A few stray *kongoni,* too, in the shade of distant flat topped
acacias; and in the far distance, what might be zebra.

BUT PETERSON was not after any such common
stuff. Those he could go out and get any day. He wanted roan
antelope and nothing but roan; and he knew that an ill advised
shot at something else might startle the very beasts he wanted
out of the nearest clump of tall grass; and then they would run
for miles. So Peterson tramped over the *veld* for the whole of
a scorching day and got nothing.

But hope springs eternal in the hunter's breast, perhaps more
so than in that of any other human. The next day Peterson was
out betimes again, and in a sweat of excitement, for the little
Kavirondo pointed at shapeless blurs in patches of sand and
said that they were the tracks of the coveted roan. His M'boko,
unaccustomed to the job of gun bearer, added to his master's
fever by pointing in the general direction of north and announc-
ing stolidly—

"*Amlikani bwana safari* come that side."

Peterson was too busy to ask the useless question of how he

knew. The little Kavirondo was giving vent to ape-like duckings and smacking of the lips. He was spreading his squat nostrils to the warm wind and rolling his eyes. All of which denoted a simian excitement at the nearness of game.

Many white men have wondered how some native hunters can detect the nearness of game where nothing is in sight. The little monkey Kavirondos scratch themselves vaguely when questioned and say they can feel it in their skin; and they often add—

"The same way a lion feels it."

Many white hunters with plenty of experience behind them maintain that the whole performance is hokum designed to impress the foolish *bwana* in the hope of getting a bigger *back-sheesh* out of him; that one will come upon game sooner or later anyhow. Many other white hunters, with longer years of experience, just look away into the distance and say they don't know; it's damn' queer.

At all events Peterson's Kavirondo led him off in a new direction and began to scramble through a country dotted with low mimosa scrub and outflung clumps of rocks, and intersected by narrow, deep little gullies. Good lion country, had Peterson experience enough to know it.

After some two hours of this frightfully tiresome going the Kavirondo suddenly flattened himself into the grass at the crest of a rise and beckoned with nervous fingers behind him. M'boko quickly pulled his master down to his knees and made him understand that caution was necessary.

The Kavirondo was pointing a skinny, copper bangled arm across the empty nowhere. Peterson, of course, could see nothing. But following the pointed direction through his field glasses, he presently discerned, marvelously blended with the heat shimmering yellow grass, a pair of magnificent reddish brown beasts with long curving horns. They were too far away to distinguish, even through the glasses, the black and white face markings which would identify them as roan antelope; but he "felt it in his skin" that the little hunter's excitement was not over any lesser game; and the excitement immediately transferred itself to him. Accordingly he acted with less judgment than even his inexperience excused.

It was a long stalk. Not altogether difficult, on account of the excellent cover afforded by the gullies and mimosa brush; yet formidable enough for a novice. Young Peterson felt that he would have difficulty enough in hiding himself alone, without the added encumbrance of two tagging along behind. He ordered them, therefore, to stay where they were, and he set off with infinite, and as yet unnecessary, caution alone.

Had his boy, M'boko, been a trained gun bearer, he would have remonstrated. A gun bearer knows that he has but one duty on earth; and that is to stick closer than glue to his master's heels. To advance when he advances; to stop when he stops; to lie prone when he lies prone; and to run away when—and only when—his master runs. There are gun bearers, few and rare, who have been known to observe that last rule. Their usual procedure is to be well and safely up a tree when the second gun is required at the urgency of life and death.

A gun bearer, moreover, would have told young Peterson that it was the sign of a very foolish novice to go off alone, with all faculties intent upon stalking game, in a lion country. But M'boko was a house boy. What did he know about such things?

As for the Kavirondo, he immediately curled himself up in the grass like a dog to snatch some moments of instant sleep. What business was it of his to question the will of white *bwanas* who went hunting? They were strange, inexplicable people, were *bwanas*, who would talk meaningless words which they thought to exist in the Swahili language, and who would thereupon fly into exasperated rages and would beat natives for no reason. The white men were the lords of the earth. It was always better to let them do exactly as they pleased. So the Kavirondo curled up in the grass and chattered contentedly at M'boko.

PETERSON CRAWLED off alone. He had tra-

versed with infinite caution an open stretch and had climbed
in and out of the welcome shelter of a gully; he had made a
hundred yards, when he heard an insistent chattering behind
him coming from where he had left the servants. In an immediate frenzy at the brute idiocy of natives, he turned to curse
the fools, although they crouched yards, hundreds of yards, too
far away for the beasts to hear. And at the same instant a sudden
tightening of the breath caught at his chest as the belated
thought came that the men were trying to attract his attention
to some danger. But it was not the kind of danger that he had,
for a moment, half feared. Both men were pointing excitedly
beyond him and away to his half left. He looked, and his heart
fell to the very soles of his veld boots.

Coming over the distant ridge was a long line of black figures
with bundles on their heads.

Peterson diverted his curse to the crawling line. The thing
was true then. This must be the *safari* of this pestilential American. Why in hell must the thing come just in this direction out
of all Africa? And exactly at this moment, too? Why couldn't
it come tomorrow, or yesterday, or just half an hour later? And
why must it be just this bally American who would be keen,
with all the energy of his race, to get roan antelope above all
other things?

Thus did Peterson curse the unwelcome interlopers and his
own luck, too. Then he began to see that the *safari* would pass
to his left anyhow, in the direction of Moyale; and with a muttered "Thank God for that," he set himself once more to his
long stalk.

But it was his fate that day that annoyances should interfere
with his sport. He had made another three or four hundred
cautious yards, when a distant shouting began to impinge upon
his consciousness. In a blaze of impotent fury he turned his
head to see a khaki shirted figure, still some four hundred yards
away, racing toward him, mounted upon a miraculous horse,
waving his arms like a maniac and shouting as though there

were no game within a hundred miles. Something or other, clearly, the fellow was trying to bring to his urgent attention.

Peterson cursed him in silent rage for a fool as well as a poor sportsman. Some idiot idea the man must have to deter him from his game till he could come up and get in on the stalk. Well, he'd be eternally damned if he'd allow that. With gritted teeth he set himself to cover just a few more yards of bush to where he could get a clear, though long shot, before the other should arrive on the scene.

Then the maniac began shooting. Peterson through a red haze of fury saw that the lunatic was using a pistol—and at four hundred yards.

"Rotten, blasted Yankee sportsmanship!" raged Peterson.

And murderous thoughts of turning his rifle upon the maniac coursed through his mind as he saw his precious roan antelope throw up their heads, jump high once as a spent bullet patted somewhere near them, and then race off, skimming the grass like brown thistledown. In desperation he essayed a futile shot; missed, of course, and turned in black fury to shake his fist at the careering madman.

The idiot was screaming at him and pointing at something. Somewhere back of Peterson. He was near enough now for snatches of words to arrive on the wind.

"Look out!" they sounded like. And, "In the long grass!"

Once more Peterson's heart skipped a beat. The urgency of the maniac's actions seemed to imply—was it possible that something— The dormant sense of danger that stays with every man in the lone African bush leaped to startled life. Peterson concentrated on the long yellow grass forty yards behind him as much as his thumping pulse would let him. It seemed to him almost that it moved. But it was impossible that anything should be there. He had crawled through that very patch just a few seconds ago.

The thundering of hoofs was in his ears; and above them the urgent voice again;

"Look out! He's going to charge! Hold your ground and take it easy!"

Then Peterson was sure of movement in the grass. Something that swished from side to side. Something like a yellow rope frayed out to a tuft, or tassel, at the end. And then just in front of the swishing thing a face took form in the yellow grass. A yellow face, huge and menacing; yellow eyes fixed with frightful intent upon his own, and with a great fringe of yellow hair that trailed raggedly off and blended with the grass.

THAT WAS when Peterson should have shot. That was his perfect chance. But he stood and did nothing. He was not exactly afraid. His mind registered the perfectly clear fact that he was face to face with a lion for the first time in his life; which would be quite as clearly the last time if he did not immediately shoot, and that, with cool accuracy. Yet his limbs refused to respond to his mental impulses. He did nothing. He just stood.

The phenomenon is common enough. Every Maine guide knows it as buck fever. They have all seen novices, brought face to face with a harmless deer, just paralyzed into inaction by their own excitement.

And just so did Peterson stand, motionless.

He was aware of a great gray horse, almost upon him; frantic with fear and utterly unmanageable, as are all horses when they scent a lion. He was acutely conscious of a khaki clad figure that slipped from off the horse with a great pistol in its hand; as it slipped, the other hand dived into a saddle bag and appeared with another pistol.

The yellow face in the grass gave forth a short coughing roar and suddenly began to grow rapidly larger as the beast advanced in the scrambling rush that is a lion's charge.

Crash! The pistol in the right hand roared in front of his eyes.

The glaring yellow face charged ahead with appalling speed.

Crash! The pistol in the left hand.

Still the yellow face came on with frightful determination.

Crash! Crash! Crash! Right, left, right.

The hurtling face hung lower in the grass now. Plowed through the scrubby tufts. Slid forward in the dust. And then at last stopped, not ten feet distant. A great claw reached forward with its last ounce of strength and dug five deep furrows in the ground in its unquenchable determination to achieve its end. Then the yellow bulk was still.

Peterson heard the khaki person's voice at his side.

"Hm. That's as near as I care to have them come. And what you've gotta do, friend, is up and give your gun bearer a stiff dozen cuts of *kiboko*. He should have been behind you and should have fired when you quit functioning. You're new, I guess. You'll be the new consul, won't you?"

Peterson began to come back to life; but words came haltingly as yet.

"Why yes, I—I'm posted at Moyale. I—by Jove, I owe you—I have to thank you for my life. I—my name's Peterson."

The other grinned tolerantly at his confusion, though he made no move to respond to Peterson's self-introduction. But Peterson expanded under the kindly grin. He began to notice things. He saw a man tall and wiry and brown, exactly as had been those turbulent hunters of the Williams Hotel in Nairobi. This one had, perhaps, a wider and harder mouth than some, and looked at the world through amused, unwavering gray eyes. Words came to Peterson with a rush.

"I'm really most awf'ly obliged to you. I don't know how to say it; but—frightfully sporting of you. Just with a revolver. If you hadn't barged in like you did I suppose I'd have been pretty sick by now. Jolly plucky thing, I call it."

The other still grinned amusedly, and there was easy banter in his mimicry of the youngster's idioms.

"Not so frightfully awfully, don't you know?"

Peterson's speech was as his national, religion—established. That was the way people talked, of course. Everybody talked like that; that is to say, all *sahibs*. It could not occur to him that it might sound curious to a mere foreigner. And anyway, he was still too confused to notice any trace of amusement in the other's voice, which was going on in, easy explanation.

"I saw this fellow slide down off a rock *kloof* and take after you. But you were so blamed intent on your stalk that you never looked around. That's a rule of the bush, my boy: never stalk more'n a hundred yards without looking to see that you're not being stalked yourself."

"But I—I never thought—" stammered Peterson.

"Yeah; so I could see. So I lit out after you. I wasn't out for meat—just covering distance—so my gun boy was trailing along somewhere with the *shenzis;* else I might mebbe have scared this beggar off with a couple long shots. I was aiming to scare your pair of buck away at long range so you'd sit up an' take notice. But you sure were sot."

Peterson thought guiltily of the unworthy motives which he had mentally ascribed to this shooting maniac, and he murmured something again about its being jolly sporting.

The gray eyes twinkled at the persistent Anglicism.

"Mm-hm. A coupla Colt .45 guns throw a pretty heavy punch at close range. Heavy enough for Mr. Simba—if you don't miss. But all the same, another rule of the bush is: never to go out in lion country with less than a .145 rifle; and if you've got one of your first class British .157's, so much the better."

A powerfully built native with a rifle slung over his shoulder came up leading the runaway horse. The man looked at the dead lion without emotion, taking it as a matter of course, but the horse plunged and snorted with white staring eyes at the body. The man declaimed something in the sonorous Galla tongue, which the khaki person answered quickly. Then he said to Peterson:

"You'll excuse me, I'm sure. I've let my *safari* out of my sight for longer than I like. I must be after them, or God knows what monkey foolishness they'll likely pull off. That's another rule. Always watch your own *safari*. I'll leave my gun boy with you.

He can skin your lion. I guess you'd like to keep the pelt as a souvenir of your first meeting with one."

He climbed into the saddle as he spoke; and Peterson noticed for the first time that it was what he would call a "Mexican," which, to his inherited insular prejudices, seemed a curious and clumsy thing; although it is the most comfortable saddle in the world for hard work. He felt that this parting, after what had happened, was astonishingly, almost scandalously, informal; and his mind, struggling to do the right thing, fell back upon the standard convention of his kind throughout all Africa and the East.

"I say—er—won't you come and have dinner at my bungalow tonight?"

The other called over his shoulder:

"Thanks much. I'd like to. I'll be overnighting in your town and it'll be right nice."

And Peterson realized that he did not yet know his deliverer's name.

THAT DINNER was a memorable one to Peterson. It was crammed full of information; about natives, about beasts and their ways; about *safari* travel; about that mysterious independent country, Abyssinia, to the north. And somehow the information carried a different impression to Peterson than that handed out by Sanford. It was not laid down as gospel as was Sanford's; it was easy, rather, and anecdotal; yet it carried unquestioning conviction.

But Peterson was forced pointedly to ask his guest his name.

"I tried to get it from your gun boy," he explained, "but he didn't seem to understand my boy's language."

The other laughed.

"Oh, my name? Didn't I tell you? Smith—" and the unwavering eyes looked into their host's with such steady effrontery that they almost carried complete conviction. "But you'll get nothing out of my Gallas. They're top hole people, the Zulus of the North. They darn' nearly cleaned up Abyssinia once; and the Abyssinians are fighters, let me tell you. They licked the tar out of the Italians in 1906 and took a war indemnity out of them, as I suppose you know. But the Gallas may clean them up yet. All my boys are Gallas, though I use Woitos for porters. Gallas are too proud to port."

Peterson was just then too intent upon other absorbing topics to notice incidental details. Smith was all that he needed to address his guest. His experience of the afternoon was fresh in his mind. He wanted to know about lions, how to shoot them, where to aim; everything, in fact, to avoid a repetition of his so nearly disastrous experience.

Mr. Smith was immediately serious. Lions were always a serious matter. Nobody knew what they might or might not do. They might run like whipped dogs for no reason at all; or they might crouch in lordly indifference to everything; or they might charge with terrible ferocity for no reason at all. One had to be ever alert and ready for every eventuality.

"There's only one way to shoot lion," said Mr. Smith. "On foot; a good heavy gun; a good gun bearer with another gun; and a good nerve. Heart or head shot if you have time; and if he charges, hold your ground and slam him on the white spot on his chin, and keep on slamming him as long as he keeps coming. That'll smash the jaw and plow up the chest and vitals. And if you don't stop him with all that, say your prayers."

The twinkle began to grow again in the quiet eyes.

"There's another way, though I don't suggest it to you. That's the way of a lot of your lordlings and our fat millionaires who come here on picnic parties to get photographs of their big game trophies into the home rotogravures. Shoot them right out of automobiles with the engine running for a quick getaway. There was a well advertised American Amazon who came out and slaughtered five lions that way. I believe she had a barbed wire fence round her car too. Vreeden took her out from Nairobi and he told me about it."

Peterson remembered something about that story and the

disgust it had left behind. There was much more that he wanted to know about lions before he turned to another subject of mystery. That great gray horse, the miraculous presence of which in this *tsetse* fly country had undoubtedly been the vehicle for saving his life. Mr. Smith's ready grin was full of pleased reminiscence.

"Ah, that's a whole story in itself. You've heard about this new German dope, haven't you? Invented by the same wizard who discovered that plasmochin stuff that the German drug people are boosting to knock the spots out of quinine for malaria?"

Peterson had not heard.

"No? Why, it was tried out right here in Kenya. This big medico prof produced it and claimed that it was the absolute goods for sleeping sickness and horse pest. So of course all the other medicos who hadn't discovered it said they were from Missouri. So the old prof showed them. He came out here and let them infect a hundred horses and mules and round up a hundred sleepy niggers; and he injected them with his bugs, and the whole darn' bunch recovered. Then the other medicos just about kissed him and said that this was an epochal discovery for the whole of Africa and, in fact, for the whole world. And the prof said, 'Yes, and we'll give it to the world when the world gives us back our colonies.' And since then they've guarded the stuff like radium. Nobody can get it for any price."

Peterson was absorbed. What a world of romance there was in that simple little tale. He recollected now having heard something about it. It was true. Highly placed personages, saddled with the burden of making *safari* arrangements for even higher placed personages, had tried officially to obtain some of the precious stuff in order that the mighty ones might ride rather than wear out the august shoe leather upon the burning plain. But the fiercely patriotic scientists had remained grimly deaf to their wiles. How, then, had this coolly smiling person managed to—Peterson blurted the question. Mr. Smith shook his head.

"Mm-mm. No, that's a secret deep and dark. Suffice it to say that the prof who demonstrated brought more of his dope than needed; and that there have been mixed into the subsequent story two Armenians and a Greek trader and a Portugee; and the Portugee won't even tell his father confessor. Enough that I've got enough of it to have a horse in *tsetse* country."

I T WA S a long and intensely interesting evening. Midnight pointed from the round tin alarm clock on the mantel shelf before the raconteur of stark adventure in the first person got up and knocked his pipe out at the open window. Peterson's heart welled over with friendliness toward his guest, so that he felt constrained to offer him that rare privilege—official assistance in so far as might be possible.

In East Africa *safari* porters have been so spoiled by extravagantly conducted parties, and their own needs of life are so small, that they can afford to be more than merely independent. A friendly government official can do much with local chiefs to fill out a crew depleted by desertion and the simple native disease of, "Me sick. Ow-how pain im gut, no can go." Which sickness always occurs near a large and comfortable village.

But Mr. Smith was easily independent.

"Thanks much; but I guess that I can scratch along all right. None of your overpaid one-shilling-one-day *shenzis* for me, with a paternally dumb government ready to back them up in skipping out of a contract as soon as they set up a howl of forced labor. No, sir, I use Woitos. He no work, bimeby I tell him he chief, he catch *kiboko*. And in my opinion that's the only way in which the African can be made to understand that he's taken up a contract to do a certain job for a certain length of time. Thanks all the same. I guess that I'll be away with my outfit before you're up tomorrow. Going eastward along the border. Guess I'll be running into your big chief, the deputy commish, somewhere along the line. So this'll be goodby, till our trails maybe cross again sometime."

Peterson lay awake far into the morning. His mind was too full of jumbled events to permit sleep. The startling day, the fascinating talk of the evening, the things he had learned—all these went racing through his brain in a confusion of vivid pictures.

And as they raced, thoughts began to take form. Idle guessings; vague surmises. This man Smith. What a colorful personality! What an impression of quiet force that laughed at the world and—with rueful admission—at most people in it; or rather, to be more accurate, at *some* of the people in it; prominent people! That innocent allusion to the "big chief." Surely there had been a hint of raillery in the gray eyes at the unnecessary adjective that qualified the word chief. Still, this man was an American; and you never knew just what their queer speech meant. But then again, that abbreviation, the commish. That was hardly a respectful way to speak of so important an official of the Colonial Government. But this man was very clearly no respecter of persons.

The unformed ideas, as they raced along the tide of thought, began to cluster themselves round this strong snag of outthrust personality and to take form. Mere shapes at first; but presently connecting incidents drifted in and began to mold the whole. Where had he heard a description that seemed to fit just this Mr. Smith?

Peterson struggled with that vague memory for awhile, and then suddenly the picture flashed through to him. The big room in the Williams Hotel. Sanford, flushed and furious in his importance. And a voice that spoke of a man who knew much about lions; who knew, in fact, what a lion would think. A man who got things done without making a fuss. A man who scorned official favor. All these things fitted this Mr. Smith most marvelously. Peterson felt pleased that he had connected up this identity.

And then suddenly the drifting thoughts bunched together into a monstrous shape, a thing of horror.

Peterson was suddenly wholly awake. Good gosh! This man about whom the argument had waxed so hot in the hotel had been that infamous slave runner fellow. This Smith couldn't be that fellow. It was too absurd. This was a splendid chap; one of the very best. And that other fellow—King, the name was—he was dead, of course. Sanford had verified that story himself.

Peterson was pleased that there could not be any sort of connection between this top hole chap and that other frightful character, that fellow who was, of course, quite dead.

But then again the insidious reflection that this man was obviously what Sanford had called a damned Yankee forced itself. And he had come down, on his own showing, from Abyssinia and—was his name really Smith? It had seemed almost as though—

There was no hope of sleep for Peterson that night. He tossed in his bed, torn with doubts; in a quandary of conflicting emotions; divided against himself in a maze of thoughts through all of which the word duty loomed.

With the morning Peterson was pale and ringed under the eyes. But his lips were set. He went straight into his little office and did a very curious thing, difficult to understand; for he was really a young man of the best of ethics. He wrote a laborious letter, full of explanations and fears and apologies; and then, summoning his East Indian office clerk, he instructed him to turn the letter over to the official messenger with orders to convey it as fast as he knew to the camp of the deputy commissioner, a full week's journey distant to the east.

Difficult it is to understand this conduct in a man of normally decent tendencies; yet understanding is possible. For the service of his country in his own little sphere in that far flung corner of the world, Peterson felt that his superior should know of the monstrous suspicion that had occurred to him, and of all the facts relating thereto.

The man Smith had undoubtedly saved his life and had otherwise impressed him as being a splendid type of man. But duty, as he saw it, demanded that he report his suspicion to his superior. And so his laborious letter, tied into the crotch of a split stick, went off by a runner with instructions that it be delivered swiftly and with all the blundering secrecy of official-dom.

THE MAN Smith sat in the shade of a giant fig tree whose broad, flat roots arched down a shelving ravine bank to a muddy little stream. Packs strewed the ground. Porters lounged in the uncouth attitudes of the African; some with ox stolidity chewing a few grains of their day's *potio,* some lying flat on their stomachs in the blazing sun, as heat proof as lizards.

Many hundreds of little white whiskered gray monkeys chattered in the higher branches of the great tree, feeding on the dusty, rather tasteless fruit and performing all the half human antics that make monkeys so fascinating to watch.

Mr. Smith lay back to smoke his after lunch pipe and watch the monkeys with a lazy smile. He was conscious of his head gun bearer standing waiting for permission to speak. He knew that something urgent was on the boy's mind, but he knew his African well enough to know that his own dignity demanded that he let the boy wait awhile before he said with stupefying omniscience:

"Well, Baroungo, it is in your mind to speak of that messenger who runs from the consul *bwana,* to the dipty c'mish *bwana;* yes?"

"*Hau tamwaku!* How does *Bwana* know one messenger fella run with letter?"

Smith's eyes twinkled. It was always good, whenever possible, to impress one's African boys with a sense of one's hidden knowledge. As a matter of fact his bluff was based on a shrewd guess. He knew his official as well as he knew his African, and he was just about sure that young Peterson's tortured conscience would send a letter; and it was for just that reason that he had made an excuse to leave one of his boys behind at the last village with orders to bring on some native tobacco which would take a few hours to prepare. All this was a simple subtlety that went far beyond Baroungo's perceptions. The boy proceeded with his eager information.

"Danakwa he come long bring tobac; he tell one messenger come quick-quick, got letter go for east. That man run sof'ly-sof'ly now 'long that side."

He pointed with his chin beyond the next low parallel swell of the plain.

"Hm," the white man commented half to himself. "That letter must be stopped."

"Yes, *Bwana.* Two spear man stand ready for run; stop um one time."

"Mm-mm. Your enthusiasm is commendable, Baroungo; but it carries you too far. He mustn't be killed. He must lose that letter—without force—or he will have a story to tell. He must lose it through his own carelessness. Then he will sit in some village for a week or so and will go back and say that the letter is delivered and that there is no answer; and the consul *bwana* does not as yet know how to get truth out of him."

Baroungo was once more impressed with his master's wisdom. As an African himself, he knew that that was exactly what the messenger would do.

Danakwa was a good man for that thing, he agreed, though with reluctance; and added almost in soliloquy—

"All same one messenger if he die through own careless, he no tell lie, no tell true."

"You render a good paraphrase of a trite axiom, my good Baroungo," said his Master. "Many wise men have so thought before you; and white men at that. All the same you let Danakwa understand that if that messenger dies through anybody's care-less, there will be *kiboko.* Send Danakwa to me anyhow. But first, what talk have you gathered from the villages about Matteo bin Ibrahim?

"Talk is, *Bwana,* that Ibrahim go by way Dawa River; he got plenty people his chain, mebbe one hunda, two hunda fella."

"Dawa River, hm? That's faster than we thought. Double trek from now, Baroungo, else we won't meet up with him. Tell the men plenty work four, five day, one piece cloth *backsheesh*. Bustle. Send Danakwa here."

DEPUTY COMMISSIONER SANFORD

was in camp near the Dawa River. In the most secret camp that he knew how to devise. The Dawa River formed the border line of that angular point of Kenya Northern Territory that wedged itself in between Abyssinia and Italian Somaliland. It was a curious river of tumbling rapids and sluggish, miniature lakes; full of great barbeled catfish and fat, pinky-gray hippopotami, which by their pig-like tameness indicated that this last wedge of British territory was a very isolated place indeed.

Across the river to the north lay Abyssinia; a good six weeks' journey from the capital Addis Abeba, and therefore as isolated as the neighboring British wedge. To the south was another sluggish river, full of mud and crocodiles, called the Dukula, or Bushbok River. Beyond it the country sloped away to the deserts of Italian Somaliland.

The British wedge between the two consisted of country cut up by deep *dongas* with perpendicular sides; dry, sandy bottom just now, forming long, winding concealed tunnels along which one might travel for days without exposing oneself on the plain. Good country in which to hide.

Farther to the east the Dukula River converged upon the Dawa at a mud village called Mandera. Important to Sanford, because it marked the extreme tip of the Kenya Northern Territory wedge, and stationed there was an outpost guard of a quarter company of King's African Rifles. Good men, recruited from the best of the fighting tribes of Africa and splendidly trained by the hard boiled type of individual whom Kipling has named Sergeant Whatshisname.

Deputy Commissioner Sanford's *safari* was encamped in the bed of a deep *donga*. It had traveled along the beds of ravines for many days. The few natives who had shown their fuzzy black

heads over the *donga edges* during the march had been immediately seized and compelled to stay with the cautious expedition. This was drastic and opposed to the regular colonial policy
of pacification. But it had been vitally necessary; for, had these
nomads been permitted to go, they would have jabbered the
news of the secret *safari* all over the countryside.

The need for all this secrecy was that Deputy Commissioner Sanford had received news that somewhere on the other
side of the Dawa River, in Abyssinian territory, lurked that
arch-scoundrel, Matteo bin Ibrahim, working his way east with
a big train of slaves. If the deputy commissioner could contrive
to lure Matteo across the river into British territory before he
passed Mandera, he would have him on the hip, red handed
with the goods; and the menace of Matteo would then be safely
disposed of in a good colonial jail for a few years.

If Matteo were once to pass Mandera before he ventured
out of Abyssinian territory, he would be safe; because then his
jockeying back and forth would be into Italian Somaliland; and
Sanford's opinion about the Italian colonial administration
would have given shame to a good ape.

Sanford's hope, therefore, his anxious dream, was to lure the
slave runner across the river before it would be too late. The
lure consisted of some forty runaway slaves whom Sanford had
rounded up and was holding as bait.

A K.A.R. man, a thick lipped Shankala with crisp woolly
hair, had been carefully coached to go across the river posing
as a dull witted runaway, to let himself get captured by Matteo's
men, and then to tell the tale of the two-score other slaves who
huddled in a bewildered heap on the British side.

It was a good trick, and it ought surely to work—if no news
of the careful ambush should have leaked across the river.
Sanford had taken every precaution. He had traveled only in
ravine bottoms; he had sternly suppressed all loud speech—
which, with an African *safari*, is close to a miracle. He had done
more; he had even prevented the howling of interminable word-

less songs at night, which proclaimed Sanford, in his way, a great man.

EVERYTHING HAD been done to preserve secrecy, and Sanford was almost sanguine, this time, of the results. With Matteo stowed away, the principal menace of the border land would be removed, and all those slaves could be released to their own devices, free and unhampered—which would be, in ninety per cent, of the cases, to drift about aimlessly near the border, yearning with animal instinct for the pasturage they knew, till they would be gathered in again by some swift raid of some alert scamp who followed in Matteo bin Ibrahim's footsteps.

The other ten per cent, would return of their own accord into Abyssinia, nurturing some dull idea that this time they would be able to hide away in some isolated village among people who talked their own language and who lived in the same unworried state of insanitation to which they themselves, by long years of heredity and personal inclination, were so lovingly addicted.

The much harassed deputy commissioner thought that he saw success; therefore he was startlingly and disagreeably surprised when a frightened boy stood before his tent and chattered that a *bwana isana* was coming to visit him.

"What's that? An important white man? Who the— Do you know this man, N'goma?"

The boy had been with Sanford for a long time and he knew most of the white men in the Northern Territory by sight.

"*Bwana*," he chattered. "I do not know this man; but it looks like the ghost of that Kingi *Bwana* who was eaten by a lion."

"What the blazing devil!"

Sanford was out of his cot as fast as a lightweight, and at the flap of his tent. And there his incredulous eyes saw a sight that dropped his heart like lead down to his *veld* boots—the man Smith strolling unconcernedly toward him through the middle of his carefully hidden and guarded camp. The man grinned at him with cheerful effrontery.

"Hello, Dip'ty C'mish. Howya? I'll bet your boy told you I was a ghost; he scuttled from me like a jackal."

Sanford's gorge rose; that is to say, his heart climbed slowly up from his boots until it stuffed his throat. This beastly apparition meant, he was sure, the end of everything. All his careful plans; all his precautions upon which he had so plumed himself; his whole long and arduous trip—all gone by the board.

The shattering of his hopes was too complete and sudden to be realized all at once. He was conscious only of a leaden hopelessness that crushed overwhelmingly all further action. On top of it all mounted slowly a growing rage; and directed, with that curious dominance of trivialities that asserts itself in times of crisis, not at the upsetting of all his plans, but at the comparatively unimportant matter of the man's easy familiarity toward him.

The dignity of his official position demanded a respectful address from all but his intimate friends—who were very few; and required a "sir" from all subordinate officials. And here was this unspeakable foreigner addressing him with cool insolence by what he knew in his secret heart was the term which the natives used in speaking of him.

Many men in Africa, most men in fact, have been content to accept their native titles and to let themselves be so addressed with a laugh, hoping only that the shrewd characterizations thus implied might not be too insulting to their *amour propre*. But the deputy commissioner was that type of aloof official that never unbends. Personal respect is their religion. And here this particular bugbear of his addressed him as "dip'ty c'mish." Yet all that he could voice just then was his poignant disappointment in the blurted words—

"I thought you had been killed by a lion."

The man grinned with wrinkled nose in enjoyment of a successful coup.

"Yeah. It was necessary for my purposes that certain people should think Kingi *Bwana* was safely dead. I drilled those two

Kavirondos in their talk for a good week before I sent them out. Did you think that they sounded fishy at all?"

THE READY choler began to rise to Sanford's face and the veins in his thick neck swelled. So he had been made a fool of by a brace of Kavirondo savages? He, the deputy commissioner of the district, who had gone to the trouble in his eagerness to question them himself, and had convinced himself to his own official satisfaction that the circumstantial tale was true. And there stood the very man who had engineered the hoax, lean and hard and disgustingly healthy, grinning widely over his scheme.

But the fellow did worse; he heaped insult upon the already grave injury to Sanford's pride in his own acumen. He fished a crumpled oiled silk wrapper from the breast pocket of his khaki coat and unrolled it with little clucks and sighs of complaint.

"I just dropped in to bring you a letter that your consul *bwana* at Moyale was sending; his messenger very carelessly lost it. I fancy he got suspicious about me. Shows perspicacity. You got the makin's of a good youngster there, Dip'ty *Bwana*. 'Fraid it's kind of wet, 'cause I had to swim that filthy river—must have been raining somewhere back in the hills there. And you just can't keep these darn' pouches leak proof, for all the lies they advertise. Dammit, my cigars are all damp too—have to pull like a vacuum cleaner. Don't mind if I sit down in your nice shiny new camp stool, eh, and powwow? Pah! My matches are just about melted. Boy, bring fire for light cigaroo!"

Deputy Commissioner Sanford choked and red swam before his eyes. And there was where he made a great mistake. There was no real reason for so much anger. Kingi *Bwana*—had been scrupulously polite. No fault could be found with him on that score. In fact even Sanford, if he had taken time to think, would have found it difficult to say for just what reason he was finding fault. But he did not think.

It was sufficiently galling that this man who, he was assured, had been a thorn in his side throughout nearly two years of endeavor, should be standing there, safe and alive and so damnably sure of himself; that he should have known, as he apparently had known, all about the carefully concealed *safari* all the time; that he should have strolled so easily into the very center of the camp in spite of all the precautions of armed sentries; and to cap it all, that he should have been so exasperatingly familiar, so utterly wanting in respect.

That last was a charge which might with justice have been brought against King. And he, for his part, would instantly have admitted it. His perfectly unaffected question would have been: just what was there to respect? An official position? A large man who could not control his temper? He was willing to treat anybody as a free citizen and an equal; but was he to come and kowtow? That was far from King's way. He was blood brother to those sturdy hunters in the Williams Hotel who kowtowed to nobody.

"Let's sit and have an *indaba*, Dip'ty *Bwana*. I've got a proposition to make to you."

The serene effrontery of the suggestion gave words to Sanford. What the proposition might be, he never stopped to consider; he was assured in advance that nothing but infamy could come from this man who, he was convinced, was a partner in the foul business of the halfbreed whom he had been hoping to catch. Burning words gushed from his throat.

"I want to hear no propositions from you, Mr. King. I want to have no dealings with you. I can have no sort of connection or compromise with any beastly thing that you may ever do without befouling myself. The bestial trade that you ply makes you unfit to talk to a decent human being—"

Such, and many more, were the scorching words that tumbled from Sanford. His face swelled and he sweated as he poured out his denunciation.

And it was therein that he made his great mistake. Kingi *Bwana* had come in peace to make him a certain proposition which the official might very well have accepted. He had come unarmed, having left his weapons somewhere on account of having to swim the river. That in itself should have been sufficient evidence that he had not come with any wanton thought of making trouble. But Sanford's hysterical hostility quite naturally repelled him. What the deputy commissioner's official acumen had convinced him of or had not convinced himself of was no business of King's to inquire, or to explain away.

He was—thank God, he thought—free, white and twenty-one. Above all, free; no bought and paid for official, sworn under oath for all the rest of his life to let unseen superiors in distant places do all his thinking for him and shape all his future deeds according to rules in a book. He was no enslaved subordinate to Sanford, to have to pander to the man's pompous ego, to explain his comings and his goings and to justify his doings.

The deputy commissioner's attitude had suddenly made the relationship between them acutely personal. Not the most reckless of the hunters at Nairobi would have spoken to Kingi *Bwana* in that manner without being ready to back up his words with something very much more substantial than talk. King remained sitting in the camp chair and sucked prodigious puffs from his damp cigar. He still grinned, though now only with his lips; but his long legs lazily drew up and tucked themselves under the stool, and his feet shuffled away the loose pebbles and sand from under them.

"Mm-hm," he mouthed over his cigar. "Seems like you don't' like me so much. Well, Mr. Deputy Commissioner Sanford, what d'you figure you dare to do about it?"

Let credit be given to Sanford. His neck veins distended more purple than ever. His shoulders hunched—and King braced his feet for a quick spring.

BUT NO fight was to take place just then. The K.A.R. sergeant came up on a run, saluted quickly and, so important was his communication, that he plunged instantly into a whispered gabble. Sanford's first impulse, in deference to his official dignity, was to push the man from him, curse him for his impudence and make his rush at King. But a phrase of the whispered message caught his ear. It arrested all other action. Without word or look to King, Sanford caught the sergeant by the arm and strode several paces away. King remained sitting, pulling at his cigar with an affectation of exaggerated enjoyment. Sanford demanded fiercely of the sergeant:

"Now what is this story? Tell me straight and quick."

The sergeant replied in urgent undertones:

"Sar, this thing true. One scout come, he say Ibrahim come cross river by Malolo *boma;* sof'ly ask news 'bout this side slave. This scout my man. He see Ibrahim self; got three, four man with. He run one time bring news."

Sanford's heart jumped. Fate, it seemed, in spite of this King fellow, was playing for once into his hand. It looked as though, deprived temporarily of King's clever brain, the other arch scoundrel had made a blunder. It was Sanford's chance to leap upon this misplay. If Ibrahim were indeed on the British side, as seemed to be miraculously true, the thing to do was to march immediately with every available man and to cut off his retreat. Sanford hardly hoped to surprise the crafty old villain in a native thorn fenced village where some chattering fool would surely give a warning. But, the man's retreat once cut off, the chances were good of rounding him up before he could get back.

Sanford commenced to give quick orders to the sergeant to get all his men ready for immediate trek.

And then cold lead suddenly dragged his flushed hopes down to dead bottom. His eyes fell upon King, sitting coolly there, puffing at his cigar patiently. That pestiferous thorn in his side hampered his every move, even here! What to do with that menace? If he were to go off suddenly he felt a chill certainty that the man would contrive in some way to outwit him and to convey a warning to his partner. Sanford's mind raced over the pros and cons of the situation.

What the devil and all could he do? Arrest him, the thought came. But on what grounds? He had no evidence. As the voice in the Williams Hotel had jeered, he would need a lot more evidence than this mere personal conviction. It was against all precedent of law to arrest a man without a single grain of evidence; and Sanford was stanch British official enough to respect the sacrosanct law. Yet the need was desperate. The man must be disposed of.

Suppose he were to manage to arrest King, and to quarrel through the legality of the action later in the Nairobi courts—what a howl would be raised about that by every turbulent free citizen in the whole colony! But suppose, in the furtherance of his duty, he were to do the thing. What would he do with his prisoner?

Bind him hand and foot? The thought lingered hopefully, but found little encouragement. Sanford had an uneasy respect for the capabilities of that coolly efficient person whose reputation was that he got things done the way he wanted. People had been tied up before by experts; and sometimes, somehow, some of them had contrived to escape. This man looked uncomfortably like one of those who would contrive.

Desperately, then, he asked the sergeant—

"How many of your men are necessary to guard that man?"

The sergeant covered his mouth with his hand as he gasped at the thought.

"*Awa!* To guard that Kingi *Bwana? M'beku!* That man like devil, sar. He know witch magic. Ten, fifteen men for guard that fella."

So that was the sergeant's opinion of it. Sanford plucked at a button of his shooting coat in his quandary. His nerves, already ragged, were beginning to get the better of him. Instant action was necessary if he hoped to catch Ibrahim; and that man sitting stolidly there, as hard and unconcerned as a stone, was driving him into a frenzy. But the sergeant had an idea to propound;

an idea born of Africa; one that had, upon occasion, stood the test of practise.

"You want know what do with that fella, sar? I tell. Batta *boma*, two hour fum heah, Malolo road. Got plenty trouble with lion. Batta fellas got one lion trap. Puttum this Kingi *Bwana* lion trap inside. He sit comf'ble shuah till you fetch."

SANFORD WALKED back to where King sat, still enjoying his cigar. The deputy commissioner's lips were set and the blood had ebbed away from his face. He was going to do an unexpected thing. In fact, a quite brave thing. The more one sized up the man King, the more uncompromisingly hard and physically efficient he looked; and Sanford was ruefully conscious of his own unnecessary weight, though he had lost much during the course of his strenuous expedition.

But the thing was necessary The effectiveness of the little K.A.R. force would have to be conserved as much as possible. He could not afford to have a sick and disabled list. It was up to him—it was his duty—to keep King in play and to hold all of his attention for as long as might be possible. Sanford therefore walked up to King with his lips set and commenced the play.

"Well, Mr. King, you were going to say something I think, when I was interrupted."

King's eyebrows lifted. He had not given Sanford credit for this. His feet gathered under him again and he said:

"Your move, Dip'ty *Bwana*. I asked what you figured you dared to do about things."

Sanford moistened his lips. King was so coldly direct. There was to be no time gained holding him in play with words. The actual physical play would have to last longer than Sanford had hoped. But he faced his trial.

"I dare, Mr. King, if you dare to stand up to me, to put into practise what I think of you."

King suddenly grinned widely.

"Good for you, Mr. Commissioner. I'll hand it to you. As for me, I take back some of the things I thought. If you like, I'll shake hands before we start in to argue."

But Sanford was not going to descend to that familiarity. He detested everything he had ever known about this man, and he felt that he degraded himself by this personal conflict which he had forced himself to undertake only on account of its desperate necessity.

"That is not necessary," he said shortly, and took off his coat.

King, unhurried, looked him over appraisingly. He saw big shoulders and broad chest, massive looking legs, sturdy calves beneath the puttees; and under the shirt, below the broad chest, more of a protuberance than an altogether healthy stomach needed.

"Humph," he commented impersonally. "You've lost quite some weight, haven't you? All the same, you won't be aiming to drag this out to an endurance test. Guess your game will be rush and slug for a quick finish. Got about thirty pounds weight on me, eh? What d'you run to? 'Bout two hundred and ten? I ought to scale around one eighty-five. That's not too much weight to give away, 'cause I'll bet I'm a lot faster on my feet. Tell you what. I'll bet you fifty dollars on the side I'll outlast you. What d'you say? Just to make it interesting."

Sanford's anger began to rise again. This unspeakable person harbored the persistent conviction that he could meet a high government official on a basis of equality. The very idea of the proposed bet was an insult. Besides, Sanford was not going into this thing with any reasonable hope of winning; he knew, better than the other could guess, how short he was of wind. His plan was no more than to keep King's attention fully occupied for as long as possible. He would gladly have strung out a little time in preliminary talk. But King slipped out of his coat with a sinuous movement of his shoulders and began to glide, to prowl rather, round him with the alert intentness of one of the greater felines.

"Don't care to bet?" he purred regretfully. "Well, all right. Up to you to start. My game'll be to tire you out."

BUT SANFORD did not know where to start. He had little confidence of being able to land on that gliding body anywhere. It was King who commenced. Like a leopard leaping at an opening it has seen, King came in. There was a swift sound of two short steps, and—*smack-thud-smack!* Face, body and neck, Sanford felt light but stinging blows. He drove a heavy right at the face in front of him, and hit only an open hand; and then, *smash!* The hardest fist he had ever met slugged in under his ear.

Sanford's head buzzed and water welled into his eyes. Through the haze he discerned the face again, head thrust forward, peering at him through searching eyes. The impersonal voice came once more.

"Shucks. Just a little too far back. I sure wished you that one on the end of the jaw. But you're slower than I thought, brother. I'll give you odds on that bet if you like."

The water in Sanford's eyes became oddly streaked with running flashes of red. That last blow had stung and—curse the fellow, he fought apparently without the least animus; as if he were engaged in a boxing bout with a friend, damn him! And the way he dissected one's capabilities was an insult. Brother!

The swimming eyes saw something beyond King's back—the sergeant and some ten of his men gathering for the rear attack. They had come sooner than he expected. Here was where he had to engage all of King's attention. He drew a deep breath and rushed, slugging with both hands. The heavy fists met flesh; hard flesh of arms and elbows that thrust the blows aside. Something hit him with sickening force in the throat, though not hard enough to stop him; and then he clung in a clinch. Quick hands covered his arms and the hated voice breathed upon his neck.

"How d'you want to do this? Hitting in clinches, or a clean break?"

Sanford answered nothing. For one thing, his throat muscles were numbed by the blow; and for another, the need for speech was past. He clung desperately in his clinch, all his energies devoted to just holding his opponent harmless.

And then clutching black arms and a hell's uproar enveloped them both.

From King came a sharp hiss of intaken breath, a gasped, "You filthy crook!" And then he fought in earnest. Like a monstrously magnified attack of ants upon a hard shelled beetle that fight was. Except that the heaving black mass howled. To the African, as to the ape, fight and noise are coincident. The one can not exist without great volume of the other. And in this case the Africans had to bolster up with noise their courage to attack a man of whom they were mortally afraid.

Every now and then above the din rose a high pitched shriek of anguish as the overwhelmed victim found opportunity to apply some especially venomous means of hurt. The strong odor of unwashed Africa hung in the still air of the *donga*. But gradually the heaving mass of flesh began to struggle with less and less violence. The end, with such odds, was as inevitable as when the driver ants make their battles.

Slowly the fight subsided. Already rope was in evidence. Presently Sanford backed out of the mêlée, disheveled, clothes torn, but elated. One after another the natives stood back, rolling white eyeballs and champing protruding lips. The atavistic impulse to rend with strong teeth was barely suppressed. One squatted, hugging a twisted knee and moaning as only a native can moan; another, with screwed face, nursed a wrenched shoulder. Minor injuries were many; but the end that had been gained amply repaid the cost.

King, the redoubtable Kingi *Bwana,* lay exhausted. Swathed positively with ropes; foul smelling, greasy cords that had been used for heaven knew what filthy purposes. His shirt had been ripped from him; his skin clawed and scratched; his mouth full of grit and dirt. A sorry figure.

He spoke no word. He looked with the one eye that was not closed with sand, as though impressing the faces of his captors in his mind. The men covered their mouths to prevent the entry of evil eye and moved out of range. Sanford's voice broke on the spell.

"Hurry up there now, Sergeant. Get your men together. You, Umgate, stay in *boma* with porters. All other camp boys come."

The start was surprisingly quick. Everything had been ready for days for just such a swift raid. Within fifteen minutes the little force was on trek. King, lashed to a pole like a captured reptile, was carried by four brawny soldiers in relays. He spoke only at intervals—with each new relay. To each unwilling four he said the same thing.

"Four men. To each one, four jackals, four hyenas, four vultures, four months."

It was gibberish. But the men groaned; and, as each one repeated King's story, horror and superstition grew. Each relay began to be more difficult to supply, till Sanford himself had to select the men and order them to their gruesome job.

King had no idea as yet just what use he could make of the fear thus engendered. He did the thing on principle. He knew that a frightened African was very close to a creature without reason; and he fired his shafts of suggestion at a venture, gambling in futures. In any case he felt not averse to making those Africans as uncomfortable as he could.

BUT NO immediate fruit was born of his craft. The time was too short. Two hours from the camp was the lion trap that the people from the neighboring Batta village had built against the marauding beasts. King was still a prisoner when they arrived. He knew, of course, from the babble of the marching men, what the plan with regard to himself was; so his incarceration was no surprise to him.

Sanford quickly inspected the trap himself in the fast falling dusk. It was in good condition. It would hold even Kingi *Bwana* in security. This matter had been worrying him throughout the march. But this trap was in such good shape that no time need be lost in making repairs. With a great thankfulness he turned to his sergeant.

"Good. Throw that goat out and put the prisoner in. On the ground will do—Good heavens! He's tough enough not to die of lying on a mud floor."

For a fleeting moment of weakness he debated whether he should remove the ropes from the prisoner. But he hardened his heart. It was a good and stout trap, built to keep a lion in; but all the same, why take any chances with this man? The whole trip was too important. He ordered only that the pole by which King had been carried should be removed. That would be all the comfort that the prisoner deserved. King, from the gloomy interior, addressed him.

"Hey, polecat! Tell your gorillas to cover me with my coat against the mosquitos."

The insult was gross and deliberate. King wanted his coat for his own reasons and he did not want Sanford to think too much about it. The very crudity of the attack brought success. Sanford's dignity blazed into fury at the affront. It is even possible that, had he been within the cage, he might in his fury have kicked the prisoner in the ribs for his impertinence. But Sanford was, after all, in spite of all his faults of inflated ego, a gentleman. And he felt, since he held all the cards, that he could afford to laugh at the insult. Sulkily he told the sergeant to cover the prisoner with the coat.

"Look to see that there's no knife in the pocket," he warned.

"No knife, sar," the sergeant reported. "He got knife in belt. I took it."

"All right, then. Cut that cord short at the door, else he'll be able to pull it up. Where are those two men who were hurt? They and one other stay on guard all night; loaded rifles. The rest march."

The sergeant cut the cord as directed. The heavy door crashed down behind its sill. The hubbub of orders commenced. King called from within his cage:

"Hey, Sanford—I'll tell you something. If you don't reach Malolo before three in the morning, Matteo will be gone. Better hurry an' run some of the fat off your paunch. You'll be faster for the next time we meet; an' let me tell you, you'll need it, big boy. An' I'll tell you something else when I get out of here. I'll tell you the story about the colonial official who went down a hole to fetch a skunk, and the skunk came out and fainted."

He heard the choked growl in Sanford's throat, and he grinned. He was in a fever really to drive the other away from there without giving him an opportunity to think coherently; and to this purpose he loosed all the poison in his tongue. An inspiration came to him.

"*Aho, Bwana M'kubwa!*" he shouted; and he commenced to call insulting messages in Swahili.

While Sanford himself did not altogether understand, he knew that every soldier of the K.A.R. would get the finer points. To be ridiculed before natives was a thing that not the meanest white man could stand. Sanford's furious cursing of hurry-up orders filtered into King through the bars of the cage. A hoarse guffaw from some appreciative soldier sounded above the confusion and was quickly shut off by a hand. It was the final straw.

"Get along there, Sergeant!" screamed Sanford. "March! What the devil is the delay?"

The confused shuffling and patter of bare feet, mingled with a low rhythmic grunting, sounded and immediately began to recede. In two minutes the last of it had faded into the falling night.

SANFORD HAD gone. He had been too furiously angry to think clearly, and he had forgotten one thing. King chuckled. Lesser shuffles and grunts sounded without the cage. King could picture the scene perfectly. Those rather bewildered natives left behind, not liking their job one little bit, and very uncomfortable. Much too bewildered with the swiftness of the departure and much too uncomfortable to remember the thing that Sanford had forgotten. King laughed outright. Immediately a low chatter of voices assured him that his three guards wondered nervously at the man who, in such a plight, could laugh.

King nodded to himself stiffly within his ropes; he knew that these men were in the right condition for him to work upon. Just how he would work or what he might achieve, he did not know yet; but he knew that a man who understood the minds of superstitious natives could work miracles with them.

He was not ready for them yet, anyhow; he was busy with his ropes. Yards of them there were, malodorous fathoms. But they gave him no anxiety. The African who can tie ropes does not exist. They will make ungainly bundles of the simplest things swathed with meaningless strings which will slip off in all directions; they will tie their crude rope bridges with a thousand knots, and will duly get drowned because some day the knots will give. The experience of their centuries has taught them a mule pack method with fifty foot lengths of rawhide which will slip twenty times in a day's trek.

Sanford of course knew enough to know that African roping required considerable supervision and revision. But he was in a hurry, goaded by that vicious tongue, and he relied on that stout cage and his three armed guards. No, King's ropes gave him no anxiety at all. Only some trouble. He devoted a steady hour of quiet effort to his ropes. Outside the night was coming on with the swiftness of the equatorial belt where there is no twilight.

Inside it was much too dark for the watchers to see between the stout wooden bars of the trap what the occupant did. In an hour's time King shook the last of the coils from his feet and rose softly and stretched. He was ready to take advantage of the thing that Sanford, in his hurry, had forgotten. It was a little thing. One that anybody, going away in a hurry, might forget.

That thing was fire.

That was the thought that King had tried to keep from Sanford's mind. Outside of his cage huddled three men. Three superstitious Africans in the open dark—without fire. Sanford had driven his force away without giving that matter a thought.

With characteristic improvidence the thought of fire had not occurred to the guards until the actual need was upon them. Not until they could no longer see did they feel the need for light; and which of them would then dare to run after the fast retreating column, or run through the goblin haunted night to the distant village to fetch a glowing coal wrapped in dried banana tree pith? And a certainty, of course, was that not one of the three would have matches. No African ever has matches; not even a house boy. They will come daily at lamp lighting time to *bwana* for a fire stick.

All this King knew. He had played for this; and the fact that no fire spluttered without his cage showed him that he had played right. He could afford to laugh, particularly since, in the pocket of his coat which he had demanded as a mosquito cover, was his oiled silk cigar case, and in it, in a camper's matchbox, sulphur matches.

HIS FIRST move was to set about establishing fear in the minds of his guards. That ought not to be difficult. Matches would help. King carried, as do many Africanders who require a light in windy places, the old style sulphur matches. These are almost obsolete now in America on account of the fire hazard; but every camp outfitter in Africa has them on sale for those whose experience demands them. King therefore set gleefully about doing a match trick for the benefit of those who cowered in the dark. Making his voice sepulchral, he croaked—

"Three men sit without and watch in the dark, and from the outer dark watch the *anu-m'kusi,* the goblins who wait for the three."

Moaning whispers greeted this announcement which every one of the three knew to be true. And then a voice—

"*Aho, Bwana M'kubwa,* that is an ill talk."

"But a true talk, O three that have no fire," croaked King. "But what have I to do with the goblins who watch from the darkness of every tree without? I am within, and safe, though I lie bound—"

He knew that African goblins never enter enclosures built by man—houses, cages, or even thorn *bomas*. It is in the open dark that the malignant spooks of rock and tree prowl and pounce upon the backs of humans.

He left them with that cheering thought for a little time which he devoted to a quick inspection of his cage. He hoped little, for he knew these lion traps, and he hardly thought that Sanford would have been so foolish as to have overlooked any weakness.

The trap was the standard construction—stout hardwood poles driven well into the earth in two parallel rows about a yard apart and brought together at the top and lashed. The shape was that of a long narrow tent with very steep walls. In order to set this trap the simple practise was to tie a goat at the far end of this tunnel where a lion, attracted by its scent, could see it through the spaces between the strong wooden bars, but could get at it only through the door at the other end. Once the marauder was inside its weight, treading upon a common trap fall, released the door.

It was this door that interested King most. A slim chance, he hoped there might be, that he could get hold of something and lift it. Its construction was crude but efficient. It consisted of a great slab of hardwood which ran up and down in grooves, like an ordinary window. At the bottom was a stout sill and the door fell, not upon, but *outside* of this; the idea being that there would be presented no projection, no bottom edge, under which a lion might hook a claw and heave the thing up.

Anybody who has ever tried to open even a counterweighted window without getting finger purchase beneath one of the windowpane frames will realize how extremely efficient such a simple lion trapdoor can be. King felt all round the door edges with faint hope and with little disappointment when he found nothing. If only, he reflected, he had been able to drive Sanford away before he had thought of a knife, he would have been able to walk out at will. A stout blade driven into the door would give all the purchase needed; and as for the guards with loaded rifles, they worried him not at all.

But no such luck was attending King on this trip. He must revert to his original plan of frightening his guards. The sulphur match trick would help. He could not delay it much longer because presently an arc light moon would creep over the flat acacia tops. This trick required darkness. Out of his deepest belly tones rumbled his voice again:

"Turn your faces, O three who sit in the open dark. Hide your heads and be afraid to look. For I lie in evil case and I summon ghosts to do my bidding. The ghosts of men whom I have killed. Many I have killed; many more will I kill. Their spirits are my servants whom I call. I lie bound but they wander free in my cage. From all sides their green eyes shine upon me. Be afraid and hide, O three whom the tree ghosts watch from behind."

Of course the guards looked. Nervously and over their shoulders; but nothing could have prevented them from peeking. They saw the pale green glow of damp sulphur matches flitting in awesome pairs behind the poles of the trap. The horrible thing was true then. The prisoner lay bound—they knew that— and here were the ghostly eyes wandering fitfully, now high up, now low to the ground.

Then they did hide their heads; and they moaned the low quavering noises of the African in great fear. This man whom their evil fate it was to guard had a reputation among the natives for strange powers. Here was a very great witchcraft. They all knew, of course, that when one killed a man, if one knew the proper witch rites to apply, the spirit of the victim became the slave of the victor. And here was proof.

THE GUARDS cowered together in the clammy dark

and groaned supplications to the *Bwana M'kubwa* not to put a haunt on them with his ghostly servants; they were poor men, soldiers; they did only what they were ordered.

"Very well," said King magnanimously. "Look. I have ordered my ghosts to loose my ropes and I am free. Open now this door and I give you promise that I shall order no spirit to sit upon your backs when it is dark."

But that was too much to demand of those men—as yet. They had been well drilled and the sense of obedience to the orders of their officer had been the most stringent of their teachings.

"*Awa, Bwana.* Tell us not this thing. We are poor men, but soldiers, and above all are we of the Kingis Africani Raifals. To open the door is against all order." And one, inspired by one of those unexpected streaks of native shrewdness, asked timidly, "Besides, O *Bwana M'kubwa,* if your ghost servants have been strong enough to open your cords, why not tell them also to open the door, and thus shall we be blameless?"

This was an unpleasant poser. A question that might upset the whole growing structure of terrorism. It would have to be disposed of at once, without hesitation. All the excuse that came to King was a lame one, but he had to make the most of it. His answer was almost immediate.

"Fools. How shall these go without to open the door? These are the ghosts of men whom I have killed in their own *bomas;* they can serve me only within. Since you are mule headed about the door, I must send for the ghosts of those whom I have killed in the open. Many they are and strong, and they come in many horrid shapes."

The piled up horrors were for the purpose of diverting the men's minds from the thinness of his excuse, and King did his oratorical best with them.

"With green eyes shining in the dark will they come and with a roaring of many tongues like the wind in the high trees.

Prepare to greet them, O three who sit alone in the outer dark, for to those ghosts will your own spirits be added this night."

"*Ahoo! A warala hoo!*" wailed the wretched three.

With native propensity for terror, they could almost see the gibbering army of the dead already. And that wicked prophesy about their own spirits was the very worst kind of bad luck, spoken even in jest. But they stuck, still, with splendid credit to the K.A.R. training, to their posts.

"Listen, O three who are nearly dead!" boomed King's voice. "Who am I? Am I not known in the land? What are the tales that men tell of me? Are they not many?"

What he wanted to draw from them was more ammunition for his thunder. To implant a new idea into the African mind takes time. King's simple plan was to find out what these men were predisposed to hear about his powers, and he could then beautifully enlarge upon the theme. Almost the first thing he drew was splendid material.

"Ow, the tales are many, *Bwana*. That you are associate with the greatest of the witch doctors. The tales tell that you know the witchcraft of the beasts; that you are a lord of lions—"

King leaped at that suggestion. The werewolf superstition is current throughout all Africa. Every native knows that certain sorcerers can either turn themselves into various beasts or can project their spirits into beasts to carry out their nefarious purposes. Upon this theory the well known Leopard Society of the West Coast is built.

"Good," chanted the white man. "Lord of lions I am. Many of my dead have I sent into the bodies of lions and of leopards and of hyenas; and at night they prowl in the outer dark. Many ghost lions serve me. What if I summon such a ghost to open this door?"

A PROPHET or a seer is in most cases an alert individual who can extract information from his public, and is quick witted enough to apply such individual information to probable future events. The more shrewdly, or luckily, he manages to fit in his cryptic sayings with the events that follow, the more marvelous a prophet he is. Working along this line, King was a miraculous prophet.

The expected moon began, as yet below the horizon, to flood the *veld* with a cold gray glow. Shadows loomed out where only blackness had been before. With the rising, the customary thin wind began to whisper in the acacia tops. Against the paling sky a fringe of upthrust shale outcrop made a ragged skyline.

Conditions were perfect. Time was right; and, such being the case, a perfectly natural thing happened. From the rock shelters of the low hills came a sound; a low booming drone that filled the air and rose to a deep, aspirated cough. It was repeated four times, rising to a full throated roar of warning and defiance; and then it died away in a series of shorter coughs and grunts.

Simba was out to the hunt.

There is probably no sound more fearsome than the roar of a lion out in the open. There is a vast, all-encompassing vibration about it that impinges upon the nerves with awesome effect. Location is difficult to determine. The menace may be anywhere. The resultant nervous confusion is, of course, just what nature intended.

Even a hardened old-timer, encamped in a strong thorn *boma*, can not hear that deep, vibrant rumble in the distance without a tightening of the skin. For a lion can scent meat an amazing distance away; and if he is hungry enough he may well jump over the thorn fence, make one devastating rush at the first meat he sees—goat or pack burro or man—and jump out again with his prey.

Out in the open, with no shelter at all, the voice of the Lord Simba is a shattering thing for the hardiest nerves. King hopped with excitement.

"Ho-ho," he chanted. "He comes. Hear the voice of my servant whom I have summoned, O three who sit in the open dark. He comes on feet that make no sound. He sees from out the dark where he can not be seen. He springs from the black shadow; he slays and he is gone. Wait for him, O three who sit without fire."

Aside entirely from the ghost theory, there was deadly truth in every word that King spoke; and no man knew it better than those Africans who had been born and brought up under the perpetual menace of Simba. Rifles they had, of course. But not the hardest big game hunter in all Africa, armed with a heavy gun and the most modern luminous sights, will venture to sit out on the ground for lion at night. A platform built high in a tree is the only perch in such conditions.

A deep booming roar sounded out of the imminent dark, apparently almost upon them. Not even the most autocratic martinet officer could have blamed those poor devils of soldiers for their instant desertion of their posts.

With gabbling yelps, they fled. Blundering into things, stumbling, staggering on, yelling in agony as they crashed into thorny mimosa scrub. Yelling, in fact, all the time. Trees were in their confused minds; tall trees where even ghost lions could not spring. But above all, trees far away; trees where they would have at least a fraction of time to feel out and climb.

King sped their parting with joyous jeers and shouted details about the ghosts that he was sending after them. Their blundering passage through the bush faded away into the night; finally even the last of their yells died away. The dead stillness of dry season Africa, when insects are not in evidence, took the place of all the turmoil.

King listened. He held his breath and listened. He waited for the faintest possible crack of twig, for a shuffle of sand, for a padded footfall. There was nothing. It was hardly possible that the beast had not winded all that aggregation of sweating meat. Was it possible that all that demoniac yelling had, as sometimes happens with that inexplicable creature, frightened him away? King wondered; and his mind swiftly grappled with plans accordingly.

AND THEN, with a suddenness that made even King jump, it came. Not a twig had snapped, not a footfall had sounded. But, right up against the wooden poles of the trap, a long snuffle of indrawn breath.

King whirled round. Almost against his hip it had been. His heart was up in the back of his palate. It was an effort to swallow it and to force himself to calm confidence. He would have to be wary. He was safe enough for the present. If a lion could not get out of that trap, it certainly could not get in. What called for caution was to be sure that no openings between the stout wooden bars were wide enough to let a great yellow paw through. That was a matter to be ascertained without loss of time.

King struck one of his matches to make a quick survey. Green eyes, not three feet from his own, instantly glared in the light. The beast coughed a startled *wroof!* and sprang back. Fire, sudden flame, is the only thing that really frightens any of the great felines. The steady glow of a dying camp-fire will cause long hesitation; but its very steadiness, unaccompanied by any violent action, will permit a return of hungry confidence.

King grunted a short laugh at the great beast's ungainly backward leap. The situation had its ironies, he thought. He, Kingi *Bwana*, reputed down at Nairobi as a lion slayer, reputed among the natives as a witch lord of lions, who had devised many methods of getting at lions in their own fastnesses, boxed up like a mouse in a cage while a lion was devising methods of getting at him.

It could not succeed, of course, and eventually it would get tired of clawing long strips of bark out of the bars and its hunger would cause it to hunt up a less difficult meal. In the meanwhile there was nothing to do but wait.

King laid himself on the floor flat on his belly to kick his heels in patience. He would need plenty, he knew, for the patience of a cat may be well nigh inexhaustible. It worried him— on account of that rising moon.

There was one space between the bars wide enough for a devastating paw. King lay just out of reach of this, his feet against the trap door, and spat in disgust. He fished one of his damp cheroots out of the oilskin case and with difficulty lighted it. Smoking would possibly help his wits to work. That moon— he did not like it a bit. It would come up blazing like a street lamp, lighting up the *veld* so that one could read print by it. Gone would be the eery blackness of night, gone the dense shadows. Even the thick darknesses under the trees would melt to grayness in which bulks of moving shadow could be seen.

And then those guards—damn' them—they might bolster up each other's courage to return. It is the ghost haunted dark that so terrifies the soul of the African; the blackness out of which unseen and grotesquely imagined horror can leap. With glaring moonlight much of the terror of the night would vanish. These men were plucky enough; they were no naked savages, but well drilled soldiers of the K.A.R. It was barely possible that the three of them together, with their rifles, might take chances with a lion where they could see him.

The brute just now was snuffling at a thin crack in the hard-wood of the door. King, with his knowledge of its habits, knew that its nose was right up against the wood, breathing in every scent that the wind carried; for that was exactly its direction. In weary disgust he softly rolled over on his back, drew up both feet and kicked heavily against the door.

The lion let out a short roar, sprang back ten feet and growled savagely. King grinned his satisfaction. He had hoped that there would be enough play in the door for his sudden kick to impart a nasty jar to that most sensitive part of any cat—its nose.

His mind returned to a contemplation of his private colored problem. He did not know to what extent he had managed to implant the idea of a lion obsessed by the spirit of a slain man. That was an all important factor. He knew that, should the men's training once suffice to overcome their material fears, his hope of exercising his skulduggery of the night would be con-siderably reduced.

Not a little bit did he like that rising moon.

A great paw slipped through the space between the bars and raked a wide arc in front of his face. Though he was safely out of reach, he automatically jerked his head back. Then he swore.

"Hell, I must be getting nervous in this damn' den. I'll have to watch that."

The taloned paw, having once found the space, came in again and raked up clods of dead grass in patient hope. King watched it sulkily. An impish thought came to him and he chuckled. Quickly he stretched out a long arm and ground the glowing butt of his cigar well into the reaching paw.

With a howl unworthy of the king of beasts the paw was snatched back; and the language of that lion was that of a hundred backyard toms with the deep added note of savagery.

SUBCONSCIOUSLY KING collected the grass tufts that the beast had clawed up; and following that train of thought he set to pulling up more of the dead grass within the trap and to peeling long strips of bark from the poles. His mind was toying with the idea of setting fire to his cage. But it would have to be the door end, for the wind was blowing freshly through the farther end. The heavy construction of the door and grooves would take a long time to burn. And that moon, the arbiter of tides, granted extra time to no man.

The lion was snuffling round the door again, where the wind blew the scent strongest. King could hear its great paw raking along the sill. He could imagine clearly the picture of an overgrown cat with hooked claws feeling out a crack under a wainscot where the scent of mouse lingered.

All at once the scratching stopped. A claw had caught upon something. The door rattled; and then—King gulped his heart back—the door lifted an inch. His feet against the wood, he had unmistakably felt it. Like a mink he scuttled round in his narrow prison and squatted to face this new problem, his two feet pressed hard against the lower edge of the door.

This thing required consideration. He pictured the construction. Inside the trap—he could feel along the edge—the door dropped behind a hardwood sill, with a good overlap. There was no chink or bottom edge under which anything could hook a claw. Outside, of course, the reverse held good. There was no need of a double sill to prevent anything from that side; it rested simply upon a log. Plenty of opportunity there for a claw, or a hand for that matter, to get a purchase.

And if once, why not again? Everybody knows the persistence of a cat; how it will try the same thing again and over again as soon as it has once learned that some advantage may accrue to it through its action. This overgrown cat was picking with a tentative claw at the sill once more.

King felt that he could apply sufficient force with his two feet pressed hard against the door to prevent any sudden heaving wide of the portal; so no great worry assailed him. But there was a thought in that thing; a thought with possibilities.

The only thing that had made King's prison a prison was the fact that he had no means of lifting that heavy door just the few inches sufficient to let him hook his fingers beneath the lower edge. But if, now, some obliging lion would give him that few first inches of lift—Yes, possibilities were there.

The thing would be no blithe game of tag at any time. Danger, swift and sudden, lurked at the edges of the thought and all around it. There would be no tiny margin of room for a misplay. But—King gritted his teeth—he could never, under any circumstances, let that Sanford man come back and find him still caught like a rat in a trap.

With decision and the glimmerings of a plan a hard grin crept over King's face. Keeping his feet solidly against the door, he lay back and felt with his arms stretched above his head. Somewhere up there was the arrangement of slats that formed the trap fall upon which a beast must step in order to release the catch of the door. King's hands found it, and after some twisting wrenched it loose. He needed one of those slats for his plan. Cautiously he removed his feet from the door, every muscle tense, ready for instant action.

"Now then, my good friend Simba," he said, "give us a lift on that door. Not too hard now, just a little one."

The lion was scrabbling industriously at the sill. Presently a claw found purchase. The door shook and rattled upward. But King in his anxiety applied foot brakes too soon. The upthrust stopped and the door dropped again.

"Huh, getting to be a nervous fool," King grumbled to himself. He relighted his cigar and puffed evenly at it to prove his steadiness. "Now then, brother worker, how about another lift there?"

The lion was doing its persistent best to oblige. In a few seconds the door rose several inches, high enough to clear the level of the inner sill.

"Good!"

Instantly King thrust a slat under the door to prevent it from falling behind again, and then pressed his feet hard against it. The crack below the edge was larger than necessary. Four taloned toes came through and worked along the edge. King hit at them with another slat. They were snatched back. The door fell down upon the restraining slat, and King applied the brakes.

The first and most difficult move toward his liberation had been successfully accomplished. He now had a clearance of a good inch below the door. He could get his fingers under it and heave it up any time he wished. There remained only the problem of the jailer outside.

An insurmountable problem, it would seem, depending entirely upon the patience of the prowling lion. But King knew things about lions—what they were likely to do, or not to do.

Down in Nairobi that other hunter had said, "Kingi *Bwana* knows how a lion thinks." So there was a definite plan working in King's mind.

THE MOON was sending long shadows from the acacia

stems, and King could see the big brute now as it padded back and forth, grumbling to itself between attempts on the door. He watched it critically; for much of his reckless plan would depend upon the degree of its hunger, its temper and so on.

"Hm! Quite a heavy whiskered old papa. That's not so bad. And not any too starved looking. That's better. Must be plenty of small *bok* around here for them. Thank Pete there's no female around with him, so he won't want to show off."

The prowl ceased and the tentative claws scratched along the door again. King felt out a narrowed sliver of split slat and jammed it between door and groove as a wedge.

"Softly, softly," he murmured. "I'm not ready yet, old boy. But I guess we'll be able to deal with you all right."

The plan was desperate enough; but King, too, thinking of the possible return of the three soldiers and Sanford's triumph, had worked himself up to a pitch of desperation. What his plan would need was steel nerve; and with plenty of that there was a reasonable chance that it would work. Nerve, King had more than enough; and he had seen something not dissimilar to his plan work with astonishing results once before.

He whistled tunelessly through his teeth as he set about making his preparations. He needed some slivers of wood. He had those from the slat arrangement that he had torn up. Grass, dry grass, was a necessity. That, too, was in sufficient quantity for his need; and the rope fiber furnished all else that was necessary for a good torch.

With wooden slats as a stiffening core he built up a torch of grass and rope fiber. Particularly of well shredded, grease heavy rope. Especial care did he devote to the business end of his flambeau. He wanted something that would light easily and would burn fast and brilliantly. A regular mop of fluffed out rope he built round the end.

The thin whistle broke out again as he surveyed his handiwork. It was good. Such a torch would blaze brilliantly with no danger of being blown out by the wind at the most urgent moment when darkness would mean swift death.

Everything was ready for the desperate dash except:

"Wouldn't hurt to have the handle a bit longer," King muttered. "He's likely to take a swipe at it in his fright; and sometimes they have a phenomenal reach."

Methodically he lashed another slat to its length; and then he had a mop with a handle nearly four feet in length.

"Good," King commented, feeling the strength of his torch. "Now for the devil or a clear getaway. Where are those darn' matches?"

Simba was facing directly toward the door, a few feet back, sniffing uneasily at the acrid sulphur fumes that the wind carried to him.

Upon the next move it would make when King sprang his plan, would depend whether the American would be alive five minutes later. Everybody has seen the lightning suddenness of tooth and claw with which a cat pounces upon a mouse let out of a trap. Well, a lion can move just as quickly.

Something, some supremely sudden thing, would have to be done to prevent that first split second's snatch of tooth and claw. If King's judgment of lion psychology was sound, if he really knew what a lion would think, his plan would give him that moment's grace. Of the rest he was sure. He had seen it happen before. Nothing was to be gained by waiting. With hard set lips he crouched over his torch like a runner at the mark and applied the match. The next moment he jerked his head back with a startled ejaculation.

The mop of greasy rope flared up almost like celluloid. This was the supreme moment. Immediately or not at all. King tore the restraining wedge out of the groove, hooked his strong fingers under the door, heaved it high, thrust his blazing mop before him and dashed out, yelling like a devil escaped from the fiery pit.

The lion was astoundedly taken aback. It woofed once and

crouched back on its tail, startled out of all normal action by the crashing suddenness of the move, blinking its sensitive eyes at the blaze. This moment of inertia was what King had counted on. That instant's hesitation was all that he needed. Yelling still with elation and anticipated triumph, he plunged his blazing mop straight into the startled lion's face.

The great beast fell back, shaking its head to escape the scorching flame. But, at arm's length, King held his torch and pushed it home. For no more than a second, of course; but the second was enough.

Blinded by the sudden glare as much as by the blazing mass in its eyes, badly burned about the face, with its mane on fire, the lion yowled in terrified anguish, plunged aside from the thrust of that desperately determined torch, and with great scrambling bounds rushed away into the streaky moonlight and in a second had blended soundlessly into the farther shadows.

With a final hoarse scream of triumph King turned and ran like a bush *bok* in the opposite direction. Escape out of the imminent jaws of sudden death was his by virtue of his supreme nerve and the surprise of his attack. But the lion might very well come back as soon as his rage should overcome his temporary fear of the fire. King, therefore, clung to his torch as he ran. Its light would serve to give hesitant reminder to the lion as long as it should burn, and the last of its gleams would help him to find a good tree for himself. Not even Kingi *Bwana* cared to wander unarmed on foot through lion country at night, despite an arc light moon.

It was not till he was securely perched in a tall acacia that he fished another wet cigar from his pocket and laughed.

"Now, Br'er Sanford," he chuckled with grim intent. "Now let's see if I can't show you something—you an' your gang of filthy gorillas who laid their paws on me."

For a long time he puffed heavy smoke and busied himself with his thoughts. Once he chuckled again.

"Ho-ho! Bet those three coons 'll have a wholesome surprise."

They did. Afterward when they came fearfully to the trap
they saw the great tracks of the lion; they saw the claw marks
along the bottom of the door. The door remained whole but
the man was gone. They covered their mouths in awe.

"*Whai, ahoo,*" they told each other. "Truly that was a *tagati,*
a ghost lion that the *Bwana M'kubwa N'kose* summoned to
open the door. Mm-mmm, he is a very great witch master."

SANFORD WAS on forced march once more. Murder,
almost, was in his heart. Never before in his official career had
so many things gone wrong in so short a time. And for all of
them he cursed King. It was King, he swore, who had been
somehow or other in evidence when each new failure crowned
his most careful efforts. If not in person, in the background.
Every time he thought that he had found an opportunity to
trap the arch scoundrel Ibrahim, King's name had cropped up.
Always his spies reported that that pestilential Yankee was
somewhere in the neighborhood. And always Ibrahim had
easily evaded him, leaving jeering messages behind.

It was the fact of the insulting messages that had gone further
than any other evidence to convince Sanford of the collusion
of the two men. He saw King's hand in those messages. No
mere halfbreed native would ever dare, he was sure, to leave
obscene insults behind him; nor would a breed's sense of humor
think of such a thing.

In this matter Sanford's perception of Matteo bin Ibrahim's
character was as much at fault as many of his other didactic
opinions. That was because his experience had been only with
the native African mind. He was of that heavy mental type that
would require another fifteen years of residence among Arabic
peoples to appreciate the subtle sense of derision that actuated
Ibrahim.

But Sanford held his views and drew his conclusions according to the judgment of Sanford. According to his conviction
there was circumstantial evidence, heaped up and overflowing,
to connect the two men together in the beastly business to stop

which he had set his whole reputation at stake. Why were they always in the same district together if they were not in collusion? Why did he never hear of a slave cargo about to be run without hearing, too, of King somewhere in the background?

And this last instance crowned his conviction with certitude. He was out to catch Ibrahim. It had been the best opportunity he had ever had. He had taken every possible precaution. Everything had been going right. Nothing had been omitted. And then came the inevitable King.

Through a despicable ruse of treachery he had caught King— he cursed himself as he thought of his personal sense of decency uselessly sacrificed. Supreme luck seemed to have played into his hands in bringing Ibrahim across the river into British territory at Malolo village. He had done everything he knew to take advantage of that luck.

And Ibrahim had left that village an hour before he arrived with his soldiers. The message, this time, transmitted by the mouth of a stupid village headman who could not understand it, was—

"How shall a ruler of monkeys catch a ruler of men?"

Sanford had gnashed his teeth. The underlying inference was apt, devilishly apt. He knew that the slave runner meant to imply that his own intelligence service always contrived to out-maneuver the best spies that the colonial government could procure. And for that he cursed King again. He did not give Bin Ibrahim, Arab, credit for so much capacity for organization; a white man's brain must direct that. He overlooked the Matteo half of Ibrahim's name.

And now news had come to Sanford again, and he was on feverish trek to take his last desperate chance. Desperate, because he was marching deliberately across an international border without due and proper authority. He knew what that meant. He, an official in high position, with an armed force, crossing an unmistakable border—no mere line on a map, but a broad, permanent river.

It meant all the grandiloquent terms of diplomacy. "Infringe-ment of sovereign rights." "Armed intervention." "Invasion of friendly territory." It meant that heated orators of the nosier little nations of Europe would rear up on their hind legs before the League of Nations and would demand to know the exact definition of that overworked term, self-determination. It meant, even, that should the outcry be loud enough, diplo-macy, that treacherous tool of nations, might find it convenient to make a scapegoat of a high government official.

But Sanford was taking these chances with set teeth and open eyes. He hoped that, possibly, no outcry would be raised. This was a remote and deserted border line; nobody lived there but a few bovine natives in scattered villages; they probably had no very clear idea to whom they belonged. A quick successful raid might be gotten away with.

The word had come that Ibrahim with his slave train had been held up at Dolo by the swollen Doria River. Dolo was two days' march beyond Mandera. At Mandera where the Dukula River flowed into the Dawa the British wedge of territory found its apex. Two days' march farther, the Dawa, forming the border line now between Abyssinia and Italian territory, flowed into the Doria River, a considerable stream that reached the sea through Italian Somaliland.

Ibrahim had easily eluded Sanford in British territory and had passed with his slave chain beyond Mandera. Now the Doria River stayed his course, and Sanford had his choice, either to infringe the sovereign rights of Abyssinia, or to invade the friendly territory of Italian Somaliland. He had chosen Abys-sinia as being the less noisy in the council of the League.

Having decided upon the serious step of possible interna-tional complications, Sanford's hopes were running high; higher then ever before. All the element of surprise was in his favor this time. Ibrahim, comparatively safe beyond British territory, would never dream that a law abiding official would outrage the very ticklish etiquette of international law. This time, surely, he would be caught off his guard.

DOLO VILLAGE was built on a little hill, a pleasing little eminence just high enough to be—above mosquito level at the junction of the two rivers. A friendly dry *donga* debouched into the Dawa River at the very foot of the hill; an ideal road for a surprise. So along this *donga* panted Sanford's little column. He could not make it a night attack this time for the simple reason that he could not get there soon enough; and sit and wait for the next night he dared not for fear that the Doria River might go down as suddenly as it had risen. But what matter? If it were going to be a real surprise daylight would serve as well as dark; better in fact, since a wily fugitive could less easily escape.

At the foot of the hill Sanford halted his raiders. A wary scout was sent up to observe and report upon the conditions. He returned with the thrilling news that this time the luck had held. Everything was quiet; nobody seemed to be on the watch; nothing was suspected. And, within the thorn *boma*, huddled some hundred and fifty men and women. Not in chain lines, it was true, but unmistakably slaves.

Sanford's elation was a prayer. At last he had the man. There was no possibility of escape. Quickly he gave orders to the sergeant to divide up his men into groups of five and to surround the *boma*. Fifteen minutes would be allowed for the farthest group to get to their positions; and then Sanford himself with ten men would rush the one and only gate in the thorn fence and hold it.

The rest would be the simple matter of routing skulking fugitives out of the huts. There was no fear that Ibrahim would show fight. He had not half as many men as Sanford and he would see in a second that he was outnumbered.

Those were the most pleasurable fifteen minutes of Sanford's life. At last the luck had turned his way. His raid had been swift and secret. No wandering Abyssinian chiefling had been encountered. There would be no injured howl before the League. Matteo bin Ibrahim's race was run; and there was no comeback.

The single drawback to those fifteen minutes was their interminable slowness in passing. But pass they did. Sanford
looked his ten men over. They were ready and eager.

"Magazines all loaded?" he demanded. "All right. No noise
now. Forward."

He led the scramble out of the *donga* and then marshaled
his men. An easy slope of about two hundred yards lay between
them and the gate of the *boma*. There was even a fair amount
of mimosa scrub cover. They might steal a hundred yards before
being seen. Sanford noted with satisfaction that the thorn fence
was high and strong. That was good; nobody would be able to
escape. Everything was perfect.

Everything continued to be perfect. The hundred yards were
gained without alarm. At the edge of the clearing Sanford gave
the order to double; and then at last, as the little force broke
into the open, a confused gabble began to rise from within the
enclosure. But what did that matter now? They were upon it.
Nobody could escape.

The gate stood invitingly, almost suspiciously, open. That is
to say, the thorn bushes that were dragged into the opening at
night, lay to one side. Everything was so quiet, so orderly, that
a fleeting suspicion did, for a moment, check at Sanford's heart.
But how needless! There were the slaves, a herd of a hundred
and fifty of them. And Ibrahim, of course, would never leave
his whole profits of half a year and run off. Not without a vast
confusion left behind. Here everything was quiet and as orderly
as an African camp may conceivably be. At the gate Sanford
halted.

"Five men hold the gate," he ordered. "Nobody may pass.
The other five with me. Forward."

Directly facing the *boma* gate was the biggest of the round
mud plastered huts—the headman's. Here, obviously, would be
where Ibrahim had quartered himself. In the background,
staring like bewildered sheep from among the other huts,
crowded the unsavory mass of the slaves, dotted here and there

by the broad palm straw hats of the villagers. The central hut would be the first object of search.

SANFORD HAD just selected his gate guard and was stepping forward with the others when a man suddenly stood in the doorway of the hut. Not Ibrahim; but a white man. Long, lean and hard, with an easy grin of confidence on his face. Sanford's heart almost stopped beating and he stood frozen.

"'Lo, Dip'ty *Bwana*," the white man greeted with maddening coolness. "I thought you'd get here earlier. You travel kinda slow with your army."

Insanity burned for a moment in Sanford's mind. His whole plan had crashed. His high hopes of success, his foolish confidence in the prevailing quietness. Everything had been wiped clean once again by the simple appearance of that diabolic man.

Insanity gripped him for a moment, then slowly ebbed to give place to a rising wave of apoplexy. Sanford's whole upper body swelled with forced blood and his limbs shook. Two of his soldiers supported him. That congestion, too, slowly ebbed and thoughts began to sear Sanford's brain.

Why should this man's presence destroy the structure of so many weeks' building? What was it that this man had to enable him to dominate every situation? Why, after all, could he not be treated as any other man? What backing did he have, here in this remote village? Sanford had made him prisoner once— he had escaped in some miraculous manner—but Sanford still had his little army. Why should he not simply be bold and arrest this Yankee again?

But this time King stood in a different position from that of their last meeting. He was taking nothing on trust. A heavy automatic pistol weighted down a holster and another one showed its square black handle above the belt of his khaki breeches. Sanford had had time to read that letter of Consul Peterson's in which the young man, amid his blunderings and suspicions, had described how this man could use those pistols.

King shook his head at Sanford, and his grin was very hard.

"Nope, it won't do this time, Dip'ty *Bwana*. I'm heeled. I try never to fall into the same hole twice."

The hard grin widened a little.

"And I'll tell you some more what you're thinking right now. You've got ten men, and you make eleven. All trained to a fine sense of duty. You give the word, and maybe they'll rush me. *Maybe*. P'raps you'd like to try. I'll tell you the truth. I've got no more'n twelve shots here—I never load more'n six to each magazine 'cause they weaken the springs. I'll make a bet with you on how many of your gorillas get their paws on me this time."

Sanford made no move. He gave no order to his men. He did not know how they would respond, and the cool admission of King about his twelve cartridges betokened an awful confidence. King continued slowly:

"Tell you what I'll do. I don't mind making it even. Eleven all. I don't like the way that man is fingering his rifle."

He snatched the pistol from his belt and fired. The man indicated screamed and jumped high in the air. Then to his own terrified surprise he found that he did not crumple to the ground, but stood, still on his own feet. Only his rifle had been jerked from his grasp and lay on the ground a little behind him.

It was theatrical. It was cheaply motion-picturesque. But King shrewdly knew the value on the mob mind of a pistol shot, sudden and accurate. He was ready now to take command.

"Now then, men," he said sharply. "'Tenshun there! All right. Now, by threes from the right, ten paces forward and stack your rifles. Hop to it there!"

And forthwith, quietly, without hesitation or protest, the command of the little army passed from the deputy commissioner of the Northern Territory, Kenya Colony, over to King, hunter and suspect slave runner. King pointed with his gun along the line; and the men, by threes, stepped forward and made the regulation tripods of their weapons.

"Good. Now then, beat it, all of you. Dismiss. Get to sudden hell outa here." King turned to the humiliated commander.

"Some of my boys will be attending to the rest of your crowd outside; so there won't be any relief expedish all of a sudden. I don't suppose you've got any hidden gun, besides that revolver at your belt, have you, Sanford? No? Well, I'll take your word, if you like, that you won't attempt to pull that one?"

Sanford was still dazed at the smashing swiftness of happenings; but his anger flared up at last at this mark of supreme contempt. Furious words choked in his throat. But King held up his hand to stop.

"Keep your shirt, Dip'ty *Bwana*. This time it's no offense. Officer and gentleman stuff. You pulled a dirty deal on me last time; but I guess I've got that figured out. Your white man word goes."

Sanford's daze became an incredulous wonder. In his silence King continued:

"Now that we're going to have no more armed intervention, we can sit and hold that powwow that I came to propose last time. But first, I guess you want to see my friend Ibrahim. That's what you came for, isn't it? Come right along, brother, an' I'll introduce you."

King led the way round to the back of the big hut. Sanford, following him, could not prevent the thought of the revolver at his belt from coming into his mind. But Sanford, after all, was a white man.

KING STOPPED at a smaller-hut outside of which one of his camp boys stood.

"Run fetch fire," he told him. In a very few seconds the boy came with a lighted torch. King motioned the boy in first and Sanford after him. Sanford saw five dim forms on the floor. From the sameness of their positions it was obvious that all of them were securely bound.

"The third one from the left is Ibrahim," said King. "You never met him before, did you? Boy, bring that fire nearer. So."

A long silence passed while the two enemies looked into each other's faces with who knows what thoughts in their hearts.

Then Ibrahim opened his mouth. Slowly and with the viciousness of a trapped snake the soul searing words hissed forth.

"*Yeth-abba-tu?* Where is your father, Commissioner-man with the head of a wild ass? *Exiabiher le Diabol yisth!* May God deliver you to the devil that his lesser imps may put the ultimate shame upon you. May the creeping sickness rot your bloated white hide—"

That and much more did Ibrahim the slave runner have to say to Deputy Commissioner Sanford. Some of it was in Amharic, the bitterly descriptive language of Abyssinia; and when the limitations of that one failed him, Ibrahim turned to his native Arabic, to the vituperative force of which there are no limitations.

Deputy Commissioner Sanford understood no word of any of it. His exalted position placed him far above any necessity of understanding native languages. Interpreters were always at his elbow for all linguistic purposes—and sometimes they interpreted what was told to them with quite some accuracy. Kingi *Bwana* listened to all of it with a stone face. But the torch boy, after a period of awe that such things should be addressed to a deputy commissioner, who was very close to God, rolled his eyes and gave vent to explosive gurgling noises in his throat. King swiftly kicked at him and he dropped the torch with a howl and fled.

King struck matches and showed Sanford out of the hut.

"Curious," was all his comment. "He said a lot more to you than he did to me when I first caught him. Queer mentality, these Arabs—Clever looking devil, isn't he, though? You can understand how he got away with it for so long."

Sanford was silent. Too many violent adjustments were going on in his mind to permit of speech. Sanford's reasoning was not of the swift and intuitive kind. Ponderously official, rather, was the grind of his machinery of thought. Here he was suddenly faced with things new to him, vast things that upset the whole structure of his preconceived ideas. Ibrahim! King! What and who were they? Ibrahim, slave runner, of course—he had been trying to catch him for two years. But King—what, who?

Kingi *Bwana*, slave runner. The words had been synonymous in his mind for nearly all of the two years. But what the devil, then, was Ibrahim doing bound hand and foot in a hut while King coolly dominated the situation—Commissioner Sanford included—with gallingly magnanimous *bonhommie?* In bewildered silence he followed King out to the long deferred powwow, the powwow forced upon him this time, to which he had to sit and listen.

During that talk he learned many things. Very many things that he had not understood for two years. Things that slowly began to grow clear to him, as there began, much more slowly, to grow the realization that nearly all of his misunderstanding had been born out of his own pompous fault. But that realization was to develop to its full extent only later and to his own very great good. The realization that smashed home to him to the exclusion of everything else just then was that Kingi *Bwana* and slave runner were not synonyms.

King pointed an accusing brown finger at him.

"One of your assumptions, Dip'ty *Bwana*, that I couldn't ever understand, was why'n hell you jumped to the fool conclusion that I was in cahoots with this Ibrahim thing. What did you ever come across that I'd ever done to make you think I was playing in with him?"

Sanford, forced suddenly to give thought to the question, found the answer not easy to give. There had been no action, no one of the many rumors about King, that could ever have been translated to place him as a ruthless exploiter of human flesh on the hoof. Sanford's only reason was true to the official type.

"Well, the news always seemed to be that wherever Ibrahim was being particularly active you were invariably in the back-

ground somewhere; you were always in the immediate neighborhood."

"And how about yourself?" King snapped. "Weren't you
always in the immediate neighborhood for the last two years?
Always just too late—like myself?"

"But—" defended Sanford with immediate justification—"I
was on official business. I was deputed by my government to
catch him."

"And of course it couldn't occur to you," King shot in, "that
anybody else might be deputed by any other government than
your virtuous own to catch the same man?"

"Well—" began Sanford once more. But King interrupted
in quick indignation.

"Shucks, you've got no excuse. I know what you've been
broadcasting for two years—my own little information service
hasn't been entirely dumb, as maybe you've found occasion to
notice. I know that you've been telling the world that the whole
shauri has been up to *your* government; that nobody else on any
side of the border gave a hang about the business. You've
preached that up and down the land as though you were your
whole propaganda bureau."

"But," Sanford was able to interject this time, "we could never
get any cooperation—"

King interrupted him again with force and with the conviction born of experience.

"Ah, now you've said it yourself. You're darn' right you could
get no cooperation. Let me tell you—now don't get all het up
about this, Mr. Commissioner; I'm not criticizing, I'm stating
fact. Nobody in all history has ever been able to cooperate with
your government. Your people have just got to do things your
own way. It may be a heap better than the other fellow's
way—I'm not criticizing it, as I told you—but it's *your* way, and
that's how you're going to do it. And I'll admit right here that
pretty often it's done damn' well.

"If I had tried to get together with your big guns down at

Nairobi I'd have been tied up with a hundred miles of red tape and I'd have needed a mule load of printed forms and a typist-stenographer to keep pace with things. And I like to do things my own way, sometimes. And where I come from it's results that count."

SANFORD'S INNATE hereditary courtesy, formal though it was and pompous, came to the front. Chagrin at his own failure as against the other's signal success overwhelmed him; but he was able to say, as though to a winning opponent in a sporting event:

"And the results of your method, sir, have been splendid. Permit me to say, very splendid indeed, and to congratulate you."

King's indignation melted from him, and he just had to laugh. He rocked back and laughed, while the other wondered anew at the queer manifestations of Yankee humor. King chuckled till Sanford was forced to interrupt him with the question—

"Well—er—how did you manage eventually to catch the cunning beast?"

King grinned widely.

"Huh, surprised him. He, too, swallowed the story that a lion had got me in the end."

Sanford grimaced. The recollection of how his own information department had been hoodwinked was unpleasant. He changed the subject.

"What are you going to do with him now?"

"I want to discuss that with you, some. Let's figure that *we* caught him. I couldn't have got him if you hadn't been so hot on his trail on your side of the border. Suppose now that I turned him over to you. What would you do with him?"

Sanford clutched at the hope.

"Why, I would take him down to Nairobi and turn him over to the executive authorities."

"Hm-m," grunted King. "And then?"

"Why, then he would be tried; and with the evidence we have, he would most certainly be convicted."

"Yeah, and then?"

"Well, *he* would be sent away, probably to the Breakwater, on hard labor for the extreme limit that the law allows."

"And that would be—"

"Why, that would depend upon the judge, to a certain extent; but I should say it would be at least four or five years."

King slammed his fist down upon the fragile camp table so that a thin leg gave way and it crumpled under the blow.

"Then you don't get him!" he shouted. "Five years is the extreme limit that the law of your soft headed paternal colonial administration allows for all that Mister Matteo bin Ibrahim has been doing for the past ten years. It's not good enough. He'll be sure to come right back here and open up his old business; and I don't know about how smart you think you are, but I know he's smart enough so I'll never catch him again. He's thirty-two years old now. Figure that he may live to his three score and ten. He's been running an average of three hundred slaves a year—and if you want to see how he treats 'em, just look over that bunch outside.

"Forty per cent of his cargoes die in the Somali Desert between here and the shipping depot at Illigh. Good old style method. When they can't be beaten to walk any more they're cut loose and left; and there's nobody bringing them any iced tea. And if you don't know it, I'll tell you how the buzzards start on them before they're dead. I could tell you a heap more things, too, about our Ibrahim's racket. Three hundred humans has been his yearly average. Figure it out for yourself, how much it'll come to in the course of his remaining years of active business. No, sir. It's not good enough."

Sanford was appalled at the thought of all that potential misery; and he knew, as did every other official, what weak kneed penalties were handed down by judges restricted by the cumbersome limitations of their law.

"Well, what do you propose to do?" he asked King.

"I'll tell you," said King firmly. "I'll give you the slaves. And if you'll take my advice, you'll herd 'em all the way down to Kimberley where the mining syndicates are in need of labor and will pay for it; otherwise they'll all come trooping back here like lonesome monkeys. And I'll give you the other four men; they're underlings of Matteo's, an' maybe you can get them their five years' hard apiece.

"But Matteo bin Ibrahim's *mine*. The Abyssinian Government wants him worse than just five years of hard labor, because it's Abyssinian subjects he's been dealing in. So I'll take him right back to the central-government in Addis Abeba where they have sound laws about slaves and sounder ones about slave raiding."

"And then?"

"And then," said King firmly, "they will judge him and will give him the extreme limit that the law allows."

"And that will be?"

"That will be," said King grimly, "that they will hang Matteo bin Ibrahim from a tree in the center of the marketplace till they are very sure that he won't come back after five years. And may the spirits of his dead attend to his soul."

There was silence. At last—

"I think," said Sanford, "that in this case the Abyssinian way is better than our way."

"A whole hell of a lot," said King. "That's the first thing we've ever agreed upon. Shake."

THE EBONY JUJU

THE TALL brown man walked—prowled, rather—like
one of the greater *felidæ*, up and down the length of the
sumptuous room. Brown from sun, he was; lean and hard from
inquisitive interest in everything outdoors in all of Africa; and
his eyes were narrow and puckered from long gazing over heat
shimmery veld. One sinewy hand hung by its thumb from the
belt of his riding breeches; the other swung a hippo hide whip
from a thong. The soft soled bush boots made no sound as he
stalked the polished floor, stepping over the strips of rich carpet
as over obstacles.

This was King—hunter, trader, guide, prospector; anything
that came along and remained out of doors. He was announc-
ing as he prowled—

"I just can't take up your proposition."

The elderly, grizzled man watched him with head on one
side, a wry smile under his clipped gray mustache. One hand
drummed on the mahogany desk while the other toyed with a
thin gold watch chain. He was dressed in the full formality of
morning attire, which sat him with uncomfortable dignity.

This was Sir Harry Mountjoy Weldon, Governor of Kenya
Colony, British East Africa. The sumptuous room was his office
in Nairobi. He turned from watching the tall man and raised
an eyebrow at a rather scandalized secretary. The immaculate
young man immediately withdrew. The governor exhaled a
breath, and with it let dignity out as from a balloon.

74

"Now look here, Kingi *bwana*," he said. "Think this thing over. There's some deviltry hatching up there and we've got to find out what it's all about and stop it before it comes to a killing."

King, too, relaxed from his nervous prowl.

"Governor *bwana*, I can't do it. Not but what it's a whole man's job that I'd like to look back on and feel that I'd pulled off. But, gosh almighty, I'd have to write a hundred page report about it and I'd have to make out an expense account down to the last cent and a daily mileage list and— Who's your man up there? Why can't he handle it?"

The governor smiled wryly again.

"Man called Fawcett. Assistant commissioner. A good youngster—maybe a couple of years behind you. But he's had only six years of Africa."

"Six years!" King exploded. "All I've had in the country is eight."

The governor smiled—wisely this time.

"Yes, but—you've had a different training. It takes some time to adapt Oxford to Africa."

King's grin cut two hard lines from his nose, past his mouth, to mark out a chin designed by a cubist sculptor.

"Sure is some handicap. Gosh, when that lad was writing Greek verse I was skinning mule back in the Dakotas and getting regularly swindled by an old Sioux medicine man on pony deals."

"That's exactly what we need," said the governor. "A man who has been swindled by crafty Indians in pony deals and has learned his experience out of it to adapt it to crafty African spellbinders. A man who knows natives like you know them; almost like I know them."

"Lord, Governor *bwana*—"

King stalked the room again. Not that he was hesitating, but that he did not know how to temper his refusal.

The governor tried again.

"If you would take government employ as a special temporary agent I could wire to Entebbe and my colleague there would make some allowances for you. But—"

"Yes, *but*—That's just it," King shot back at him, pointing with a long forefinger. "I'd still have to wrap myself in a gaudy silken cocoon with sacred red tape. Gosh, I'd suffocate."

The governor sighed. He could understand this restless man. He was not one who had been born to the splendor of colonial administration; he had won his way along the line from the long ago days of the Boer War.

"That's the damned American of you," he growled. "If you wouldn't be so bally scornful of necessary authority you'd find some of our youngsters to be jolly decent chaps and this driveling red tape wouldn't bother you. But you're too dashed much like a leopard to change your spots. Well, if you won't, I suppose you won't. I'll have to see if I can find one of our more experienced officers to fill the job. But remember, not a word outside. This thing is an official secret as yet."

King grinned.

"Governor *bwana,* how many years have you been in Africa, that you talk of secrets?"

The governor smiled whimsically.

"Oh, well, of course there's nothing hidden in Africa for those that have ears to hear. I suppose you'll pick up a lot of underground talk. If you hear anything real I would be glad to know about it."

King chuckled.

"Anything that your blawsted British officials are too high up to hear, yeah? Sure thing. I'm going upcountry after some ivory that I've heard about, and if I happen on any bush telegraph I'll pass the word *pronto.*"

The bush loper left; the secretary returned; and dignity fell over the office once more. The governor sat long and made holes with a pencil in his spotless blotting pad. A worried frown puckered his forehead; then the wise smile spread slowly.

"Ivory?" he mused. "I wonder just where— By Jove, I wonder whether maybe we won't have to detail anybody up there?"

FROM NAIROBI a lumpy railroad track straggles northwestward to vast Lake Victoria, which only sixty years ago was Livingstone's Heart of the Dark Continent. Two weeks after his interview with the governor in Nairobi King sat in this train and damned its dreary rattle, bang, crash.

It is about two hundred and fifty miles from Nairobi to Kisumu, the port on the great Kavirondo Gulf of the inland sea. A day and night run if one is lucky, but to weary travelers it seems like a week. Mile after crawling mile of burned brown veld and sparse, flat topped *acacia* and countless dry *dongas*—the bridges over which make African railroad building so expensive; and every now and then antelope or zebra in the distance; and dust. Over everything dust. Fine white dust; over the lumpy coach cushions, in the food, sticky around one's collar, smarting in one's eyes.

Quite one of the most unpleasant railroad journeys in the world. Yet since it can cover in two days a distance that a *safari* could hardly accomplish in twenty, one travels perforce by the train and curses it as one doctors one's eyes against infection from the pestilence of flies.

From this train King alighted at Kisumu and cursed it with mechanical finality. A big, strongly built native grinned all over his face at him. He was dressed in an old khaki shooting coat and the scantiest possible loin cloth. Below each sinewy knee and above the right elbow was a garter plaited of monkey hair leaving a flash of white tuft. He carried a long, beautifully polished stick, which was really a spear with the head removed, since the regulations of well policed Kisumu town did not permit natives to go armed.

But King knew very well that the two-foot long, razor sharp blade of that spear was somewhere not far from the shaft, for a Masai and his weapon do not part company. King was too judicious to inquire.

"*N'kos bwana,*" the man greeted. "*Maleff?* Train this time good?"

"Ha, Barounggo. Never good. *Dak* bungalow. And after bath time come and tell me what the talk is in Kisumu."

King gave the man a baggage check and was away while the rest of the tired passengers still fussed with bundles and gun cases and extra hats and all the cumbrous mess that collects in an African railroad coach.

One of the first men King met in the screened veranda of the bungalow was Raynes, Africander and trader. Raynes bellowed a joyous greeting.

"Hello, Kingi *bwana!* Hel-lo—boy, one long chair and a whisky peg— Heard you had a job with the government. Howzat?"

King grinned wearily.

"Yeah, most of Nairobi heard that one. What's talk on the lake?"

"Nothing at all. Locusts at Jinja; navigation company boat aground on Lolui Island; some yarn about gold in Western Province somewhere; lions bad at M'bale—eating up a couple villages; and trouble brewing up by Rudolf. Usual stuff—new leader with mysterious powers going to put the white man out of Africa. It's a big government secret. Nothing new at all; country's as dead's a convent and only half as wicked. What you doing upcountry?"

King grinned again. This trouble brewing had been the important and very private matter about which the governor had wished to speak to him. But he knew and Raynes knew that there were no secrets in Africa which didn't leak throughout the country faster very often than the white man's telegraph.

"Me—" he told Raynes his business frankly—"I've got hold of a talk about some buried ivory up Elgon way and I'm going look-see." Then, musingly, "Trouble about these little bush troubles is that they usually bump off a couple of white men before the colored gent gets walloped out of his rampage."

"Well," Raynes said, "that's a chance the white man takes when he comes here; and he comes for his own profit, so he's got nothing to complain about— That tall fellow your boy? He looks 's if he wants to make plenty *indaba*. My bath time, too. Come to my table for chop when you're clean."

King nodded to his man Barounggo to approach.

"After bath time, Barounggo, I said."

The Masai raised his stick in the sign that was salute as well as deprecation.

"Yes, *bwana*, talk is for after bath. But there is a gift and— maybe some talk goes with the gift."

He opened a grass basket and showed two beautiful melons, luscious luxuries in that parched season just before the rains.

"Ho, good! What friend sends this gift, Barounggo? And what talk should there be about a gift of two melons?"

"*Bwana*—" the man hesitated and looked up and down the long veranda and uneasily about the compound planted with laboriously cultivated shrubbery.

King's eyebrows flickered and he, too, shot a glance along the veranda. It was deserted; all guests had gone to their baths in leisurely preparation for their dinners. King stepped down to the veranda stoop and seated himself on the edge. He knew his man. The Masai, besides being the most warlike, are some of the most intelligent of the African peoples. Barounggo had been with King for many years and King knew that he was no wild goose chaser.

"Tell me this talk that belongs to two melons. All the talk."

The Masai glanced about the compound once more, poked with his stick into a couple of nearby clumps of palms and bamboos, and came nearer.

"*Bwana*, there is talk, first, that trouble is growing up among the jungle men of the North."

So the great official secret was all over the bazaar? Of course it would be. But what had trouble in the Rudolf province to do with melons, King wanted to know.

"*Bwana*, the trouble is a young tree as yet; but it has a strong rain in the words of a new witch doctor. This *amatagati* has a strong witchcraft. A new *juju* has come to the land."

THE MASAI, like the Zulus, love to orate. If given a chance they will declaim all round and about a story in order, as they say, to wrap it with meat before they come to the bone. King stopped him.

"Melons," he said simply.

Barounggo resigned himself. He had a most gorgeous story to wrap with rich meat; but he knew that King was wise, so he came to the point as directly as his innate sense of drama would permit him.

"The talk is, *bwana*, that we have taken service with the government to go up and stop that trouble."

"The hell!"

This time King was startled. Though not accurate, this was the fastest bush telegraph that he had known. Barounggo, with the air of one who has distinctly scored a point, pulled a wooden plug from the end of his spear shaft and tapped a pinch of snuff on to his thumb nail.

"Melons," King reminded him.

"Yes, as to the melons," Barounggo agreed. "A Kavirondo savage came to me in the bazaar and said he was the servant of that Banyan trader Khoda Bux who has the garden and who remembered you with a full heart and sent these melons as a salaam."

That seemed innocent enough. King had indeed done some service to the East Indian, and a delicate compliment of a small gift was an Oriental custom. But he knew that more lay behind that innocence.

"But," continued Barounggo, piling in his swift climax, "that Banyan has been dead a month and that savage lost himself in the throng of the bazaar."

"O-ho! And so?" King was interested more than on the surface now.

"And so, when talk is of trouble," said Barounggo sententiously, "the wise man looks for trouble. Therefore—" he cast a fierce glance round the compound once more, came nearer and lowered his voice—"observe that melon, *bwana*. This one; here. And consider that this is the *limbwa* melon which the white men say is spoiled by the taste of a knife, so they but score the skin and break it open in their hands."

King looked closely and saw that a clean round hole had been punched in the fruit just over the stalk indentation and that the plug had been neatly replaced. He whistled a thin, tuneless rhythm through his teeth.

"O-ho! It is possible, Barounggo, that you have been very wise. Now what trouble, think you, can come into a melon through a round hole?"

"Many troubles, *bwana*." Barounggo was whispering. "A good witch doctor, such as that one where the trouble is, who might wish that we should *not* go into his country, could put a strong devil into it. A fool could put a poison into it."

"Or," King supplemented softly, "if he were a white man, some kind of a contact bomb. It won't be a bomb; still, precaution would suggest cutting this interesting melon with a longish knife." He looked at the imperturbable Masai.

"If we had a knife now, Barounggo—a long blade, say, on the end of a long stick—that would be safe, wouldn't it?"

He looked at his man fixedly. The Masai tried to appear not very interested; but King's gaze bored him through. Finally, with another of his fiercely cautious looks around, Barounggo reached his hand behind his neck and, apparently from out his spinal column, he produced two feet of shining steel. The great blade fitted sweetly on to the end of his stick and he handed the weapon to King.

"If a man of the poh-lis should come, this thing is a toy that I have brought for *bwana* to purchase."

"Quite so," agreed King seriously. "A toy for a small child. Now lay that melon over there; make a hollow so it won't roll. Stand clear now and we shall see what we shall see."

Carefully, gingerly, for who could tell what might be the meaning of a plugged hole in a melon pretending to be sent by a man who happened to be dead, at full spear's length King sawed at the fruit with the keen blade. The denouement came with sudden swiftness. The fruit split softly open and fell apart disclosing its pale yellow inside which ought to have been speckled with large, dirk purple seeds. Not a seed was there. Instead an incredibly swift watch spring thing, colored bright red with a thin black stripe down either side, wriggled free and coiled in compact but deadly menace.

"God!"

Almost as swift as the brilliant coiled death, King lunged the great blade at it. The steel buried itself in the ground a bare inch from the vibrant thing, and it, like a watch spring again, flashed once in the sun and was gone.

"*Whau!*" from Barounggo. "A *limpo'-olu!* The snake whose evil is as great as his belly is small. But, *tck-tck*, a pity. *Bwana* lacks practise with the spear. Had I held my—the toy that I brought for *bwana* to see, its one wicked tooth would even now be cleft from the other."

King was breathing hard through his nose, still looking at the spot where the beautiful death had coiled. Mechanically he tugged at the spear shaft, thinking, muttering to himself:

"Hm. There must be a heap more to that fuss brewing up there than even the governor's outfit thinks. Still, none of my funeral—as soon as they quit connecting me up with it." Then, aloud:

"Barounggo, you have shown wisdom. I am pleased. There will be a blanket with stripes as brilliant as that snake. Make no talk with any man. This trouble is not our *shauri*. We make *safari* to the Elgon Mountain. We go fast before all the water holes dry up and we come out fast before the big rain. Six *shenzis* are enough for the going. For the return the number depends upon luck."

11

WITH THE morning of the third day King was striding out of Kisumu at the head of six porters who carried bundles on their heads, Barounggo, who carried only his ever present stick, and a wizened, monkeylike Hottentot who carried an extra gun and the splendid name of Kaffac'-enq'uamdhlovu, which in his queer, staccato language had something to do with the slaying of elephants.

Old-timers who knew King cocked their eyes and wondered what big venture he was set upon with all that equipment. Others, accustomed to seeing the mountainous impedimenta of rich sportsmen, wondered how far this rangy looking fellow thought he could go into the interior with that insufficiency of food, and how long he hoped to keep up that speed.

As a matter of fact King proposed to keep up that speed until eleven-thirty, when he would camp under an umbrella *acacia* to let the heat of the sun pass over. There was nothing surprising in the proposal; but there was surprise in its accomplishment—to those six *shenzis*. Four miles per hour had been the pace set; and the porters had swung along easily enough. Experienced sportsmen's porters they were, all of them.

Presently, they knew, this white man would wander off into the veld and would tramp a few miles in order to shoot some buck or other; and in the meanwhile they would lie on their backs and smoke and wiggle their toes in the good dust; and when the white man got back he would be tired and would not go much farther and they would make early camp and there would be meat for them. It was a good, easy business, this portering for white hunters, and the government saw to it that their pay was twenty-five cents a day with *potio*.

But this white man did not wander off to shoot anything. At a steady four miles an hour he stalked ever toward the horizon of brown, burned plain. The porters gabbled among themselves. It was just as well to establish their rights at the very beginning. It was not that they were tired or that they couldn't keep up that pace. When upon their own business they would carry heavier loads and would keep it up from dawn till dark.

But white men, they knew, were beyond reason; if a foolish man should once show that he could do a certain stint of labor the white *bwana* would imagine that he could do it again. So they began to blow long moaning whistles between tongue and teeth and to sigh high pitched sighs, and to straggle out till half a mile separated the last of them from the tireless white man.

King wasted no breath in futile admonition, or even the energy to turn round. When he came to a shady mimosa he sat quietly under it, lighted his pipe and fanned himself with his sun helmet. The porters judged this to be the time to come up with lagging footsteps and with great heaving groans of relief. When the last of them had arrived, King rose. He spoke only to Barounggo—reflectively, almost impersonally.

"Does it not seem to you, Barounggo, that some of these *shenzis* think we have arrived in this land but yesterday?"

The Masai grinned.

"All *shenzis* are the offspring of porcupines," he said. With deliberate enjoyment he reached his great hand behind his neck and drew forth the rest of his polished walking staff. Lovingly he fitted the blade into position and fixed it with an iron pin. "In my country," he murmured, "we fatten our dogs upon *shenzis* before we sell them to the bushmen for their corn planting feast."

Kaffa, the little Hottentot, rolled on his back and cackled like a chimpanzee whose feet are tickled. This was a recurrent joke with him and the humor of it never lost its savor.

"Hee-hee-hee-ee! The father of all the *shenzis* was Mek the turtle. Not till the half hour before noon does the *safari* stop, O porter men."

And so it was. At eleven-thirty King found a suitable umbrella tree, and the caravan, right at his heels, was within its shade almost as soon as he was.

"Three hours rest. Let any man sleep who will. But first, in that load are mealies, already parched. Each man gets a half portion of *potio*."

The surly looks of the porters altered with African light heartedness to grins. This wasn't so bad after all. This white man was not one to be made a fool of; but on the other hand, he knew what other *safaris* never seemed to understand—that food was good at any time.

PROMPTLY AT two-thirty King rose.

"Three hours trek," he announced briefly.

The porters took up their loads. There was no murmuring. Three hours of steady going saw the party on rising land twenty-eight miles from Kisumu town. Good going; nearly twice as far as the cumbersome sporting *safaris* made in a day's trek.

To the northward, miles and miles away, a pale cone of ghost gray without any tangible base stood up out of the dust haze. Almost transparent it looked at that distance. It might almost have been a freak of cloud; but the cool wind that blew from it even at this distance established it as the snow mass of Mount Elgon; and the water beside which King proposed to camp was snow water on its way to feed the Lake of Victoria.

There was a little more than an hour of sunlight left. Just time enough to make camp in comfort. Four of the shenzis under the direction of Barounggo King told off to cut thorn bush and build the customary *boma* against lions. An hour allowed just time enough to build an impregnable circle of some fifteen feet across and eight high and to stock it with sufficient firewood to last the night through. Kaffa, without bidding, scratched together a few sticks and commenced cooking; the circle would grow around him. The other two *shenzis* King astounded by saying—

"Go and fetch in that bushbok; the young one under that small tree."

The men stared at him with the ape expression of their kind. The little herd of red-brown antelope were feeding between four and five hundred yards away. How were they, not hunters but porter people, to carry out this peremptory order? They stood therefore and stared dumbly.

This was another never failing joke for the Hottentot. Over his half started fire he chuckled and clucked till he blew bubbles instead of breath at his feeble members.

"Heh-heh-ho-ho-ho—ahuu-uu! Go, turtle footed ones, go when my *bwana* says it. Else the *elmoran,* the Masai, will show you how the sun glints upon his great spear when it strikes. Go. Perchance that buck will wait for you. Indeed it will wait for you if the *bwana* says it."

So the men went. Theirs not to reason why or what foolish things the white men said; particularly this white man. They set off, looking back at every few paces expecting they did not know what.

"And," King called after them, "bring it back whole; without disemboweling it."

This was another foolishness that was beyond understanding. One always cleaned game where it fell. Why carry useless weight? The men with quick African superstition began to be uneasy about all this mystery—which was just what King wanted.

He smiled thinly to himself as he watched them go. Then leisurely he walked to a little knoll, sat and kicked himself comfortable heel holes for a steady position. Carefully he wiped the day's dust from his rifle and blew sharply through the peep sight. He used the precise Lyman .48 and the little sums that went with its use came to him automatically. One point subtended one inch at one hundred yards, was the basic rule. Two inches at two hundred, and so on. For open veld shooting he kept his gun sighted in for point blank at three hundred; he knew his ammunition trajectory to drop three and a half inches between three and four hundred and four inches between four and five hundred.

Very well, four-fifty; six points would just about do it; and the little breeze that persisted was not of sufficient strength to figure. No old fashioned guesswork about this. All that was required was the ability to hold steady. Good eyesight, unshakable nerves, and taut muscles. King had all the requirements.

Taking it easy and without hurry, he fired. The young buck leaped high in the air and fell, and the rest stood staring stupidly at the distant report. Not till the *shenzis* began to approach did they up-tail and race off.

The little Hottentot, who noted everything with a monkey-like curiosity, pretended to be engrossed with his fire. Squatting as no white man can, with his knees up behind his ears and between violent blowings of the flame, he ventured the question:

"*Bwana,* for what purpose must those *shenzis* bring the entrails? There will be meat enough without."

King smiled grimly.

"For magic," he uttered momentously. "There will be a witch smelling this night."

"*Aho! Wo-we!*"

The Hottentot tended his fire in silence. His master, he knew, had many mysterious powers.

And since King had not expressly ordered to the contrary, this news communicated itself to the little camp before ever the *boma* was finished. The men, as they worked, looked at him with uneasiness. The gloom deepened. The *boma* was completed; all but the entry way, before which lay a thorny sapling ready to be shoved into place.

Meat was broiled on sticks and eaten in gloomy discomfort. King sat wrapped in black silence. The *shenzis* squatted apart and whispered to one another. The last of the day disappeared and the tropic night swept over the land. The atmosphere was full of apprehension. King sat without motion and let it all soak well in.

SUDDENLY HE lifted his head and glared across the fire at the huddled *shenzis*. Upon his forehead they could discern, marked in white, an oval with a spot in its center.

"Aho, look! It is the eye! The eye that sees within!"

They muttered to one another and huddled closer. This was witchcraft such as their own witch doctors practised.

"Bring those intestines!" King's voice exploded into the uneasy gloom.

Kaffa scuttled forward with the mass. Not without a certain disgust King pored over the offal.

"A young buck," he mumbled. "Without horns, without guile, one that had not yet learned the way of lies. The truth unwraps itself."

With his forefinger he made a vast pretence of tracing out the windings of the intestines. With meticulous care he followed the thin tracery of the fatty tissues that surrounded the paunch, bending forward with eagerness, starting with *ahs* of surprise and *ohs* of conviction, breaking off to glare across the fire at the wretched *shenzis* who watched with the fearful fascination of the African for gruesome mystery. This was divination of the surest sort. Only the best of their witch doctors could work this magic. And that this white man should know it too! *Whoora-alu!* This was fearsomely horrible.

The slow moving forefinger traced the fatty nodules and thin windings of veins.

"This is the house of the evil one," intoned the magician. "This the road that he follows. Here is the fate that awaits him. I smell him out. I see the evil in his heart. Nothing is hidden. Ha, it is finished. I make the test—the test of truth. His death sits in his shadow and is ready."

With that he sprang up and stalked before the wretched *shenzis* who rocked themselves on their hams and gave vent to moaning misery. In King's hand appeared six white pellets—aspirin tablets.

"Up!" he shouted. "Stand up and take the test of the magic that does not lie! The guiltless ones will grow strong from it; the one with evil in his heart—his belly will swell with his own poison that he carries and he will surely die. Up and open your mouths and let the guiltless have no fear."

With something like relief the men stood up. They knew all about this kind of ordeal. Their own magicians always smelled out wrongdoers that way. And it was true, the innocent ones never suffered; and if one did, why, there was proof of his guilt. The thing was infallible.

The first man opened his mouth obediently. King muttered mumbo-jumbo and popped an aspirin into it. The man gulped and waited, half uneasy in his conscience for past wrong doings, though innocent enough in the present instance. Feeling no sudden cramp in his vitals, he began slowly to grin his relief.

"Good! The first man is clean of evil and he will be strong. But the evil one knows that his ghost grins behind him. Let the second man show his innocence."

The second *shenzi* took the test with flying colors. The third. But the fourth man in the row was gray with terror. His eyes rolled white and the sinews of his neck distending dragged down the corners of his mouth in a horrible grimace. Suddenly, while the third man was still awaiting the verdict of his stomach, the fellow gave an inarticulate howl and bolted out into the night through the opening in the *boma*—which King had not closed with thorns for that very purpose.

"*Whau!*" from the men.

Even Barounggo and Kaffa were impressed. It was a real magic. This had been a true witch smelling and the evil one had fled rather than take the test which would have swelled his belly and killed him in agony.

"So," said King portentously. "His wickedness turned his

heart to water. Let him go. Let the ghosts of the night eat him up."

To himself he ruminated:

"Hm. That was a good hunch and the bluff worked. I figured damn sure that that Rudolf crowd, if they thought I was important enough to stop with that melon trick, would have sense enough to work a man in with my porters. Must be a slick bird running that rumpus up there. Glad it's none of my worry. Wonder just what this goof's plan was? Arsenic, I suppose. Wish I could have searched him. Just as well he ran, though. I'd have had to do something pretty horrid to make my bluff good about swelling him up. Well, if the lions don't get him a tough night in a thorny tree will be right good for him."

And then his ruminations were broken in upon by the remaining two *shenzis* who came diffidently, yet as with a right, and wanted their share of the magic pills which would make them strong because they were innocent. King, laughing at the eternal childishness of the African and which was ever cropping up in some new phase, gave each one a five-grain tablet of aspirin.

THREE DAYS found the little *safari* on the northern slope of Mount Elgon.

From there King had to pick up old trails. The information that he had gathered about this cache of ivory was sure and accurate; there remained only the exact locale to trace. The story that had come to him about the ivory was an alluring leftover from the days of the great scramble for Africa. Great Britain, Belgium, France, were all playing the vast game of intrigue for control of Central Africa. Nominally they were great trading companies who were just trying to open up business. But the trading companies were supported by troops of employees who knew how to salute smartly to young clerks who openly carried the titles of lieutenant and captain. Besides the business of stealing marches upon each other, these "business men" were faced with the always treacherous opposition of the Zanzibari Arabs who had got into the country before them.

The most infamous, perhaps, of all these traders, was Tippoo Tib who, nonetheless, under the urge of business policy, was appointed governor of Stanley Falls by no less a personage than Stanley himself, who, though an American citizen, was acting nominally for the Khedive of Egypt, but with funds supplied by the president of the British-India Steam Navigation Company.

The whole situation was a scrambled mess of intrigue and counter-intrigue, with vast interests jockeying for control. It can be imagined what a glorious time was had by such a man as Tippoo Tib. A clever organizer unhampered by any inhibitions at all, he sent his raiding parties north and south and east and west. The trail of slaughter and pillage that they left in their wake has been written into the annals of African history.

Their methods were simple and effective: to rush upon sleeping villages, shoot down all opposition, torture the survivors into confessing the local store of hidden gold and ivory, and then carry them all off, men, women, and children, as porters for the loot, and eventually to serve as slaves. Livingstone reports such a caravan of more than five hundred shackled men, each carrying an ivory tusk, and some two hundred women with wrapped bundles of other loot.

Sometimes one of these raiding parties never came back. Fate or weather or desperate natives overcame them. The Buganda, a tribe of a surprisingly advanced state of civilization, who lived along the shores of Lake Victoria, put up an organized resistance to these raiders. The story that had come to King was of a large party who had ravaged the country for a year and had amassed an incredible amount of loot. And then the Buganda hordes came upon them. The raiders swiftly buried their loot, murdered the workmen in approved fashion, and moved out into the best fighting position they could find—and were there very properly wiped out by the Buganda.

Only about fifty years ago, this had happened. Old men lived who had seen that fight. The locale was known. King had checked up descriptions of it from more than one source. What he hoped to find now was some old man who had survived the slave chain and who could perhaps give him some clue as to where all that ivory had been buried before the battle.

When King required information he always went to one of two basic sources: missionaries or witch doctors. Both, he maintained, were excellent people and had many points in common, the most useful of which was that both had more downright accurate knowledge of their people than the most scientific observer could ever acquire.

He made inquiries, therefore, for the oldest witch doctor in the north Elgon district and put himself out to make friends with him. Nothing clumsy or patronizing about his method; he knew the jealousies and vanities of all people who controlled their less intelligent fellows through superstition.

He had met his hundreds of white men whose religion and conviction it was that the African must be dealt with only from the position of lofty dominance. It was a good rule, and he knew all of the arguments and citations with which it was so uncompromisingly supported. But King knew, too, where to make the isolated exception. So he sent Kaffa to the old rain maker's hut with a present of tobacco.

KAFFA KNEW his ambassadorial duties as well as any diplomat. First he told the old man how good he was; then how good his own master was—a brother of the craft, no less; and that he sent a gift to express his admiration of the other's powers. Thus properly appreciated, the old magician, instead of secretly opposing the superior white man's every move, sent him back a goat, and the way was open for social amenities. So King paid a call and sat on the three-legged stool of honor before the doorway of the hut festooned with bones and dried snake skins and claptrap, and took snuff with the old faker while the uninitiated common herd of the village squatted in a wide circle out of earshot to let the two wise ones discuss the inner mysteries.

The mysteries consisted of the local gossip and the previous rainfall and the movements of game and the chances of a good mealie crop—all around the block and back again for an hour before King broached the question that was uppermost in his mind. He had drawn a lucky number at his first venture. This old man knew all about that battle of Elgon and all about the ivory, too. But there was disappointment in the very definiteness of that knowledge.

Oh, yes, the ancient said, it was all true. He had not seen the fight himself because he had been serving his novitiate in the village of another witch doctor far away; but the ivory had been buried, all right, and the Buganda, having foolishly speared every last Arab, had not been able to find it and had gone away. But some information had somehow remained alive; for after some seasons had passed—he could not remember how many seasons—a strong war party of the Tappuza, who were a branch of the great Elgume tribe, had come down from the north and had dug it all up and taken it away. He had seen it himself; a vast treasure; many hundreds of tusks—thousands, in fact. The warriors of the Tappuza covered the plain and each man carried a tusk; and there were many loads of gold besides.

Aha, what a looting that had been! And the Tappuza were now the strongest of the Elgume peoples because—this was a secret—they had for some time past been carefully trading ivory for rifles which the Armenian and Greek traders smuggled down from the Sudan. Still, there must be an immense treasure left, because it was difficult to get guns; the Inglesi were so stringent about such things. But all the same, the Tappuza were a strong people. And thus and so on for a garrulous hour.

King came away from that interview and was thoughtful. Not because that buried ivory had been removed; as far as that went, one hole in the ground was as good as another. Not because the Tappuza tribe who now had it were a "strong people",—he had dwelt with many a strong tribe before now.

Not because these people had it and recognized its value; that merely made a trade proposition of the deal rather than a treasure hunt.

No; King was thoughtful because he believed in luck or fate or whatever it was. In Africa, every now and then, things happened. Without one's own volition; outside of one's knowledge; against one's direct precaution. They just went ahead and happened and one was drawn willy-nilly into the vortex of that happening.

This was one of those happenings. These Tappuza lived up north of the Elgon Mountains. They lived, as a matter of fact, along the western shore of another of the huge lakes of the Great African Rift. None other than Lake Rudolf. That was where King did not want to go; had refused to go. For it was just these Tappuza people about whom the governor of Nairobi had spoken.

Fate; that's what it was. It was too circumstantial to be co-incidence. It was just one of those happenings of Africa beyond the molding of mere man. Man proposes and Africa disposes. King felt that he was being pushed up to the scene of smoldering trouble. And that was what gave him thought. Caution never hurt anybody, was one of his rules; another one was: figure it all out in advance and then jump with both feet. That was why he was so seldom hurt.

To be or not to be? There might be profit; there might be danger; for those people who were smart enough to make two attempts to waylay him—

So that settled that little question right there.

"Try to pull their funny stuff on me, would they?" was King's growl.

Well, then, should he go back south to Kisumu, steamer across to Entebbe, see the chief executive there, and go officially with the lavish pay and expenses that the Nairobi governor had offered? He thought of the old Æsop fable about the dog who invited a wolf to dinner; and the wolf marveled at the other's ease of life—comfortable kennel, good food, protection from the constant fear of being hunted, plenty of leisure—until a whistle sounded and the dog jumped up and said he had to go instantly because his master was calling. So the wolf preferred to remain a free lone wolf. King called Barounggo.

"Barounggo," he told him, "from tomorrow we must catch guides to show us the water holes, for that country to the north is bad country and the road is not known to me."

The Masai remained impassive.

"Good, *bwana*. It is moreover a happening of fate that in this village is a Turcana bush dweller who would return to his country. For his *potio* and a present at the end of the journey he will show the good places; so I have engaged him." King flicked an eyebrow at such prescience. The great *elmoran* continued, "It is already known to me that we go north. For three days I have smelled blood on my spear blade."

To which King grunted:

"Humph! Helluva cheerful prophet you are."

III

THERE IS just one advantage to travel over "bad country" in Africa. The quality of badness is contingent by no means upon the roughness of a country; where roads are non-existent, rocks and ups and downs and *dongas,* or steep walled dry water courses make little difference to the man on foot. Badness in arid country is qualified by the distance between water holes and by the degree of foulness of these holes. Animals drinking at water holes wade in very often up to their bellies. A pool, therefore, with rocky or hard pan sides, is a good hole; for it is tainted only by the animals. A bad hole with sloping muddy shores is thick with ooze and trampled dirt as well as dung. Such water must be strained through a cloth before it is fit to drink.

It would seem, then, that there could hardly be any recompensing circumstance in bad country. Yet there is a very outstanding compensation to the traveler. Where water is poor and scarce, game is correspondingly so; and where game is scarce, lions know better than to waste their time. There need be no thorn *boma* built every night; no constant watch against prowling danger.

It was a long trek through bad country to the region occupied by the strong tribe of the Tappuza. In point of distance no more than a good day's run in an automobile; but to a *safari* traveling on foot, a journey of many parched and thirsty days; so desperately thirsty that one drank gratefully the water of the water holes. But that burned out plain began to give place to rolling higher ground, the beginning of the escarpment of Lake Rudolf; trees other than thorn bush began to appear; seepage of water showed among sheltered rocks; green herbage grew. The country began to be fit for human habitation. Another stiff march and one would come to rain forest.

At the edge of the forest, on the highest available ground overlooking the great lake fifty miles away, to take advantage of whatever breezes might blow; yet no closer, for that again meant descending ground and more heat, was the little outpost station of Lo Bur.

At Lo Bur, for his sins—which he did not know—was domiciled Mr. Sydney Fawcett, assistant commissioner of the colonial administration, and Lo Bur was his headquarters station from which his duty was to rule and keep in order a district as large as Massachusetts, studded with scattered villages of the unrestful Tappuza.

To assist him in this hopeful little chore he had a slim, sallow Eurasian, three *babu* clerks and a black sergeant and six men of the King's African Rifles. Total pay roll seven hundred and thirty dollars; total expenses, traveling allowances and so on—all regularly disputed by the comptroller of accounts at Entebbe—three hundred dollars. All of which accumulated money was sent up every three months under escort and lay in the office safe until disbursed, a temptation to the whole surrounding district.

The official residence was a large, low roofed bungalow with latticed veranda and a corrugated iron roof, perched high on ten-foot posts. At a discreet distance was a row of adobe cubicles, servants quarters. On the opposite side at a yet more discreet distance, a similar row and a stout, square, iron grilled block of masonry—the barracks and guardhouse. There were a well, a vegetable garden and some scrawny banana trees. The whole was surrounded by a strong barbed wire fence. For a hundred yards in all directions every tree had been felled and all brush cleared. An austere, cheerless place that dazzled in the merciless sun. Good for defense but ghastly for residence.

AT LO BUR, also for his sins—which he humbly admitted—lived one Father Aloysius van Dahl. He was a member of the Jesuit Belgian Mission and here he had built a mission house from which his hope was to make as many as perhaps fifteen converts in the course of a year, and to win them to his mission settlement by teaching them to grow better yams and mealies and bananas than they knew how to grow before.

To assist him in this almost hopeless task he had Lay Brother Leffaerts and—a new acquisition—D'mitrius Stephanopoulos, zealous convert from the Greek church in Alexandria, who had shortened his name to the form more in keeping with his present affiliations, Stephen. Total payroll of this establishment, *nil.* Total expenses, about thirty dollars a month. All of which accumulated wealth was stored in a wooden box under the good father's bed; and which, incidentally, was turned out of a small profit made on carved wooden beads and plaited baskets made by the converts and exported for sale in Belgium.

The mission station was a long, low barrack built of split bamboo daubed with a mixture of clay and lime, and whitewashed. It had a thatched roof and stamped clay floors covered with bamboo matting. It nestled in the shade of great flat leaved *euphorbia* trees, and was protected from the hostile world by tall fences of string beans and a miraculous grove of *papaya* and *guava* trees. A blazing *grenadilla* vine straggled over most of it, usurping its windows and toning down the glare of its white-wash with a delicate pattern of blue shadows. It was an impossibility for defense, but a place of rest for overheated man as well as for countless flashing birds and scorpions and flat toed *gecko* lizards and brown wood ticks.

It is etiquette in African colonialdom for a traveler to call upon the local government authority; a pleasing convention which disguises the harsh necessity of reporting arrival. For where natives are many and turbulent, and white men are desperately few, with, among the few, the inevitable percentage of those who would sell their own treacherous souls for gain, it is a wise administrative precaution to know the who and the why and the where of each newcomer.

In some of the fussier European colonies in Africa the process is brutally direct. One presents oneself at the local police station, is severely inquisitioned, and is registered—and sometimes even fingerprinted—in a huge tome in which all future movements are marked up. In British Africa one pays a polite call and discloses one's business in the process of conversation.

King, therefore, presented a rather crumpled card to the barefoot sentry at the barbed wire gate and followed him in to the shade of the veranda. Dilapidated brothers of that card were known in many parts of Africa. Some men—like the governor in Nairobi, who knew men—were glad to see them. Some others who had heard stories about this strenuous man from the moving-picturesquely wild and woolly West of that uncouth and inexplicable country, America, viewed them with misgiving.

Assistant Commissioner Sydney Fawcett received the card with a feeling of dismay that was akin to panic, which turned to smoldering irritation.

"Good heavens!" He sank back in his chair and frowned while he fidgeted with a carefully clipped blond mustache. "That man here! As if we haven't trouble enough already. There's always trouble where that fellow is. What the deuce brings him up here, I'd like to know?"

The assistant commissioner's statement, on the face of it, was true; though fault could be found with the nicety of his wording. It was not exactly that trouble was where King was, so much as that that restless man was so often to be found where trouble was. Mr. Fawcett pushed his chair back and called sulkily to a boy to bring two whisky pegs out to the veranda and went to meet his caller.

King had been received by district officials before; he had a quite accurate comprehension of what many of them thought of him; he knew that they thought it because he came and went his own way, that he did whatever he did without explaining means and motives, and that he went away again without making clear exactly what he had done. Or, to paraphrase his words to the governor, because he would not write a hundred page report about his doings. Such procedure was disturbing to the peace of mind of district officials whose business it was to read hundred page reports upon what was going on in their districts.

Yet King just could not bring himself to be the tame dog of the Æsop fable. So there remained the inevitable clash between the regulation bound official and the free citizen who had a strong conviction of his inalienable rights to life, liberty, and the pursuit of happiness.

MR. FAWCETT received his caller with formal courtesy and made the formal Anglo-Saxon gesture of good will by offering alcoholic stimulant. To which:

"No peg, thanks very much," said King. "Not so early in the day. I'm a confirmed sundowner."

And right there, in the perfectly courteous offer and refusal of a drink, was a source of irritation to a mind already predisposed to antagonism. A little thing in itself; yet a universal cause of hostility throughout the tropics. To any man whose system feels that a stimulant during the sluggish heat of the day is advisable and perhaps necessary, it is a subtle reproof, a never admitted sense of inferiority, to meet a man whose more robust system does not need that stimulant.

Mr. Fawcett was unconscious of resentment; yet this impalpable barrier had been raised. Courtesy could continue to govern all dealings with this foreigner, but there could be no cordiality. Neither could King, for his part, confine himself to the banal preliminaries of polite conversation. He proceeded directly to give the information required by law.

"I report two rifles, Mr. Fawcett; a .457 and .300, and a sixteen shotgun. About three hundred cartridges all told, and two dozen sticks of dynamite."

Mr. Fawcett's jaw dropped to disclose large even teeth and he fussed with his mustache. It was his duty to know, yet he shrank from the barbarous necessity of the direct question. Things just weren't done that way. These matters should always come out in the process of conversation; or, at least, after a decent period of persiflage.

"You, ah—er—are you thinking of prospecting for gold here, Mr. King?"

King felt easier. The stiff preliminaries done with, he felt that he could talk.

"Shucks, no. There's no gold around here—not in the ground, that is; I don't know how much the high muck-a-mucks have got hidden away somewhere—not as yet. I carry the dynamite 'cause I never know where I may be going; just part of my regular kit. I came up here on a yarn about some ivory."

Mr. Fawcett's jaw dropped still farther. He had heard some disquieting rumors about that ivory himself; but if this—quite clearly trader person should come stirring up ancient legends and if he should discover anything, there would immediately be confusion and argument and dissension about property rights and heaven only knew what else. So he set out to explain to King with great patience all about the difficulties and the secrecy of the people, and the almost prohibitive transport problem—and even a hint about the "little temporary unrest."

King nodded appreciatively.

"Uh-huh, you seem to have quite a bit of underground something on your hands. And I picked up a talk about getting guns in. Sounded pretty authentic, too."

Mr. Fawcett shot a quick look at King. From where did this uncompromising fellow get so much information that was private news known only to the official elect? However, he commented only polite surprise.

"Yeah," King supplemented. "Some sixty, seventy guns, I'm told. Martini-Henry carbines mostly, with plenty ammunition. If as many as fifty per cent of them don't blow up there's still enough to make heap big trouble."

Mr. Fawcett was suspicious. This was damnably explicit. More even than he knew. Was this man trying to pump him? Mr. Fawcett was the unfortunate victim of a tradition which the governor in Nairobi could understand. He had been reared in the knowledge that in every outlying colony might be found a certain class of white man who would smuggle guns and liquor to the natives. No white man of his own class would ever descend to such a despicable business. Here was a white man distinctly not of his own class; therefore potentially he might belong to the other class; *and* this white man seemed to possess much suspicious knowledge.

As official lord paramount of an immense district, with all its lives in his keeping, it was his duty to protect those lives—even at the risk of his own. This King man, therefore, a man of another caste whose reputation anyhow was one of turbulence, must be—until proven—regarded with official suspicion. Mr. Fawcett set about officially to question the not proven alien.

"Why, er—you make a very definite statement there about the number of guns which you say have been smuggled in. What basis, permit me to ask—"

King sensed the thing immediately, of course, and responded accordingly. There it was again, the same old clash between intrenched authority acting according to prescribed rule and its honest convictions, and the individual with an indomitable sense of personal liberty. King's reaction was always that of the boy who dares to tease the policeman. His expression was one of innocent mysteriousness.

"Gossip, Mr. Fawcett, just gossip. Native village chatter. *You* know natives, of course; and *you* must know how many guns have come into your district; I'm just retailing scandal."

Mr. Fawcett was not at all sure how genuine was this perfectly true statement. King fired a metaphorical sling shot at a wicked chance.

"And I'll tell you another bit of gossip that'll give you a laugh. Your reenforcements from Karamojo are having trouble with the monthly mail truck and it's pretty sure betting that they'll have to make it on foot; twenty days of foot slog over Africa if they're fast."

That shook the assistant commissioner from his precise reserve. He gagged. Words stuttered in his throat. This man was a devil. How could he know about an urgent appeal for twenty more men—and what did he mean by his certitude of car trouble? If it were all true it would be a condition of desperate seriousness. But he thrust that thought from him. It couldn't be. This unofficial fellow could not know.

As a matter of fact King didn't. He had picked up a story about a runner having been dispatched two weeks ago with a letter going toward the headquarters of the next district. He knew that regular mail communication was by monthly auto trucks, with an escort of two rifles. From this his simple deduction was that news that could not wait for the monthly mail must be very urgent. What urgent need might there be in the existing situation other than a call for help? And the bet about car trouble, then, was no more than a logical sequence. Having his own little experiences about the cleverness of the man, whoever might be organizing this unrest, in trying to keep him out of the game, he felt confident that, if reenforcements had been sent for, the same alert mind would surely plan to delay them; and since their leader would be no more than another native sergeant, he would quite probably succeed.

King left the assistant commissioner wondering darkly just what was his purpose in coming here, and what might be his connection with the smuggled guns about which he seemed to know so much. He chuckled as he went. It was so seldom that the bad boy could put anything over on the policeman. Authority always held all the cards—all the might of government; all the sources of information; all the mutual assistance; and limitless funds. The lone hunter had nothing but his wits and such knowledge as he could dig out by diplomacy. That was what made the game so interesting a contest of skill.

I V

FROM THE formal report to intrenched officialdom King went to make a social call of one white man to another at the mission. There was no card of announcement. Father van Dahl was standing under the long fringe of thatch eave over the door. A slight, pale figure with deep brown eyes, visible above a flowing brown beard and mustache, robed in the prescribed habit of the order, which had once been black but which many suns and many washings had faded to a rusty brown, the priest blended into his surroundings. There was no alien note of color or of newness or of harsh superiority; the quiet low house and the quiet little man belonged in that far African setting.

"Mr. King?" The priest held out his hand. "They told me you had not long arrived. I have heard much of—Kingi *bwana*. You will come in, yes; and the boy will prepare the bath. Very shortly we eat our little tiffin. You will partake with us, no?"

King took the proffered hand that he could have broken easily in his own brown fist and marveled, as he always did, at the spirit that could keep so frail a man in so thankless a place. The cool dimness of the house called to him.

"Yes to all of them, Padre, and heaps thanks. Exactly what

my system needs. I hope that all that you've heard about me hasn't been as bad as some other people have heard."

The priest smiled wisely.

"We who live in Africa," he said, "after we have lived a long time, we understand what to hear and how to hear, is it not?"

He pulled, almost as a bird, at King's sleeve; and the dimness of the house swallowed them.

A native boy who had been squatting under a listless banana tree—the kind of boy who is always to be seen squatting about in mission compounds doing nothing—got up, picked up his shield and light throwing spears, scratched his knee with the toes of his other foot, and trotted off along the well trodden trail that led to the native town.

It was a simple little lunch, simply served by Lay Brother Leffaerts, a tall silent man, and convert Stephen, a rotund little person, sallow skinned, with a pair of keen black eyes, and full of laughter about everything. The meal over and the sonorous Latin blessing pronounced, Father van Dahl rose with the self-conscious smile of a child about to perform a trick, fetched a black box and pushed it toward King. In his eyes was pride of achievement. The box contained no less exotic a marvel than Belgian stogies; long, shapeless, speckled, with a straw built into the thinner end.

"Of our own manufacture," the priest beamed. "One accomplishes little in Africa, yet so much we have reached. Our maker is without skill of hand but our tobacco is much better than of the monopoly in Belgium. With the good smoke we can talk. Much news we expect you to give us."

"News, Padre? There is nothing new in Nairobi except the government secret of an uprising fermenting amongst these Tappuza. It's up to you to give me all the gossip that hasn't got as far as the official secret service yet. What's the lowdown about this new *juju* that the natives are hanging their courage on to?"

The priest looked troubled.

"So? It is uprising that they in Nairobi talk? I still hope it will not come so far. If only this Mr. Fawcett— But tell me first, my friend, are you—" the hands lifted in a pleading gesture— "there was a story that you had taken contract with the government to come and put down this rebellion."

The ready grin reduced King's eyes to slits.

"Hm, that's a nice flattering one. And the story shows a healthy growth, even for Africa. That would be some contract, wouldn't it? Well, it isn't so, Padre. There was a thin basis for the yarn, but that's all. I came up here on the trail of some old Tippoo Tib loot. Things being as they are, I don't know whether I can negotiate a deal. I'm not going to run guns for them, and I don't know whether they'll trade on any other basis till that madness has been walloped out of them."

The priest nodded.

"Yes, yes, the ivory, is it not? Somewhere there is some. I do not know, but our Brother Stephen will be able to tell you. He was, before he came to us, a merchant of the Nile."

Brother Stephen was all eager to oblige, but King checked him.

"Ivory can wait. The little question of transport will keep that weight comfortably right where it is. What about this *juju* magic? That's more important."

The priest was immediately grave. His eyes were those of a pleading spaniel.

"Yes, yes, that is the most important. They are children, these people; they run to follow a show. This idol, it makes some tricks. The man is clever, and my people leave me. Look, more than a hundred of them I had gathered so slowly with so much care. How many are left? Perhaps twenty, perhaps ten. They have left their good houses, their little plantations that we made with the scientific method; and every day two more, three more, leave off their white clothes and take their spears and go to howl in the night before that devil made of wood. It is the story of Africa. Let Brother Stephen tell it. I will leave you. I still have some small duties left."

Brother Stephen was well informed about the idol. An alert mind with no hallucinations, he dissected the situation with clarity and in fluent English.

THE *JUJU* was an unusually large one carved out of some black wood, apparently ebony; it was probably not new but quite antique, and had been produced from some witch house by its present high priest who was a cunning old highbinder. It stood upon a roofed platform some thirty feet up in a solitary "ghost tree"; it was hung about with the usual collection of bones and offerings; and it did tricks.

What kind of tricks, King wanted to know.

Well, it's most spectacular trick was that it's arms and jaws moved and it ate offerings—some simple system of strings or levers, no doubt, manipulated probably from the tree against the trunk of which it stood. And at certain times, proclaimed in advance with all its attendant hokum, it talked and gave messages to the people. Stage effects, no more, put across by a smart knave; but quite spectacular enough to capture the infant imaginations of the Tappuza savages and to bend them to whatever purpose the highbinder had in view.

King sat with narrowed eyes. A deep straight line ran from his nose up into his forehead.

"There's just two questions come out of that," was all his comment. "The man or men, whoever they are, are playing up to starting a fuss. Why? And the organized intelligence back of it all is more than the common witch doctor has. Who? If Mr. Fawcett knows enough to find those two answers he'll know how to put the skids under the trouble."

Brother Stephen thrust out his hands, palms uppermost, and his round dark face twisted into a grimace that was not complimentary.

"Ah, yes, if he knew but enough. But Mr. Fawcett is of the 'heaven born.' By reason of the very difficult examinations which he passed in London in order to gain his appointment into the government service in Africa, he knows too much about everything native. He thinks that the way to stop this trouble is to confiscate the ivory so that it can not be traded for guns; and he is hoping to find it."

"That," said King with certitude, "would cause an immediate riot."

"Yes. Immediate, at once. But he will never find it. I could—" he checked himself—"If he were not so high and mighty toward a Greek trader I could perhaps help him. He had even planned to confiscate *the juju.*"

"And that," said King, "would have meant that you would all have been wiped out. These people have too many guns against his little force."

"Yes, but I—but Father van Dahl agreed with my opinion and persuaded him to do nothing so hastily before he had many more soldiers. So, you see, we stand upon a gunpowder mine. My advice to anybody would be to go away before the mine blows up."

King tapped the ash off his cigar with meticulous neatness. His tone was impersonal.

"Yeah, that would be the *wise* thing for a man to do. But I came up to look into this ivory yarn."

Brother Stephen's hands were eloquent.

"My friend, let me give you my opinion on that matter as a trader of experience. Consider. This ivory is no longer a buried treasure; it must be bought from these people—under government supervision, remember, and the government tax must be paid. If there is not so much of it as you hope—let us say maybe a hundred tusks—the small profit is not worth the distance involved. If there is enough of it to make it really pay, you would need a whole tribe to transport it. Slow travel with the weight; one month's journey to the railway at Kisumu.

"This is not the good old days when you could *dash* a chief a few gaudy gimcracks and have him order his men out. You would have to pay the rate prescribed by a grandmother govern-ment; seven hundred men at one shilling a day apiece with *potio* and half pay coming back; and you can figure that out—if the government would ever permit so many men to leave their fields at once.

"The gold in quills—that is to say, if there is any—would be taken in by the government as specie and the face value would be disbursed by the benevolent administration for the benefit of the tribe. No, my friend, I assure you, as a business man, this is not a trade proposition."

King remained in silent cogitation, absorbed in intent ex-amination of the end of his second stogie and in the great rings he blew to enormous distances in that still, warm air. At last he said:

"I think you're dead right in everything you say. And I think I'll go and see if this Fawcett gent is possibly as good an egg beneath his cast iron shell of caste as the old governor at Nairobi."

Brother Stephen's shoulders showed his disapproval.

"I would not advise you to do that, my friend. I assure you he will listen to nothing; he will take no advice—" rising passion darkened the sallow face—"he will but treat you with conde-scension; he will insult you to your face with his politeness; he will— What do you want to go to him for? You are not inter-ested in this thing, you say; not officially. As a trade it is not possible, I tell you. Then leave the official to take care of his own troubles. Go away before trouble comes to you. It is not your affair."

He ceased abruptly and blinked his round eyes, swallowing to control his emotions. King blew some more smoke rings in silence, then:

"You're right again in everything you say. Dead right. All the same, I think I ought to have a pleasant chat with him. And there's the hundred men to be remembered; it would be a pity to have them led astray by a trick *juju*, the good hundred who have learned to wear white clothes and to grow bigger and better yams."

That apparently forgotten consideration was beginning to dawn in Brother Stephen's fate as King left him.

SO THERE was the whole truth about affairs. Witch doctors and missionaries. Those were the people who always understood the rest of the people and who had the information. King came from the missionary interview even more thoughtful than he had come away from the ancient witch doctor at the Elgon Mountain. He smiled thinly to himself as he walked.

"So that's the answer to the first of the two questions. Clever lad, that; knows quite accurately about everything—" the thin smile stretched to a grin. "Friend Fawcett must have upstaged our Stephanopoulos pretty stiffly at that. Guess I'll take mine tonight after he's had his dinner; he'll be all dolled up and at his best then. I wonder why the Greek doesn't want me to go up?"

At the mission outskirts one of King's *shenzis* met him. He had been sent, he said, by Barounggo, to lead the way through a jungly path to the camp. They had moved from the hasty halt of arrival and had taken possession of a deserted *boma* with a couple of huts in it which they had repaired. It was a strong place.

"Good," was all that King said; and he wondered what his two boys had heard that had induced them to move into a strong place, for there were, so close to human habitation, no animal menaces other than the ubiquitous hyenas.

Arrived at the camp, he asked no questions. That would come in its own good time; it was better for the present to betray no anxiety. He washed up, rested, shaved, ate leisurely; which brought him to the time for his after-dinner visit to the assistant commissioner. He signed to Barounggo to accompany him. The Masai was ready; all that he needed was to pluck his great spear from the ground where it stood upright at the entrance to the *boma* and to stalk behind his master. A thin moon cut black and white silhouettes out of the jungle path. They walked awhile in silence. Then King asked—

"What talk has been this day that you moved the camp into a strong place?"

"A small talk, *bwana;* yet such as I have heard before a letting of blood. Talk was that the Black One of the ghost tree will talk this night."

"Hmh. That is a talk that must be heard by you or by Kaffa, and I must know what is said by this witch doctor."

"Nay *bwana*—" the Masai was positive—"the witch doctor does only the *bonga,* he calls the names and the titles in advance; it is the Black One himself who speaks."

"Hmh!" grunted King again and walked on in silence. Then, softly, "How many men, think you, are following behind us?"

The Masai showed no surprise.

"It has been in my mind that three men come running softly."

"Good," said King. "Now therefore at that bend in the trail where the moon strikes do you step swiftly to the left and I to the right, and we shall see what manner of men come behind us in the night."

Some thirty paces farther the trail took a sharp curve. No sooner round it than both men ducked into the bush and crouched. In a few seconds padding footsteps sounded and the followers trotted into view.

King's eyes narrowed in the dark and he took a quick breath. He had seen this kind of night runner before. Three strongly built savages, naked except for their gee-strings; each carried a short, heavy stabbing spear; their heads thrust forward, the moonlight glinted white upon their eyeballs, distended with excitement, and upon strong white teeth showing between curled lips that panted wide, though not with the exertion of their stealthy running. Killers they were, and the lust of hot blood gleamed from each dark face.

"Well, of all the damned nerve!" King muttered, and hurled

himself out of his hiding place in a flying tackle at the foremost runner.

The man crashed down with a startled yelp and King instantly rolled with him into the black shadow of the underbrush.

At the same moment a coughing "*whaugh*," the war shout of the Masai, told him that Barounggo had not hesitated. His own man was a burly fellow who, after his first surprise, fought in ferocious silence. In the darkness King, clinging to his spear hand, found some difficulty in locating the fellow's head, holding it down with his free hand and smashing his knee hard under the ear. The squirming figure went limp.

King leaped from that place, ten feet in one great bound, to another patch of shadow beside the path and crouched for whatever might come. Running feet receded farther up the trail. A tall dark figure stood with his back to a tree, head forward, great spear poised. King was at a disadvantage. He tore his automatic from his belt holster, though under the very shadow of the established law, as it were, he hesitated to get himself involved in any premature blood spilling.

But the dark figure in the half-shadow of the tree did not move. The head hung in the same forward strained position. The threatening spear pointed not at King but curiously horizontal. In the same second King knew. He whistled thinly and pushed his pistol slowly back into its holster. He stepped close softly. The spear was not one of the short stabbing spears of the killers, but the great weapon of the Masai. Four inches of the blade's butt, a handsbreadth wide, showed darkly red before the man's chest. The remaining twenty inches of steel were through him and fast in the tree trunk behind.

KING WAS levering the blade loose when running steps sounded again. Single footsteps. It was the Masai, eager, face gleaming with excitement. He stood and regarded his handiwork critically.

"*Hau,* that was a good stroke." He began to stamp his feet

in a savage rhythm and to declaim his exploit in an impromptu sort of chant.

"A good stroke; a fair stroke. In the dark I smote, yet my blade has eyes to see in the night. A nose it has, a keen nose to smell out the heart of my enemy. Who is the dead dog who lifted spear to me? To me, an *elmoran* of the Masai. His point scratched my breast and I smote. Ha! Where is he? *Hau!* He is gone—"

"Shut up!" King told him tensely. "Cease this bragging. This is a bad business. What of the third man?"

The slayer stopped, balanced on one foot, the other ready to beat the next rhythm. King noted a thin gash in the breast of his khaki coat, the edges of which were tinged with blood. But his wound would be the last thing that the Masai would pay attention to. His reply was in an injured tone.

"That one's ghost sits beside him and moans. My hands were empty and he came at me with his spear. With his little spear like a fool he came, as one who hunts an ape. I have seen many spears. I moved my body—so; and with his own toy I let the cold night enter his breast." Triumph began to possess him again. "Aho, it was a good fight. Swift but merry. Scarce the space of three good breaths that a man may take and three men lie dead. Surely a good little fight."

"Please, great slaughterer," King checked him. "It was not good. And three are not dead. This one in the shadow we must take and bind. It is a bad business. We sit under the very mantle of the *Inglesi serkale,* and much trouble will be made over spilled blood. Sure justice will come in the length of days; but there will be talk and bother and interference at this time when I want no interference with my doings."

The Masai put his balanced foot to the ground and scratched his buttock. The excitement of battle was giving place to penitence.

"That is indeed so," he agreed. "I have seen the *serkale* do its work. Men will come together with many papers; they will sit as do the rock baboons and will make a great *indaba;* they will weigh useless talk as the monkeys weigh rotten sticks and they will throw words to all the four winds for many days. In the end one will pay blood money and go free. Yes, I have known this thing."

King stood frowning at the body of the killer who was still pinned to the tree. A trickle of blood crawled the length of the spear shaft and fell with a plop on to a dry leaf. This was a nasty dilemma. The three men had quite obviously followed them with murderous intent in the third attempt to keep him out of the fermenting trouble. Everything could no doubt be proven and cleared up; but the one certainty of the whole affair was restrictive delay.

The Masai spoke from the shadow where he was tying the unconscious man's hands with a quickly twisted rope of grass:

"*Bwana,* there is a word in my mind. I have many times listened to the talk of the *m'zungu mon-pères,* the white priests who say that their great white spirit who rules all things has put all things into the world for a good purpose. This is a hard talk to understand, but a little is clear to me. For this good purpose has he put these many hyenas into the land. Let me throw these twain dead dogs into the first *donga* and in one hour it shall not be known how they died. And if *bwana* will permit likewise that this third dog who would have murdered us from behind—"

King grunted a short laugh and came to a decision.

"You'd make a swell convert for the good *padre;* you have the faculty of acceptance of fundamentals. Listen now, Barounggo. Thus it shall be. Give these two to the hyenas; this third one take back to the *boma;* bind and watch him well. He must be questioned and we may learn something. I go to talk with the *bwana Inglesi.*"

THE ASSISTANT commissioner sat in his veranda in solitary after-dinner state. King could see the pale glow of his shirt front, a white splash in the deep shadow, long before he reached the steps.

Like any other man, he had grown up with certain traditions, himself. One of these was that to wear anything white was a foolish invitation when trouble was abroad. The formal greeting concluded, the formal drink accepted, King ventured a well meant warning.

"Mr. Fawcett, you ought to be able to step out there and look at yourself once. You've no idea what a target a boiled shirt makes for any sportively inclined coon who's got one of those Martini-Henry's."

Mr. Fawcett's reply was stereotyped, as one expounding a creed.

"Oh, I suppose it is visible at quite a distance. But then, Mr. King, one can not drop all the conventions of decent civilization just because one happens to be posted in a savage country."

King, dressed in breeches and shooting coat, and with frayed cuffs at that, grinned to himself in the darkness. He had met this same thing all over Africa. It was the proper thing to do and it was therefore done. Tradition again; and unswerving faith to it.

But he had come to talk, not to quarrel with another man's religion. He approached his subject placatingly.

"Will you let me ask you a few questions, Mr. Fawcett—and let us look at question and answer quite impersonally?"

Mr. Fawcett inclined his head.

"Well, then," began King, "have you formed any idea of what is the real bedrock reason for this unrest here?"

Mr. Fawcett weighed his answer.

"I don't mind answering that question, Mr. King. And I say, no, I do not know. I believe it to be the work of a crazy witch doctor inflated with a sense of his sudden power over his su-perstitious people. And in turn, I would ask you why you are interested in this unrest?"

King weighed his answer in turn.

"I'm interested only, as I told you, Mr. Fawcett—that is to say, I *was* interested—only in so far as it affected this ivory story. But—" the eyes narrowed to the same hard thinness as the mouth—"some nervy gent connected with this fuss is so interested in me that he's begun to warp my judgment. But let's continue to be impersonal for awhile yet. Let's suppose, for a moment, that everything was quiet here and a man should locate this hoard and deal for it legitimately, would you sanction his hiring porters here?"

"That would depend," said Mr. Fawcett judiciously, "upon how much ivory he wanted to take away."

"Well, suppose that man should tell you that there were seven hundred tusks; what would you say?"

"I would say first, Mr. King, that I don't believe there is any such fortune of ivory in the district; next, that that man knew very much more about this secret than I do; and finally, that I would refuse to sanction any such number of porters. Why, my good man, that would be a migration. You have no idea what such a tribal upset would mean."

King nodded.

"Well, leaving out the ivory, suppose a man should tell you that somewhere in the tribe is a store of gold in quills. What would you say to that?"

Mr. Fawcett was positive.

"I would tell that man, first, as an officer of the government, that he might as well forget it; because the government would not permit the tribe to be exploited. That gold would have to be paid for at its face value. And secondly—" Mr. Fawcett's tone was pointed—"I would demand from that man how he knew so much about the ivory as to be able to state its quality and so much about the gold rumor as to know that it was put up in quills? I would regard that man, Mr. King, with suspicion, and I would watch his every move. In fact, I would cease to regard the question as impersonal; and I ask you flatly, Mr. King, as the administrative officer of this district, how you come to have all this information which has not even been reported to me?"

King laughed shortly.

"I have *not* all that information, Mr. Fawcett. I don't expect you to believe me, but I repeat, I'm following a thin trail of a story and I'm guessing. But I have one piece of information now which I will tell you. I'll tell you the rock bottom reason that's back of this unrest."

King pointed his statement with a long forefinger.

"This whoever it is who is stirring up trouble is aiming to bring about an uprising—it don't matter how quickly suppressed or who pays the piper afterwards."

Mr. Fawcett permitted himself a smile.

"Uprisings are always possible in Africa when the natives are excited about something; but you ascribe an unusual intelligence to the agitator. Why, Mr. King, permit me to ask, does this witch doctor wish to have an uprising? What would be his possible gain as against his very sure future punishment?"

King pointed his forefinger like a gun.

"Suppose, Mr. Fawcett," he said slowly, "that it isn't the witch doctor who is the bedrock. Now then, this man who's supplying the brains wants to get the administration out of the way for just a little while—no, let me finish please. He wants to get it out of the way so that he can make his own dicker with whatever nigger will be the big chief. He will arrange with the chief for porters at about four cents a day. He'll fix up to snaffle all that ivory and that gold, to pay for it in trade trash, and to make his getaway before the government can restore order and come back to control things."

THE ASSISTANT commissioner gasped. The statement was too audacious. That the unrest might develop into an uprising he knew only too well; but that the whole thing should be a deliberate plot, so diabolically clever—and going on right under his nose—that was more than he could assimilate all at once.

Revolting from its acceptance, his mind searched for difficulties in its conception. He found one almost immediately and it was so conclusive that he was afforded a laugh.

"That is a very ingenious theory, Mr. King. But you forget an important point; I might say a prohibitive point. Admitting for a moment that this Machiavelli of yours should succeed in temporarily dislodging the administration of this district—of *this* district mind you—where could he go with his loot? The jolly old transport problem, don't you know? He couldn't upset all of British Africa, could he? And one can't *safari* several hundred men with elephants' tusks hidden about their person; or even a few men with gold in quills, for that matter.

"To the northeast across the lake is Abyssinia, where they would take everything away from him in the first day's trek. To the north and northwest is the British Sudan and desert. Not a single water hole in many hundred miles. All the rest around us is British Uganda or Kenya Colony—*not* upset by your intriguing genius. And, dash it all, we do know what is going on in the country. So where, Mr. King, would your man go?"

"That," admitted King, "is the big hole in the argument. That's what maybe I can find out. But let's suppose for a little bit longer. Suppose that that is the plan, how could you stop the trouble before it came to an uprising and a white killing?"

Mr. Fawcett's triumph in the argument had put him in a more tractable humor. He was willing to disclose a corner of administrative policy.

"That is at present a problem, I don't mind confessing. You know, of course, that all these African disturbances are the work of some single dominant personality who understands how to excite the monkey mind of the herd. These poor fools have nothing against us; they are infinitely better off than they ever were before, and if they would stop and think they would know it. But the excited African can not think. Some dominant mind is exciting these people by an appeal to their superstitions. Eighty per cent of the African wars have been started that way.

"We do not know the person in this case. But it is obvious that his instrument of excitation is this blasted *juju*. The people's courage is being bolstered upon their belief in its magic powers. Unfortunately—the missionary here has convinced me—any overt action against it will be the signal for an immediate riot. As soon as my reenforcements come I shall confiscate the bally thing and that fact in itself will blow up its whole prestige. It would blow up if I dared to confiscate it now; but since you seem to know about the guns that have been smuggled through from somewhere I may as well admit that I'm not strong enough just now to risk the ensuing riot."

There spoke Africa. King understood and nodded. He knew the old story by heart. Here was this stiff necked official sitting, as the Greek had said, upon a powder mine; yet the thought never even came to him that he might desert his post—or, to put it diplomatically, that he might temporarily retire and come back with an adequate force. Nor did that thought occur to the missionary. Nor, for that matter, to King. That was why the white man dominated Africa.

"So the question boils down," said King slowly, "to who gets there first; the dominant mind with this uprising, or your re-enforcements."

"Well, er—I suppose that is so, Mr. King, since you put it that way."

"And believe me," said King. "Your reenforcements are going to take a long time getting here."

The assistant commissioner was immediately belligerently suspicious again.

"What do you know about my reenforcements, Mr. King? There again you display an unwarranted knowledge. I have a right to know your source of information, and I demand to know."

King held up disclaiming hands.

"I don't know a darn thing, Mr. Fawcett. I'm guessing. You

don't believe my guesses. When I know anything definite I'll tell you. Good night, and thanks for your information."

The assistant commissioner listened to the crunch of King's retreating footsteps on the gravel—the khaki coat and breeches had melted into the darkness.

"I wonder," Mr. Fawcett cogitated. "I wonder whether that fellow is all right after all?"

King walked back through the moon streaked jungle path alone, alert with ready gun, but not unduly anxious. The dominant mind, the dispatcher of the three killers, would hardly have had time yet to ascertain the result of the mission and to have made new preparations.

"Gosh," King thought to himself with a certain heat, "this highbinder is sure asking me to horn into his game and bust it up."

But he did not devote much time to indignation. His mind was engrossed with other things. Thoughts flew from point to point in his brain; guesses formed, worked themselves out or remained as reckonable possibilities. Certain things adhered together in an as yet intangible train which he voiced to himself.

So friend Fawcett would regard with suspicion a man who knew that there were seven hundred tusks and that the gold was put up in quills. I wonder. And the Greek doesn't think of himself in his own mind as a missionary, but as a man of business, a trader. I wonder— Still the hole remains. Where could he go with the stuff if he got it? Wonder if the commish has a good map?

At his camp *boma* he inquired about the prisoner. The man had been put into one of the huts with thumbs bound behind his back and was safe. He would keep till the morning. King turned in to sleep, for he intended to devote the next night— when the *juju* would talk—to wakefulness.

V

MORNING BROUGHT an interview with the prisoner—entirely unsatisfactory from every angle. King had to look at the man's face but once to know that there was little hope. It was a brutish gorilloid face with wide cheek bones and prognathous jaw. Had the fellow been white he would have been a gunman. Dull witted enough to take orders without asking why and animal enough to be callous and physically courageous.

He knew nothing. He had been told to go out and do a job, and he had gone accordingly. He was to have received a piece, two and a half yards, of print cloth in payment. He did not hesitate to state the name of the higher up who had given him his orders—a certain Umbale, a native of the village. It meant nothing. King had never hoped that the guiding genius would have been foolish enough to deal with his stupid tool directly.

And that was about all that the man did know, King was convinced. He knew better than to try to extort further information under threat of death. It is only the civilized mind educated to dread of after torment, that fears death. Primitive man lives in too close contact with sudden death to be terrified by its imminent threat.

"A spear and the *donga,*" Barounggo growled.

"Shut up," said King. "Put the fool back in the hut. Feed him and hold him safe. If he cries out drop sand in his mouth for a lesson. Perhaps later we give him to the *bwana Inglesi* for justice."

King went to the official residence and requested to be allowed to look at maps. Permission was granted readily enough, though with unmistakable suspicion as to his motives. A *babu* clerk took King down to the office and turned over to him an enormous map roll, the familiar "Kitchener Survey." King spread it out on a table, weighted the corners and pored over it.

What Mr. Fawcett had said was true. Except for a little corner

of Abyssinia abutting on the lake, the rest was British territory. Miles upon thousands of square miles colored pink. Good
Lord, they seemed to own half of Africa, these British! And it
was true, too, their far flung territories were well administered.
Any large *safari* movement would be reported and quietly
checked over at some point by some outlying resident white
official; most particularly if the word had gone out that something bulky was being smuggled out.

No, it was impossible. Except—King strained his eyes over
the map and visualized roads and ways and means. *Safaris* could
not just disappear into the uncharted wilderness; they were
confined to certain definite trails by the inexorable circumstance
of water holes. Kenya Colony? The sinewy brown finger trailed
off hundreds of miles in a wide north-east-south arc. Uganda?
Westward clear to the Belgian Congo. All of it quietly, effi-
ciently policed. Up to the northwest there were no water holes
at all. The Tappuza wooded country gave way to desert. Four
hundred miles of blazing sand and rock and rubble to the mud
village of Rejaf on the white Nile. Not a water hole, not a tree,
not a blade of grass. An empty, deadly, barrier.

Yet—an idea began to grow. Desert. That meant no water.
No water meant no rain. No rain meant no *dongas;* no steep
sided washout ravines criss-crossing the country. That meant
level, or at most, rolling ground; sand dunes. No nourishment
for man or beast. But—the idea flashed to climax. What was
four hundred miles to an automobile truck? Had not a French
Count Somebody-or-other crossed the Sahara with a train of
trucks?

King whistled his tuneless melodies through his teeth and
his eyes contracted to almost sightless slits. Was there any hole
in that idea? Rejaf? The Nile? Too far up for regular river
steamer traffic; but native boats plied up and down all the time
with a worthless assortment of upriver trade. Dried mud fish;
papyrus reed; pottery. All kinds of junk. Miles of barren, unin-
habited stretches above and below the mud town. Many ivory
tusks could be loaded into the bilge of a native boat, covered

over with any kind of junk and could keep going without question until doomsday.

King removed his weights and the map rolled up with a conclusive snap.

"Hmh!" muttered King. "That fills in that hole. I'm ready to bet on question *why*. Remains question *who*."

He went to have tea at the mission. He talked with the good missionaries about nothing in particular; the gossip of interior Africa. People and tribes and local customs and railroad developments and isolation of distance and *safari* travel and autos and airplanes. Airplanes would be the salvation of the interior. All agreed to that. As to automobiles which had opened up the rest of the world—the trouble with automobiles, said Brother Stephen, was the prohibitive expense of bridging the countless *dongas*. If it were not for that, there were many makes of cars that would stand the rough going over the veld.

And Brother Stephen was able, out of his experiences of his trading days not so long ago, before—with a flashing smile— before his reformation, he was able to name some of these cars and discuss their merits.

King came away mumbling to himself.

"He has the knowledge. I wonder if he has the nerve?"

Away to his left he could hear a steady drumming. He knew the rhythm. It was the notice of an *indaba*. It would continue all day, and that night the *juju* was going to talk. Decidedly both Barounggo and Kaffa would have to go and hear that talk. He told them so once again; and they were only too eager; as eager as white folks to go and see a mystery play. So were the six *shenzis*. Good; he gave them all leave to go.

WITH THE beginning of dusk they went. King lounged in indolence till full dark—till no possible watcher could note his movements. Then he too got up with the eagerness of one who contemplated a show. First he went to the prison hut and assured himself that the captive was safe. Then he opened one of his *safari* bundles; one of his secrets that even his own servants must not know. From a cloth roll he took a fat black stick and proceeded to make a black face of himself.

More than once before in his experience he had found that the glow of a white face in the dark was almost as noticeable as the glow of a white shirt front; and he was going where a white face would be a swift passport to a particularly horrible death.

The ghost tree stood alone, a giant wild fig with enormous horizontal limbs and wide, buttressed roots, between some of which one might have pitched a tent. Half of the spreading base had been built up with crooked sticks and thatch to form a witch house. Bones, human skulls, dried monkey mummies, snake skins—all the horrors dear to the African mind hung about in gruesome suggestiveness.

For fifty yards around the tree was a clearing, stamped hard by the pounding of many hundreds of naked feet. The dark clearing was packed just now with naked, shuffling, heaving bodies; and they all stamped a dull rhythm on the hard ground. A sweaty odor of goat pens eddied in the hot night air over the human mass.

Back of the clearing was a treeless scrub of tangled bush and stunted thorny mimosa. In the scrub King lay on his belly. It was pitch-black in the shadow, for which he was properly thankful. This was as near as he dared to come; he had no hallucinations about any sleuth ability to disguise himself so that he could mix in with the crowd. A white man detected in that hysterical mob would be torn apart by clutching blunt fingernails and big white teeth.

From where he crouched King had a clear view of the *juju*. Halfway up the giant tree was its platform—high enough for the hocus-pocus of manipulation to pass muster. At either corner of the platform a smoky wick in a saucer of oil lighted the awesome idol; a squatting figure carved with all the savage talent for the bizarre; a huge grotesque of jutting angles and vast opaque shadows. High lights glittered blackly from the knobby, drawn-up knees, from the curve of a great pot belly, and reflected out of the higher gloom from the outlines of a bushel-basket mouth and glaring eyes. A clever stage effect of a voodoo horror.

The thick arms which hung between the splay feet moved jerkily. The heavy jaw chattered on a hinge like a ventriloquist's dummy. For a space the thing confined itself to these antics while the crowd below shuffled and milled in suspense.

An overwrought savage, nerves taxed beyond endurance by the awe-inspiring suspense, screamed a high pitched hyena laugh, slavering through blubber lips, and fell to the ground. He writhed unnoticed. His howlings were smothered out in horrid gurglings under hard feet. The mob moaned in minor keys and closed over him. He screamed once again and was silent. Shoulders heaved; heads tossed like cattle before the break of thunder; eyeballs glared white like those of the *juju*.

King crouched in his shadow, tense. He knew the danger of Africa in that temper. This was more than he had come prepared to see.

The looming idol tired of its chatterings and its jerkings. It yawned cavernously to show inset bone teeth as large as dollar pieces.

The packed crowd shivered. The thing was going to speak.

The jaws clicked woodenly. A hollow megaphonic voice issued. King could make out most of its mumblings; for the Tappuza dialect was an offshoot of the Masai with a sprinkling of Kiswahili. The message was meat for the attendant congregation. It flattered their strength; it praised their courage; it promised them wealth, and above all indolence. There would be nothing to do except sit in the shade of their huts and eat. And soon, soon, *soon*, would all these good things be forthcoming. Tomorrow it would eat offerings—King grinned grimly at the inevitable priestcraft—and soon would come the sign.

Africans do not cheer. The crowd seethed and its grunts of ejaculation rolled back and forth like summer thunder. King was grave. This matter was closer to bloody riot than even he had guessed. The *juju's* trick was most dramatically impressive. Its great jaws opened once more and commenced on another harangue on the wrongs of the black man. King listened, and wonder dawned upon him. He thanked his various heathen gods that he had come. Never would his Barounggo and his Kaffa have been able to report the important essence of this speech. His suspicions crystallized. This talk made everything clear; everything possible—and infinitely more dangerous.

T H E   V O I C E   that mumbled from above was an unmistakable African voice; but the claptrap that it dispensed was pure bolshevism. The African in himself has no inherent sense of his wrongs; he has not evolved to that state. If he is starved, and if he is beaten and robbed, he resents it with dull apathy. If the starving and beating and robbing reach a point beyond human endurance he will rise in a howling mob and will rend and slaughter everything within his reach.

He will rise and slaughter for other causes, too. But, of his own volition, never because some intangible authority claims to own the land upon which he lives, which his fathers reclaimed from the jungle; nor because he has to pay a tax to that intangible authority for the privilege of growing yams upon his own land; nor because that authority prevents him from killing his neighbor if he doesn't like him, and if he does kill that neighbor, relentlessly executes him.

The primitive African is not convinced that he is an oppressed proletariat. But if he is told that he is; if he is told it carefully, in words of one syllable; and told often; and told the same thing again; and with all the force of awesome skullduggery to back up that telling—then the possibilities of the primitive African are devastating. No witch doctor could think those thoughts; they would be beyond his ken. But any African spellbinder could put those thoughts across to the herd if some more sophisticated intelligence, which knew how potent such rhetoric was to inflame the primitive mind, would coach him along.

King's lips framed to a soundless whistle. The intelligence behind this cunning propaganda—the same intelligence that had guided three attacks upon his own life—was indubitably a white man, or men. It was white intelligence that could see a huge profit in all that ivory and gold if it could *dash* the jubilant local chief a present and make a getaway—maybe by automobile—across the otherwise impassable desert.

King's blood chilled. So that was the seed of that plot. A perfect plan, carried out with devilish cleverness. Inexorable in its progress, and certain, from present indications, of success. And the little white community that would be obliterated by the first wave of that mad orgy sat helpless. What if King should tell the government authority all that he knew and all that he suspected? What if the authority believed every word of it? Authority sat with empty hands, with a black sergeant and six soldiers against who could tell exactly how many fairly modern guns? What could it do? Apprehend the guiding spirit? Who was the guiding spirit? If, acting in desperation upon suspicion it should succeed in arresting the evil genius, had not the deluge already gained sufficient momentum to carry it blindly forward? Authority could watch it come; but lacked sufficient force to stem it.

Authority could also run away. But King laughed silently. The same tradition that made authority wear a boiled shirt for dinner in the wilderness would make it stick through hopeless odds and against all reason to the end. Kingi *bwana's* night prowl had given him much to make him very serious indeed. So he laughed again out of a crooked mouth.

Suddenly he stiffened. His never dormant hunter's instinct made him aware of a presence near him. Something breathed in the black shadows, softly, cautiously. It was not an animal; he knew that at once; this was no sniff-sniff-snuffle of any beast. It was the slow, careful exhalation of a human under the exertion of moving in dead silence.

King cursed himself for a fool. Not because he was there, but because he must have in his absorption, in craning for a better view, made some noise to have betrayed his presence. Some sharp eared savage must have detected something in the bush and was crawling to investigate; some unusually nervy fellow to go prowling about in the outer dark when magic was afoot.

King had been through too many violent experiences to have any hallucinations about any sort of certitude in the matter of a fight. It was only in the motion pictures that the intrepid hero could be sure of seizing an adversary and choking him into instant silence; and silence was desperately necessary to King. A single cry, a scuffle, and that hysterical mob only a few feet in front of him would hurl itself, screaming and fighting one another, to lay clawing hands upon the intruder who had cared to spy upon their black mysteries.

King had seen a dog once torn into little pieces of rag by the infuriated males of a troup of rock baboons. He had no foolish shame of flight. He rolled softly over from his stomach, and over again. His legs felt the prick of a thorny stem. Carefully he drew them up and clear and rolled again. He listened. In the clearing the crowd still shuffled and murmured. From where he had just been his straining ears fancied they detected the click of a breaking twig.

On his knees now. How he thanked his stars for those days of his youth when he had played Indian with real Indian boys from the reservation and had labored so earnestly to vie with them in stalking the hostile brave. He had to feel his way, reaching with cautious hands to locate bush and overhanging branch and to sweep dry twigs from his path. For a moment he thought he had lost his skulking follower; then a soft scrape of thorn upon cloth came to him.

HE WRIGGLED under a bush, breathing hard. Curse his foolishness in getting into such a trap! The man was good. King himself was far from a clumsy stalker; but this fellow managed to keep right on the trail. Could he smell him? King wondered uneasily. He had heard many natives claim that a white man's smell was strong and unmistakable. Was this fellow following him by scent? He rolled with drawn up knees through another opening—and stopped in the middle of the turn.

To his left, farther away, sounded another swishing of disturbed foliage. Good Lord, was the bush full of silent stalkers in the dark? And why so blood chillingly silent? Why didn't they yell an alarm and call the howling pack? But this was no time for questions. King scrambled hurriedly in a right angle direction. His hand came down hard on a two-inch mimosa thorn which immediately pierced clear through the heel of his thumb. His tortured nerve responses forced a hissing intake of breath. He lurched on through the passage into an apparently more open place—and the presence was there.

It breathed heavily. Soft pats indicated a groping hand. Something touched his boot. He snatched his foot away. Leaves rustled above; a straining grunt; a swish; and a soft chuck in the ground where his foot had been.

King scuttled desperately from there; he didn't know where; and the noise he made seemed to him appalling. There was no mistaking those sounds. He might almost have seen the action in broad daylight. That had been the vicious stroke of a knife. Limping on two knees and a hand, King contrived with his teeth to get a hold on the broken end of the thorn. Its drawing out seared like a hot needle. A tangle of thorn barred his progress. He wormed to the left of it. A bristly stem radiated low hanging arms. Farther to the left. More thorns. He was in a *cul-de-sac*. Beyond him sounded the rustle and crackle of the other stalker. This fellow was not so skilful. Behind him came the stealthy crawl of the expert with the knife. It was a trap.

King was unarmed, to all intents and purposes. He had his automatic, of course, in his belt holster; but, as well as use that, he might stand up and shout his presence. The only weapon to this situation would be a piece of soft lead pipe.

King reached out a cautious hand and groped the ground for a stone; something to give weight to an empty hand. In this hope his luck was with him. The groping fingers closed on a large oval that fitted nicely to the hand. King crouched on knee and one hand and waited.

Before him, skyward, the far glow of the *juju's* footlights showed blurry patches of foliage in silhouette. Around him the shadows were black. The very blackness took form and swelled and shrank and shifted. It was hopeless to try to discern anything there. King's heart thumped and he took long inhalations to still its pounding. Stillness was the most difficult thing in his life.

Suddenly out of the black a hand pawed his face. King, shaken from his nervous tension, nearly yelled. In the next second the other would yell his discovery. A faint odor clung to the hand; not of goat, not of sweat, not of plain African dirt—but of sandalwood perfume!

All that came to King out of that startling discovery was the flash that it explained why a knife and not a spear. He visualized the knife again, heaved up for the instant stroke, and not, this time, at where a boot had been. The issue depended upon swiftness of decision; upon which of the two would recover first from the momentary shock of actual contact. King judged his distance and direction, heaved his shoulder and swung his long arm over with all his might. There was a hard *thuck* as the stone struck; a stab of excruciating pain where an overreaching fingernail had impacted; and a soft, knuckly sound of subsidence.

Out in front the *juju* mumbled gutturally; the crowd shifted and stamped. This thing had been as silent as the best talking picture could have wished. To the left sounded the scuffling of the other, less skilful, stalker, clearly in a tangle himself. King began his precarious retreat from the trap into which he had crawled. A certain elation filled him. He had discovered much. The exhilaration of having gotten out of a desperate trap was with him. That other clumsy stalker worried him not at all. He

left him fumbling in the dark and felt his own way out from
the so nearly fatal scrub.

VI

KING SAT in his tent, without light, thinking. So it
was established that the directing intelligence behind all
this trouble was white. A knife and sandalwood perfume were
not native attributes. And that explained, too, why the stalker
had not settled the issue by simply giving the alarm. However
friendly with a more intelligent chief or witch doctor whom
he directed from behind the scenes, he would be, as a white
man, just as forbidden as King himself to a voodoo ceremony
of the herd. And the herd, further, should it be known that a
white man was directing operations, would with natural suspicion be less amenable to the spellbinding of their leaders.

Yes, he was a cunning devil, whoever he, or they, were. He
overlooked nothing. King supposed that he had hidden himself
in the scrub to overhear whether his lessons were being put
across properly and to supplement omissions in future lectures.
Clever. Not a mistake anywhere, except—King scowled into
the dark—except the mistake of starting hostilities against him.
Three times; three attempts on his life. Somebody would have
to pay damages for that.

If—there was always that terrible *if*—the trouble did not
break before King could, or the assistant commissioner could,
or somebody somehow could do something. The situation was
very near its climax. The directing genius would never have been
so foolish as to announce a practical declaration of war unless
he knew for certain that no reenforcements would suddenly
arrive out of the south to spoil his plans. All that was needed
now was the last straw; the final match. One good manifestation
of the *juju*—some spectacular miracle—and the blue flame that
glowed just beneath the dark crust of banked fuel would blaze
out in an orgy of destruction. Let almost any little excitement
start, and that insensate herd would stampede to the kill. To

stab and thrust and mutilate long after the last white man had been killed. That was the history of Africa.

Yes, the situation was bad. And no bright ray of hope in the immediate future either. Well, anyway—King was able to bark a short laugh—there was one crafty plotter, who, just about now, was carrying a horribly sore head in a sling; he would remember that for awhile.

King's men came home jabbering in awestruck tones about the wonder they had witnessed. He sat still and said no word. Thinking. Once, long after the men's chatter had died down, he got up, fumbled among his duffle, carefully made up a packet in wrappings of trade cloth, and returned to his thinking.

"Slim chance," he muttered. "But the only one I can see—if the *padre* will cooperate."

With earliest morning he went to visit the mission. He knew that missionaries got up at an appallingly early hour to commence their meticulous labors of the day. Father van Dahl met him, frail, quiet, smiling a welcome through tired eyes.

"So early, my friend? It is nothing of seriousness I hope."

King was forced to smile in return to the greeting, but the smile quickly left his face.

"Pretty bad, Padre. I've come to make *indaba*. I took in the *juju* show last night."

"So? That was, no doubt, difficult—even for Kingi *bwana*, no? Myself, I have never seen this; nor any other white man."

"Hm! Don't be so sure, Padre. Your—er—are your people up yet? Lay Brother and Brer Stephen?"

"Oh, yes; certainly, yes. Even Brother Stephen." The priest smiled indulgently. "Though he finds it not so easy as yet. He has been not long with us; and our devotions, yes, they come earlier than those of one who has been in the trade world."

King's eyebrows flicked wide. He had somehow expected after last night's encounter in the bush that Brer Stephen, as he now tabulated him mentally, would be—but he didn't know exactly what he expected. Why should he have connected

Stephanopoulos with anything at all? And just at that moment Brother Stephen himself appeared. He was passing the door; full of health without a care in the world. He flashed his ready smile, bustled in, shook hands, remarked cheerily on the early hour, and bustled out murmuring something about morning duties.

King was nonplused. He had been building a theory upon a suspicion which he thought had been clinched last night. Had it been correct, Brer Stephen—Brother Stephen, he amended himself—would have been a sick man this morning; very sick indeed.

The priest was talking with fond benevolence.

"Yes, he is a great comfort. He has a way most wonderful with the natives; his great experience as a trader—yes, it was a firm making much money; Stephanopoulos and Righas. Perhaps you have known the name, yes? Already we consider him as one of us, though he is not really a lay brother as yet; but the appellation pleases him; and he is a great help, a great comfort."

King's brows contracted.

"Righas," he muttered. "Righas. No, I don't know the firm; they didn't operate in Kenya anywhere."

"No, no, not in Kenya. In Egypt and the Sudan. They were well known and were making much money—and he has given it all up for our work."

THE SUDAN. That resumed a persistent train of thought. But King had come on a more important errand than one of vague speculations. He told the priest all that he had witnessed; the impressive performance of the *juju;* the temper of the crowd.

The priest was very grave. He nodded with understanding.

"Yes, yes. That is bad. That is very bad. I did not know; I hoped— Yes, at any time now it may come. My poor people."

King spoke swiftly, trying to put conviction into an argument that he knew was hopeless.

"But there is still time, Padre. You're not tied down. You're not a government official glued down to his job. And one can't reason with that bird, anyhow. But *you* can get out. Grab your valuables and go. You haven't much to carry and enough of your converts remain to act as porters."

Father van Dahl smiled slowly, nodding.

"Yes, yes, you are a man of the world; I you do not understand. *You* can go while you have opportunity. But I—have I not also my duties? More even than Mr. Fawcett. My people who for the moment have been misled—"

King was impatient.

"But, Padre, have some sense. In a couple of months it will be all over. You can come back and—"

The priest interrupted in turn.

"In a couple of months? In one day, my son, my people will have lost their confidence in their pastor. My hundred whom I have so slowly won. Shall the shepherd desert his flock?"

King swore, and made no attempt to apologize. He had known it would be so. Let battle and murder and sudden death come or let it pass, the priest was just as much an inexorable fixture as was the government official. That, too, had been written into the history of Africa.

Father van Dahl laid a thin brown hand on King's knee.

"And you, my friend, I do not perceive you making preparations to go, is it not?"

King swore again.

"Padre, there's just one chance—a slim chance, if I get all the breaks. And since your damned hundred nigger men whom you've taught to grow bigger and better bananas than the rest of the savages are more important than your life and your assistants' lives—though I never heard you asking them—I'm going to take my hat off to you and I'm going to take the chance.

"Now, listen. Wasn't there some prophet in the Old Testament once whose people were sliding out on him in favor of an idol that pulled magic stuff? Baal, wasn't it? And the prophet called miraculous fire from heaven and burned the *juju* up along with a batch of its priests and so cut the sticks from under the opposition prestige and won his crowd back?"

Father van Dahl perked his head in bird-like query. He could as yet see no analogy. King continued with totally unconscious lack of reverence.

"Well, now, you give out that you're going to do a miracle and set a magic fire to this idol; and if my luck works, your people 'll come crowding back on you so fast—"

The priest held up his hand.

"My son, my son, do not blaspheme."

King jumped up. He had never any patience with matters or sentiments unpractical.

"Gosh almighty!" he stormed. "How can I get you to have some sense and understand? It'd take all day—and then you'd have some inhibition about it. Listen, Padre, I've got no time to argue. Things are buzzing right along in these backwoods. I'm going out to take a long chance; and I'm going to prophesy the miracle for you. If it works you win—we'll all win and save our scalps. If it flops you'll be past worrying."

He stamped out; and behind him came the priest's urgent entreaty that he refrain from the awful sin of blasphemy.

IN KING'S *boma* the boys waited expectantly; children anxious to relate all the wonders of the show they had seen. King sat on a camp stool and listened with exaggerated boredom. Not the most spectacular of the marvels moved him, even when embroidered by African imagination. He flouted the super-*juju* powers of the idol.

"That is not such a great witchcraft. I have seen many better. This is but a little jungle *juju*. Thus does it move its arms, thus its foolish mouth, and the words that it talks are winds." King imitated the spasmodic antics of the thing and its megaphonic voice.

"*Aho! Wo-we!*" The boys were impressed. How did the white *bwana* who could not have seen know these things?

"I had heard much talk of this toy and it wearied me. I slept and sent my spirit to look while I rested."

"*Arra-wa!*" Yes, that might well be true. The greater of the witch doctors could do this thing, and the white *bwana* surely had this magic too.

Barounggo stood up. He had a speech to make and he required space for action.

"If this is but a little witchcraft, *bwana,* then it is well. For that Black One of the Ghost Tree—" King noted that even the Masai hesitated to name the thing—"the Black One makes an ill talk; a talk of the slaying of all the *m'zungu* in the land. Now it is in my mind that we in this *boma* could make a proper fight. We three alone; for these *shenzi* six will run as do the dogs when the lion speaks—"

King could not but admire the loyal fellow's cheerful insult of the porters and their meek acceptance of it. The Masai gave himself over to declamation:

"A very proper fight. Or, perchance, in the wire *boma* of the *serkale,* a better fight; for these soldiers of the Raifuls are true men; I have spoken with them. Yet these Tappuza dogs are many and in the end their spears will be red. Therefore, *bwana,* if the Black One is not so strong as he says—"

King yawned carelessly.

"It is nothing. It is a small matter. For us it has no interest. But I have told the *m'zungu mon-père,* the white priest, of these babblings and he has said it is enough! I have given him a small witchcraft and he will burn up this little *juju* with magic fire. Tomorrow, perhaps; maybe today. It is nothing."

"*Aho?* A magic fire?"

The men were awesomely impressed. It was sufficient. King knew that this planted seed of a counter magic to the Black One would sprout and spread throughout the community faster than the civilized magic of the telephone.

Kaffa, the little Hottentot, had a word to say. He squirmed uneasily making his request.

"That is good. The *mon-père* will make a magic and the Black One will burn up and die. *Bwana* has said so and it is without doubt true. Yet—" he writhed in his abashment—"suppose that the *mon-père* does not work his magic right; suppose that the Black One does not die. An offering, a small gift—today he eats offerings—a gift today might well be counted in our favor when trouble comes."

King chuckled. It flashed upon him that maybe his luck was beginning *to* work. At the same time the everlasting adherence to type of the African held his attention. On the one side the Masai, the fighting man, loyal to the death, facing the imminent danger with a fierce nonchalance. On the other the Hottentot, the bush dweller, loyal, too; but as cunningly full of caution as a monkey. Maybe this caution was playing right into King's hand.

"What is the manner of this eating of offerings?" he asked.

"It is a strong witchcraft, *bwana.* Those who give place their gifts upon a flat basket. In full daylight then a servant of the Black One ascends a ladder of bamboo with the basket, at no time touching the gifts, and places the basket before the Black One's feet. The servant retires and the Black One takes up the gifts in his own hands and eats them up. It is a great magic."

King laughed outright. He quoted in English a familiar patter:

"Nothing in my hands, gentlemen; nothing up my sleeve; at no time, you will perceive, do I touch the card— Gosh, what children! But it works. It works every time."

Kaffa was emboldened by the laugh.

"Therefore, *bwana,*" he pleaded, "I would ask an advance against my pay. A piece of cloth; a small gift, *bwana.* On behalf of these *shenzis,* too."

King held himself to pose in judicial contemplation, control-ling his impulse to whoop. Then he announced in a matter of fact tone:

"Good. I will give you a piece of cloth. But it is a waste; for the *mon-père's* magic will surely burn up this little jungle *juju* this very day."

He went into his tent and there he pounded his fist into the other palm. Lord, his luck was running strong! He had been racking his brain to think of a means to introduce his miracle plan to the *juju*, and here it came to his hand. He took the little packet he had made overnight and unwrapped it.

"Two sticks ought to be a plenty," he uttered. "But these detonators 'll stand some doctoring."

He proceeded to "doctor" accordingly, and his tuneless whistle broke out. His plan was simple; as simple as are most great strategies. He knew from his youthful experience of Independence Day that torpedoes were a lot cheaper to make than to buy. A pinch of fulminate and a little fine gravel wrapped in a paper ball provided the most delightful material to explode at other boys' heels and to send girls screaming down the street.

With a certain cynicism he translated all his percussion cartridges into giant torpedoes; and he began to feel that he had an almost foolproof miracle. The *juju*, he reasoned, from his observation of its movements, whether actuated by strings or by internal levers or whatever it might be, would pick up these offerings and would drop them through its cavernous mouth into its hollow interior. The figure squatted at least five feet high. King knew from experience that a drop of less than that was ample to detonate a fulminate bomb. With a dozen oversize bombs and two sticks of dynamite surely something ought to happen. At about four o'clock that very afternoon, then, the predicted miracle might be counted upon to disintegrate the *juju's* death laden prestige into a great many very little pieces of hardwood.

King chuckled. He would have to witness that miracle. He wrapped his surprise packet carefully in a gaudy strip of trade calico, tied it with string carefully against monkey meddling, and came out from his tent and told the Hottentot:

"Here is your gift. A good gift. This order only do I place

upon you. Carry it with care. Do not drop it, on your life. Place it softly in the gift basket. And return and report to me that it is done. Later you may all go and watch the eating."

The Hottentot took the packet gingerly. Already it was becoming imbued with the sacredness of sacrosanct property. King turned in to snatch some sleep.

VII

WITH EARLY afternoon he gave his men leave to go and watch the eating of the offerings. As soon as they were well out of the way he took his field glasses and set out himself. He was going to watch this show too, if from a distance. His way took him past the government *boma*. He had not intended to stop in; but a soldier ran after him. The assistant commissioner wanted to see him. That gentleman was in a condition of bewilderment, and in his predicament was much more cordial than before. Something had happened that had given him a considerable measure of respect for King's judgment. He came to the point without preamble.

"Mr. King, a very extraordinary thing has happened. I am taking you into my confidence because—er—you seem to know a great deal of what is going on. A man was picked up this noon in the bush in front of this *juju* thing. The natives would not touch him—some nonsense about witchcraft. My men brought him in—a white man."

King's eyes flickered. He held his surprise with an effort. He had not expected this.

"So? A white man, eh? He was—"

The assistant commissioner nodded.

"Yes, dead. Killed by a blow with a club. There's the usual secrecy, of course. Nobody knows anything about him; never heard of him; and everybody is ox dumb. And as for me, I didn't even know that any strange white man was in the district. Where could he appear from? What could he be doing?"

King frowned into space without answering. So the man

who had stalked him in the bush was dead. At mention of the man having been killed with a club he impulsively squeezed his blackened middle fingernail into the palm of his hand and winced with the pain. He had hardly expected that. At most he had thought of a very sore head. Well, the man had not been exactly stopping to consider whether he would perhaps be hurting somebody with that murderous knife.

But even that was not exactly what was occupying King's mind. What he was cogitating was whether the death of one guiding genius would undermine the trouble at its source. Was there only one? Who had been the man in the bush with him at night? Native? White man? Partner, possibly, in the great plot. It was a big thing for a single man to tackle. Damn it, if only the fellow had been captured alive! He was a white man, not an African; he could have been made to talk.

At all events there was definite proof now of some of his theories. With a certain triumph he asked the assistant commissioner—

"Well, doesn't that begin to fit into what you called my fantastic theory about a guiding genius behind this trouble?"

"It does, Mr. King. I admit it. Otherwise why did the fellow not come up straightforwardly and report his presence? In fact I don't know from where any white man could have come through without some report coming to me."

King smiled thinly. He thought, if the rest of his theories were correct, that he could guess from where a white man—who had perhaps a sturdy automobile—could come without passing through a populous and well patrolled country. But Mr. Fawcett was asking another embarrassing question. The law training essential to his studies for his appointment had rendered him adept in picking the holes in any situation.

"All the same, Mr. King, if this man were, as you suggest, the guiding genius of this unrest, he would be obviously *persona grata* with the natives. Who, then, would kill him?"

King did not feel that he could enter into explanations and

delays. Time was passing. During the last minute conviction had come upon him about more than one of his cogitations. The death of one man, one wheel in the carefully built machine, would not stop the progress of its function. Not at this stage. It had gained too much momentum. There remained at least one other wheel which, to insure its own safety, *must* now carry on. And there remained the *juju*, potent source of hysteria and latent slaughter. He turned the subject.

"Any sort of identification? Name? Business? Where from?"

"Not yet,—" Mr. Fawcett made a face. "I dislike that sort of thing myself. My men are looking him over in routine form."

"Well," said King, "I'll look in later. I've got to hop along and see the Reverend van Dahl's miracle do its stuff."

The assistant commissioner raised his eyebrows in interrogation; but King was gone. He was aiming for a scrubby little knoll which he had noted before as being suitable for his purpose. From it a clear view of the ghost tree could be obtained and it was there that he proposed to plant himself with his glasses. The small delay at the government office had not made him too late. At all events he had heard no explosion, so he would be, he hoped, in time for the performance.

He was. He selected with instinctive habit a bush which screened him from casual observation. Under it he stretched himself luxuriously on his stomach and took his glasses from their leather case. Far away from the direction of the ghost tree the confused, sublimated thunder of drums sounded. This was no call to an *indaba*, to hear a speech. This was just noise; *fiesta*, sideshow about to commence. King grinned in anticipation.

"Guess they'll get a bigger show than their tickets entitle them to. It's not every day that these frisky coons see a white man's miracle."

HE WIPED the lenses of his field glass and leisurely adjusted focus. It was one of the newest Zeiss eight-power hunting glasses; the kind that showed the approximate range of the focused object. Instinctive habit once again made him note it. Between seven and eight hundred yards. Well, that was plenty near enough to see everything that went on. Many a time had he observed the intimate movements of game at a greater range.

He could see the ebony figure clearly; its inset shell eyes; its thick jointed arms; even the white tips of the big teeth between loose sagging lips. The drumming boomed distant thunder and faded out to nothing as the hot breeze eddied about. It rose to a crescendo and mingled with a sudden volume of far shouting. Something was going to happen. Either the servant of the Black One was about to climb up with the basket, or, if that had been done, the magic performance of eating was about to commence. Then King noted that no ladder stood against the platform. He grinned again—cunning precaution that no overwrought worshipper should climb up to present himself as a Juggernaut offering and so discover the hoax.

Good; the thing would soon move then. And it did. A furious howling came on the wind and the *juju's* jaws chattered in anticipation. King was keenly interested in the mechanism. Elbows firm on the ground, he held the glass motionless.

The thick right arm moved. With a slow clumsy motion the thing groped at the basket between its feet. It seemed that the thumb worked on a hinge against the rest of the hand; a sort of lobster claw movement. Presently the claw found a hold on a small bundle. Stiffly the arm heaved up; the jaws fell open; the bundle hung between the big teeth, then was sucked down. The jaws champed wooden appreciation.

King was troubled. From the nature of the movement he guessed that the mechanism was man. A man within the hollow figure worked a hollow arm and then, when the offering was between the jaws, just took it in.

"Poor devil," he muttered.

But he was consistently practical. Better, a hundred times better, the immolation of one malignantly scheming savage— or, for that matter, of a dozen men—than the rebellion of a whole tribe that would mean a slaughter and its aftermath of blood in the reestablishment of control.

A further thought troubled him; a more awful thought. The man might not be immolated. The jaunty cocksureness left him. With growing anxiety he watched each offering in turn lifted clumsily to the gaping mouth, and disappear. With his glasses he could distinguish various packages of colored print cloth take their turn with carved wooden bowls and painted gourds and ax heads, but at that distance he could not identify his own prize package.

With each gaudy packet he tensed. Would it come? Would a sudden explosion tear the sky? Or, since quite obviously the man inside took each bundle in his hand and presumably laid it down, would he jar it sufficiently to set spark to any one of the fulminate torpedoes?

For a long dragging hour the thing ate with gusto. Nothing happened. It remained full of health and horrid,appetite. The last of the offerings disappeared. The crowd howled; the drums roared. The miracle of the eating had been accomplished. No counter miracle as threatened by the white priest had occurred.

King hovered for a moment on the verge of panic. His fool proof plan had failed. Nothing stood in the way of revolution. One white man was dead; but he was surely not working single handed on so ambitious a scheme. His associates, so near to success, would carry the cold blooded business through. Everything was ready. The very threat of the priest's counter miracle, by its failure, would enhance the prestige of the *juju* and raise the courage of the natives to a howling frenzy.

King bit his teeth together till they hurt and forced himself to calm thought. What would happen now? What would be the next step? The *juju* man would obviously have to remain in hiding till dark. Then he could slip out. King thought that the ebony figure stood close enough to the tree to enable an undetected retreat. It must; the trick could never be worked otherwise. But the packages? The offerings? Would they be smuggled out at the earliest opportunity so that the greedy priest could look over what he had drawn; or would they remain till a more favorable time?

"One chance," King muttered. "One thin chance left."

HE CRAWLED from his shelter and sprinted through the bush for the home camp. Then as he ran and his thoughts raced ahead he slowed down. After all, the thin chance that remained depended upon the lighting of the footlight lamps on the *juju* platform. There was to be another speech that night. Possibly the last one; who could tell? The carefully planted rumor about the white man's counter miracle might be the last straw, the match that the blaze of riot awaited.

Still, there was a dim gleam of hope in the forthcoming speech. The crowd would begin to gather early, before darkness set in, and the opportunity for the magician to remove the day's loot from the belly of the idol would be unfavorable. The explosive packet might well remain there for awhile. In that hope lay his one chance. King decided that he would have time to stop in at the government *boma* to urge the assistant commissioner to be prepared for anything and to make arrangements, if necessary, to bring the missionaries in by force.

Mr. Fawcett thanked him coldly for advice that was neither asked nor needed. Everything for defense had been done as far as might be. But there was an item of information. The search of the dead man's clothing and pocket effects had revealed the fact that his name was Theophilos Righas.

King stiffened. His eyes narrowed to the characteristic slits and in spite of his anxiety, the thin grin seamed his cheeks.

"So-o? Righas, yes-s?" That fitted exactly into his guessed theories. That was the last crooked key piece to the jigsaw puzzle. With assumed carelessness he asked:

"Ever hear of the firm of Stephanopoulos and Righas?"

The names conveyed nothing to Mr. Fawcett, though King's tone told him that something ought to connect somewhere.

"Mm-m, no," he said. "They didn't operate anywhere in Kenya

or Uganda—Wait a minute, though. There's something about—" he turned a key in a confidential steel file case and flipped over the cards. "Yes; here's a report that a firm of that name bought a hundred rifles from Daniel Leroux and Company in Port Said a year ago. That's French administration; we can't control those sales."

"Mm-hm; in Port Said?" said King. "And from Port Said up the Nile to the extreme limit of the Sudan and to your borders; how about that?"

Mr. Fawcett considered for a moment.

"It could be done," he said. "That is to say, except for that strip of desert."

"Then," opined King, "if this Theophilos Righas who bought a hundred guns in Port Said got bumped off in Tappuza district where somebody has sold guns to the natives, somebody did a pretty good job, no?"

Mr. Fawcett was aghast at the untold treacheries that this train of reasoning opened up. Indignation and disgust shook him like a fever.

"I think the scoundrel received no more than his just deserts," was his unreserved official opinion. "Why, what a foul thing! Unspeakable hell hound! What a bestial cunning!"

King was not listening to any confirmation of what he knew. Another confirmation outweighed everything else. There *was* another partner then. Equally cunning, equally callous; who must now push the thing to its desperate climax. Perhaps the more cunning of the two; he had certainly played a bold and brilliant part. Possibly the brains of the outfit.

This was no time to dally. Unceremoniously King left the still raging Fawcett and ran.

Straight to his camp he went. Only Barounggo squatted in the *boma*. The rest of the boys had gone; scuttled off without leave to see the *juju* show again. And since, after all, they were but small boys mentally, King could not be very angry. To Barounggo he gave a short word of commendation and told him to run off to the circus. Barounggo was eager. But he waited to say a word.

"This is an ill talk that will be this night, *bwana*. It has been said—all men have heard it—that the Black One will give word for a war."

King forced himself with an effort to nonchalance. It was the white man's creed in Africa never to show anything but confidence before a native.

"There will be no war, Barounggo. The magic of the *m'zungu mon-père* will burn up this jungle *juju* with a great noise and a fire this very night while it makes its monkey chatterings. Go and watch it. And tell all men that it will happen."

Barounggo was impressed with his master's power. He lifted his great spear in salute and departed.

King looked after his broad shoulders melting into the dusk and his face twisted in a wry grin. He wished he could be one tenth part as confident as he had bluffed. A chance there was that he might avert disaster; but the chance was a thin one.

IT WAS his rifle that he had come home to fetch. Very soberly he took it, flipped its sling over his shoulder with familiar certainty, and started out. His objective was his observation post of the afternoon; the mound from which he had obtained a clear view of the *juju;* the knoll between seven hundred and eight hundred yards distant. Nearly half a mile.

It was dark by the time he arrived. He sat down and set slowly to kicking heel holes at the exact places for a comfortable rest. He had never been able to accustom himself to the Army sharpshooter's prone position; the sitting rest for him every time; and who, after all, since it was results that counted, could argue with him?

The distant drone of voices came to him from the ghost tree; but the lamps had not been lighted yet. With methodical habit he wiped off his sights. By meticulous feel and by ear he turned the little micrometer screw and clicked off the required elevation.

Between seven and eight hundred yards. Well, that was easy enough and no guesswork. All he had to do was to count the clicks correctly; the elevation rule was absolute. A certain glow of contentment began to come over him as he worked. This was something he knew. He commenced to thrill to the test of his skill, of the surety of his hand and eye and nerve. His thin whistle broke from between his teeth.

Eight hundred yards, call it. There was nothing to be alarmed at in that. If an Army marksman could be expected to hit a bull's-eye at that distance and even greater, surely the squat *juju* was a mark large enough; and it would be nicely centered between two lights.

And that was one little worry. Suppose the lights were not set in the regular positions? To an African a foot or so one way or the other would make no difference. But the main cause for anxiety was the conjecture whether the offerings had been removed from the belly of the *juju* or not. If, by God's grace and good luck, *not*—a hard grin split the hard face—well, a bullet carefully planted anywhere near the middle of that bulk would jar that fulminate off like a bolt from heaven.

And since the dynamite would explode upward none of his men looking on would be hurt. King didn't want to hurt any of those poor fools unless it were necessary. Nobody would be hurt, unless perhaps a chunk of falling *juju* should hit somebody on the head. King whistled some more. From his pocket he took a little bottle of radium paint and spotted a careful bead on his front sight. He squinted through the peep at it. Good, that was not too big.

Wind? Wind was in his face and therefore negligible. Perhaps one point of elevation. Click. He was ready. The issue depended upon his luck. King began to feel confident. His luck had been running with him. Surely it would continue.

A point of light began to crawl fitfully up the wall of distant blackness. A swelling hum came downwind. King shuffled his heels into secure position. The point of light mounted interminably; it moved horizontally; became two lights; moved again; became three lights. The swelling hum became breakers on a rocky shore. The first light descended and left the two horizontal ones.

King tried his glasses. Just dimly, he thought, he could discern the ebony bulk between its illumination. It looked to be middle. Good. Luck had held that far; and King felt that he was not asking too much of the wayward goddess in hoping that the offerings had not been removed from the *juju's* belly. On the contrary, it would have been difficult for anybody to remove them between the eating and the after-dinner speech. That was all that King asked. If his bomb were there he would hit it, or near enough to it.

Distance worried him not at all. With modern weapons and sights there were hundreds of men who could pump seventy-five per cent, of a string into a bull's-eye at eight hundred yards. Darkness troubled him hardly any more. There stood those providential twin lights; two sharply marked sighting points with the added advantage that, in the dark, there was no intervening heat flicker above a scorching veld.

Only one question caused any anxiety. Exactly where was the inner floor of that *juju?* Where did the offerings lie? The thing was a squatting figure some three feet wide. Its inner hollow would be, say twenty-four inches. Since it was about five feet high and since a man had crouched within it, it was reasonable to assume, King hoped desperately, that it was bottomless. The carving, the hollowing out, would naturally have been done from that end; the open shell, therefore, probably stood upon the platform itself.

Well, if that were so—King raised his rifle and squinted critically through the sights—if luck would admit him but that much accuracy in his reasoning, his bomb would be lying amid a jumble of hardwood and iron and some cloth—damn the cloth—within a rough circle of some twenty-four inches in diameter and upon the floor of the platform, level with the lights that stood on the same platform.

HE WOULD have to shoot middle and about six inches up. If he missed—well, he wouldn't miss the target—but if his bullet did not smash through near enough to his bomb to set it off he could shoot again. A one hundred and eighty-grain bullet arriving into that assorted mess of hardware—even with a few packages of cloth—would disrupt things quite considerably. It was just a matter of his luck how many times he would have to shoot.

At that distance with wind against him, and the crowd howling, nobody would be likely to hear anything. And if one did, what matter? It would be no more than a foolish *m'zungu bwana* shooting at a hyena or something in the dark. If his first shot struck right nobody would hear anything because a high velocity bullet arrived at eight hundred yards quicker than sound, and the explosion would occupy everybody's attention for quite the next few days.

King snuggled his cheek down to the stock and held his breath. This was to be the supreme test of his skill, of his judgment, of his luck. He was cool and unhurried. Evenly he pressed on the trigger. He felt the final small resistance, steadied to the last little fraction of immobility, and pressed it home. Instantly with the shot, stock on shoulder, his right hand shot up to the bolt, slammed it out, in again, ready for the next shot.

But before that lightning maneuver was one half accomplished a yellow glare split the sky before him. It winked once like an enormous eye and closed down on empty blackness. A roar hurtled downwind in a furious hurry and was gone. And after the roar came a prolonged yow-wow of shrill yelpings—the cry of Africa in its terror.

King whooped once and let the remainder of his pent breath escape in a long hiss.

"Phee-ee-ew!"

He wiped his forehead. His immobility had vanished. He found a tremor shaking his whole body, and at the realization a dry laugh croaked from his throat. Then he scrambled to his feet in a panic and raced for the home camp. It behooved him to be innocently within his tent when his men arrived with the portentous news.

The *boma* was silent. He went into his tent to await the boys. Suddenly he remembered. In one of the huts the killer was still a captive. King flashed a match in the man's startled face and looked him over; he was securely tied to the hut's centerpost. With his hunting knife King cut the cords.

"You can't do any damage now," he told the man in English, which he could not understand. He held him by the back of the neck and pointed him at the door. "Beat it, you poor fool. And the next time you go gunning for a white man make sure he's not one of those pestiferous Americans. Shoo! Git!"

He kicked the man hard; and like a thankful rabbit the fellow bolted. King chased him across the *boma,* got in one more kick, and then the night swallowed him.

King lay on his cot and laughed. Laughed till his belly muscles ached. Reaction from nervous tension and the exhilaration of success were upon him. His luck had held good—he attributed it all to his luck; the consummation of the white priest's miracle would thoroughly cow the natives—must already have; the effect would be instantaneous. Not the most unscrupulous scoundrels would stir this tribe up again as long as the memory of that wonder lived.

He was forced almost to admiration. Clever devils, those two. That had been a slick scheme to take cover under the mission and work right under the eye of the administration. An almost perfect plot the precious pair had hatched. A queer thing, fate. If they hadn't overreached themselves in their anxiety and tried so hard to get him disposed of he might never have come there. Yes, he would, though. It *was* fate. It was one of those "happenings of Africa."

The wandering thoughts clouded with a tinge of regret. Since he had come; since he *had* taken the risk and done the job, he might just as well have taken up the governor's proposition and have done it at government expense.

But, no—a million times no. He would have had to write a report about it. Many driveling pages of explanation and detailed repetition of something that had already been finished. No, that would be unthinkable. Sufficient was the satisfaction of having done a job that would put stiff necked officialdom under an obligation to him—an obligation which he would never permit it to repay.

And better satisfaction still in that the good old priest would be a veritable prophet in the land. Ho-ho! How that backsliding flock would come crawling back to its bigger and better yam patches, and would bring a lot more with them to boot. That was the way to civilize the savage—appeal to his belly. All the same, the *padre* would reprove him sadly and would pray for his soul for having called the thing a miracle. Well—

King's ruminations were broken in upon by his returning boys. They trooped into the *boma* jabbering in awestruck whispers. King let them chatter for awhile; they discussed whether they should wake the *bwana* to tell him the wonder. They decided that it was a matter of sufficient importance. Baroung-go stood at the tent flap and rang his spear blade like a bell.

"Well?" King called sleepily from within. "Has it happened? Some sort of noise I heard. Was it the *m'zungu mon-père's* magic?"

"*Awo, bwana*, we do not know what happened. From the sky came a fire as of a lightning; only more fierce; and the Black One was eaten up."

King chuckled silently.

"And that, if I remember rightly, was just about how that Baal miracle happened." And to the men, carelessly, "I told you that thus it would happen. It was a good magic. Let one man light the lantern and go before me. I go to the *mon-père's* house to give him joy and to bring back my magic that I gave him."

WITH THE morning King was at the assistant commissioner's office, grinning all over his rough carved face like—well, like a *juju*. Mr. Fawcett, for the first time in their acquaintance, met him with a smile—a rather twisted smile of inquiry, hands in pockets, head on one side. These miraculous happenings had passed beyond the pale of official reserve.

"What in hell, Mr. King, have you been doing?" the assistant commissioner wanted to know.

"Nothing, Mr. Fawcett, nothing," said King. "Er—I did a little shooting last night; damn good shooting, and I'm proud as all heck over it. But I've come to talk business. I've located this ivory at last. In a couple of weeks, I take it, this flurry will have settled down to normal; and so I want to ask if you'll let me have six hundred men for porters?"

Mr. Fawcett was pained. He felt in some vague way that King had done something commendable. He did not understand the whole of it yet; but he disliked having to refuse. But administrative regulations were adamant; decision was not in his hands.

"I told you before, Mr. King, that I could not sanction such a migration. And why six hundred men? I thought that your very accurate information had made it seven hundred loads?"

King grinned; he had played for just that question.

"Oh, I can get a hundred men from the mission; I require your sanction for the six hundred only."

Mr. Fawcett shook his head.

"Government regulations, Mr. King. I would have to apply to the governor in council for so great a local upset, and it would take weeks to get action. Under no circumstances may I permit so large a body of men to move more than one day's journey out of their district."

King was satisfied.

"That's quite all right, Mr. Fawcett. All I need is half a day out into the desert side."

Mr. Fawcett looked his amazement.

"I have many proofs, Mr. King, that you are anything but

insane. I am prepared to find further proofs at any moment. So why not sit down and explain the joke or the catch or whatever it is in this thing?"

"No catch at all, Mr. Fawcett," King assured him. "I've got an auto truck out there. A Rugby six-wheeler, all comfortably stowed away under a canvas cover and weighed down with stones. Brother Stephen tells me it's an excellent car; and, believe me, that boy knows trucks."

"Brother Stephen?"

"Yeah; he sold it to me. I've got a map how to find it, and I was careful to get a bill-of-sale—Stephen knows all about the business intricacies of these things—and my man Barounggo ought to be well on his way to sit on the property till I can get over."

King produced a paper upon which, sure enough, was scrawled a correctly worded bill-of-sale. And it was signed D'mitrius Stephanopoulos.

"Of the late firm of Stephanopoulos and Righas," King explained.

Mr. Fawcett began to see light. With stolid British control he withheld himself from evincing any undignified curiosity or ignorance of happenings. Time would come for explanations later—over the dinner table would be appropriate. Yes, over the cigars and whisky peg King would talk. Just now he asked only—

"What sort of services?"

"Negative, Mr. Fawcett," said King. "Mostly negative. His chief appreciation seemed to be that I didn't twist his filthy neck for making three attempts to bump me off. I had a mind to, too; but I allowed that a good truck would balance the annoyance."

"Humph," said Mr. Fawcett. "Perhaps I shall do so officially."

"Maybe, Mr. Fawcett, maybe," agreed King. "But I'd almost bet against it. Brer Stephanopoulos went out into the dark some time last night, and I'll bet that boy is melting into the African landscape right smartly. But to come back to the point. Now that I've got a fine new truck and a map to the Nile, how about those porters for seven hundred tusks of ivory?"

"Well," said Mr. Fawcett judicially, "I suppose you've earned them."

THE LOST END OF NOWHERE

THE BEARDED man spoke fluently, appealingly, with only the faintest trace of a foreign accent. He was even convincing.

But the other man, King, sat back, hugging a cord breeched knee in his two brown hands and observing the speaker through thin slits of eyes from behind a smoke screen made by his pipe. He heard the man out; led him on to talk about distances, directions, costs of *safari* and so on. Then leisurely he changed knees and said pointedly—

"Why don't you go in yourself and get him out?"

The bearded man shrugged deprecatingly.

"I, Mr. King, am a man of science."

King let go his knee and grinned at the man quizzically.

"Yeah, I know. Herr Professor Reinsch, director of anthropology of the University of Heidelberg. I've known that ever since you came here to Dar es Salaam a month ago. And you've written three books on your subject, and you've lectured over most of Europe."

The professor raised his eyebrows.

"Your information is very accurate. You will see, then, that for a man such as I a *safari* into Central Africa is no—"

King, with head on one side, continued to grin with such sardonic amusement that the professor stopped in confusion. King took up the unfinished sentence.

"You were going to say that for you a *safari* is no novelty—at

least, I hope you weren't
going to try to tell me anything else."

The professor stared at
him with round eyes for a
moment and then he threw
up his hands with a rueful
expression and laughed.

"I perceive," he said,
"that what they told me
about Kingi Bwana is true.
Very well, I admit. I have
safaried before. But tell me,
please, from where you get
your so accurate informa-
tion."

"Shucks," said King.
"What do you think I
gabbled such a lot of hot
air about *safari* for? Just to
see how much you knew about it. The other is no gumshoe
work of mine. They checked up on you as soon as you came
here."

"They? Who is this they?" asked the professor quickly. King
chuckled as he spoke. He had found his own moments of irritation from the same source.

"His Britannic Majesty's very careful government of the
mandate territory of what used to be German East Africa."

"Aa-ah! So?" A long breath of understanding came from the
professor. "But how do you know this? You are not one of them."

"Well," drawled King, "things are different from what they
were in your time. Now there's a whole lot of East Indian clerks
and Eurasians in the offices and in the telegraph and so on.
Things leak, and if you're not too high up to listen you can hear
them hit the ground."

The professor nodded absently. He was connecting up in the light of this new knowledge the long circumstantial chain of hindrances and delays that had reduced him to despair and brought him to King. The latter added an item—

"And just about that time Biggs, inspector of police, took a holiday and went by train to Ujiji to make *safari* up to Emin Pasha Gulf on Lake Victoria."

"Ss-so," hissed the professor. "They know something, then."

King's mood of banter changed. He pushed back his chair and prowled with long and singularly noiseless strides up and down the room, his thumbs hooked in his belt, his lean, angular face impatient, and his wide mouth a thin line. He stood and shot a long finger out at the professor with the suddenness of a gun.

"Now, listen, Professor. I don't like this deal on its looks. To begin with, you're offering me too much money. Why? To go on with, the British authorities are too much interested in you. It's none of my business, but I want to know why. Now if you'll cut out all the clever stuff and play cards on the table I'll listen to you, though that don't mean that I'll take up your proposition."

The professor lifted his hands in quick apology and defense at the outburst. He had already decided that he must tell all the truth to this man.

"Sit, please, down again, Mr. King, and I will tell you everything. Everything, at least, that I know. It is all true as I have said. We of the university received a letter from our colleague, Doctor Hugo Meyer. In this letter it said that he had discoveries of such a great importance to science that we should please send an expedition to bring him out with his proofs. Unfortunately the letter was so worn out and tattered that we can not guess at the date. It may have been a month; it may have Iain in some hut for years—you know how a letter is that is entrusted to an African runner. We receive what is not worn out. The date line is gone; and of the address we have only Deutsch Ost Africa.

"Our colleague, it seems, is one of those not reconcilables who will never admit that we have lost our colonies. You see it was before the war that he went up there into the interior, and we had since then heard no word from him until now."

"Umph," grunted King, still suspicious. "How come you haven't his war record for at least the next four years, since your people hung out till the end and surrendered only after the armistice when Von Lettow was guaranteed military honors and repatriation for every German in his command? How come you have no repatriation record? How come the university didn't see him before he came out again? Come clean now, Doctor, or I can't waste time talking to you."

The professor held up his hands again.

"Please, my dear sir, please. Listen and I will tell you true. The very extraordinary circumstance about our colleague is that he had no military record. You understand that. No military service in a time when every German in Africa was a soldier. We of the university received a letter at that time—that was fifteen years ago—in which our Hugo Meyer said that he was not interested in this stupid war; he was interested only in a study of botany and zoology—especially of anthropoid apes, and he would go into the deep jungles and would not waste time with marching up and down.

"We there in Heidelberg, we laughed and said to each other how fine he would look in a kitchen uniform; for every man of us within the age was immediately in the army. But the very strange circumstance was that when Von Lettow came back after it was all over and we who were left made inquiries; it was true; our Hugo had disappeared and had escaped service; and from that time on we have no news until this letter."

"Good Lord," murmured King. "Fifteen years in those jungles! Alone! How do you know he isn't dead long ago? How d'you know that letter hasn't been lying in some native hut for years before some one had a whim to take it out?"

"This, we do not know," agreed the professor simply. "Except that Meyer was a young man and of a very unusually strong physique to withstand the sickness of the jungle. But there is one more thing that we do not know; and this I will tell you true. We of the university were debating what we should do. For *safari* expeditions cost much money; and we have not so much money nowadays. We were almost thinking to wait for another letter, when suddenly from somewhere the university president told our department of zoology that all the money we should need would be available and we should make this expedition immediately to bring out these discoveries of so great importance to science with all the proofs. Particularly must we bring all the proofs."

"Hmph!"

King's steel gray eyes narrowed to gaze into distant nothing as a thought came to him in connection with the sudden mysterious source of money for an expedition, and the equally mysterious interest of the British government in the colony.

"You say this man was a zoologist and a botanist? He wasn't by any chance a mining man, was he? Or an oil expert, huh? Could he locate oil, maybe?"

"No, no, my dear sir. Positively not. He was what you call a crank on the anthropoid apes; and he was interested in botany from the point of food—the food of nature as the monkeys eat it and keep their health; you understand? Dietetic botany, you say, is it not? Nothing else. Nothing else at all. The man was of a very single purpose mind."

"Then that upsets that little theory," grunted King. "Well, what else?"

"That," said the professor, "is all that I know. I was quickly sent out with sufficient money to make this *safari* to look for our colleague in those not so well determined jungles. I arrive. I find only obstructions. Everywhere I meet with the greatest politeness from all officials, I am invited to the race meet, to the club, to the sacred ceremony of tea. But I get nothing more than politeness. I receive no permits to make *safari*. I am unable to hire porters except through the government agency; and the agent does no more than invite me to accept many whisky pegs and to play billiards and tennis at his club. I am not a fool. I see that there is an obstruction. I do not know why."

KING'S HARD face cracked in a wide grin of appreciation. He had his experience of that masterly method.

"Yeh, that's their way," he chuckled. "Always polite and good fellows; no rough stuff. But, golly, how gracefully they can stall when they're tipped off from higher up."

Then a certain exasperation came over him and his face set hard again and his chuckle changed to a grumble.

"They give me an awful pain. Not only they—I mean all governments, all officials. Stuffed out like bullfrogs with the importance of their jobs. If they've got some private deal on why can't they come to a fellow and say, 'Hey, lay off, this is private?' Anybody'd say, 'All right, brother, it's your business, not mine.' But when they go stalling around, giving each other the secret high sign on some huge diplomatic maneuvering that is already common bazaar gossip it sure stirs the wishbone in me to buy in on the game."

"And so, Mister Kingi Bwana," said the professor, stepping adroitly into the exasperated mood, "I come to you. You are American; you owe no loyalty to these diplomatic maneuvers in a colony which is only mandate. You will carry through this business in which I am so from the underhand prevented."

King's quick grin broke through his irritation.

"Wait a minute, brother. Not so fast. You haven't bought me yet. Let's talk some more. Tell me exactly what it is you want me to do."

The professor was quite candid.

"It is simply that you go in, that you find our colleague, if he is alive, and that you bring him out. I do not know why he can not come out alone. It is perhaps that he needs money or that he needs *safari* to bring out his collections, his proofs, whatever they may be. There is only one proviso—these scientific discoveries, if they are of such importance, they must be delivered to us of the university. In Germany these days much of our activities are restricted by treaty. We wish very jealously to retain our credit for scientific discovery."

"Hm-mm, that's fair enough."

King frowned into the distance, musing. He could see no objection. He believed that the professor had been open with him and had told all he knew. The only possible fly in the ointment was this mysteriously obstructive interest on the part of the mandate government. And that, if anything, was an attraction.

Nobody had come and confided anything to King; he was an outsider, not of the great official family; and not, therefore, bound by any loyalty to a confidence. If officialdom chose to make a ponderous mystery of some trivial thing, that was—he grinned—well, that was just their hard luck. He had suffered so often from restrictions set up by an autocratic officialdom, too proud to explain why, that his natural sympathy was with the underdog who, without official backing, suffered under similar restraint.

His mind was made up. He pointed his terms as though taking aim with his forefinger.

"All right. I'll play with you. I'll go in and find this scientific nut of yours. If he's dead, I'll find his cache or whatever reports there are about him. And I'll deliver to you in Heidelberg. You'll turn over to me now about a thousand dollars expense money for *safari*—better make it fifteen hundred in case there's a lot to bring out. I'll collect the balance when I deliver the goods. That's how I prefer to work. No tickee no washee. And—" the long forefinger aimed a final shot—"don't let any methodical skinflint at your end ask me for any piffling account of expenditures, 'cause I won't keep 'em."

It was the professor's turn, now that the thing was settled, to find misgivings.

"Do you think, my dear sir, that you can accomplish this? They will try to stop you, as they have hindered me."

The deep lines and abrupt angles of King's face stiffened to the semblance of crudely carved hardwood. He grunted rather grimly.

"I've done nothing they can lock me up in jail for; and I don't see anything else in sight that'll stop me. Don't you worry about that; that's my *shauri*. You go and holler your head off to the high muckamucks and keep them busy stalling you off with tennis and tea. I'll see you in Heidelberg. Always wanted to come to your country anyway to buy one of those three barrel shot and rifle combinations."

"Also, *auf Wiedersehen*," said the professor. "I shall have one waiting for you when you come—a handmade 'Drilling' by Sauer."

"It's a bet," said King.

KING WAS enjoying scenery. He sat on a high, rocky bluff, smoking a pipe and watching a red sun smolder through misty layers of thin vapor that floated upon long, torn streamers of violet, from beneath which radiant shafts of hot orange flared over the edge of a dead flat, ash-gray cloud.

Behind his back gray parrots squawked discontentedly in huge, blue-black euphorbia trees and an occasional shriek of a terrified *colobus* monkey indicated that the creatures of the night were beginning to prowl forth on the hunt.

The flaming sky mirrored itself in the waters of a deeply indented lagoon that stretched away beyond vision into the dusky gloom.

This was the gulf that Stanley had named after Emin Pasha of Egypt. It reached in a crooked, lava broken creek out of the southwestern corner of the vast square of Lake Victoria Nyanza. King knew that there were two thousand miles of that jagged waterfront of which less than two hundred miles—and those mostly at the northern end—could be said to be inhabited.

Somewhere in this unmapped maze Dr. Hugo Meyer had last been seen—fifteen years ago. Fifteen awful years in the silence. And now a great university wanted him and a government was interested and King was looking for him. It was almost as much of a needle hunting in a haystack as had been Stanley's search for Livingstone.

King was alone. That is to say, it is the custom of explorers in Africa to speak of themselves as being alone if there is no other white man with them—no matter how many dozens of porters, trackers and camp boys they may have.

It was King's peculiarity that he did not consider himself to be alone. With him was Barounggo, his Masai henchman, an unusually powerful great fellow, a member of one of the most warlike peoples of Africa. Also his cook, whose whole grandiose name was Kaff'enq'uam-undh-lovu, a Hottentot as shriveled and dried up as the Masai was huge, possessor of uncanny bush lore and cunning as an ape.

They were just niggers to most of the lordly white men who ruled the land. But King had a queer quiet way all his own of making a distinction between Africans and just niggers. He had niggers with him too; forty of them; many more than he needed; more than he had ever had on a *safari* before. Most *safaris* had at least that many. But King had learned his camping, not in the luxury of tropical cheap manpower, but back home in the Western hills where a pair of tough old prospectors would go out with a single pack burro, and contrive to stay six months.

The forty were *shenzis,* dull oxen who carried thirty-five pounds of camp duffle apiece on their thick heads in country where the *tsetse* flies would kill horses or cattle in a week.

Forty of them at thirty-five pounds apiece, with all the attendant trouble of looking after and controlling them, were as great a surfeit of worry as of carrying capacity. So much so that King seemed to have gone quite crazy, and most of his *shenzis* carried upon their wooly heads, instead of the assortment of canned foods that burdens the greater part of most *safaris,* nothing more valuable than grass with a few large stones to bring up the regulation weight.

King had collected them at Ujiji and, since there were no orders in his case to the contrary, had set out for the tip of Emin Pasha Gulf before a rather bewildered local official had interfered. But he knew that heliographs had winked across the hilltops behind him and that the scattered native constables in the villages ahead of him had not been surprised at his coming.

Nor was it any surprise to him, therefore, when his Hottentot took form out of the shadows and announced:

"*Bwana,* that man whom we sent out has come. He says a white *bwana* comes. In one hour he will be here."

"Good," said King evenly. "Prepare food and hot water for the bath against his coming and send Barounggo to me."

The Masai was already there, blending with perfect match of color into the deeping shades behind him. Only the flutter of the plaited monkey hair garters above his great elbows and knees and the breeze ripple along the furry edge of his leopard skin girdle denoted that something moved that was not entirely natural to the wild. That, and two perpendicular scintillations of light; one thin sharp one at the ground and the other, a broad stab of flame, in a direct line seven feet above it. These were the glint of the last sun on the iron spike at the butt and the broad two-foot blade of the Masai spear.

The man leaned motionless upon his great weapon. King asked him what he knew to be a superfluous question.

"Barounggo, is all ready as I have ordered?"

"All is ready, *Bwana.*"

"And the twelve men, they are the strongest of the lot, and you can surely hold them that they do not run away?"

The Masai laughed a deep rumble in his great chest.

"Surely I can hold them, *Bwana.* I have picked only Banyoro men and Baseses. Their fathers were the slaves of my fathers."

King laughed silently at the man's shrewd selection of men of these two tribes. Since all time—as far back as their grandfathers could remember—before the white man came these fierce Masai had enslaved their people and had slain them relentlessly for the least of misdeeds. They might run away from a white man, as *shenzis* had often done as soon as there had been a hint of the least little procedure unusual to their dim minds.

A white man would never chase them with murderous ferocity through the woods; the most he would do would be to try to catch them and perhaps beat them before putting them back to work. To run from that great spear flashing at their heels would be worse and infinitely more certain death than taking their chances of doing the most usual thing that the wildest white man might order.

King laughed.

"Good," he said. "Take the twelve and travel swiftly, and hold them till we come; it may be one day; it may be two. And do not, on your life, forget to make the trail of the secret sticks that the Hottentot has taught you."

WHEN THE white man came hotfoot into King's camp he found all the litter of an African *safari* getting ready for supper. This was not the open plain country of farther East, favorable for lions; so there was no need of a thorn *boma*. It was heavy stunted mimosa bush; and King had selected the tiniest possible natural opening that just gave room for his diminutive tent and his simple needs.

"Ha, hello, Big Chief Biggs," King greeted the police inspector. "I got word you were coming, so I've got a hot bath ready for you and then we can eat."

"Hello, Kingi Bwana." Biggs shook hands. "You heard I was coming? The deuce you say. I wish I could get the service out of my niggers that you seem to get out of yours. How do you manage the thing?"

"One way," said King lazily, "is not to think of them as just niggers. But go ahead and clean up and let's eat."

During the meal both men tacitly agreed not to discuss the business that both knew brought them together. When it was over and Kaffa had removed the enamel plates King lighted his pipe, stretched himself comfortably on the ground and said—

"Now then, shoot."

The police inspector hesitated. His mission was, to his inherited principles of courtesy, an awkward matter to bring up to a man with whom he had always been on friendly terms.

King laughed at his confusion and helped him out.

"Hell, Chief, you know I've come up here to find this Meyer man, and I know you came up a month ago to look for him yourself. Now let's start from there on."

The inspector was relieved. King's open minded attitude made things easier.

"Well," he said, "he isn't anywhere around here; and unless you have some information which we have not, I believe the man must be dead. I've come to find out what you know and what you propose to do."

King was relieved, too. Immensely relieved. He wanted just that information; it saved him many weeks of fruitless search. If the policeman, with his connections and his channels of inquiry through native constables and headmen and so on, had established the fact that the lost scientist was not there, that eliminated an enormous district. In fact, had it not been for the need of this information which he could have got in no other way, it is probable that King would not have been there when the policeman came. King was willing to trade news for news.

"You want to know what I know? It's darn little. Except— d'you know about the letter the Heidelberg crowd received?"

The inspector did not. King told him frankly. He explained the content of its quite ambitious claims about the value of the discoveries, and the condition in which it had been received; also the unexpected and unknown source of funds.

"I thought it might be gold or oil; but it seems that this bird knew nothing about such things. Now there's my cards on the table. That's all I know and that's why I'm looking for him. It's up to you to tell me why your people are officially interested."

"That might be a few months old; or it might be a few years," said the inspector, referring to the letter. "It establishes nothing. What is your opinion of the professor from the university?"

"I believe he's on the level," said King. "His crowd is interested in the scientific findings, if any. He doesn't know where the money comes from; though his higher-up probably does."

The inspector ruminated. He was inclined to believe with King. As to why officialdom was interested, it seemed to him that since King already knew so much and was there on the spot, there could be no harm in telling the secret.

"I'll tell you, Kingi Bwana, since you've been so candid. The professor thought it was queer that their man wasn't just picked up and shoved into a uniform. Well, after the trouble was all over and our people got to straightening up and looking over whatever records there were, we came across a notation to the effect that this Hugo Meyer was to be let alone because he was doing something or other of immense possible value to the German arms.

"That was all. It didn't say what; only that he was not to be bothered. Now that it is all over, the thing is possibly useless. But we made a note of it, of course; and when this professor suddenly cropped up after all these years to look for him we thought we'd better find out what it was all about. But now that the man is dead, I suppose that closes the chapter."

"I have a hunch," said King slowly, "that he isn't dead. I think you've looked in the wrong place. He dropped out of sight here; but—he was interested in anthropoid apes—the fighting around here drove away every live thing that the Heinie troops didn't have to shoot and eat—and from what I hear those birds ate about everything. Why wouldn't it be reasonable that this scientist nut moved west, up toward the Ruwenzori foothills? There's supposed to be more of his apes there, anyway. That's where I'm to go look-see."

"Good Lord!" gasped the inspector. "My dear fellow, you can't do that. That's Urundi and Ruanda districts. Positively ghastly country. Nothing but solid jungle for hundreds of miles. It would take an army ten years to find a man there if he wanted to hide. You could go in there and in the first day you'd be lost to the human world. It took our whole African army, helped by the Belgians, four years to round up the Fritzies in the comparative open country around here; and still they were holding out after they had given up in Europe. Nobody lives in that frightful country."

"Pygmy tribes do," said King stubbornly.

"Oh, pygmies, yes; but they are half monkeys, anyhow. And for that matter a missionary once told me a fairy story about giants. But good Lord, my dear chap, that is the last, lost end of nowhere. You don't mean to tell me that you hope to find a white man in there after fifteen years?"

King's face wore his hard look of determination.

"I've hired out to go and look, anyway," he insisted. "And if he's dead I'm hired to look for anything he may have left."

THE INSPECTOR relapsed into silence. He knew King. He knew it was useless to argue. He thought the matter over from his official angle and finally he said—

"Well, I don't suppose there can be any objection to your going idiot if you want to—er, provided, of course, that, if you should find anything and come out alive, you'll let our fellows look it over—just in case, you know; if this fellow might after all have found something of military importance."

King was positive.

"Hell, no! I deliver my findings, if any, to the crowd that's hired me. Just the same as if I was a mining man or a plain business scout, I'd be bound to turn in my reports to my employers."

The inspector was officially thoughtful; out of which grew a great embarrassment. He looked at King's dogged expression and found it difficult to give words to his decision. At length he forced himself to mumble—

"Well, my dear fellow—er, I know it's no use trying to dissuade you; but—I'm awf'ly sorry, I'll have to detain you—er, at least until I can communicate with headquarters and find out whether they want to go any further into the matter themselves."

King took the announcement with surprising coolness.

"Yeah, I figured you'd think that way," he said. "Although Urundi and Ruanda are Belgian mandate and you've got nothing to do with it at all."

The inspector was more determined and more embarrassed than ever.

"Sorry, old man, but—by Jove, that complicates things. We'll have to get in touch with the Belgians—because, you know, there might be something in all this. It might be a matter of the gravest international importance. Dash it all, I wish you could see this thing my way."

"Oh, I do," said King. "I can see your point exactly. I figured just that anyhow. And I suppose the negotiations will take weeks and months."

"I'm afraid they will, my dear chap. But—I'm really frightfully sorry—but it's my duty to stop you until the thing is settled. I'm beginning to think it may be much more important than we had thought—that mysterious money, you know; and the insistence upon bringing out all his proofs, whatever they might be. Somebody besides the university is interested. Sorry, old man, but I've just got to stop you."

"And just how do you propose to stop me?" asked King pointedly.

The inspector was excruciatingly embarrassed. Not because he had any doubt of his ability to stop King. This was not any wild and woolly West of America where men settled such personal issues at the swift point of a gun; this was British territory and the British policeman had the ingrained conviction of his kind that all and sundry persons would be amenable to the majesty of the law. He was embarrassed at the need of displaying his authority.

"Oh, come now, my dear fellow." He laughed constrainedly. "We don't have to fight about a thing like this. But, if I must, of course, the simplest thing is to order your *safari* men not to go any farther with you and to send word through the villages that you don't get any others. And you'll have to stay with me, of course. So—" He finished his exposition of authority with another constrained laugh.

"Yeah," King said resignedly. "We don't have to fight. I figured you'd do just that."

"Sorry, old man," apologized the inspector. "But there's just a chance that the thing might be frightfully important."

King grinned at him without a trace of rancor.

"Oh, that's all right, Chief. You're acting just like I figured you'd have to according to your best lights. But we're deadly enemies, and I won't ask you to share my tent—haven't got room for two, anyway."

"Awf'ly glad you take it that way," said the inspector with huge relief. "I'll pitch my tent in the next little hole in the bush. My sergeant will take care of your *safari* men."

The next nearest available hole in the bush where a tent could be set up—King had carefully seen to that—was a hundred yards away.

So that night, when everybody was asleep and contented and secure, King and Kaffa quietly rolled up the tiny tent with the few cooking pots in its center and melted away from that place, leaving twenty-eight *safari* men with their loads of grass and stones in care of a trusty sergeant of police.

"Now then," whispered King to the Hottentot, "see to it, little monkey man, that you don't fail to find the secret stick trail that you taught to Barounggo."

"Keh-heh-heh-heh," giggled the Hottentot. "If that great man of more war than wit has not forgotten it I will surely find it. Have no fear, *Bwana.* Surely will I follow it."

THE LITTLE *safari* had arrived. The queer Hottentot code of broken sticks had been surely laid—the man of war had not forgotten—and as surely followed. The twelve *shenzis* had remained intact, wondering and fearful under the shadow of that great spear.

That was a week ago. No angry minion of the law had followed. As the inspector had said, one could go in there and in the first day one would be lost to the human world. King was lost in the lost end of nowhere. He did not know where he was. Nobody knew. He had traveled westward from Lake Victoria Nyanza, crisscross, zigzag and around, as the lesser densities of the jungle had best permitted. He had covered many tedious miles; he did not know how many.

Perhaps he was twenty miles away from the lake, perhaps a hundred. Maps were indications of nothing. In mere unsurveyed country maps are a help in that when one comes to a river one may figure that this may be such and such a river and that it may be perhaps within fifty miles or so of where a random cartographer drew it.

This map showed but one river, the Kagera, which rose theoretically somewhere near Lake Kivu, the "gorilla lake", and flowed generally northwestward and emptied into the Victoria Nyanza by the swamps of Bukoba—at least the map thought it was the same river. King had already crossed three rivers, three quite sizable *lu-anzas*—or maybe it was the same river three times. He had skirted round the shores of five large *ni-anzas*, two of them salty and one whose edges were heavily encrusted with potash. The map knew nothing about these.

King knew something about the elements of ascertaining position by sextant observations; and he was wondering rather grimly just now how some explorers could come back with such confident traverse notes out of dense forest country where one could scramble along for days without ever catching a glimpse of the sky, to say nothing about horizon, or stars, or sun.

Positions, however, are relative; their scope and usefulness is in connection with other known and established points. Had King been able to establish his accurate position to a pin prick on the map, what good would it have done him? It would not, since the rest of the map was vague, have told him how far he would have to hack his way through the jungle to come to the next water or to a pygmy village.

He was looking for a village. He thought he was in pygmy country. If he could find a settlement of these queer, shy little people he hoped to inquire whether anything was known of a white man alive somewhere in the district. If anywhere within fifty miles—which was about the life and trade association radius of these forest dwellers—so unusual a phenomenon existed, it would surely be known.

For all that King knew he might be surrounded by the little people at that very minute. Furtive and aloof as animals, they might skulk in their own fastnesses and peer cautiously at strangers for a week before they would permit themselves to be seen—or rather, might grow careless enough to be surprised. It has happened that the first intimation strangers have had of their presence has been a poisoned arrow from a diminutive bow or a blowgun dart out of the night.

But if one stopped to think of the possibility of treacherous natives one would never get anywhere. That is a chance that the stranger must take, and he must be careful in his slow progress to mind his jungle p's and q's; to do nothing, not even any unknown anything, that may offend the unsuspected conventions of the suspicious denizens of the forest.

King was being very careful. His course was an erratic zigzag. He picked openings where he found them; he pushed through where he could; he detoured rather than let his men chop a path; for all forest dwellers are of necessity tree worshippers. How could one tell when a blade might chop some sapling whose evil spirit required to be propitiated, or might scar some tree whose tutelary deity called for reverence? Until the people had been met, how should these things be known?

Fortunately for his progress this was rain forest, not *liana* jungle. The elevation was nearly four thousand feet and was gradually ascending to the lower flanks of the Ruwenzori range. The trees were tropical giants of silk cottons, tamarisks, yews; the underbrush was sapling and bush growth rather than the awful interlaced thorny vines of the lower levels. Now and then occurred spaces where the overhead growth was so dense, the light that filtered through so dim, that undergrowth struggled but feebly for life. Here one could progress almost as fast as a slow walk.

Suddenly King, in the lead, stopped and held up his hand. Kaffa at his heels immediately did the same. The first porter behind Kaffa followed suit. And so the signal passed along the winding line to the Masai who brought up the rear with an ever watchful eye upon stragglers. The shuffling line came to a halt and stood to listen.

For awhile there was nothing. Then from far ahead came the sound again; a swishing of branches and a crackle of dead leaves. King looked at Kaffa. The Hottentot listened awhile and then nodded.

"Yes, man," he whispered.

"Ba-m'bute or Ba-nande? Dwarf man or forest man?" inquired King.

Kaffa weighed the question.

"I think forest man," he pronounced. "The moving of branches is too high up for dwarf."

"Guess you're right," agreed King. "Now if you know any forest talk like you've always bragged, call to him."

Kaffa grinned his readiness to show off his accomplishment and gave forth a throaty barking hail. Instantly the growing noise stopped. The jungle was as still as if a deer had crouched in hiding. King was wise. He made no advance toward where the sounds had been. He motioned Kaffa to call again. After a long hesitation a voice came questioning.

The Hottentot was wise, too. He made no blundering statement about a white man with a *safari;* he said only that he wanted information about where there might be habitations and that he would give a piece of meat if the man would come forth.

"Nay, come thou to me," the man called with innate suspicion. In this way he would avoid falling into a trap and would be able to hear whether one man approached or many.

King signed to Kaffa to go. The rest would be up to the astute little fellow's power of persuasion. King sat down and lighted his pipe. He knew that all the questions that could come within the scope of the jungle dweller's reason would have to be satisfactorily answered before he would even begin to consider the advisability of coming forward. And indeed an hour passed before the sounds indicated two men coming back.

Kaffa came grinning his triumph, clucking like a hen to encourage its offspring to advance. The man came cautiously into view, but remained standing at a little distance, ready to make an instant dash for safety. He was very black. His scrawny body was short and pot bellied, but abnormally long legs brought him to normal height. His forehead retreated into overhanging crinkly hair; enormous lips protruded in counter proportion; a nose flattened over half the face, was slit by great elongate nostrils. Except for the lack of the cranial ridge and the over developed canines the face might have been a gorilla's.

THE FIRST thing King did, before putting a single question to him, was to give him a large lump of cold meat. With animal intentness the man fell to gnawing at it, watching over its top with wide alert eyes.

"He says," announced Kaffa, "that a white man came long ago with a *safari* four days' journey to the south. He does not know how long ago; he did not see that white man; he never saw any white man; but he heard about him; and that man went away."

"Hm. Right useful piece of news, isn't it," grunted King.

"He says also," continued Kaffa with triumph at all the information that he had elicited, "that he has heard about another white man who came long ago and he has never heard about that man's going away."

"Ha, that begins to sound like friend professor."

King's eyes sparkled. He had not in his most sanguine dreams hoped to strike the trail at his very first effort. It was almost too easy.

"Ask him if he knows anything about where that white man may be, or if he knows where there are people who may know."

Kaffa translated and the man mumbled back at long length over his meat, pointing with his eyes and with inclinations of his head.

"He says he does not know. The jungle people were afraid of that man because the *Ngai* had looked into his eyes and he was mad." King knew that the *Ngai* was an almost universal Central African name for the great Nature god. "The *Ngai* had looked into his eyes," continued Kaffa with prosaic indifference," and so he married a monkey and went away to live with them."

"What? What's that you say?" King's shout was so suddenly vehement that the jungle man sprang back and crouched ready to run for fear he had in some manner offended.

"He says," giggled the Hottentot as though the thing were merely funny, "that that white man married a chim'panze and went away to live with her people in the jungle."

"Good Lord!" This was news with a vengeance. And told with such simplicity that the astounding thing sounded true. "Went crazy and married a chimpanzee." Good heavens, what wild and weird things could happen in Africa!

And then, as reason began to assert itself and to interpret this stark statement of the native, King began to nod with slow understanding, to smile as he nodded, and then to laugh. He leaned back against a tree and held his sides as mirth rocked him. Of course he understood it all now. The professor absorbed in his study of the anthropoid apes, prowling in the deepest forests all the time: That was quite sufficient for the primitive mind to set him down as having been touched by *Ngai,* the Nature god.

There were plenty of civilized people who were quite ready to set down as crazy any fellow human—and particularly a foreigner—who acted so radically differently from their own established conventions of life.

The good professor was quite possibly a bit eccentric, too; a man would have to be, to come and immure himself in the jungle for so long in order to pursue a study. Even though he had never intended to make fifteen years of it, circumstances had just so happened. That was Africa.

Man proposed and Africa disposed. How many men were there who had come to Africa for a year of business and had stayed the rest of their lives? Cursing it, many of them, moaning about exile, longing for home; but there they had stayed. Africa had just reached out and taken them into her maw. Here was himself. If anybody had tried to prophesy to him that he would stay in Africa for eight years he would have laughed—he would, in fact, have called that person crazy.

Of course the natives would say that the professor was crazy. And when he went away, when he withdrew to some other part where the opportunities for his study were better, they would say—what was more probable than that he had a tame ape or two?—they would naturally say with perfect African logic that he had married it. Why not? They unanimously insisted that apes stole their women. It was true that he, King, had never known of such a case personally; but more than one white man had vouched for the story; and King had heard plenty of sly stories about bush natives who had reciprocal unholy tastes. Why not—in their simple minds—a white man too?

Of course that was it. King was quickly persuading himself. That was the explanation. Ha-ha, what queer ideas these primitives could evolve out of the simplest things. That, without any manner of doubt, must be the whole truth of the matter.

Still—King laughed less whole heartedly—this was Africa; the lost end of nowhere in the very center of Africa. Nothing was sure in Africa until one had seen and talked and knew for oneself. He turned to Kaffa.

"Ask him about any people who might know something more about this white man."

Kaffa had already done that. One of Kaffa's greatest assets was that he did not need to have each item of order detailed to him one by one. The little Hottentot had a thinking apparatus within his monkeylike head and he frequently used it.

"He says that one day's trek to the north is a village of the Ba-m'bute. The white man went away with his wife to the north. There is a trail. He will show us. I have said that *Bwana* will give him *potio,* the same meat and mealies that the *shenzis* get and a strong knife."

"Good," said King. "Tell him to start."

THAT TRAIL was a godsend. Crooked, aimless, scarcely more discernible than an animal track, much overgrown, often requiring crawling upon hands and knees; none the less it more than trebled the distance that could be covered in a blind blundering about the forest.

Even at that, it was not till well into the following day that they began to reach indications of human habitation. King had expected no more than that. He knew that a native stating the time distance of any journey always states it in terms of how fast he can do it according to his usual mode of travel, walking, running, canoe, or mule back; he never thinks to translate it into the probable speed of men with packs or of slow footed white men who flounder through unaccustomed bush.

Indications of a village began to be plentiful enough. Little trails crisscrossed; piles of refuse festered in the hothouse air— for these were simple people who disposed of their garbage by throwing it out at the very doors of their crude shelters; and when the stench became unbearable even to their nostrils they just moved their habitations to a less polluted spot.

Over all hung the pervading effluvium of rottenness which the wind, howsoever fiercely it might rage above the far treetops, never got a chance to blow clear in the dim, humid lanes below.

The jungle man stopped and explained to the Hottentot that he had better go ahead and announce the arrival of so unusual a thing as a *safari,* making clear not only that its object was pacific, but—much more important—that it knew how to treat jungle natives; otherwise some startled villager might send a blowgun dart whispering through the leaves as a stop message; and with those things just a touch, as light as the whisper of its coming, was sufficient to stop its recipient for all time.

"Go ahead," grunted King, and sat down.

To the wary Hottentot's suggestion that the man might be going in advance to arrange an ambush—for the little *safari* gear would mean fortune to the village during the lives of all that generation—King grunted again with malicious humor—

"For that purpose do you, little bush man, walk in front, and so shall your cunning which you boast be the security for all of us."

At which Kaffa twisted and wrapped his knees around each other like a shy schoolgirl and grinned with less good cheer than usual.

That interview between the jungle negro and the dwarf village took up half a day. Time, of course, was a nonexistent element with them. Tomorrow there would be daylight again. It might rain or it might shine; what difference did that make? One could fight or one could run away and hide in the woods equally well in either case. To run or not to run, that was the weighty question.

The village elders had to squat in conclave and jabber that matter over from all possible angles. In the meanwhile any impatient advance on King's part would mean a hasty blowgun dart or two before running.

So King smoked many pipes and kicked his heels in the patience that is bred of Africa. In the course of weary time the messenger came back and clucked at the Hottentot. Kaffa translated with sly malice.

"He says the little people are prepared to make talk with the *bwana* but they are afraid of the Wa-kuafi."

The Masai gave vent to a noise like the explosive grunt of a buffalo. The Wa-kuafi are a branch of the Masai, pastoral tribes, rich in cattle and in tilled fields, and therefore envied and looked down upon by the fighting men. Barounggo was an Elmoran, a warrior, who owned nothing, but took what he wanted with his spear. He rumbled deep in his throat.

"Many people are afraid of me, little monkey man. Why should not your relatives in this place of stinks also fear?"

"Keh-heh-heh-heh," chuckled the little Hottentot.

It was one of his most enjoyable amusements, to excite the somber ferocity of his master's other servant; although he had in reality a great regard for the Masai's loyalty and courage, as the Masai in turn envied the little man's superior cunning which he acknowledged with a lordly condescension to be a necessity to a man who could not wield a seven-foot spear.

And indeed it was not to be wondered that the little people were nervous about the great fellow. From some mysterious place he had produced a single black ostrich plume which he had bound over his left temple so that it nodded above his plaited hair to exaggerate his height, which was already twice that of the pygmies. To them he typified the stories that had filtered in even to their forest fastness of the fierce great men of the plains who condescended to no work but slew for their needs.

"It is well," said King. "Barounggo stays with the *shenzis* and makes camp in a clean place. You and I go and make *indaba* with these Ba-m'bute."

The village itself stank with a concentrated force much worse than its surrounding middens. It consisted of tiny huts of interlaced brush, hardly more than rain and wind shelters, scattered among giant tree trunks. No sun ever came here to sweeten the air by dessicating the litter of refuse. Everything lay as it was thrown and rotted in the humidity.

What impressed King most about these people was the extraordinary vitality that they must have, their resistance to disease. They must be very close to the lower animals to be able to live in such conditions without dying off like flies in the fall. Their shelters, except that they were on the ground, were not much more than the nests that the chimpanzees of the same district built in the trees.

What, indeed, separated them from the apes? The faculty of reason? There was no doubt that they did possess a certain dull quality of reason. But might that not be a matter of degree rather than kind? Various learned professors had recently made elaborate experiments to prove that the greater apes could distinctly reason. What, then, was the great dividing line? Something mysterious in the structure of the body cells? King did not know. Perhaps Dr. Hugo Meyer, after fifteen years of close study, would know.

A GROUP of the little people waited for King under a tree. No other live thing was in sight. The reception committee wriggled their toes with nervous tension through the moist muck of mud and rotting banana pulp that made a malodorous slush on the ground. Monkeys did just that in their cages when visitors came to the zoo.

They were sturdy, little, quite naked creatures, most of them well under four feet, and—King was quite startled—they were not black. Reddish yellow, rather; though some tended to brownish black; and the hair of some of them was distinctly russet. It was an amazing discovery to King.

Bristly black hair grew on the upper lips and chins of the older males; heavy and curly on their chests; and—extraordinary again—fleecy yellowish on their cheeks and limbs, quite a mat of it on their backs.

King's thoughts, as he looked, were running curiously riot. Chimpanzees were black, he reflected; but the gorillas of Mount Karisimbi, not so far distant, gorilla beringii, were often no more brownish black than some of these creatures, whose faces, too, were remarkable for their long upper lips, their depressed broad noses with enormous alae and their heavily prognathous jaws.

Where in the scale of evolution would Dr. Hugo Meyer place these people? He had to try to make clear to them that he was seeking information of Dr. Hugo Meyer.

First of all he distributed gifts, little coils of copper wire that he brought out of his pockets—they were that far ahead of the apes in that they did make crude arm bands of beaten metal. And they carried weapons. Each man held either a diminutive three-foot bow or a long eight-foot blow tube. But for that matter King had seen a reddish brown orang-utan carry a club; the difference was in degree again, not in kind. The little men took the presents and chattered to one another, showing their teeth under lips which turned up as they grinned.

King motioned to Kaffa without speaking; he felt almost as if a human voice would frighten these creatures. The Hottentot clicked and clucked to the Ba-nanda man and he in turn made staccato noises at the Ba-m'bute folk.

There seemed to exist a confusion in their minds. The question required to be assimilated. That required time. They pointed inquiringly at King; they thrust out pointing chins to the surrounding jungle; they acted out comings and goings and climbing of trees; they shook their heads; they accompanied all their wealth of motion with chatterings in high tenor voices. At intervals the Ba-nanda man gabbled to the Hottentot and the Hottentot back to him. Fifteen minutes it took to put over that question and answer. Then Kaffa reported the stunning disappointment.

"They say they have never heard of any white man as far as they travel or as far as the people whom they meet travel. There is no white man here. There are no people here except their own people and the chi-m'panze. The Ba-nanda man told them that his people had heard that the white man had married a chi-m'panze, and had come here; and they say, well then it is clear that one must ask the chi-m'panze, but they themselves are civilized people and do not know how to talk to the chi-m'panze. Perhaps the white *bwana*, who must know everything, knows how to talk with them."

King's high hopes dropped to zero. He had dared to let himself hope when he had first heard the Ba-nanda man's vague story, although he had felt the insistent warning that his quest was shaping up too easily. Things did not fall out as easily as that in Africa. Surely the curse of Adam had concentrated in the African jungles. In the sweat of one's brow one had to labor. Health and life and the indomitable will to carry on had to be heaped in the balance. Only in payment for continuous toil and high courage would the jungle ever yield a grudging return.

All these things King knew from experience. It never occurred to him that possibly the patience and skill and judgment
that had gone into his arduous journey into this lost end of
nowhere might have appeased the jealous gods of the land.

He made Kaffa question again from every possible angle that
might overcome any misunderstanding. But the reply was
definite. There was no white man. There had never been any
white man. The little people were positive. The one ray of hope
that they offered was that perhaps he had gone by another way
up toward the foothills where his wife's people were plentiful.

They themselves did not go to the foothills because the Ba-
n'tongo lived there. The Ba-n'tongo were bad people, big people,
bigger even than the big black man who had stayed with the
porter men, and they did not permit the little people to come
into their country.

The big people? King's eyes widened. Those must be the
giants of whom the police inspector's missionary acquaintance
had told. They could not be so hostile, then. If a missionary had
penetrated to the country there was no reason why another
white man should not have done so; and particularly no reason
why yet another white man should not follow. And the apes
were plentiful in the hills? Quite likely then that the professor
had worked his way up there.

King's hopes began to rise again. He told Kaffa to see whether
he could find out anything about directions, routes of travel,
trails, anything. Kaffa relayed the question. But the little people's
minds had tired of concentration upon the one subject. They
had gone off on another tangent and nothing could shake the
new thought from their heads.

They were glad, they rambled on, that the white *bwana* had
come; because he was without doubt a *bwana m'kubwa*, a very
great white master, and he had guns; and they were going to
make a war and they wanted him to help them. This very night
they had been planning to make their war and it was surely the

sending of the ghosts of their fathers that so strong a white man had come, and he must surely help them in their war.

"To which, tell them most surely not," answered King. "If they are out for trouble that's their affair and I'm certainly not going to bring white man's weapons into play to slaughter their enemies for them. Tell them they're fools and that their silly quarrel, whatever it is, can probably be arbitrated, and I'll go so far that I'll see the other side and we'll sit in white man's judgment over the quarrel."

The long winded answer to that boiled down to that the matter could not be settled by talk because the other side could not understand.

"H'm, that's what all our most civilized belligerents say," said King. "Besides—" with a sudden suspicion that fighting might be some sort of an excuse for treachery—"ask them what kind of a yarn is that; since they said that there were no people around here but their own people."

The reply was startling in its insight into some of the mental processes of these folk. Oh, they were not planning to fight with any people, they said; they were going to war against certain marauding apes; and since the great apes were very fierce, they wanted the help of the white man's guns.

A war it was in their minds. Not just an expedition of humans to hunt some animals; but a conflict against creatures who fought back.

But King was one of those who objected on principle to the unnecessary killing of the great anthropoids. The advance of man into their jungles had already exterminated them from all but a few of the remotest fastnesses; and even to these more than enough millionaire sportsmen came with a covering excuse of collecting specimens for little tank town museums. One of the great indignations of King's life remained against a European prince who came at vast expense into the western flank of the great mountains on whose less accessible slope he now was, and murdered fourteen gorillas and then posed all over the landscape to be photographed with his carcasses for the delectation of his admiring subjects.

King, in common with many other people, had heard and read a vast amount of hysterical propaganda about atrocities committed by the Belgian government in the Congo; most of which propaganda he considered to be lies circulated by a rival power in Africa. But, lies or no, he was inclined to forgive them all in return for the splendid action of the Belgian government in setting aside the whole of the Karisimbi Mountains as a sanctuary for the great apes.

He would certainly not be a party to any war on them. But he wanted to know for what reason the pygmy people were so intent upon a war. The reason was simple enough, crude and direct. The apes were robbing the pygmies' melon and yam patches. And they were foreign apes; not the local apes of their own trees; that was what made the crime the more unforgivable. If they would permit this insult, the ghosts of their fathers would bring sickness upon them.

THESE PEOPLE were becoming more amazing every minute. They stood at the very dawn of human reason and yet in this matter of war and killing, these almost Neanderthal men reasoned exactly as did the most civilized statesmen of today. Foreigners. That was the major crime. Their own monkeys might be shooed off; but when foreign monkeys—astounding thought that; foreign monkeys—when strangers looted their land that was a matter that touched their honor and could be settled only by war.

How could these astounding little savages know that the marauding apes were not the same cunning beasts that lurked in the thickest of their own jungles, King wanted to know.

Oh, that was easy—the little men tossed their heads and grinned in open boasting—they had long ago disciplined their neighbors in their own trees; those apes were wise enough to have learned that punishment followed melon thieving. These overbold marauders always swooped down from the hills where there were no melons and yams, traveling fifty miles in a day along their tree roads and retreating just as fast when they were routed.

Not the best warrior of the little people could follow half as fast along the jungle paths; and besides, up in those hills lived the Ba-n'tongo, the big people who allowed no man to enter their country.

The Hottentot translated everything with perfect seriousness. Why not? He knew that in his own bush country far down to the south monkeys were a pest to his own people. Only there they were the big hamadryas baboons and they raided the mealie patches with immense damage. Many a time had he sallied out with the rest of his village—by no means ever alone—to chase off the robbers.

It was King who laughed, almost giggled. The idea was so ludicrous.

It was just as if he were transported to the beginning of the world and was observing one of the major causes of war that had persisted throughout the rest of the world's history. It had always been the bold mountaineers who had swooped down from their barren hills to raid the comparatively prosperous habitations of their more civilized neighbors, and had fled back into their inaccessible haunts when defeated.

The little men saw him laugh and took heart to press their plea. Would he not help them with his might and his knowledge, for the raiders were very fierce and cunning? If one of them could drop from the thick foliage of a tree upon a pygmy man alone it would give but one tug of its great hands and would tear an arm from the socket; or it might hang from a branch by one hand and clutch a man round the throat with a great strangling foot.

And the leader of these apes—the little savages were building up their case—he was a particularly huge and cunning devil; he could see through every trap, forestall every strategy. From the hills he came; from those hills where that other white man must have gone with his ape wife; perhaps this leader was a son of theirs—that would explain his cunning. It was, in fact, practically the duty of the white *bwana* to help them against this aggression.

King laughed no more. He could not tell just why. He did not entirely believe all the horrors of ape warfare that the savages recounted; that was sheer sympathy seeking craft on their part, he decided. These things might well have happened within the memory of their generation. Anything could happen in these dark primeval jungles. Still, he could not accept them as habitual tactics of malice aforethought.

It was not that that chilled his mirth. It was that recurring reference to the white man's ape wife. The thing came so naturally; it was accepted so easily, without demur, as a commonplace that called for no argument.

Was it remotely possible that— No, the thing was monstrous. A native perhaps, one of these pygmies who were not so very far advanced beyond the tree stage—with only a little more of that horrible brown-yellow hair their faces would be absolute ape. Yes, he had heard plenty of such stories of miscegenation. But a white man? Never! Impossible!

No, this was just the primitive mind ascribing to others what might be quite natural to itself. But Africa— Fifteen terrible years alone in the jungle. Absorbedly interested in the anthropoids—for the sake of science—possibly crazy....

King shook himself. He looked around rapidly and blinked his eyes. He was becoming morbid. These dim sunless jungles, these debased dwarfs. They were hypnotizing him into a condition of bizarre unreality. He turned to Kaffa.

"Tell them," he ordered, "that I will not use my guns against these monkeys who rob a few yams. But I will come with them; and if any man is in a great danger from which he can not escape then I will shoot to save his life."

That was a concession, though King scarcely realized it, to the dramatic ability inherent in these savages. They had told a good story; they had built up, unknown to themselves, a situation of man against nature; and King responded to it. As man, howsoever far removed from these naked primitives, he stood by man to the extent at least of defending human life.

That was as far as he could go; and with that the little savages had to be content. Very well then; the war party was to steal out that same night. By night because the apes were too cautious to be surprised by day; and they, humans, had so far progressed beyond nature that they could postpone the time for sleep; while the apes, evolved beyond the nocturnal creatures, had not yet gone far enough, and slept with the coming of the dark.

I T I S a phenomenon among savages that their little patches of cultivation are frequently astonishingly distant from their habitations. Travelers have wondered why. Does anybody know just why a farmer will sometimes walk a mile or more to some outlying field when untilled land lies at his elbow? Possibly he has persuaded himself that the distant soil is more fertile than the nearer and prefers to go according to his hard ingrained "experience" rather than let the government analyst test his soil and give him a true report of its values.

Savages whose analyst is their local witch doctor go according to his expert whim. This crooked branched tree harbors a benevolent spirit; or that curious outcrop of rock is a good omen. And so one finds little hidden patches of crude clearing scattered in a wide flung radius around every village.

The pygmies had located a small troupe of apes that were looting a distant field. They were cunning enough to avoid all traps and ferocious enough to attack any small boys who might be stationed as scarecrows. An armed party of men could keep them off; but then they would simply go to another field. The only recourse, therefore, was war; a surprise night attack upon their roosts. A scout had discovered the group of giant silk cotton trees in which they slept.

King was all eager to see how these primitives conducted a war. And a war it was to them. Man to man, a chimpanzee was as big as a pygmy, much heavier and infinitely stronger—and, King reflected, not so very much less intelligent.

The little people set out with as much precaution and stealth as though they were attacking a neighboring hostile tribe. Their fear exaggerated the intelligence of their enemies; the apes kept a spy posted to give warning of their movements, they insisted. It was a serious business for them. Every man knew that, as in any war, death was a grim factor that played no favorites.

King stumbled along an unseen track in a grotesque dream. He was at the dark dawn of civilization and these were dawn men fighting to maintain their hard won superiority over the apes. He could just discern shadowy little shapes that hurried along and he followed the pattering of their hard feet.

There was a thin moon. Not that it could be seen through the dense mat of foliage; but a pale glow filtered through sufficiently to show shadow masses where otherwise everything would be the utter blackness of the pit.

Good for them but bad for the apes, the little men chattered gratefully. That seemed to be an enigma born of some queer superstition. But Kaffa's woodcraft knew the answer to that one. Monkeys always crouched desperately still on moonlight nights because the great snakes, the tree boas, which were unable to see in the pitch darkness, hunted like cats in the dim glow.

King was hard put to it to keep up with the pygmy army. His stride was twice theirs and his walking speed proportionately so. But those twisty trails had been cut to suit pygmy stature. At six feet of height sudden unseen branches rasped across a tall man's face. More than once a thick limb, like some ghostly arm reaching out of the night, thudded against King's chest and staggered him.

After an interminable stumbling and ducking through the dark jungle maze the swift patterings of little feet began to slow down. Shadows gathered in groups and hissed sibilantly at each other. The groups congested, broke up, melted out into deeper shadows.

There seemed to be no order, no plan; nobody, apparently, was in charge. Shadow groups formed, larger or smaller, according to whim of individuals. They moved away according to mob impulse.

King judged that they had arrived and that the flitting shadows were surrounding a certain group of vast trees whose thick limbs hung low to the ground. Nobody paid any attention to him; nobody suggested any vantage point. These primitives made war each man according to his own unrestricted desire.

King had always been under the impression that chimpanzees were pacific creatures. But he had seen them only in zoos. A big male ape in its own jungle might be a very different beast from the consumptive creature in a cage. At all events, these pygmy people ought to know; and small wonder, then, that their night foray was a matter of serious moment to them. So formless an expedition, without thought, without plan, was bound to leave a loophole for disaster to strike somewhere.

Kaffa whispered at King's shoulder.

"There, *Bwana,* but a little distance to the right is an open place. No tree is there from which anything can drop. That is a good place. This is a fool's war that plays with death in the dark."

King felt his way out in the direction indicated, Kaffa with him and the Ba-nanda man so close to his heels as to impede his stumbling progress. King wanted to curse him for a frightened fool, but he had not the heart. Fighting with apes was outside of his experience; but he did know that the big hamadryas baboons of the plains gullies would not hesitate to attack a single man or two. These chimpanzees were twice as big as the biggest dog baboon; and there was something creepy about the thought of a black demoniac something dropping, all tearing hands and feet, upon one's head out of a tree in the dark.

Suddenly a spark of fire winked between the farther tree trunks. Another glimmered out, and another. They formed a rough circle round the tree group. Goblin figures showed in silhouette against the light, stepping cautiously under the trees—not too close-peering upward, poised with toy bows and deadly little arrows.

Stealthy shufflings commenced among the high branches. The goblin figures darted about beneath, hoping to catch a glimpse of a moving mass between the deeper abysses of blackness. Gibberings came from above. Excited chatterings answered from below. In the trees a springy creak of wood, a threshing of branches and leaves as a heavy body launched itself through space to a farther branch. On the ground a frenzied patter of feet as the goblins huddled in a protective mob.

King felt as if he were in a nightmare of ghouls. It was weird and unholy warfare. Shadows flitting in the firelight hunting shadows. It was not of the material world, this thing. It was gloomily unreal; a flickery moving picture of a maniac director's inferno.

King did not blame the dwarf people for being afraid of this war of theirs. In that dark setting any horror might happen.

An angry coughing bark sounded from a low hanging mass of foliage. A flurry of pygmies fled that spot. Gibberings answered the bark. The fling and crash of heavy bodies took a definite direction. The angry bark sounded with insistent command.

It seemed to King that there was more purpose and direct plan among the tree folk than among the dwarf mob. He was telling himself that it was as he had expected. The apes were clearly trying to get away and, unless cornered with retreat cut off, would not show fight. And he could then picture the howling, tearing, fury of that fight.

He was just beginning to relax from the tension of an unwarranted expectation of danger, when the horror that he had imagined might happen in the ghoulish setting materialized out of the dark with a suddenness that was the more horrible because it exceeded the wildest probability of his imagination.

The apes were moving successfully along their line of retreat. The goblins were unable to keep up with their fresh fires to light the attack. It looked like a clear getaway, when a lucky arrow flew truer than the rest. There came the shriek of a wounded animal and a frenzied scurry among the branches. The dwarfs yelled in shrill chorus and rushed in a mob to keep up with the scurry.

The arrow, of course, was poisoned. Its effect would be to paralyze the nerve centers within a few seconds or a few minutes, depending upon the freshness of the venom. The inevitable result would be that the victim, unable to hold on, would fall from its tree. The venom on this particular arrow was fairly fresh and so the end was swift. The ape, feeling its weakness growing apace, began with the last fading of its instinct to climb down in order to avoid a heavy fall.

A dark shape could be discovered lowering itself slowly down the bole of a tree a little beyond the rim of the farthest fires. Desperately it clung; reluctantly it slipped lower. Inevitably lower.

Hobgoblin shadows howled and danced in infernal jubilation. They ringed the tree and leaped in grotesque antics, throwing vast shadows of devils on the farther greenery. The picture required only the master fiend to complete it.

He came. A half human bellow of rage burst from the nearest bushes as a monstrous shape rushed from the blacker darkness and hurled itself upon the leaping shades. In the smoky gloom it looked to be twice as huge as it really was; but allowing even for that, it was enormously bigger than the dwarfs.

Screaming its fury, it charged into the thick of them. Vast arms and feet clutching, swinging, it swept half a dozen little figures whirling into the air in its first rush. After one long second of awful silence the yells of jubilation broke out in shrill yelpings of fear. For a moment a massed mob formed. Not with any idea of attack; it was a huddle of horror.

A bow or two twanged, but without apparent effect. The monstrous shape roared again and rushed the huddle. A luckless dwarf came into the clutch of its vast hands. In a moment it dangled high by one foot. Holding it so by the ankle with both hands, the monster flailed at the mob with the limp body, screaming its fury.

It was enough to terrorize braver people than the dwarfs. With high pitched shrieks the mob broke and fled like devils at cock crow. In an instant every shrieking imp was swallowed into the surrounding blackness. In the same instant the monster made a leap and was gone. A crashing in the bushes, smaller scuttlings in other directions, and the night was as silent as a cave. The devil's nightmare had vanished as suddenly as it had come. Only the flicker of the encircling fires was proof that the thing had happened at all.

KING EXHALED a long shuddering breath.

"Twist a grass torch, Kaffa, with speed," he ordered; and when it was ready he advanced warily to the scene of the awesome fight.

It had all come about so suddenly and so far in the gloom that to use his rifle had been out of the question. But there would probably be some first aid to be given, and he was quite sure that none of those pygmies would return to give it.

The torch disclosed six twisted bodies. Dead. Horribly dead. Crushed. Distorted in impossible positions, with broken backs or necks. If there had been any wounded, they had crawled off into the bushes. At the base of the tree huddled the black hairy form of the chimpanzee, already stiff.

As complete as it had been sudden had been the typhoon of death. King was awed. He had never seen anything so sudden even in Africa. Kaffa chattered at his elbow.

"*Bwana,* this is an evil place of devils. We have yet to find our way back to camp through these imp trails without a guide."

"Let us go," said King. "Let the Ba-nanda man make torches as fast as you burn them up."

Occupied as King's faculties were, finding the way back through the jungle maze by sheer trial and error, the thing that he had seen found place to intrude. Anything could happen in

Africa, he had often said. But not this thing. This was too impossible.

That the pygmy people should organize a hunting party to chase away some marauding monkeys was nothing. It was their superstition and their own limited mentality that ascribed a proportionate super-intelligence to the apes and built up their expedition in their minds to the dignity of a war.

But what was this other thing? This sudden avenging monster? No chimpanzee had ever grown to half that size. This creature must have been at least six feet in height; possibly more; though in that gloom it had been impossible to gage with any accuracy. And there had been more than ape intelligence behind the ferocity of its fight. Was an ape physically built so that it could stand on wide spread legs and swing a body round its head with both hands?

Kaffa, trotting along with the torch, might almost have been reading his thoughts.

"In my own country," he broke out of a long silence, "the monkeys have a god whose name is Han-Hau. We give him mealies and pawpaws to keep his people out of our fields. This great one is undoubtedly the god of these chi-m'panze. It is good that we took no part in that war. He is a very fierce god."

"Which is about as far as we shall ever get with any explanation," grunted King. But to the Hottentot he said for the sake of morale, "Monkey gods for monkey people. This was an ape as great as you are a fool. With the morning the little people will make it clear."

And with the morning it was his amazement that the pygmy folk bore him out to the letter. Yes, they said, this was the leader of those apes about whom they had spoken; very big and very terrible and very cunning; had not all men heard him barking his orders to his people?

King, forgetting his reproof to Kaffa, said—

"Rubbish; who ever heard of a chimpanzee growing to that size?"

They answered with perfect readiness, of course not; this was not a chi-m'panze, but a wo-m'panze, one of the greater apes from the big mountain, and the chi-m'panze had chosen it for their leader. Was not a greater ape wiser than a lesser ape even as a big man was a better leader than a small man?

To which sound logic there was no answer. What though King growled irritably that no gorilla would herd with chimpanzees any more than hamadryas baboons would herd with chacmas. The little people would not even argue the matter. There it stood; they had seen with their own eyes and he had seen; what more was there to talk about?

More important was that since the white *bwana* had miserably failed in his promise to shoot his gun and save their lives, he should now come with them to give a belated protection. They had to go and bring in their dead. And the body of the ape would have to be skinned and the hide stuffed with grass and hung up in a tree as a horrible object lesson. The skull would be brought back and decorated with yellow and white clays and kept in the tribe as a trophy.

King was not averse to returning to the scene of the nightmare by daylight. He wanted to convince himself of the impossible by looking for gorilla tracks. The distance which had been an interminable torture by night was agreeably shortened by day. The pygmies approached the battlefield with caution and a certain awe; but took courage from the presence of the white man who towered in the center of their mob.

But once upon the scene and satisfied by throwing stones into the trees that no vengeful enemies lurked in ambush, they dragged their dead aside with animal callousness. Death was something that came in its various forms of suddenness and horror; and the dead would have to be properly cared for according to tribal convention and tradition; otherwise their ghosts would come back and make things unpleasant.

But all that could come later. Just now was the occasion for the quite as important matter of offering indignities to the body of a slain enemy with all the proper ceremonies so that his ghost would suffer an unpleasant time and would not be able to come back.

Ordinarily King would have been intensely interested in watching these ceremonies and in finding out the why and wherefore of each move. It was a necessity of Africa, he considered, to know what all kinds of natives did and why they did it, and from that to reason out in what queer manner they thought. More than once he had been able to apply his accumulated knowledge to the working of some simple hokum that had gained for himself a considerable reputation as a white witch doctor.

But just now he was busy on a more absorbing matter. For the sake of his peace of mind he wanted to see those gorilla tracks. He prowled, therefore, over the ground, searching for footprints. In the immediate vicinity was only a mess of trampled mud. No hope there.

At the base of the tree where the ape had been shot were a couple of prints of foot and knuckle before the sagging body had blurred the rest. King studied these carefully. A gorilla print ought to be very similar to these, only larger. He cast around for larger tracks without success. Going back to the actual spot of the demon fight, he reconstructed the direction from which the monster had charged forth.

From that heavy underbrush it had come. King went there and dropped to his hands and knees so as to miss nothing.

And there it was. Startlingly King saw it, and he froze. Stiffly on all fours, like a trained dog, he tensed over his find.

There it lay, quite clear and sharply outlined; and a little behind it was another deeply impressed by a heavy weight, unmistakable.

King gave a thin, hissing whistle, and in a moment Kaffa was at his side—also on all fours, gazing incredulously at the tracks, broad nostrils twitching as though to find a clue by scent. King spoke no word, but looked at his man. The Hottentot slowly turned his head and puzzled wonder was in his eyes. This track that shouted out loud at them from the silent ground was just not possible.

The imprints were clear all round, easy to read, unmistakable. The wonder lay in that there were no long prehensile toes, no great opposed thumb as in the prints of the chimpanzee. The marks were long and quite flat with sharp edges, slightly wider in front than at the heel. There was no possible room for error.

This thing had worn shoes!

Or moccasins, rather, would be more accurate; for there was no sharp indication of a heel. These were moccasins such as a man might make who had long been out of touch with a shoe store.

KING SQUATTED back on his heels and his eyes narrowed to long, barely open slits. What wild and impossible enigma of Africa was this? A thing that had worn moccasins and had rushed out to murderous battle on the side of chimpanzees? What ancient Roman was it who had written, "Out of Africa always some new thing?" As long ago as that this dark land had startled the world with its bizarre unrealities; and what new manifestation was this?

King strode to the busy group of pygmy skinners and frightened both the leader of them and the Ba-nanda interpreter by taking them both by the arm and leading them to look at those inexplicable tracks.

But the little leader was in no way nonplused. He had the explanation in a second. He looked, and a great understanding broke in upon him.

"Why, it is quite clear then," he said. "It is not a wo-m'panze from the hills at all. It is without any manner of doubt the son of that white man who married the chi-m'panze and went up into the hills. That is why it is so cunning."

King pushed away the dwarf with an exasperated mutter.

He stood looking with hard eyes in the direction of the hills where the man had pointed. After many minutes he called Kaffa.

"Little man," he said, "you are wise; wise in the ways of the woods and of the people of this dark land. Tell me now out of your wisdom. Would any native of Central Africa ever wear a foot covering like that?"

"No, *Bwana,* never," answered the Hottentot with instant conviction.

"Who, then, would?"

"Only a white man, *Bwana.*"

King nodded. Slowly and with deliberation he nodded, still looking toward the hills which he could not see.

"Well," he breathed at last, "I don't know what weird mystery of this unbelievable land this is. But to those hills we must go. The trail leads to the hills. Little man, go swiftly and tell Barounggo to bring along those *shenzis.* I wait here—on the hill trail."

11

T HE LITTLE *safari* toiled up a long slope of a vast lateral ridge that reached from the high shoulders of the Ruwenzori to splay out into the far plains of the southeast. It was still the same limitless rain forest, but its nature was changing. King felt a thrill of home to recognize an occasional witch hazel. A scattered grove of junipers gave a tang to the air. Begonias grew in sheltered limb crotches as cosily as in parlor window pots.

But the reminder of Africa was ever present in enormous, somber *podocarpus* trees and in thorny vines; in the grating squawk and clear whistle of gray parrots and the thin cough of toucans.

Now and again the long lost sky became visible where some decrepit forest king, falling, had torn a hole in the green canopy. Gray clouds hung sullenly over these openings. These Ruwenzori Mountain flanks were beyond the terrible monsoon belt;

but a hundred inches of rainfall distributed themselves fairly evenly through the twelve months with a preference for Spring and Fall. This was April. The relentless gods of the land substituted extreme wet in place of extreme heat.

Wet clothing—wet bedding—wet tents—wet food. It was not cheerful. Ammunition alone was dry; and that was almost a miracle. But the outstanding achievement of King's organization was that he traveled with the same twelve porters with whom he had started.

These were men of the open plains; people who traveled not at all during their monsoon. They shivered like wet monkeys in this permanent damp. Their normal food was maize, with meat as a very occasional treat. Here King kept them supplied with plentiful meat; but, animal-like, they moaned at the substitution of yams for their mealies. Still, here they were, all twelve of them. Barounggo, cheerfully grim, saw to that.

The *safari* slowly topped the windblown back of the ridge. A wide valley that rippled and tossed in waves like a green sea spread before them. This was bamboo. The solid ground was a hundred and fifty feet below its liquid surface. A far, sublimated yelping came up with the wind. It sounded almost like the jolly chorus of fox hounds. But King's eyes narrowed and he looked keenly to the far right and left to see whether that bamboo jungle could be avoided.

Kaffa was appraising the same forest with glistening eyes.

"There will be elephant in that jungle, *Bwana*. Much meat for many days."

The *shenzis* awoke to a hungry interest with thick red grins. There spoke Africa. Meat. A gorge or two before quick decay would turn even those calloused appetites; and the remaining tons of waste would be left.

King had heard of the curious subspecies of straight tusked elephant that might be found in these jungles; but he was slaughtering no vast, inoffensive beast just to feed his *safari;*

there was plenty of smaller game that would be picked to the clean bone at a single meal.

Beyond the bamboo forest another ridge swung in a slow heave to a higher escarpment, blue in the misty haze; and beyond that another again. Those were the true hills. There would be—if the little pygmy men spoke true—the lairs of the great apes. And there—God alone knew—perhaps the haunts—or rather, the home—of this dark mystery that had worn moccasins.

The long descent commenced. The grade was not steep; but going was difficult on account of the long trailers of thorny vines that stretched, as though with the set purpose of impeding, always across the choicest openings where one hoped to pick a path. Not high, low creeping things they were, seldom more than knee height; more usually hidden under the sparse grass tops, and tough as wire. Many people will remember how a barbed wire entanglement impeded advance.

Once in the bamboo jungle, however, going was easy. The giant grasses grew in clumps, twenty or thirty knotted stems as thick as a man's thigh in a close bunch. Between clumps the ground was clear, carpeted only with the fallen leaves of all the centuries.

King paced silently in the lead. This was excellent ground for getting a snap shot at a buck or a pig, so avoiding the later delay of hunting meat. But King carried his rifle by its sling over his shoulder; he was not hunting—he was listening. The *shenzis,* far behind, feeling the first easy going in more than a month, the ground soft underfoot, broke into a grunting rhythm of song, one man supplying a short impromptu verse and the rest barking a chorus.

King cursed venomously and ran back to stop the idiots. He did not shout at them but, as soon as within view, signaled with his both hands to shut up. The *shenzis* blundered cheerfully ahead and kept up their barking. It was not till their master was almost upon them and they could see the impotent rage in his eyes that they came to a confused halt in staring wonder.

Barounggo, man of the open plains himself, had not known of any need for silence, and he too stood wondering, but outwardly emotionless. King cursed the men with silent ferocity for fools, and hoped that perhaps luck would be with them.

But it was not to be. A thin ki-yi of yelping came from far down the valley. An answer followed quickly; many more answers. King damned loudly, then:

"Make *boma* swiftly," he snapped. "Tree *boma*."

Kaffa, with the first yelp, was alive to the need. Under a barrage of obscene invective he drove the now frightened *shenzis* to the task.

In bamboo forest, fortunately, to make a tree *boma* was easy. It required but to scramble up a clump and to chop half through a few of the great hollow tubes at a height of eight or ten feet; to wedge them fast or, if necessary, lash them, where they fell into the next clump; and to lash cross pieces of split bamboo to make a rough platform, using twisted strips of the tough green cortex for the purpose.

King was taking no chances. He had recognized those distant yelpings in the first instance to be the terribly destructive hunting dogs of Central Africa. These ever hungry brutes had been known to range in packs of fifty or more and in those numbers to attack men. It might well be that the present pack would not be large enough to molest a party as large as his. It might, however, just as well be the record pack of all time. It was by not taking unnecessary chances that King was here.

With the same number of white men he would have collected them in a compact body and would have pushed on. But with twelve panicky natives who could be held together no better than sheep, King was taking the precaution of being sure. It was for just such reasons that he had his same twelve porters.

"Up you get, monkeys. Squat and dangle your dumb feet. Pass up those packs first."

A quite close yelp of the scent discovery punctuated the order and sent the men scrambling with frenzied haste. At the farthest visible opening between the bamboo clusters a rangy, tawny creature sat back on its haunches with red tongue lolling and watched.

I T W A S plain dog; nothing wolfish about it. Just long haired, underfed hound dog; and its tongue lolled in a grin of friendly looking interest.

Barounggo stood his ground. His eyes rolling white, nostrils twitching, full lips protruded, he gripped his great spear and stood to give battle. It was beneath Masai dignity to take shelter from a big dog, or from an army of dogs.

King grinned at him and pointed at other shapes that sat still, expectant. No yelping now; only watchful waiting with long lolling tongues, and in the farther, unseen distances, a pattering of many feet.

"This is something, old blood letter, where your great spear will avail you little. I, too, make a monkey of myself."

And with that he swung himself on to the platform. With his master's example before him, the Masai could not but unbend. Yet he did it reluctantly—those chattering *shenzis* must see no haste. Scowling ferociously and with cold deliberation, he prepared to hoist himself to safety.

There came a rush of quick feet, a clicking of teeth, as a hungry red beast, seeing the last of its hoped for meal escape, mustered courage to charge in, snapping at the Masai's dangling foot.

With iron nerve the great fellow never hurried. With the same slow deliberation he lifted his foot clear, only inches from the white teeth. Then with the sudden speed of light he whirled up his spear and drove down. The wretched creature yelped once in agony, rolled over twice in desperate effort, and then stretched in its last convulsive tremor. A hell's chorus of howls answered the yelp, and the lean brutes closed in to see what had died.

"One," said the Masai.

"But forty are left," said King.

He was being sincerely glad of his swift precaution of the *boma*. With so large a pack in attendance, had he been caught on trek, nothing would have prevented the panic crazed porters from dropping their loads and scrambling, belated, for trees; and nothing then could have saved at least one of the number from being dragged down.

As it was, King lighted his pipe. Seeing which, the Masai with a vast show of unconcern drew a little tube of ivory from the lobe of his ear, pulled its wooden plug and tapped a meticulous measure of snuff on to his thumbnail.

"What now, *Bwana?*" he asked. "Do we grow tails and become *shenzis* and stay in the trees, or do we cut, each man, a stick, and drive these dogs before us?"

The *shenzis*, looking down through the wide openings of the hasty platform at the red tongues and clicking teeth, chattered horror at the thought.

"When they are fed and full bellied," said King, "they will go their ways in search of water."

"Wherefore," Kaffa chimed in quickly, "one of these who by their ape song called these beasts forth, we might well throw down quickly in order that the delay be short—keh-keh-keh-hee-hee-bee-ee-ee."

The porters rolled fearful eyes at him and then, slowly grasping the idea, tittered with faces averted. They were used to Kaffa; but the great Masai they never understood, whether serious or not. His somber ferocity that lay just beneath his calm exterior kept them in a condition of permanent awe.

"If we should lose a *shenzi*," said King seriously, "then would Kaffa have to carry his load."

This, to the *shenzis*, was brilliant repartee. If their master could joke it meant that he knew some way of getting them out of the nasty situation, as he had so often done before. So they guffawed their appreciation. When King drew his Luger automatic and shot one of the gaunt hounds, and quickly another and then three more, their minds grasped the stupendous strategy almost at once.

"Awo! Meat for their full bellies," they told one another, and gabbled for an hour thereafter about the astounding wisdom of their master who could think of such a brilliant maneuver.

Wild dogs, of course, like wolves, are cannibalistic. And King's nature craft, too, was correct. The great brutes snarled and gorged and fought and gorged again, till, surfeited, they began to drift away in a search of water and a secure lie-up. Only a few, that thought gluttonously to wait awhile until their distended bellies could hold some more, made themselves comfortable in the immediate vicinity.

To chase a full fed dog, of course, is no very difficult feat. With snarlings and ferocious growlings and all the noisy bluff of canine belligerence, these few got to their feet and slunk into the farther jungle. The total delay had been less than three hours; the loss, *nil*. The whole thing had been no more than an inconvenience.

But Kaffa knew. He was astute enough to perceive what would have happened had it not been for the prompt order to construct a tree *boma*. The Hottentot theology, almost as complex as its grammar, recognized various gods of woods and trails. To them he would give a goat, a pure black goat with no blemish on it. And when he told his laudable plan to his master as he trotted alongside and explained that the offering was really in thanks that no *shenzis* had been eaten—not that *shenzis* mattered; but that the whole *safari* would have been slowed up on account of the heavier proportionate loads—his master said:

"Good. I will give you the money to buy that goat, for I no longer know what gods or devils guide this quest for a thing which is not possible."

CAMP WAS made that night in the rain, well away from the bamboo valley and up the side of the farther ridge in a grove of conifers. The next day's going was worse than it had yet been.

It was not that the slope was steeper; it was the thorns. Those terrible barbed entanglements. Something in the soil there, or the rainfall, just suited the growth of these tough vines. They crept insidiously through the grass; they spanned every opening between the underbrush. And they grew higher here than on the other ridge; at waist height almost they plucked at the clothing and raked the tenderest skin.

For a white man, well cord breeched and high booted, it was bad enough; for bare legged, bare footed natives, the going was well nigh impossible. King, in the lead with a bush knife, was forced to cut a path. Kaffa remarked wisely:

"I think, *Bwana,* that the little man said true. Here indeed must the great apes take refuge, coming by their tree roads, for here no man can follow."

It was beginning to be literally true. The thorn vines grew in tough tangles to the exclusion of all other growth. Turn which-ever way they would, the barrier grew worse with each new cast. King was realizing the hopelessness of progress and consider-ing a return and a detour, possibly of many days, to come up on the other flank of the ridge, when he chanced on a heaven given trail.

There it was, hardly discernible through the encompassing bush, but still a trail. Little used and faint, but obviously a human road through the otherwise impassable barrier. The vines had been cut with a sharp instrument and forced apart.

Whose path, or why a path at all, was a matter for surmise as one went along. The important thing about it was that it led in the right direction; the direction in which King was deter-mined to go, detour or backtrack or around, north-northwest by his little pocket compass to the hills. King accepted the trail thankfully. He was almost inclined also to accept Kaffa's quick suggestion that this was the direct and immediate result of promising that goat.

The providential trail led unerringly over the back of that ridge. From its high point a vista of tremendous country spread out. Green—all the various shades of green. Treetops, treetops, miles beyond rolling miles of them. From the far west a cool breeze washed the cheek; and there, beyond the ridges that turned from green to blue, from blue to purple, a ghostly white broken cone glimmered out of the gray sky. Toward the north the grayness was accentuated to a sullen storm darkness.

King breathed the fresh air with a crinkling of the nostrils. That smoky blackness must surely be the one of the M'fumbiro craters. The snow peak would then be Ugali, or maybe Ubungo. He must be in the Ruanda country. If that were so, then farther to the north again, behind the smoke screen, would be Kari-simbi, the gorilla mountain. This began to be like getting some-where.

Kaffa pointed silently. King followed the line of the skinny finger. At first he could discern nothing besides softly waving high lights and deep shadows of green. Then his eye picked it out—something that did not wave. Motionless it hung and peered through an opening in the high branches; a black face with round wondering eyes.

"It seems that the little people spoke true," whispered the Hottentot, "and here the great monkeys live."

"Maybe then this path goes some place where people live," murmured King. "People who can tell us about a something that wears shoes."

For an hour the *safari* followed the trail diagonally down the flank of the great ridge. Without it progress would have been impossible. The thorn vines grew in an impenetrable mat. Kaffa sniffed with head high, quartering the breeze.

"I smell man," he announced.

King knew that this was no superhuman power of scent that the Hottentot possessed to detect, as a dog might, the actual scent of man; but that he had distinguished a whiff of the ef-fluvium that surrounds the habitation of African man.

In another minute the path opened out into a small clearing. Yam vines and a great yellow cucumber thing grew along one side. The path went straight across the clearing and dived into the thorn tangle on the other side as into a tunnel. At the mouth of the tunnel was a wattle-and-daub thatched hut around which lay the usual litter of fire wood and gourds and oddments of bone and dirt.

At the noise of the *safari* a man came out of the hut, bending low under the opening and leisurely covering a yawn behind a long hand.

King was startled as the man unbent himself and straightened up; and a gabble of wonder came from the porters behind him.

It was an immense creature that stood up. King himself stood his good six feet, and the Masai was a couple of inches taller. But this man towered from the shoulders above them both. Well over seven feet his height must have been, and the spear that he held was longer even than the Masai's, though the blade was a tiny thing compared to the great Masai weapon which was practically a sword, four inches wide and two feet long, stuck on to the end of its polished shaft.

Enormously naked and black he stood, except for a wisp of loin cloth; and it was easy to see that his growth had gone into his great height. He was not as broad as King or the Masai.

"By golly, the Ruanda giant that the missionary told the policeman about," murmured King.

THE MAN was unpleasantly self-possessed. There was a wonder in the rather protruding eyes in his long, bony face; but it was a wonder not at a white man and a *safari*, but a surprise that a *safari* should be there at all. There was calm hostility in his bold stare.

"See if you can make him understand anything, Kaffa," ordered King.

The Hottentot tried various of his bush dialects. The man shook his head; he understood nothing. He wanted to understand nothing. Imperturbably, like some huge traffic policeman, he pointed with his spear along the road they had come. There was no mistaking the command that they should make no fuss about it, but should quietly turn back.

Kaffa whispered—

"The little people—they said there were great fierce men who let no man pass."

The wide corners of King's mouth began to take the faintest possible downward turn, and the beginning of a thin, vertical line appeared between his brows.

"Try to make him understand we don't want trouble, that we're looking for a white man. Tell him that we bring gifts."

King smiled with outstretched, open hands; he showed his own hunting knife and indicated that there were similar things in his packs. He tried in a questioning tone all the words meaning white man he knew—*m'zungu, bwana, bakwale,* and a half a dozen others—which Kaffa supplemented with a variety of clickings and chatterings.

The man seemed to understand something of it all, for he repeated one or two of the words that Kaffa had uttered, and pointed with his long spear to the slopes behind him. It was done with an impersonal air of disinterest, and with the same swing of the spear shaft he pointed inexorably again to the way the *safari* had come. It was the traffic policeman admitting that the desired goal might well be there, but the road was definitely closed.

The thing was common enough. King had met isolated tribes before who desired to maintain their isolation. Usually such tribes, if a superior party forced an entry, resorted to ambushes, sniping at night, poisons, anything. This tall fellow did not at all seem to feel that he was confronted by a superior party. He was confident and becoming rapidly more hostile. He held his spear threateningly and spoke in a curt tone, that clearly indicated there was to be an end to all fooling and the intruders should get out.

The corners of King's mouth drew lower; the line between his brows deepened; into his eyes came the wary, alert look of one who faces conflict. If his goal were there, as he had come so far to find out, he was not going to turn back. He could not turn back. As a white man, leading a party of natives, he could not afford to let himself be ordered from his objective by a single spearman—or, for that matter, by ten.

The bold front, the sheer weight of white man's prestige applied with determination, had carried through many thousands of such situations in Africa. Delay and argument would be only a sign of weakness.

King advanced without further hesitation. In an instant the point of the giant's spear was over his heart—and in no half hearted warning, either. The man was by no means afraid; his point pierced the khaki shirt and pricked well into the skin. King knocked it aside with a quick sweep of his left hand and stepped inside of its range.

That was the last move in this game of bluff. If determination and prestige would win, well and good. If the man shortened his weapon for a thrust King would have to decide upon his instant next move and then carry the thing through to its finish.

Neither thing happened. Instead the man gave a great shout, obviously a call, and with splendid courage, in view of the numbers that opposed him, dropped his hold on his weapon and grappled with King; just as might a policeman who knew that reenforcements were behind him.

King found himself in the grip of this huge man whose strength, in spite of his leanness, was quite as great, if not greater, than his own.

The sling of his rifle slipped from his shoulder and hung on his arm. He let it go, feeling even in that strenuous moment the pang of dropping the meticulously oiled bolt mechanism into the dust.

He was not flurried. He had been at grips with strong men before; and he had found that a cool head and a quite extensive knowledge of rough and tumble methods could offset most handicaps.

But this giant fought in a manner entirely new. Owing to his immense height and his tremendous reach, he could bring into play an unexpected and murderous trick.

He brought a bony knee up against King's chest and, twining his long arms behind King's back, was able to join hands and exert a terrific pressure against the chest.

Wrestlers given to foul tactics sometimes in desperation bring into play a similar principle, with the head against the opponent's chest. If not swiftly broken the hold is capable of crushing in the chest wall. It can be broken, if the opponent retains sense and strength long enough, by the equally foul defense of battering under the hugging arms at the unprotected face and jaw.

With this giant, face and jaw were out of reach. King gasped under the sudden pressure. It was his salvation that this man had not the huge biceps of a wrestler; but, at that, he felt his chest cracking under the strain and spots danced before his eyes.

He could still reach the pistol in his belt holster; but there remained inexorable in his mind the white man's religion—prestige. Hand to hand the sudden fight had started. Hand to hand he must finish it. In the presence of his native following he could not, would not, take unfair advantage of a gun. By the sheer, indomitable faculty of winning against odds he held his people together and commanded the loyalty of his followers. If he could not continue so to hold it, he might as well be dead as far as his successes in Africa would be concerned.

Through the gathering mist in his eyes he could see the form of Barounggo circling with poised spear. To him he gasped an order to keep off. Against the pounding pressure in his head he must force himself to concentrate on some method of combating this deadly hug while he could still stand on his feet.

That was it. He was still on his two feet. His own wide spread legs and his opponent's one formed a firm standing tripod, with the advantage on the side that could use the free leg as a deadly weapon.

King collected his strength for an effort and threw himself with all his force over to one side, twisting as he fell. The third leg of the tripod whirled a circle in the air. Both bodies crashed to the ground together. The terrible knee slipped from King's chest and passed under his armpit. The awful pressure was broken. Like an anaconda King's arm encircled that thigh and hugged it close while he lay for a moment to gasp his relief.

The advantage was now his. The African knew nothing about fists. Fists are a weapon evolved by a civilization that has discarded arms. The giant clawed futilely at King, battered at him with wrists and elbows. King was able to drag close enough to bring a short chop to the base of the man's ear. The great arms and legs jerked galvanically to the shock. Both King's hands were free. He picked his spot and smashed his right fist at the protuberance behind the man's ear again; and then quickly again.

The great limbs dropped away from him. King rolled off.

"Tie him," he was able to pant, and he lay and drew in great lungfuls of life-giving air.

But weakness would not do. He pushed himself to a sitting position, leaning on one arm, and forced his voice to direct the operation.

A quick thudding of running feet sounded in the farther tunnel of the path. Barounggo turned to meet the menace, as another tremendous man burst into the clearing, brother in every way to the first giant; if anything, a little taller, and a broader built man.

At sight of so many people he stopped short and glared with wondering eyes. He saw only black people. The white man sitting on the ground was partly hidden by Barounggo's burly form. The black men were clearly maltreating his fellow tribesman.

Once again the analogy to the policeman was evident. The

newcomer did not howl and rush at the strangers with his spear
as a supremely brave man might have done. He acted as though
his sheer immensity gave him authority. He took a great stride
forward and with a long arm made to brush the obstructing
Barounggo aside.

The Masai stood on braced feet, immovable, and growled
out of his belly at the giant. The firmness of the resistance
stopped the huge fellow in quick surprise. Resistance to authority.... The giant looked a moment, then snarled impatient
truculence and struck the obstructor with closed fingers and
wrist on the side of the head.

A rasping noise like a threatening lion came from the Masai's
throat, and his instant retaliation was to lift his foot high and
kick the aggressor in the stomach.

The giant let out a hoarse scream of fury and rushed to the
side of the hut; he snatched up a great oval shield and turned
to take immediate vengeance. Barounggo faced him, shieldless,
crouched forward, balancing warily on his toes, and hissing
softly between his teeth.

KING STRUGGLED to his feet. But even as he did
so he knew the futility of any interference. He himself was in
no condition to take on a new fight, particularly against an
armed man. His pistol! The thought came, but with his hand
on the butt he dismissed it.

The ancient code of all fighting men checked him. Mortal
personal offense had been received and given. How few years
ago was it even in America that duelists claimed the sacred
right to avenge their personal honor. Did it make any difference
that the duelists were black men?

The giant hesitated. The sudden appearance of a white man
complicated things. He stood, half hidden behind his big shield,
and eyed King suspiciously. Barounggo, out of the corner of his
watchful eye, noted the hand on the gun butt and, as his master
had checked him a little while ago, he demanded his right to
non-interference now.

"Let be, master, let be," he growled with a whine in his throat. "This dog has put hand upon an Elmoran of the Masai. Look, I have seen dogs before; are not their marks upon my breast? Where are they, those who struck? Their bodies have been eaten by other dogs."

The giant still stood and watched suspiciously.

"Take at least a shield, Barounggo," said King. "Look, there is another great shield beside the wall. I hold him off with the gun."

"A big shield for dancing among the women," growled Barounggo. "A little shield for fighting. What does this jungle man know about fighting? But hold him, master, till I shed this garment that chokes my shoulders. But a moment, master, and I will give this great fool instruction."

King drew his pistol, while with a deft wriggle the Masai shook his old shooting coat from his shoulders and stood only in his leopard skin girdle. The velvety black skin of his chest and shoulders and thighs was scarred with innumerable thin white cicatrices, the marks of those who had once struck and had paid the price.

He moved his big scarred arms in the shoulder sockets and drew a long breath of comfort. He exhaled with a soft hiss.

"It is well, master; let him go."

King shoved his pistol back into its holster with a gesture of hopelessness. The Masai crouched again. His big chest indicated lung capacity, stamina; his rippling shoulders, driving power; his flat thighs and knotty calves, speed; his wide spread toes, sure footedness. And the white scars were evidence that all had been many times proven. It was an ominous figure of poised alertness, the Masai made.

He sounded the sibilant fighting noise of his kind and stepped on wide splayed toes to maneuver into a more favorable light. He held his great spear in an unusual and novel manner. Not with the point forward, as a lance for a thrust; but diagonally across his body with hands wide apart.

The giant towered immense over his crouching form; only his perplexed face was visible over the edge of his shield, and his long spear projected from the side. He was at a loss to understand what this curious pose meant. It looked to be defenseless, yet the growling man behind it seemed to vibrate power and confidence.

But the Masai was working into the better light. The giant made up his mind that attack, from behind his shield, was the proper move. He made a sudden, enormous lunge. The Masai swayed only his body, and with a swift stroke of his vertically held spear shaft diverted the giant's point to zip past his side. At the same moment he stepped in and with a heaving thrust of his lower hand brought up the spiked butt of his weapon to stab at the inside of the lunging leg.

The giant recovered with astonishing speed for his size and hid behind the lowered shield, alert for defense or attack. But a thin trickle of blood began to run down that leg.

The Masai turned back red lips and grinned at him. He taunted him with words the other could not understand.

"Ho-ho, thou jungle fellow that would deal blows without thought. Thou tree. By cutting the stem has many a tree been felled. Strike again, thou long wood, and receive instruction in spear play."

Though he could understand no word, anybody could understand the scorn in the tone. The man gave a great war cry and charged forward with the intention of bearing his opponent to the ground by superior weight, his spear held short for stabbing behind the shield.

The Masai defense was to crouch quickly, quite low, so as to trip up the attacker by the knees and then to stab him from behind. With an ordinary man this trick would probably have succeeded. But the giant sprang high in the air and clear over the Masai turning himself in time to make a long thrust at Barounggo as he still rested on one knee and hand.

The Masai ducked in the fraction of time below the point,

but the blade, flashing over his shoulder, cut a red gash in the muscles of his back.

For the moment King's heart stopped. The Masai's confidence in himself had bred a similar feeling in King, despite the frightful handicap of his opponent's enormous length of arm coupled with the defensive shield. It seemed now that the handicap was more of a factor than the over-confident Masai had been willing to admit.

Barounggo, too, astounded him by roaring over the cut like a wounded lion. It seemed to be an outcry out of all proportion to the seriousness of the hurt. But the incoherent bellowings began to make themselves clear.

"My back! Oh, my back! I am wounded and my life is gone! Never have I been thus wounded."

Screaming in his anguish, he rushed at his huge opponent and, whirling up his spear in both hands, drove at him with all his force. The giant took the stroke on his shield, and such was its force that the great blade pierced the tough double hide and protruded a foot in front of his startled face.

That was the giant's chance for swift victory. Had he retained sufficient presence of mind to drop his shield he would have left his opponent's weapon stoutly held in its cumbersome weight and his opponent helpless.

But the man knew no tactic of spear play other than the crude thrust and shield defense. He clung desperately to his defense and tugged to wrest it free. His precious moment was lost. Barounggo, tugging at the other end, tore the blade from the hide.

King saw the need for jolting his man out of the blind rage that consumed him.

"Does an Elmoran fight with his mouth?" he called. "Does he frighten his enemy with words and beat at his shield like a fool?"

The sting in the words brought the Masai to his senses like a douche of cold water. In an instant he dropped back and circled warily. Only the glare of his eyes and the dog grin on his lips showed the rage that filled him. A growling came from his throat.

"Count thy last ten breaths, thou tall spear dancer. Thy recompense is that thy ghost may laugh when the women point to my back and say, 'Lo, there was one who ran faster than he.'"

The giant felt that he had learned that when the other man talked was the time for him to attack. His blade and arm flickered out in another enormous lunge—this time with shield low to counter that swift return of the spiked butt.

The Masai swayed his body as before, pushed the thrust aside with his spear, and this time slid his hands together along the shaft, swung his blade in a whistling, horizontal stroke at the other's neck.

THE GIANT threw up his lowered shield in a panic and ducked behind it. The Masai's great blade, whirling like a medieval pike, sheared clearly through the apex of the oval, exposing the scared face behind it.

The giant, feeling his safety, was just beginning to grin his fierce derision when the blade, curving in a swift return circle, bit with a soft chuck deep into his unprotected thigh.

"*Hau!*" shouted the Masai. "A good stroke! Five breaths, I count it, O tree. Five more I have promised thee."

The giant staggered as the gashed muscles gave. Then in his last desperate hope to bear his smaller opponent down and finish it at hand grips on the ground, he charged in once more with shield held close and all the weight of his vast body behind it.

The Masai gripped his spear in both hands and braced himself like a bayonet fighter to meet the shock. As the mountain of man and shield bore down on him he drove square at it with all the force of his loins and legs and shoulders.

The combined impact gave a tremendous power to the thrust. Through the tough hide the great blade went like paper; through muscle and gristle and bone of the great chest behind the hide, and stood out half its length behind the back. It would have gone farther if the Masai's hand on the shaft had not smacked hard against the shield.

The giant jerked up short in his rush; a grating intake of the breath gagged in his throat. Then, slowly, he straightened up— and slowly, like a tree, fell backward. The Masai spear stood straight in the air, transfixed in the wide shield that decently, quietly, covered the death beneath it.

There followed a long minute of tense silence. A tiny rivulet of blood made a crooked path from under the edge of the shield. Then the hissing, steam exhaust sound of many breaths slowly escaping.

"Ss-ss-so," said the Masai, breathing hugely. "Upon my back did he put dishonor; but what shall the ghosts of his women say to the hole in his back?"

His nostrils were flaring wide and his eyes glared white against his fierce black face. A bass humming noise commenced to issue from his throat. King knew that he was preparing to launch into one of those impromptu declamations of braggadocio which are an outstanding trait of his people. Being stolid and undemonstrative, King always felt that these brag-fests, as he called them, were unworthy of a brave and strong man; but nothing, he knew, would stop the Masai before he had worked off at least a portion of the heroic emotion that remained as the aftermath of a good fight.

"*Aho,*" chanted the warrior, stamping his feet in heavy rhythm. "*Aho,* it is I. It is I. I heard a noise and I looked. My spear said to me beware. Lo, one came running swiftly. *Ow,* he was great; *Whai,* he was fierce. He put forth his hand and touched me. An Elmoran was defiled. Where is he, that great one? Foolishly he flourished a spear. Lo, I have seen many spears. Like an elephant he charged in his rage. What is this turtle that lies at my feet? This turtle under its shield? What is this that stands so straight before me? *Hau,* it is the spear of an Elmoran!"

This pæan of victory would have gone on for an hour. The

Masai would have recounted in flowery detail every action, each separate move—while the immediate future could bring whatever the gods of battle might send.

But King had other considerations to weigh and decide swiftly. How many of these hostile giants were there? How far might this outpost guard be from a village? There were two of the great shields. From that one could easily deduce two men to the guard. But how soon might others come? Were these men relieved every hour or every week?

That path, did it lead direct to a nearby village? Or was it only a distant entrance into this inhospitable country? If strangers penetrated into that country, would they be just herded out—or would they be incontinently speared? And if one entered anyhow, was it in the farther hills that the great apes congregated and would it be there that one might pick up the trail of Dr. Hugo Meyer?

And then King knew that that one was the only consideration. Was the lost scientist somewhere in those hills?

It seemed that he might be. The trail had led consistently there. Vague and evanescent, scarcely more than a rumor, yet there it had steadily pointed. And now at the last it had seemed to be definite. That first giant guard who now lay bound had distinctly understood the reference to a white man and had indicated the hills behind him.

King's frown sat deeply between his eyes and the pugnacious droop twisted the corners of his mouth. That settled it, then. If a white man were there, a white man of any sort, King was there to find out about it. So into those hills he was going; hostile giants—or monstrous mysteries of the dark that wore shoes—notwithstanding. And the sooner he went from this place the better.

"Peace. Peace, great slaughterer," he told Barounggo, who had reached his fortieth stanza, all about the disgrace that had come upon him because of the wound in his back and how people would jeer at him for it and how he would instantly slay them.

"Peace. Cease this bragging. And, since it was a good fight—though it should never have been—I will now quickly wash it and put a white man's medicine upon it so that no scar will show. Kaffa, there will be water in the hut—and open the medicine pack."

The Masai ceased his chant and looked his incredulous hope.

"*Bwana* has such a medicine? *Whau,* then there is no sorrow to this great fight. *Aho,* a good fight it was. A good stroke I smote. Like a—"

"Shut up!" shouted King. "Like a woman grinding corn do you sing. This is time for work. Bring here that shoulder."

Quickly and not too gently he washed the half congealed blood from the wound and swabbed it with iodine. It was a long, though not serious gash. Left to its own African devices, it would fill up with many kinds of dirt, and when the strong vitality of the man had finally thrown off the resultant infection it would leave a neat white scar. With simple hygienic treatment there would hardly be any mark visible. Sticking plaster, that godsend among bush remedies, completed the treatment, and the *safari* was ready to go.

The captured giant was a problem. He lay his enormous length on the ground and looked sullenly at King. He did not cringe, although in his mind there could be but one fate in store for him. Inherently the man was brave enough, as had been shown by his sturdy opposition to so large a party; but there was a certain awe in his eyes, an almost superstitious fear at these men, so small in comparison to his vast tribe, who yet were able to win against all the odds.

King looked down upon the man, biting his lip with a sardonic crooked smile at his own limitations. He knew what decision now confronted him; he knew how he would decide; and he knew his decision would inevitably rebound to his own detriment, perhaps even to the extent of death. He had been up against such decisions before and he had always suffered for his action, and he was going to do the same foolish thing again. And so his smile was bitter as he knew that his rule of taking no unnecessary chances must be broken on account of his white man's inhibitions.

Certain principles of civilization, he knew, and thousands of others like him knew, to be inapplicable to African conditions. The white man who so applied them placed himself under an inevitable handicap. Here was just another one of those situations in which the white man had to take up the burden. The African method was so much simpler.

"A spear stroke and the thing is finished," growled Baroung-go.

And Kaffa quoted the Hottentot of a universal proverb—

"The tongue that does not wag makes no trouble."

"Shut up," King snapped irritably.

He knew these things from long experience; and he knew that his followers would blame him—as the white man's followers have always blamed—for the trouble that would follow upon impractical squeamishness. He cursed inhibitions the more bitterly because he knew that when the white man's government went to war, then such squeamishness went by the board. It was when the white man found himself involved in a matter of life and death without the solemn sanction of the graybeards of his government that the "civilized" code must hold.

"Tie his hands behind and hobble his feet so that he can walk but slowly," King ordered.

And to himself—

"Damn it, I wish we knew how far his village might be."

To Kaffa again:

"Is there food in the hut? Put some in a basket. If he needs it for a long trek he can carry it in his teeth." And once more to himself, "He'll probably wriggle loose anyhow and bring the gang down on us. Hanged if I know, unless I set up a gangrene, how to tie a man so he can't get away.

"Come along," he shouted. "Speed it up there. We must get out of this and travel far in a hurry. There's nothing that we want here."

"One moment, master, one moment and I come," grumbled the Masai. He was standing upon the shield that covered the dead giant, carefully prying his great spear loose from the tenacious grip of wet earth and stiffened muscle and tough hide. "This is a thing of which we shall yet have need. Surely we shall have need."

Kaffa left King inspecting the thongs that bound the other giant, and came and whispered quickly to Barounggo. The Masai stopped short a moment in his tugging at the spear while the thought soaked in. His eyes showed white as they rolled furtively to the prisoner; then a ghost of a fierce grin played over his face and he continued nonchalantly to disengage his spear. Kaffa flitted back to fuss around King.

"Try him again," King told him. "The first time he was too full of fight to listen. See if you can find out anything about his village, and try him about the white man again."

The Hottentot chattered and made inadequate signs, while King fretted that in Africa there had not evolved any semblance of a universal sign language like that of the American Indian. The giant listened stolidly. If he understood anything about a village he made no sign; but to the reiterated question of white man he pointed with eyes and lips to the hills as before.

That was all they could get out of him, though King bade Kaffa set the basket of food beside him and indicate that they were going to leave him so, unhurt and alive. The man accepted the gift of his life with ox-like indifference.

"All right," said King briskly. "That's all we can get out of him. March."

Kaffa sped a quick look from under his brows at Barounggo

and herded the *shenzis* together with their packs. King stood at the mouth of the tunnel of thorn.

"Barounggo," he said quietly without looking round. "Do you go first with that ready spear—in case armed men spring upon us. For a little way I come last."

Kaffa exchanged a baffled glance with the Masai. The latter passed into the tunnel before King with a sheepish expression on his face.

"Keh-heh-heh," giggled Kaffa, unabashed. "What use? The *bwana* knows all things."

IN THE hills—at last the true hills beyond the long ridges of toil and tribulation. It was good country. Not too hot, though wet beyond comfort. The forest was forest, not jungle. The thorn belt had been left behind. That path had wound down the valley to habitations somewhere. King did not know how near or how far. He had struck directly across and made for the next ridge, and the next. He hoped he was lost.

It was easy country to get lost in. Trees were close enough and high enough to conceal all landmarks. Rounded green pericarps were evidence that nuts of various kinds would be ripe later in the season. Fruition in that climate seemed to be permanent. Vivid, heart shaped vine leaves indicated wild yams.

And apes were there. Solemn black faces looked down out of round, wondering eyes at the scarcely more intelligent black faces of the *shenzis,* who looked up out of equally wondering eyes and chattered with no more understanding. Nor were the tree folk any more afraid of the humans than the latter were of them. Long and steadily they looked and grunted, and when they moved it was with the heavy leisure of contentment.

It seemed at last to be the promised land. Good country for the great anthropoid apes—or for a white man who might be eccentric enough to belong to the school of raw vegetarians.

"The apes," King deduced, "have never been hunted; therefore they aren't afraid of man—which means again that this would be the ideal place for a scientist to come and observe them. But why—" musingly—"did those pygmies say that they came to loot their fields because there were no yams here? And why would the apes go so far afield when food is plentiful right at home?"

Kaffa quoted a proverb again from the wisdom of his people.

"When one's own food brings no appetite one visits one's relations. Their food may be worse, but it will taste better."

"I wish," said King, "that we had brought one of those relations along so he could ask them about this white man who must be somewhere around."

It did seem to be something of a hopeless task to find one particular person in those miles upon miles of forest, where one could not see forty yards through the trees. But King had been thinking of a plan which was quite simple and ought to be practical. He proposed to fire his rifle at intervals—the ordinary requirements of hunting meat should be almost sufficient—and then, if the lost professor were anywhere within hearing, he would surely know that his relief party had arrived.

The Hottentot's thoughts ran along entirely different lines. They persisted upon the humanness of the great beasts that observed them with the same slow, ruminative speculation that village elders bestow upon tourists.

"Look, *Bwana;* see that old one who gazes without fear? If I talk to him as I did to that giant of little wit whom *Bwana,* alas, left alive, will he not understand as much? And is he not much more friendly? Surely he will carry the word of our coming."

"Go ahead and try him," King acquiesced; and Kaffa, with perfect seriousness, clucked and chattered at the ape who balanced on a high limb, one long arm holding on to a branch above, and looked solemnly at the gesticulating human below. Then it emitted a croak and moved away.

"See, *Bwana,* see?" the Hottentot gabbled excitedly. "It told me, *kor au-au,* which in the bushman talk means 'all right.'"

"And surely," supplemented Barounggo with lofty prejudice, "that new friend of our Kaffa knows as much as a bushman."

King had to laugh. It was seldom that the Masai was able to score a verbal hit over the quick witted little Hottentot, who this time had fallen so completely into the trap of his own imagination that he had no repartee to make. In place of which he muttered obstinately—

"Even if he does not know the bushman talk they will talk among themselves and the word will come to the she of their people who is the wife of this white man whom we seek."

King said nothing. There it was again, that persistent reminder of what the black man accepted as perfectly natural fact; and King had seen too many weird things in Africa to lay down any didactic law that some new thing was positively not so, just because he did not know of it himself.

He was content to travel up and down this good forest country, to quarter the ground, spacing his routes by the approximate carry of gunshot explosions. If the lost professor—or, as Kaffa insisted, any of his family—should be within hearing, they would come.

I T WA S to the second camp that something came. It was growing dusk. The *safari* had eaten, and lay in sensuous enjoyment of the camp-fire in a grove of scented junipers. King sat on a folding camp stool before his little tent flap and smoked his pipe. The evening was still, except for the tree frogs that piped their thanks for the afternoon's rain. The faintest possible crackling of tiny dry twigs came downwind.

King reached quietly for his rifle. The *shenzis* had been trained at that sign to stop their uncouth jabbering. The whole camp stilled to listen. Something was moving softly in the brush. King's lips framed the question—

"Man?"

Kaffa shook his head. He rolled over and came up on his knees to whisper:

"Man would know enough to hunt upwind. Lion would know; leopard would know."

King nodded. It was true. The predatory creatures had learned to make their approach so that the wind would carry away their scent. Some non-predatory beast it was, then, that stalked the camp with such caution. There was comfort in that thought. The thing, whatever it was, settled down with the tireless patience of the wild to watch before it would make another move.

There was nothing to do but to match its patience and wait. Any move in its direction, since it was clearly nervous of approach, would bring about immediate flight.

More than an hour passed before the thing had gathered confidence enough to move again. By this time it was dark. The most cautious movement could be heard carefully working its way nearer. Kaffa hissed softly and pointed. It was at a sound in the shadows rather than at anything he had seen; though King had often thought that the little devil could see in the dark. King reached a long arm and groped in his tent for his field glasses. With their aid he could distinguish a dim shape that moved.

A form, no more. He could make out the size of it, not the outline. It moved quickly, through a lane of the flickering firelight. The sight was blurred, though he thought he perceived an upright figure. But Kaffa was crouching in the greatest excitement.

"Monkey," he whispered. "The man ape with whom I made speech."

King signed to Barounggo to gather an armful of dry brush and kindling wood and to hold it in readiness. He fixed his glasses on the moving shadow and waited. Presently his chance came. It stood in a clear alleyway between the black tree trunks.

"Now!"

Barounggo dumped the kindling upon the fire and blew a long breath into it. It blazed up. The figure gave a startled leap and was gone. But King had caught a fleeting view.

"Man," he announced. "A pygmy."

"Monkey," said Kaffa with equal conviction.

"Monkey would not be prowling in the night," said King.

"Man would not come from upwind," insisted Kaffa. "Moreover there are no dwarf men in these hills. They said so themselves."

"Bring a torch, and the tracks will tell," said King; and there was an uneasy wonder in his mind as to just what impossible tracks this indeterminate creature might have made.

But the ground under those trees was covered with the springy needles of the conifers. There were no tracks other than vague indentations.

So the talk round the camp-fire reverted perforce to what a man or an ape might, would, or could do; each side citing instance and experience, and the *shenzis* offering among themselves proofs that the thing could be no other than a wood devil. The last word was with Kaffa. All arguments, one side or the other, having failed to be convincing, he was left with a firm conviction. There could be nothing else.

"Very well, then," he said. "It could not have been man for such and such reasons, and it could not have been monkey for such and such reasons. Yet with our eyes we saw it. Therefore it must have been the offspring of that white man who married the monkey. Who else would be interested in us?"

And that logical solution satisfied them all, with the exception of King, who sat in his tent in deep cogitation as to what this new mystery of the woods might be.

Those pygmies, they had offered the same solution for the monstrous thing that had rushed out of the dark to do battle with them. To them the solution was perfectly natural and proper, as to the Hottentot it was a satisfactory explanation of this smaller creature.

But that first furious creature had worn shoes—if this thing were remotely possible; if so astounding a combination could exist—and King would have taken no oath that, in Africa, it could not. He was convinced, however, of one thing, and that was that it most certainly would not have worn shoes. He was building his own theory about what that other thing might have been. But what, then, was this? Good heavens, the woods could not be full of these incredible hybrids!

Only one decision could he arrive at before turning in. This inaction was all wrong; he was sure now. This sitting quiet in fear of scaring away the night visitants would discover nothing. He went to sleep on a plan to ambush the next scout, or whatever it might be; and he would then at least know whether he was dealing with furtive dwarfs or with some new creature— possibly some new ape, hitherto unknown to zoology—that could transcend some of the laws that bound the animal kingdom.

King's proposal was to go about the evening camp preparations as usual; to build the ordinary little fire and to lie around it in the abandonment of relaxation. Everything as usual, except that he and Barounggo—the latter on account of his superior physical strength—would lie out, perhaps in a tree, at some favorable point outside of the firelight, and stalk the stalker.

It was a good plan. If the night creature was an ape, the same curiosity that had impelled it in the first instance would bring it round again. If it were man, spying out the newcomers, he would come again to find out more. If he had already found out enough and if the night would bring an attack of his fellows, an unexpected sortie from the rear would be most valuable.

Kaffa, in charge of the *shenzis* in the camp, would indicate to the watchers by means of simple signals with a glowing stick in which direction the stalker might be approaching.

An excellent plan. And it might have worked had not the night stalker been so much more skilful than the watchers, both within and without the camp, that nobody was aware of his presence until his sudden warning arrived out of the darkness into their midst.

The first that King and Barounggo knew about it was a

yelping and crying among the *shenzis* and the shouts of Kaffa cursing them into silence, punctuated with the whacks of the cane that symbolized authority.

King tensed. If this were a night attack, it behooved him to give a little thought to his best move. Barounggo leaped down from his tree, ready to charge into anything that might be battle. But it was immediately evident, from Kaffa's energetic action to control the frightened porters, that no attack was taking place.

CAUTIONING THE Masai to be wary about blundering into any trap, King ran to the center of disturbance. The camp was in confusion and consternation—the reason of which stood starkly apparent. Out of the silent dark—even Kaffa had heard no sound—had whizzed a great spear which stuck now straight out from the bole of a tree.

"Douse the fire, fools, and lie flat," King snapped at the prancing *shenzis.* "Kaffa, scout a half round this side. Barounggo, there."

With all the caution at his command King wormed his way out in the direction from which the weapon had come.

He found nothing. No movement; no sound. He came back and found the others already there. They too had drawn a blank. The forest was as darkly silent after the coming of the portent as before.

"Well—" King gave his opinion—"whoever it be is as clever as a devil and this thing is a warning—he could just as easily have got a man as a tree."

He leveled the spear loose from the tree and tendered it to the Masai, the expert. Within the tent he lighted a campers' candle lamp and said—

"What, now, do you read from that spear?"

The expert examined it carefully, went outside of the tent to feel its heft and balance, and then announced:

"It is not a spear of those giant folk. It is better balanced and the blade is better set in the shaft. See, an iron pin holds it fast in the wood. Thus do we of the Masai set our blades. The blade, too, is not of this land. It is a blade such as the Banyan traders sell in the market in Nairobi. The steel is much better than of this land; but the style of the blade is foolish. Those who make such toy blades have never used one. The wood is of the black tree such as grows here—good, but too heavy. That is all that I read."

"Read yet one more thing," said King. "Could a dwarf man such as we saw last night—or a half ape—wield such a spear?"

The expert was immediately positive.

"Never, *Bwana*. To wield such a spear with any skill would require a man such as I; though for me the blade is too light for the shaft. To throw such a spear would require a man greater than I."

"Humh," grunted King, and sat in thought. "Not a Ruanda spear. Then the giants are not after us—yet. A trade blade, imported by the Banyans—those things are all made in Germany... Thrown by an unusually big and strong man...."

Those descriptions were definite and they pointed in only a single possible direction. What particularly big strong man who used a German made blade might there be in this lost end of nowhere?

The Masai broke in on his cogitation.

"One other thing does this spear tell, *Bwana*, though that, for *Bwana*, makes no difference. It says, 'Go from this place swiftly.'"

The corners of King's mouth dropped and the vertical indentation sprang into being between his brows. Then as quickly they passed, and he looked at his henchman with speculation.

"Would you go?" he asked.

The Masai stared in wonder at the question; as though the baffling developments of this thing, the dark mystery of it all, had driven his master off his normal balance to think in such a manner as he had never known him to think before. He spoke in almost a frightened tone.

"But nay, *Bwana.* How can this be that we should go away, having come this far and having accomplished nothing?"

King's hard grin dissipated the obstinate frown. The sturdiness of the Masai's intrenched viewpoint was a comfort.

"Good man!" he grunted shortly. And then his troubled mind harked back to his thoughts of a moment ago, and to himself he wondered, "But why should Dr. Hugo Meyer throw a spear as a warning to get out of here?"

ONE BENEFIT, at least, came out of that latest addition to the tangle of guess and surmise and enforced belief in the utterly incredible. If indeed it had been Dr. Hugo Meyer who had thrown that spear—and who else could it have been—who else could possibly fit into all the circumstances?—then there was no further need to go hunting through the limitless forest for the lost scientist.

The object now to be achieved was to have speech with him. But this was Central Africa and the way of man in Central Africa is not easy. If Dr. Meyer threw spears at people out of the dark and disappeared into the silence again, how difficult was it going to be to attain to that speech? And furthermore, if that speech should be attained, what sort of speech might it be? What gruesome thing might Africa have done in fifteen years to the scientist that first he sent an indeterminate something in the night to spy out the white man's *safari,* and then came and threw a spear into it?

For the moment King could see nothing ahead. Here he had arrived into the hills that had been his hard won goal. The difficulty had seemed to be the finding of a single man in that wilderness. But now, having found him, the new difficulty seemed to be a hundred times greater than ever before.

This lost scientist had of his own volition managed to get a letter out to his fellow savants in his home country, a fairly recent letter, for the man was still alive and apparently in the most vigorous health. The letter called for a relief expedition to bring out the results of fifteen years of study; results which the doctor in his letter claimed were of immense scientific value. The relief expedition had come; it was here—and the doctor crept in at night and threw a warning spear at it. The mystery of the whole thing was more than just discouraging. It was enough to turn any man back.

King ground his teeth together and swore to himself that he would stay in that forest till he could, if necessary, track down and capture the mysterious scientist and find out what the whole mess meant. Tracks once again. In the morning he must hunt for tracks and hang on the trail of his quarry till the final showdown.

But for this one time, that difficulty was spared him. The morning showed upon a distant tree trunk an irregular, lighter smudge that had not been there before. King went to inspect the product of the night and as he came near enough to distinguish it his pulse quickened. It was a piece of paper. A very crumpled, very much stained and torn piece of what had once been white paper. It was pinned to the tree trunk with slivers of bamboo. There was writing in pencil upon it.

The writing was in English, the broken English of a foreigner, wild and threatening, but perfectly coherent. It read:

> To the sport hunter, warning. You shall not these apes in this forest murder. If you will not immediately go away I make with my people war against you. My power have I shown. I can yet much worse perform.

The ultimatum was unsigned. But what signature was necessary? King read it and his pent breath broke from him in a great laugh; a whole hearted laugh of vast relief. This truculent warning made everything easy. Kaffa and Barounggo stood in the helpless wonder of the illiterate at the magic of script. King in his lightness of heart translated the ultimatum to them just to get their separate reactions.

Kaffa, the wise and cautious one, said—

"It will be necessary to sleep in *boma* and to set spring traps of the sharpened bamboo until this enemy be wounded."

Barounggo, ever belligerent, murmured appraisingly—

"This great spear thrower, if he has any skill, ought to make a good fight, a very proper fight."

King's heart glowed to know that neither of the men harbored the thought of obeying that warning and going away, and he laughed with carefree abandon again. To him the note made everything clear; it explained everything—or at least a part of everything; for nothing in Africa is ever completely explained. The writing explained nothing of the furtive, half human creatures of the dark; nothing of the insistent mystery of ape wives. But it did very clearly explain this latest development that had seemed to be the most baffling mystery of all.

King understood it perfectly, now. The scientist, his life devoted—fifteen awful years alone in the jungle—to his study. His secure retreat broken rudely in upon by a white man's *safari;* not a relief *safari* of German colleagues—that was what the indeterminate spy in the night must have reported. What else could this white man be but one of those so-called sportsmen who had penetrated at last into this lost haven of the fast vanishing anthropoids?

King could well understand the devoted scientist's rage; and he did not blame him one bit. He knew more than one or two such sportsmen whose necks he would like to twist himself. He was able to laugh, therefore, out of a full heart, and he felt an immense weight slipping from his shoulders. He was beginning at last to see the end in sight. This warlike warning could be quite easily settled.

King had with him, as credentials, the letter from the Herr Doctor Director der Naturforschung of the University of Heidelberg, which commissioned him to come in and bring out Doctor Hugo Meyer.

That night, therefore, King spiked his credential letter to the same tree of the ultimatum and hung above it as a guiding beacon his camp lantern. Then he withdrew his camp to a little distance and sat down to wait. And for the first time in many nights he let himself relax and take his full measure of unworried sleep.

THE DAY brought the expected result. And, though expected and awaited, it was startling in its suddenness. King was sitting smoking in front of his tent, listening to pick up any sound of approach from the forest. He heard nothing, saw nothing, till from behind a tree not thirty yards away stepped the figure of a man.

An enormous man. Not particularly so in height—though he topped the six-foot mark—but enormous in bulk, with massive shoulders and thick, corded arms, huge thighs and knotted calves. A tawny, bearded Hercules dressed in skins.

He stood a moment and took in every item of the camp through quick, flashing eyes. There was suspicion in his poise. Then with a lithe animal grace, in spite of his bulk, he advanced.

King sprang up to meet him, desperately ashamed at having been caught napping, and with unconscious mimicry of a world famous phrase said—

"Dr. Meyer, I presume?"

The huge man's eyes lighted in quick recognition of the words and strong teeth showed for a moment under his Viking mustache. Speech came to him haltingly, dug with an effort out of a memory of a language known long ago.

"*Ach*, so, the finding of Doctor Livingstone, no? From here not so very far. This also is a—a—how says one?—a like feat, yes? *Ach*, you Americans!"

King offered him his battered camp chair; but the man sank by preference to his heels and squatted native fashion. King called to Kaffa to bring the coffee which had been in readiness for the past hour, and to serve what was left of the previous day's broiled pig with the leathery corn flapjacks that took the place of bread, where wheat flour necessitated the labor of a few porters who would carry but thirty-five pounds apiece. The man's eyes lighted again.

"Ha, coffee I have since many years forgotten. Bread I have

from yams made but in the past. Since years I have no fire used. I thank you, I am not flesh eater. I have already a long time ago learned the raw vegetables to eat; and so, like my friends, I keep in the jungle good health."

King experienced a vague uneasiness. He had, as a matter of fact, been making up his mind to find the long lost scientist to be a good deal off the normal. He seemed, so far, to be normal enough. But that reference to "his friends"... That was the second time. In the ultimatum on the tree he had written of making a war with "his people." What friends? King wondered. What people? There was, of course, no reason why the doctor should not have established himself with some isolated forest tribe; but somehow that expression rang uncomfortably upon King's ears.

The doctor, of course, wanted to know everything. King found it difficult to adjust his answers to the incredible fact that fifteen frightful years of darkness had to be sketchily eluci-dated. Some major events the doctor knew with a certain modicum of accuracy; but all were most amazingly colored by the African minds through which they had passed.

He knew, for instance, that the war was long since over; that the *Bwanai Inglesi* now controlled all the country to the east of him and that the native chiefs were becoming strong again— absorbing insight into the native acceptance of the British pacific policy of colonization. He knew that the *Bwanai Belgani* controlled all the country to the west. But he did not know who controlled the immediate district in which he was—Which satisfied him well enough; for he inferred that nobody cared very much about it.

His contacts with natives had been sporadic and less and less frequent since the servants whom he had originally brought had died off—the fools would insist upon eating meat, he swore with sudden flare of rage at the recollection.

Natives, the doctor explained, never came of their own free

will into this retreat. It was necessary to make long journeys to catch them.

"And," wondered King, "what the devil did the man mean by that—journeys to *catch* natives?" That sounded as queer as the talk about his people. And with that connection the uneasiness that had assailed him before sprang into life as a strong sense of disquiet. "If there were no natives, who were his people?"

The doctor asked a thousand questions, mostly from a scientific angle—world events were of minor importance. Some of them King could answer in a superficial manner; but his answers never held the doctor's interest. While he spoke the other's attention wandered off the subject to gaze with acute interest at some trifle of camp gear, to look into the distant treetops, to scratch himself with absorbed intentness.

It came to King with a qualm of realization that the man, living that way, must be verminous.

But the doctor always brought himself back with a visible effort to ask some new question; and King began to find a definite connection running through all of these inquiries. They tended, every one, to inquire into the most modern developments in the study of anthropology, with a special curiosity about what was being accepted in the theory of man's evolution.

It began to be clear to King that the scientist's mind clung to a fixed idea. Accurate answers to these technical queries were beyond King's knowledge. But his answers did not matter. The doctor wanted only answers which he knew to be wrong. He chuckled to himself out of the satisfaction of a superior knowledge that was his alone.

What was being said about the apes? The doctor wanted to know. What were these complacent scientists deciding about their place in the scale? This was his subject and an excitement was growing upon him as he questioned.

King happened to know such of the more outstanding arguments, *pro* and *con,* as had furnished newspaper copy; and through his connection with an animal collector he knew that some remarkable experiments had been made with a young gorilla. But the doctor leaped to his feet with a single springy bound and strode immensely back and forth, his skin garments flapping raggedly in the wind of his own making.

No, no, that was wrong, he shouted; all wrong. The gorillas were all very well; but they were an inferior tribe. It was the chimpanzees that possessed a far superior intelligence. To these chimpanzees here an obstinate science must look for the link, the infallible connection. And he, Dr. Hugo Meyer, he would show to the thick headed world that—

He strode up to King and shook a thick finger under his nose, as though lecturing to a headstrong pupil.

"Look you now, sir. I will show you—I will before you place the proofs which I have now with certainness established. With your eyes you will see, and you will believe what—" With a huge inhalation the doctor recovered a certain measure of control over himself. His voice fell to an angry mutter. "But what use? What use? My papers, they have all. I have it written down. My experiments, they live. They will to those stubborn professors who know nothing give proof; and these murderings shall cease."

He came again to King, apologetic.

"You, my friend—you do not understand. But I shall show you, and you shall then my papers guard with your life. As I too, with my last life. Look you. I thought in the first sight that you were hunter—" at the hated word the doctor's excitement began to grow again; his voice rose—"a collector, come to murder these anthropoids for their skins; where so long no hunter has come. That is why I made you a warning. I shall not permit this murder!" The doctor stamped up and down and shouted, "I shall not permit! I shall defend. With my life I shall defend—" the thick arms raised themselves high, the fists clenched, the tawny, leonine head lifted back and the great voice roared its warning—"to the death I shall my friends defend."

T H E   H U G E figure stood on its tremendous, wide spread

legs, great chest outflung, eyes glaring, unmistakably snarling its defiance to the world.

And in that moment King knew it for the monstrous maniac thing that had rushed from the dark upon the pygmy mob that had hunted the apes with their poisoned arrows.

Kaffa, shrinking away from the little folding table where he was clearing up the meal, knew it too; but for another reason. He edged up to King and whispered:

"Look, *Bwana;* look at the feet. It wears shoes of rawhide."

The only sentiment that King experienced was pity. A vast pity for the man, overlaid with a certain awe. This was Africa. This man had matched himself against the dark gods of Africa, had adapted his living to the hard conditions of their jungles; and the inexorable gods, unable to touch the splendid physical specimen to put the mark of Africa upon him, had reached out quiet, insidious fingers and put their mark in his brain.

King's one thought was to calm the man down. When not excited he was perfectly normal. King told him a piece of news.

"But, Doctor, here is something that I'm sure will please you. You don't know perhaps that the Belgian government has formally set aside the whole of the Karisimbi Mountain as a sanctuary for the great apes, where no man may hunt under any circumstances."

For a moment it seemed as if this information would increase the raving man's excitement rather than diminish it. He glared into King's face. One hand gripped King's arm as though to wrench it off if there should be any trick about this thing.

"What is? What do you say there? Lie not to me!"

King repeated the information at great length. How a famous American explorer had campaigned to raise public interest and how the Belgian government had responded to the appeal to create this great sanctuary for the vanishing anthropoids against all encroachment for all time.

The scientist drank in this information. Slowly he absorbed all of it; and as he understood its whole significance he quieted.

"You will mean to tell me," he asked, still half incredulous that the white man in Africa could have shown so much foresight, "that all the anthropoids who live in—or who to Karisimbi may go—shall remain by the law from killing protected?"

King nodded. The scientist sank slowly to the squatting posture on his heels. It astonished King to see tears in those fierce eyes.

"*Ach Gott, wenn ich gewusst hätte.* If I had known. If I had this known, I would have—but it is not too late. I will immediately tell them and they shall go. *Ach,* yes, there will be a *Völkerwanderung.* We shall emigrate."

The great man smiled with an expression of singular benignity, as of some kindly nomad patriarch arranging for the moving on of his tribe to better pastures. He was apologetic again.

"You must excuse, my friend. I am angry when I think of these murders. My good friend, this is a very beautiful information. It is progress. Yes, it is good. But it is not enough. They must be everywhere protected. But you shall come. You shall see my papers, my proofs. You shall meet my Cri-ack, my halfbreed. You shall carry to the world my proofs; and they shall by law be protected. Come, it is far, my house."

He started off at a tremendous pace, walking King along with him, holding him by the arm. King hung back.

"Wait a minute. Ease up. I've got things to attend to here first. I can't barge off like that at a second's notice."

The big man checked his stride.

"*Ach,* your *safari?* It shall follow. My people shall show the way."

He lifted his head and barked up toward the treetops, and King was awestruck to hear a gibbering answer from above. The man started off again in a vast impatience, but King shook free.

"Barounggo," he called. "I follow this wild man. Kaffa comes with me. We mark the trees with a knife. Do you bring the *safari*. Explain to the *shenzis* that there is nothing to fear."

The Masai, watching all this extraordinary happening, leaning imperturbably on his spear, boomed comfortingly:

"It is well, *Bwana*. We follow. To these *shenzis* I explain that there is more to fear from me if they think not to follow."

The German was already disappearing through the trees. King stepped out after him. Kaffa trotted at his heels.

"*Bwana*, look; his wife's people are thick in the trees above us."

"Shut up," snapped King, and exerted himself to keep up with the tremendous pace set by their guide.

His head swam with speculation. Well might the Hottentot wonder. One thing, of course, was pitifully clear; the man's highly strung brain had broken down under the stress of intensive study of a single subject and frightful conditions of living. How badly or how permanently King could not guess. He hoped fervently that when he should get the man out—and that was going to be more than a small job—proper attention and rest might restore him to normal.

But how much was there to all this talk about his people. What were all these half spoken hints about proofs? Proofs of what? His people must be protected legally from being murdered—the man insisted upon calling it murder. Good Lord, that sounded as though he really considered them to be people. The Hottentot's firm acceptance of that forest negro's yarn about marrying a monkey. Absurd! Insane! But—what was the impossible meaning of "my Cri-ack, my halfbreed"?

All these almost insane thoughts raced in a confused maelstrom in King's brain as he struggled not to lose sight of the German. And above him the swoop and swish of heavy bodies through the branches indicated that the "people" were coming along.

King felt that he was walking in a Grimm fairy tale—a particularly grim African fairy tale, he punned to himself with a strained laugh. The laughing did him good. It released some of the tension; and the relief enabled him to think more clearly, to sort out the confusion in his mind. An explanation of the ape people's presence grew out of a simple application of wood lore.

It was perfectly possible that the doctor, living in isolation among the apes, never molesting them, knowing their habits, had established a certain sense of his harmlessness among them. Many a hermit had been known to tame the wild creatures of his environment. It was perfectly possible, too, that certain of the bolder apes—there were certainly not more than a score of them above, in spite of all the noise—having learned that the man often had food for them, or could lead them to food, followed him about whenever hunger prompted them.

And as for the apparent answer to the man's bark, which so impressed the Hottentot, King had seen native hunters locate *colobus* monkeys by giving vent to a sudden ringing call in the silence of the jungle, which the monkeys would invariably reply to with indignant chatterings at the disturbance.

The explanation pleased King. It refreshed him. It removed some of the gruesome mystery of the whole thing. Possibly there might be similar perfectly normal explanations of some of the mysteries that remained.

THE GERMAN strode on. His tremendous vigor was a tribute to the efficacy of vegetables as a salutary diet for the jungle—raw vegetarianism at that. A thought flashed into King's mind that possibly that was why the great apes never survived long in captivity; because they were given, among other things, cooked vegetables—those little understood vitamins, or something, were lacking. King stored this theory away for future use.

The wild man evinced no desire to talk. Apparently he had nothing to say until he was ready to demonstrate his proofs, his papers which were to be of such vital value to the world. What were these proofs going to be? Would anybody but a scientist understand them? The wonder stayed with King throughout the most strenuous day's march of his life.

It was approaching evening when the tireless guide suddenly stopped before no less a miracle than a woven wattle cabin of extraordinary symmetry. The vertical upright poles were of perfect thickness and alignment and the corners were of a sharp squareness that betokened a phenomenal skill in bush carpentry.

And then as he came close to examine the phenomenon, King was astounded to see that the thing was an iron cage; a great iron cage, the bars which had been interwoven with split bamboo to make a very compact wall. And then he remembered. Long ago—he had forgotten how long ago—he had read a newspaper account about some professor who had gone into the interior of Africa with a hare brained proposal to live in the jungle within the security of a cage to make a phonetic study of the noises made by apes and to trace, if possible, a language out of them.

He seemed to remember that this professor had come back with a claim that he had established a vocabulary of some twenty or more words. Was this Hugo Meyer the same wild philologist come back for more words, or was he another and more persistent enthusiast? The doctor indicated the cabin, apologetically again.

"In the early times I used here to sleep; but that fear is no more. The house is, however, of value my writings to protect— my valuable papers from the curiosity of my friends. I will show you. You shall see and you shall believe. Come, while yet there is light left."

The man paused as an idea came to him; an idea of not much moment, but one to be disposed of before proceeding to the important matter of the papers.

"You do not, I suppose, require to eat, is it? Or is it not?"

King could, at a pinch—and frequently had—gone without food for many more than twenty-four hours. But just now he saw no need. Papers that had waited fifteen years could wait a little longer. Furthermore, he wanted to see whatever there was to see by full daylight; he wanted to talk a lot more to the professor first, so that he might get an inkling of how he should receive the information contained; what sort of replies he should make so as not to occasion excitement; and particularly did he not want to have an excited madman on his hands in the gathering dusk. Therefore he claimed a consuming hunger that left him weak.

The eager professor was disappointed. But, except on his one subject, he was normal. Hospitality's claims could not be ignored.

"Fruit I have; nuts I have; yams I have. Nourishment for all needs of the body. Somewhere it is possible a tin plate I have, but I do not know. If cooking is for you necessary you must, alas, your own matches have. For fire I have not in many years known."

King was amazed again at the simplicity to which this man had reduced his life. Fruit, nuts, yams; all the food content for a balanced ration. If this single track man had so controlled his appetite that it needed none of the variety that civilization has gradually evolved with all its coincident ills, so much the better for him; and he certainly most abundantly testified to the benefit of his diet in his own person. But perhaps no one but a man single tracked to the point of mania could ever so have controlled the impulses of his heredity.

King had often made a meal less tasty than that which the doctor enumerated; though yams, to his mind, did very much need to be baked. Kaffa, turned inside out with hunger, made a fire; smelled out, or by some other process of wizardry discovered the store of yams and some plantains and had them baking in the embers while the white men were still talking about the need as against the dispensability of fire.

After the meal King smoked. The doctor evinced no desire for tobacco; he seemed to have reduced his desires to the simple needs of an animal—of one of his apes. It was dark. King was glad. Those disturbing documents would have to be postponed till the next day. He was willing to talk; or rather, to listen to the fanatic talk about his subject that was of such vast importance to the world.

"Look you now," said the scientist. "Tomorrow I show you and you shall believe. Tonight I tell you and you shall laugh. It does not matter. Those others, those doctors of the university who know so much, they shall laugh—until they my papers have seen.

"Listen now with care. *Imprimis*—" the lecturer was to the fore—"*Imprimis* I have a full vocabulary established. One hundred and six words. In my papers it is written down—System Hugo Meyer, upon the phonetic of Gaston Larue based; every known sound can be thus written. By a study of the phonetic and a good practise of the tongue a man may the anthropoid sound also reproduce and he will understand. Presently I shall from the tree one summon and you shall hear. Good. But that is small things. That is nothing. Wait yet and I tell you."

"Nothing?" thought King to himself. If the man called that stupendous achievement nothing, what marvel had he yet to disclose? If it were actually so that the man had isolated as many sound groups as he claimed and had connected a meaning to each, or even to half as many, why, then, that would be a language; that would mean the power of consecutive thought; it would mean—King hesitated to let himself speculate what it might mean, if all this were not the imaginings of an overenthusiastic brain.

King wondered. The man talked so sanely. It was only when he was excited upon the subject of killing that he went into maniac rage. Could it be possible that he was normally balanced when he spoke of a vocabulary?

He was talking with perfect normality now. His great hand fell upon another packet of papers, a fat notebook with many inserted sheets, all neatly bound together with twisted grass fiber.

"Here, my friend, I have—" he looked at it and stopped.

His mood changed. The feverish eagerness with which he had been expounding his thesis lost its interest. He smiled in his tawny beard, half pityingly, disdainfully. He shrugged his big shoulders.

"This is—yes, this also represents a labor. But—it is foolishness. *Gott,* how foolish is man! Look, here is complete description with drawings from microscope of a fungus. A very unusual fungus of mold. In the time of war I was for this fungus searching; but I did not until long afterward isolate it. It does not matter.

"In the native condition here where I have isolated it with much trouble, the rain keeps all things so moist that the fungus does not grow. In foodstuffs, which must above all things be preserved dry, you see, my friend, how this thing is a danger. For eradication the complete burning of everything is necessary.

"Look you, this fungus, it is very extraordinary; it propagates in the dry, not in the moist. It is of the family of the dry rot; and it propagates with a quickness like the devil and in time of war this fungus—one little pinch, so—if it shall be placed in the food supplies of an enemy, will quickly spread through everything. This is a weapon more deadly than guns; for it is silent and it can with only very great difficulty be stopped."

The scientist was deadly serious.

"My friend, I tell you that who in a war has this weapon can spread the mold in all the foods of his enemy. This is a terrible thing, is it not? But—" the mood changed swiftly again to a lofty pity for the follies of man, and the strong, blond, hairy hand swept the packet aside—"this is nothing. It is of no importance. I tell you something better. I tell you something of very much bigger importance." Enthusiasm glowed in the fierce eyes again. The leonine face lighted with interest. "I tell you— no, I do not tell. You shall not laugh. I show you my Cri-ack."

HE WENT to the steel door of his queer composite home and called out into the night. King's eyes were glued in fearsome fascination upon that deadly packet. That was the work, then, that had been so important as to render this man immune to military service. That explained the notation which the conquerors had found in the records. That explained, too, the mysterious source of funds to the impoverished university.

The thing came over King with sudden horror. Good Lord, could this be literally true?

He was living through a fairy story now; a wild romance of men and apes and jungle, far from the known world. But, great heavens, could it be possible that this scientist with his deadly concentration of purpose had actually discovered a new and terribly insidious weapon of destruction? A weapon that he brushed aside as of no importance in comparison with his obsessing interest in his apes?

The monomaniac was calling into the jungle.

"Cri-ack!" he called, and King could distinguish other sounds which seemed to be restricted in their gamut to various renderings of grunts and squeaks; no scale between these seemed to exist.

Perhaps they were words; perhaps no more than calls in various tones. King could not tell. A dread expectancy encompassed him.

"Cri-ack," the doctor called. "*Kom mal her, du.*"

Something rustled in a low bough of a tree and plopped softly to the moist ground somewhere beyond the circle of Kaffa's firelight. Kaffa left the fire and edged closer to the steel cabin.

The doctor called again, persuasively, affectionately. The something came hesitantly into the outer fringe of the fire light and stood upright, peering under its hand, but fearful of coming closer. It stood in the dim outer fringe and made cricket-like noises. King cursed himself that in the hurry of leaving he had left his prism glasses in his tent. The figure, as far as he could make out, was a pygmy man; not the same as those of the earlier jungle; a lower type, longer in the arm and shorter in the neck. But the firelight flickered horribly; King could not be certain.

The doctor stepped out to reassure the hesitant savage, to bring him in. Kaffa slipped close to King and whispered—

"The same monkey who came to spy upon the camp."

"The same," agreed King. "But man. He stands upright."

"Monkey," insisted Kaffa. "He is afraid of the fire."

It was the same difference of opinion as before; and it was settled the same way.

"Look, *Bwana*," the observant little Hottentot compromised. "Listen how with affection he calls. Surely it is his son. But like a monkey it runs to hide."

"Rubbish," snorted King. But into his mind flashed the doctor's own words, "My halfbreed." It was with a fascinated horror that he watched.

The doctor strode back through the gloom with that extraordinary litheness of step, annoyed but self-possessed and calm.

"He is afraid. Fire is a new fear to him. But no matter. To-morrow you shall see close and you shall believe. Now I tell you."

He paused, the lecturer once more, arranging in his mind his discourse so that his pupil might understand.

"I do not into the pathology enter. That is all in my papers for my colleagues to understand. All. With slides for the microscope. Sufficient I tell you this elementary. Those doctors, those *Dummköpfe*, have always said the difference between the man and the anthropoid is absolute. There is no link. It is in the blood construction. For them it is finished. The science has spoken.

"But I tell you, my friend, I, Hugo Meyer, have the science to be a liar proved." He thwacked two thick fingers into his other palm to emphasize his statement and his strong white teeth glinted in the firelight above the mane of his beard as he chuckled his triumph. "My friend, to you, since you have first come, is the privilege to be the first man to hear what is a—how says one?—a revolution, *ja,* an epoch, in the thought of man, in the science, in the religion, in everything.

"Listen." His deep voice sank to a portentous bass of authority. "You have seen my Cri-ack. Not good; but you shall see him better. You shall see others; not so clever like my Cri-ack, but similar. What do you think he is? Man? Or do you think he is ape? I will tell you."

The great voice whispered the secret.

"He is halfbreed."

King sat silent. He was spellbound, hypnotized by the tremendous force of this man. Whether crazy or sane, King was in no condition to judge. He knew only that there in the black African night, with only the fire flicker for light, this huge shaggy scientist convinced him of truth. The thick finger laid down the details of explanation.

"In the blood cell construction is the not-to-be-overcome difference, say those doctors of the science. *Unsinn.* Stupidness. They know nothing. Listen. I, Hugo Meyer, have made experiment where the difference is the least. I have the lowest type of man selected and the highest type of ape—I have the pygmy men kidnapped."

King was beyond surprise any longer. Anything was possible in that African night. It came to him, as a pleasing solution of a puzzle that that raid upon the pygmy people had not been for the useless and paltry purpose of looting a few yams but in order to obtain specimens for an enormously important scientific experiment.

The calmly convincing voice continued to state cold fact.

"*Ja,* it has been difficult, the men. They are so cautious to catch. Formerly I have the women kidnaped; they are easy; and they do not so much trouble with the mating make. But that was my mistake with which I have many years wasted. The progenys die—they are weak. The true reason I will tell you. The pygmy man for the male parent is better; for the anthropoid mother has the instinct for the rearing instead of the savage superstition. So are the progenys stronger.

"*Ja*, it is more satisfactory so. The men I can then let run away; the women I would have to keep four, five years. They have made for me much trouble. Always they wish with their progenys to their tribe to run. And I, ho-ho-ho, you can see, my friend, I am for a nurse not so good."

The natural, normal laugh brought King out of a dream. He shook himself to shake off the hallucination of reality. But the thing remained so damnably real. The more he thought over it the less improbable it seemed. The scientist was stating callous fact. Why not? Other scientists with the loftiest aims performed hideous experiments of vivisection upon living animals. They had coldly proposed to perform various experiments with condemned criminals. Who could say that this scientist's experiments had not been inspired by an equally lofty—or perhaps loftier—aim?

The scientist proceeded to lay his claim to the latter.

"And so you see, my friend, my Cri-ack and the others, they are proof that the so not-to-be-overcome difference in the blood construction *can* be overcome. I ask you then, is this not proof that the blood difference does not exist? And if this blood difference does not exist—" The scientist took a long breath and held it. This was the supreme conclusion, the ultimatum of fifteen years of awful devotion. His voice vibrated with his strong emotion and he enunciated his words with incisive precision. "Where, then, is the difference between pygmy and anthropoid?"

Excitement began to overcome him.

"What man shall say that between European and pygmy is a less difference than between pygmy and anthropoid? Where does man cease and monkey begin? You understand, my friend, do you not?" Passion shook the voice in a fierce gust, and the man strode hugely up and down before the dim fire glow. "One may not, by the law, kill pygmy. The law says murder. One *must* not, by the law, murder anthropoid who is a tribe not so much different from pygmy."

The fanatic gesticulated with his arms and shouted the challenge of his proven thesis into the night. And from the farther darkness his furtive proofs chattered to him in support.

Hurriedly King agreed with the shouting, stamping enthusiast. In the face of that cold logic—of those apparently incontestable proofs—in the looming African night, he was convinced. Or at any rate he was in no condition to argue with himself whether or no. He agreed. He said that it was indubitably so; that it was murder; worse than the killing of a pygmy, because the apes were peaceful, defenseless, unprotected—which, had he thought of it, was not so very far from his real conviction.

The German calmed down. He stressed the importance of his discoveries.

"You see, my friend. It is so, is it not? My papers, my proofs, they must before the world be brought. The science shall recognize. With your life you will now this so important trust guard."

King promised. At that moment he was convinced. Those documents and those living proofs—whatever they might be—must be brought before the world of science. Murder must cease.

Far into the night the scientist lectured. He gave details of his experiments, of his earlier gropings in the dark, of his progressive loss of human contacts, of the dying off of most of the native servants whom he had at first thought to be necessary, of the frightened flight of the rest, of his loneliness, of his gradual adaptation to the requirements of the jungle, of his slow winning of the apes' confidence, of his mistakes, of his weary reconstruction, of his troubles with his human captives—there was where the cage had been so useful. The whole story was an amazing jungle tapestry of a tireless energy, of a perfectly astounding fortitude, of a fanatical singleness of purpose.

To King came the thought: Where did fanaticism cease and mental unbalance begin? But he dismissed the thought; and he dozed over the tireless recital of technical details of cell construction which he could not understand. He dreamed fanatic dreams of debased savages and cultured apes and of a voice that droned on with an awful conviction of impossible things.

KING AWOKE to a confusion; to a hurrying and scuttling in the trees; a grunting and barking of orders and a gibbering and a squeaking of response. He was immediately wide awake and on his feet. Dawn was turning the blacker shadows to gray. The doctor strode back and forth, collecting various objects of his primitive life and throwing them into the big cage.

King looked quickly to the bolt of his rifle, wiped it over with his handkerchief and stepped to the scientist. That one barked a terse explanation.

"The Ruanda men. That at this time they should come. Never before have I had with them trouble. But only now I receive word that a war party comes. *Gott*, what a bad luck."

King did not ask in what mysterious manner he had received word; this was no time for questioning. He swore whole heartedly with the scientist. It was his white man's inhibition that he cursed. The penalty had come as he had hoped against hope it might not come. That wretched prisoner whom he had let live solely because his heredity and his upbringing had inculcated in him a certain code that distinguished between killing in hot blood and killing in cold blood. Of course the man knew that he was looking for the lost white man and so the reprisal party knew just about where to come.

Gratitude on the part of the man who had been spared? Bah! This was not an uplift story. This was stark, savage Africa. The white man had accepted the disadvantage of his inhibition and the white man must pay the price.

King did not feel that it was necessary just then to tell the fuming scientist that his trouble with the giant people *en route* had brought this visitation upon them; but to Kaffa he snapped the information—

"The giant men from the place of thorns."

The Hottentot let out a long hiss. He was humanly savage enough to rub it in.

"Ah-h-h. If *Bwana* who is so wise had but been wise enough not to let his eyes see or his ears hear."

The scientist, cursing his luck and his ill fate in a deep, continuous growl, called to them to come within the cage.

"Better here. These people have only spears; they do not know bows. These walls of bamboo are proof against such. Here we hold a fort."

"How many of them, do you know?" asked King.

"*Verdammt*, no, I do not know. They count not with ease, my people."

Even in the tense atmosphere of expected attack King felt the surge of wonder whether this bizarre thing could be true— this was daylight today; the hypnotism born of the night's fierce personality no longer swayed him. This hybrid Cri-ack creature who had presumably brought the news, was he a crazy creation of the fanatic's brain, or was he no more than a pygmy halfwit who hung about the doctor's home for the sake of shelter and food?

The doctor was bolting the cage door. He grumbled grimly:

"Your rifle, I see it is good. A rifle I also have; but my ammunition since many years is finished. For weapons I have no use. Only my friends live in these hills. They have the leopards chased away. There is nothing else. My weapons are these."

He lifted from a corner, both in one vast paw, a builder's broad ax, rusty from disuse, and a light lumberman's swamping ax still shiny along the edge from occasional wood chopping. A flashback of schoolbook memory brought to King a picture of a huge Goth ancestor with matted long hair and tawny flowing beard wielding just such an ax and shouting the names of heathen gods as he hewed his foemen down. Himself a good

woodsman, well used to swinging an ax, he knew what a terrible weapon it could be in the hands of such a physical specimen as the forest hardened scientist.

But all that was idle speculation. There was going to be no
foolish hand to hand encounter here. This was a matter of
holding a fort with arms and ammunition. The white man,
having accepted the disadvantage of his inhibitions, had a right
to accept the advantage of his weapons.

That was why King was anxious to know how many there
were in the war party. His store of ammunition was with the
safari which had been forced to camp overnight somewhere as
soon as it had become too dark to follow the trail of the blazed
trees. In his rifle King carried six cartridges. They were all he
ever needed. It was seldom that he required more than a single
one for the day's supply of meat. He carried a Luger pistol in
a belt holster, also with only six cartridge in the magazine; for
he adhered to what was probably no more than a superstition
of his father's, one of the old-timers of the six-gun days in the
West, who thought that more than six cartridges to a gun was
not quite decent. And since his father had taught him to shoot,
he had found that six shots were as many as a man might need
in a pistol.

Twelve shots. How many men? Would twelve be sufficient
to discourage the rest?

He was soon to know. Lank figures of abnormal height could
be discerned among the farther tree trunks. The number of
them could not yet be determined in the density of the forest.
An unfortunate thing, too, was that the doctor, with his simple
needs, had never found it necessary to make a clearing round
his cage. It was the sheerest luck that his native servants, while
he still had them, had felled the nearest trees to give sunlight
to their mealie patches.

King—so strong are the qualms of hereditary conscience—
still hesitated to take the advantage of the first offensive while
there remained the possibility of the parley which the foolish

white man always hopes for. But the Ruanda men had no stupid inhibitions; they were out to make a war.

The cage had a little square opening cut in the bamboo wattle of each of its four walls to admit light, making neat little barred windows. A light throwing spear whizzed through one of these and stuck in the farther wall.

King whirled with a certain grim joy that he was free at last. His rifle found his shoulder as he spun. It cracked like many whips in that slatted enclosure. The spear thrower flung his long arms wide and embraced the tree from behind which he had stepped. Then slowly, like a drunkard, he slipped down the trunk, sagging ever lower, till he clutched its roots.

"One," counted Kaffa in imitation of Barounggo who always tallied off his dead.

"So," said the doctor coolly. "You shoot well, my friend; as well as one would expect from one who has come here as you have come. But these holes we must with something defend."

The cage contained a couple of sturdy folding camp tables of wood such as the German outfitters used to supply to *safaris* in the days when they owned territory to which *safaris* might go. The doctor carefully removed his methodical piles of papers from these. With a wrench of one great hand he tore the lid from a box. These things could be propped or jammed between the bars to form shutters.

While he worked King's rifle cracked twice more.

"Three," counted Kaffa, without glancing from his work.

Three was true. But only three shells were left. King decided to hold these in reserve and drew his pistol. Thanking his stars that his father had taught him to shoot, he discarded right there his father's superstition about six cartridges. He swore to himself that if he should ever get out of this he would in the future carry his pistol magazine jammed to its full complement of nine, and one cartridge in the chamber besides.

A snarled oath from the doctor following on a rattle of spear heads against wood caused King to spin on his heel. His own front was clear. A volley had been fired at the table top that the doctor was fixing in place, and the tip of a particularly well hurled shaft had pierced the wood sufficiently to prick his hand.

"Quick," snapped King.

He snatched the board down and two fast shots dropped their men before the rest vanished behind protecting trees. The horrible proximity of the cover gave the one advantage that it was impossible to miss at that range.

Kaffa, on his front, was hopping before his window, holding his box lid as a shield and catching the spears as they came. King darted to his side and relieved him of three overconfident attackers who had thought that side almost safe enough to rush.

"How many, *Bwana?* I have lost count," panted the Hottentot. "These great men are devils; they have no fear. Would that Barounggo were here."

The scientist stamped from one shutter to another, peeping hurriedly through the narrow slits that he had left and fretting at his inaction.

"*Gott in Himmel!* You shoot *hundert pro cent,* my friend; but I—I can nothing help. *Verdammte Schweinehünde,* why must they just now come when all the departure is at last ready?"

The big man, inherently a nervous organism of enormous energy, could ill stand the ordeal of attack without retaliation. His anger rose with each minute and his great limbs quivered as he fought with himself for control.

King was husbanding his ammunition. Only one pistol shot and three rifle cartridges remained, and it seemed to him that quite a dozen giant figures still slunk among the trees.

American Indians in that number, as he had heard his father relate, would have had enough of that unerring shooting and would have drawn off, if not for good, at least to consider a safer plan of attack. But Africans—the warrior tribes—less intelligent, possessed greater animal courage. And these Ruanda giants had shown themselves, from their very first contact in the thorn belt, to be physically brave.

A YELL from Kaffa called King's attention to the hitherto undefended side of the cabin. He rushed to the shutter
board in time to see a long figure that had crawled, flattened
out under his shield, almost to the very wall. The last shot in
the pistol, fired straight down through the shield, must have
broken the man's spine; for he lay without a move and the shield
settled quietly over him.

Kaffa yelled a triumphal count of nine. But King was very
grave. His eyes were nearly closed slits and the corners of his
mouth were tightly drawn and white.

For that man had been earning a weapon far deadlier than
a spear. In the hand that protruded from beneath the shield a
twist of grass glowed red under a thin blue spiral of smoke. The
man must just have been blowing upon it preparatory to sticking in between the dry bamboo slats. King watched with a
nauseous fascination while the dead fingers tensed and curled
slowly over the bright flame and crushed it dead.

The doctor called to him.

"Those devils there, they are some hell thing doing. I do not
know what."

But King knew and he waited with ready rifle. From behind
the sheltering tree an occasional giant elbow showed, and once
the curve of a long back bent over a horizontal spear shaft. The
attackers seemed to be grouped together in that place, their
combined brains engrossed in their task.

King might have snapped a rifle bullet into one of those
incautious elbows; but he waited for the surety that was deadly
necessary.

A spear thrower suffers under the great disadvantage that he
must expose all of his body in order to throw. A rash warrior
thought to dash from behind an unexpected tree and make his
cast. But the rifle cracked and he lurched forward before the
spear left his hand. It buried its point in the ground and its
twist of grass went out in harmless smoke.

"*Gott!*" came from the doctor in a strained gasp. "*Gott!* That, also, they have thought of. My papers! *Du lieber Himmel,* my papers!"

Two shots left. Ten men, as far as King could make out; perhaps nine. It was very hopeless. Two shots would quite surely not frighten those men away.

But their minds had at last assimilated the lesson of that deadly gun. They were cautious, very cautious. And they were becoming crafty. The group showed themselves just enough to show that they were there. They stayed farther away among the trees and all that remained visible for any length of time were the shafts of their spears as they worked assiduously upon them.

King watched like a hawk. The doctor strode mightily in his cage, at times growling his awful rage and then trembling in fear for the papers that were his very life.

Time passed. The group of tall forms beyond the trees began to move as though on some concerted action. Something was about to happen. King held his rifle for a snapshot at the first advance.

The thing happened to one side of him. A heavy thud sounded low in that wall. A spear point projected through the wattle. While the doctor still looked at this aimless cast, a wisp of smoke crept between the chinks and curled lazily into the room.

But King had already torn the improvised shutter from its place. A lank figure was running for shelter. The rifle spat viciously after him, and he pitched forward in a long dive and slid on his face in the gravel.

The group of men yelled their derision and triumph. One more had fallen; but his spear stuck in the wattle and the red flame was beginning to lick higher with more fuel than the grass that it had brought. His fellows flung their arms high and danced in uncouth glee.

"*Verpfluchter Gott!*" It was an animal scream from the doctor. "My papers!"

He stood for just one moment in an agony of horror. Then

he went berserk. With one enormous bound he snatched up his broad ax, tore open the bolt of the cage door and rushed screaming out to the giant gang that massed together to meet him.

His mane of hair streamed in the wind; his yellow beard streaked over his shoulder; his garments of dressed skins fluttered behind. So must his ancestors have rushed roaring forth to battle to slay until they should themselves be slain.

King fired his last shot into the group. A man fell. Seven seemed to be left.

"Kaffa," he yelled. "Look to that fire. There is water in jars."

Then he, too, snatched up the only weapon that remained in the house, the lumberman's ax, and raced out after the screaming scientist. Passing a fallen man, he stooped and grabbed up his shield. He knew little enough about its use; as he ran he wished it were as familiar to his hand as the swamping ax.

He saw the raging doctor brace himself mightily on his legs to meet a giant who rushed toward him. The giant lunged with his spear. He seemed to miss. The broad ax whirled in the air, swung in both great hands. The giant went down, spouting blood, seemingly hewn in two from chest to thigh. Other giants stood in the way. The maniac roared on to meet them.

And then King found a tall spearman in front of himself. The man made a tremendous lunge at him. King caught the point somehow on his shield. His impetus carried him beyond the glade and inside of its scope. The man's great shield was up before his body. King swung his ax in with an underhand stroke. He felt surprise and a savage joy to feel it bite deep under the man's arm pit. The man screamed like a stricken horse and dropped below his line of vision.

He heard the doctor roaring somewhere close by, and a fierce shout following a crunching sound. A long black arm worked at him from behind a shield; a spear shaft rasped along his neck. He struck savagely at the arm and saw it turn suddenly red.

Clutching arms were round his waist, dragging him down.

He struck at them, but his ax fell on a shield. A rank odor of sweating African sickened him even in that fierce mêlée.

And then he heard the most welcome sound that he had ever heard in his life.

Long drawn and high, it sounded over the roaring of the berserk scientist and over the hoarse shouts of the Ruanda men.

"*Ss-zwee-ee, m'bale! Ss-zwee-ee!*"

The strident, hissing war whistle of the Masai.

The clutching hands slipped from his waist to his knees. His feet felt something that might be a face. Savagely he stamped upon it. He could see nothing. In front of his own face a great shield was pressed. He hacked at it with his ax.

Suddenly the shield disappeared of its own accord. In the space it left he saw a fierce, eager face under a rearing black ostrich plume and a great blade that he knew.

"*Hau!*" shouted the face. "*Jambo, Bwana?* A good fight is this!"

The great blade glittered a streak and disappeared.

"*Hau!*" shouted the Masai again. "*Ss-zwee-ee!*"

And then there were less of the lunging Ruanda giants. And then only one. His back was toward King and was going away fast. The Masai bounded after it and the great blade whispered *ss-s-whee*. Then there were no more giants.

King stood panting in the shambles, splashed a spotted red, nauseated with the reek of hot blood. The Masai with wide nostrils breathed it in. He stepped high footed over the sprawled bodies with ready spear—he was taking no chances of an escape this time. But there was no need. He grinned joyfully at his master.

"*Whau, Bwana.* A good fight, a very proper fight. But these people are fools. With their long spears and arms they should fight at long distance and apart. Massed thus like saplings swaying in a wind, the ax hews them down. Truly a good fight. But, *tche-tche*, it is my ill fate that I did not come sooner. Already had *Bwana* and that great man there slain—look, *Bwana,* the great one is hurt."

The big man stood, braced on massive legs leaning on his terrible broad ax. Face and hair and yellow beard were red from the spouting of that first man whom he had hewn nearly in two. The massive forearms were bathed in blood. The raggy skin garments dripped red. But the dripping continued in a steady tiny stream. Then King saw that the broken neck of a spear protruded from his right side, and that the man stood with closed eyes, fainting as he stood.

"Quick, Barounggo, hold him."

King jumped forward and caught the swaying figure. Together they helped him on sagging feet back to the cage and let him slip down to a patch of grass. Kaffa, unbidden, brought water and a grimy cloth. King washed some of the blood from the leonine face. The eyes opened wearily. Uncomprehendingly they looked as far as could be without moving the head. They saw the cage that had been home for fifteen years, intact. The tired eyes lighted up and looked their wonder.

"The boy managed to put it out," King explained.

A long breath filled the straining lungs. The doctor nodded.

"Good boy. In the box is still a little money—I give it to him."

He smiled slowly with closed eyes and nodded many times. He strained another bubbling inhalation.

"Yes, it is good. My papers. My friend, you make me now a promise. You will my papers take— By the Semliki forest you shall go out. North, three days; then east, ten days—Uganda—safe. Thirty more days to the English railway. My life, it is nothing. In my papers it is all written down. Those so stupid doctors will understand. You will my papers with your life defend. They are many lives worth. My proofs, my Cri-ack and his brothers, that will be now more difficult. But—you will tell—with your eyes you have seen. The science will believe—and this murder shall cease."

The tired voice stopped and the shaggy head rolled over. King thought it was finished. But the eyes opened once again and held King's commandingly.

"The science is pighead. It will demand with its own eyes to see. You will bring them. But not here. My people, I have told them. They go to the reserve of Karisimbi."

The lion eyes glowed a last flame and the voice took on sudden strength.

"My friend, you are a brave man. You give your promise?"

King nodded silently. The eyes smiled and closed still smiling. A whisper came from the lips—

"The murder shall cease."

KING SPENT a long day in that place; a day of cleaning up and of burials. He was glad of the strenuous work that made it unnecessary for his mind to think. He did not want to think about anything for awhile. But in spite of his resolution, an insistent question groped in the back of his mind—the question of this dark riddle of Africa that had reached out and drawn him into its maze. Nor did the succeeding days tend to elucidate one single item of it.

That night, as the collected *safari* sat about the camp and moaned in fear of the ghosts of the dead who must be prowling about the scene of their last fight, a something howled a high pitched shriek at intervals from the high trees.

"It is his wife who mourns," said Kaffa with conviction.

"You are a fool," said King. "He had no wife—and apes do not howl in the night. It is the man thing, whom he calls Cri-ack."

"Men do not howl in trees," said Kaffa.

And so the old argument was on, the question which must be settled; for its importance was vast.

Still another day King spent in that place, and another. He was trying to lure the Cri-ack creature to a nearer approach. At times he would catch a fleeting glimpse of it; but always in the farthest woods; never clearly. Was it hybrid, as the scientist claimed, or was it halfwit pygmy? King could never decide.

He tried to trap it. With all of Kaffa's craft and ingenuity to help him he constructed snares and traps of half a dozen kinds and set them with all the care of their joint command.

They were good traps; they would have caught the cunningest monkey or ape. But—it was weirdly extraordinary—*there were no apes.* The solemn black faces that had looked down upon them so contentedly had all disappeared. Kaffa said—

"His people have gone to shave their heads and to put clay upon their bodies for the period of the moon, as is due to the passing of a great chief."

King said:

"You are a fool. They have gone to Karisimbi." And he did not know why he said it.

The traps remained empty. The Cri-ack thing was too clever for them. They would have caught an animal, but not even a weak witted man.

King had a fleeting hope that he might glean something from the scientist's papers, some word of friendship, of reassurement for the creature, from that astounding vocabulary. But the explanations were all in German. Perhaps those German colleagues would understand and perhaps some student among them, with the stolid pertinacity of his race, would master that miracle language.

At the end of a week King's mind was made up. Whether the dead scientist were crazy or whether he were coldly sane, here was one mystery of Africa that science must settle so definitely that the world would know once and for all.

He gave orders to pack up the camp gear; to burn, as a careful camper should, the week's litter in the last of the breakfast fire. He packed very carefully the scientist's collection of precious papers and notebooks, wrapping them in a rubber ground sheet. In his hand he held the notebook.

The innocuous looking fat notebook with its many inserted

leaves tied with grass string. King paused in his operation of packing and looked into distant nothing through thin slit eyes.

Was there anything in that? Was it possible that a new and horrible weapon was contained within those closely written leaves? When the scientist wrote it all painstakingly down— that was years ago—had his mind already succumbed to the awfulness of the African jungle? Had it, for that matter, succumbed at all? King did not know what he thought.

But that book. That deadly, innocent looking book. The power behind the German university that had supplied the funds to get it out; would it find within those pages a ghastly weapon for some future conflict? Or perhaps—suppose on his way out that his ingenuity failed to avoid an overhauling from the British authorities and an investigation of his finds—would this weapon be theirs by right of seizure?

King pondered long, frozen in motionless introspection. Who had a right to this weapon, if any? Or had anybody a right to so evil a thing?

Then decision came. King shook himself out of thought into action. A hard grin split his face.

"Heinies or Limeys," he muttered. "It's all one to me—and I'm darn sure *we* don't want it. And Hugo Meyer was right; the other things are more important."

He stepped to the fire and dropped the deadly little package into the flames with the rest of the litter. He watched the string char and burst asunder, the stiff covers curl up as they blackened, the little lines of blue flame race along the edges of the paper sheets. And he laughed out whole heartedly.

The rest was easy. All these other papers; all that he had seen and would report. That was for science to decide; to come out with an expedition properly prepared, and to investigate and decide and publish. He called Kaffa and Barounggo to him.

"I place an order upon you," he said. "From here we go to Nairobi. From Nairobi I take train and steamer to this great man's country. If I should die on the road, as death may come to any man in this dark land, this is the order: You will wait in Nairobi. Whether I come or no, men will come speaking my name. The *Ngai* will have looked upon all of them, as upon this great man. You will bring them to this place with all the care that you know and you will tell them all things that you have seen. Is it understood?

"It is an order," said both men.

"Good," said King. Then to himself, "And I think, whatever they find out, whatever they decide, there will be sufficient interest so that the murder of the great apes shall cease."

CORRESPONDENCE

This note anent lion traps properly belonged in the same issue as "The Slave Runner." The incident Mr. MacCreagh refers to, if you remember, dealt with the imprisonment of the American, King, in such a trap by a treacherous native.

HOW DO I know what it's like to be in a lion trap with a big cat prowling about?

I know the best way possible. I've been in one. Only it wasn't lion and I wasn't shoved in by the infuriated local savage. I went in all of my own accord.

Why does any lunatic go into a lion trap of his own accord and stay there all night? That one is easy to answer too. Because it's safer in than out.

It was in the Shan Hills of Burma. I was out and everything went wrong that day. It got late. Camp was ten miles away. Darkness came faster than I could run. It was bad tiger country. Less than two weeks ago a Chinese caravan muleteer had been jumped and carried off a few hundred yards into the jungle. I bought him from the gang and sat up in a tree over him for three nights in the hope that the tiger would come home to dinner. But the wily beast must have winded me. He stayed clear.

When the bitten out parts of the Chinaman began to glow all phosphorent in the night I quit my useless vigils—and on the fourth night the tiger came and finished up his kill. Tigers are filthy feeders anyhow.

S O I knew that there was at least one healthy man eater in those woods, and probably a few others. But one was a plenty, thank you.

Ever been out in the woods and afraid of the dark? Let some movie hero try it when he knows that some four hundred pounds of striped hunger are padding along where he can't see his hand and where it can see the white of his eyes.

I knew where there was a trap. A nice new strong trap of stout poles with a fall door. If a tiger couldn't get out, it was hopeful to suppose that it couldn't get in. So I stepped out right smartly for that trap. I threw out the goat—and golly how that trap stunk!—and I let the door fall. Now let them all come.

And they did. Things that snuffled in the dark. Feet that stepped on dry leaves like pistol shots. Little feet that scampered off when bigger feet came. Eyes that glowed out of black nothing, motionless for long years at a stretch, and then winked in lazy indolence and went out like lamps. Spooks that wailed and whispered in the trees and prophesied bad luck.

How do I know what kind of feet or what kind of eyes? Maybe "tiger burning bright," maybe jackal, maybe porcupine— and don't let anybody tell you that a porcupine's eyes won't shine as big or as bright as a tiger's.

Tracks next morning? How could I pick out a track in close jungle—vines, rank grass, fallen leaves—I was never a Boy Scout. If I had been I would have known enough not to have been caught out far from camp in the dark.

—GORDON MacCREAGH

In connection with Gordon MacCreagh's story, "The Slave Runner," in the April 1st issue, a reader contributes some interesting information on lion hunting.

Pattison, Mississippi

I HAVE just completed reading Mr. Gordon MacCreagh's fine story, "The Slave Runner," in April first issue of your magazine. Before speaking my little piece, I wish to compliment you on your excellent magazine and its well written and entertaining stories. I have been a regular reader for some past years.

It is not my intention to find fault with your magazine, or to censure your authors for technical errors; I am sure that there are more than enough chronic fault-finders who will busily attend to those details. But I do have one complaint to make.

In brief, I refer to the passage in Mr. MacCreagh's yarn, in which he states, "But not even the hardest big game hunter in all Africa, armed with a heavy gun and the most modern luminous sights, will venture to sit out on the ground all night. A platform built high in a tree is the only safe perch in such conditions."

IN SO far as the above statement is concerned, I fear that Mr. MacCreagh has either been misinformed, or has never had occasion to hunt lion at night. He doubtless penned those lines from a knowledge of an East African statute which forbids any and all hunting between the hours of sundown and sunup; thinking perhaps that this was passed to protect ignorant and foolhardy hunters. On the contrary, however, it was meant to prevent the unsportsmanlike hunting of Leo by so-called sportsmen perched safely in a boma a score of feet from the ground. To such an extent has this practise been followed, that all night hunting has been brought to ascertain amount into disrepute.

But there is another method of hunting his majesty at night which is both fair and sporting; and I can name a dozen men who have gotten their trophy in this manner. For the benefit of Mr. MacCreagh and those others who are not acquainted with this practise I shall try to explain it in brief. First the territory is scouted for the proximity of lions, and if possible the remnants of a kill are found (in most cases lions will return to the spot of their last kill before making a new one). The next step consists of building a boma near the kill, or if none is found, in a spot likely to be visited by Leo in his nightly wanderings. This boma is made of thorn brush, and is usually four or five feet high, in the rear, about eight feet in diameter, and two feet high in front. A dead zebra is dragged to within ten feet of the front of the boma, and the hunter lies down to await the coming of Simba. In most cases the hunter has a companion who is placed slightly behind him.

WHEN THE lions have fed for a short time on the bait and have become accustomed to the presence of the men, the hunter signifies his readiness to his companion, who, holding a flashlight just behind and over the hunter's rifle, flashes it on the lion, thus enabling said sportsman to see both the hunted and the sights on his rifle at the same time. And although night hunting has been condemned, due to the use of tree bomas, the man who sits in a low ground boma, affording only imaginary protection, and gets his lion, has been fully initiated into the true sportsmen's fraternity, and is worthy of their regard.

It is a thrilling experience and not soon forgotten, for the low deep growls, the noise of breaking bones as they feed, the dim shapes seen scarcely an arm's length away, and over all the fetid odor which always betokens the presence of lions, is something which lingers on and is likely to be lived over again, particularly after a large dinner of too rich foods.

AMONG THOSE, who have shot lions in this manner are Al Klein (mentioned in Mr. MacCreagh's story), and Chas. Cottar, famous hunter and guide of Kenya. Mr. Cottar has shot more than a half dozen lions at night while sitting in a deck chair, with no more protection than a blanket pulled over him as a means of concealment. Too, I have gotten part of my bag from behind a low brush blind in the wee hours of the morning. And though I did it illegally, I am more proud than ashamed of having done so, for the night is the lion's setting, like all cats, and he is far more at home in darkness than during the bright

light of day. What with the continued use of the motorcar for
Safari work and the rapid decrease of African game, it will soon
become imperative that one hunt lion at night if he desires to
fill his bag.

It was not my intention to detract from Mr. MacCreagh's
fine story, but rather to correct the impression that many persons
hold of the malevolence and mankilling tendencies of African
lions. A lion is dangerous. Sometimes he's poisonously mean.
And when riled or wounded a killer. But he *seldom charges* unless
molested, and is *rarely* a man-eater. Let's have some more of
Mr. MacCreagh's stories. He writes exceedingly well even if,
like all things human, he does err occasionally.

—Russell L. Fox

*Following our custom, I sent the letter on to Mr. MacCreagh. Here's his
reply:*

New York City

THANKS MUCH, first of all, for your good word about
my stories. I'm glad that you do read them—even though I err.

Can't I argue with you a little about the erring? Let's admit
I ought to have said that a tough hunter wouldn't sit out on the
open ground. I mention the boma practise a few paragraphs
earlier. I don't go into intimate detail about just how a man may
hunt from a boma because of the requirements of a fiction story.
This story was not built round lion hunting. A pause at that
place to go into a little dissertation on ways and mean's would
have held up the flow of action. It would have been that frightful crime in fiction—irrelevant.

I did *not* know that the Kenya government had made illegal
all hunting between sundown and sunup. This is news to me,
and good news. I'd like to know how far the rule is enforced.
Up near Magi—that's on the Sudan border Of Abyssinia—a
certain official of the Sudan administration—Cambridge University at that lays out his kill under a tree and uses the platform

method. In Portuguese East, I suppose you know, that method is universal.

HOWEVER, WE can't quarrel with local conventions in sport any more than in conventions for the dinner table.

Personally, I think that with modern guns a man ought to have nerve enough to give his lion a chance. I'd like to see the rule about getting out of the automobile before shooting enforced to standing at least, say, a hundred yards from the car before shooting.

Though I don't say that I would have all that nerve myself.

Shooting from an automobile—and with the engine running, at that, as some bright scions of wealth have done—is one of the most disgusting things in modern African sport. Many jumps worse than shooting from a tree.

Incidentally, about the tree. My man in the story doesn't advocate that method to any aspiring hunter. My comment is only that it is the only *safe* place. Which is true. The boma is not safe; and that is what makes a sport of it rather than a slaughter.

Reverting again to local conventions. The Sahib who sits up for his tiger in a tree isn't looked down upon by any compatriot in India. In fact, that is the way the thing is done. Yet it is an astounding anomaly that in *French* Indo-China a feeling has grown that one ought to sit out for tiger in boma.

AS TO "correcting the impression" of the malevolence and man-killing tendencies of a lion. I haven't intended to give this impression. In fact, on page 18 paragraph 3, I especially mention that a lion might do anything; that he might "run like a whipped dog for no reason," might "crouch in indifference," or might "charge with ferocity."

And right after that I have *Kingi Bwana* expound what ought to be the real nervy way of shooting lion.

How come you missed the horrible blunder about the calibre of big game guns? Or didn't you? Or did you perhaps guess the truth that it was a typographical error? Page 15, sixth paragraph: *Kingi Bwana* tells the youngster that nothing lighter than .145 or .157 is safe. I've already had two most godawful bawlings out over it. My typist, copying my script, typed ones instead of fours. And I can't fire the typist 'cause she's my wife. I can fine her one new dress though; and that's what she's got.

—GORDON MACCREAGH

A further letter in the correspondence between Gordon MacCreagh and Russel L. Fox on the subject of sportsmanship in big game hunting.

Pattison, Miss.

DEAR MR. MacCREAGH: As you say in your letter, there is too much of this unsportsman-like propaganda foisted on the minds of the public. Most of it done by a group of millionaire sports, lusting after trophies and caring little how they get them as long as they have them to crow over and boast about to their foolish and admiring friends. Big game hunting under such conditions degenerates from a field of true sport to wanton brutal murder.

Yes, there are laws both in Kenya and Tanganyika now which forbid the hunting of any game between the hours of sundown and sunrise. These laws were passed with the indention of preventing the unsportsman-like practise of hunting game from tree bomas. I can not say that I approve of the law as a whole, but I suppose that it is the only effective method of combating the pernicious habit of hunting from trees. The other method (that of hunting from the ground) I consider quite sportsman-like, for in most cases the boma is low enough to permit one to see over the top of its front wall from a sitting position, there being no top on the boma.

The primary object of such a structure is that of a blind, and the only protection afforded is psychological. A friend of mine, Mr. Chas. Cottar, of Nairobi, has shot lion without any other light than that of the stars or the moon, without other concealment or protection than that of a blanket thrown over the steamer chair in which he was sitting. But I suppose that he takes chances which many men would avoid, and too he has been mauled badly on several occasions as a result of his indiscretions.

HOW BITTERLY true are your conclusions as to the practise of shooting game from motor cars. The tragic part of it is that this is followed mostly by our own American citizens, that is, among the scions of wealth of whom you spoke.

They have a rather efficient system of keeping tab on hunters out on the East coast now. Simple and very, oh very expeditious. The game department offers a very liberal reward to the native or natives who secure the conviction of a game law violator. The hell of it is that the natives, being without morals and withal quite greedy, oftentimes swear to a deliberate lie in the hopes of profiting from a conviction. It is needless to say that a white man's word (particularly that of a defendant) is often discredited by the testimony of his shenzie accuser. One would naturally and quite correctly infer that under such conditions the game department does not have the hearty cooperation of the settlers.

RATHER AN amusing incident happened recently, while I was out in Kenya. A game warden passing near a poor settler's farm stopped for a drink and a bit of a chat. While there, he noticed a fresh eland-hide rug on the floor. The family being naturally courteous and not wishing to offend the warden's feelings tried in a tactful manner to get rid of him. But being possessed of a very thick skin, and seemingly unaware of their delicate hints, he lingered on. At last in desperation the family were forced to serve lunch (already delayed an hour) and to invite the warden.

At first they served no meat but were at length forced to, due to the warden's comments on the delightful aroma emanating from cooking meat. They served the meat (eland steak). The warden finished his meal. Then asked the host for his license.

The poor devil had none—not even a 10 shilling license for hunting on his own land. I sincerely doubt if he had the price. The warden confiscated the rest of the eland flesh, took the unfortunate fellow into custody, and naïvely admitted that he had practically forced the family to invite him to lunch so that he might obtain enough evidence for a conviction, as the hide alone was not enough evidence to warrant an arrest. You can imagine how tickled the other settlers were to hear about the warden's little joke.

The game department is simply rotten with graft (if I am informed correctly), concessions to hunt in Tanganyika, professional guides licenses to hunt there; these being issued at the discretion of the head game warden, who may grant these privileges to whom he pleases, but may not be compelled to issue them to any one.

—RUSSELL L. FOX

Somebody questioned Gordon MacCreagh about that vast double barreled gun shooting a bullet weighing a quarter of a pound, mentioned in his recent story, "The Slave Runner." He thought his answer might be of interest to the rest of us, so he sent this note along:

New York City

I MEANT the vast double barreled *smooth*-bore, the identical gun used by Sir Samuel Baker, greatest of old-time British hunters. Himself a very large and strong man he had guns built especially for him which were rather heavier than the average hunter would care to carry. But Sir Sam was a gun crank. This identic gun is now in Nairobi. It is a six bore; that is, six spherical balls to the pound; not quite a quarter pound to the ball.

The charge was about 100 grains of the powder used in Sir Samuel's time, *and*, as in the case of the gun, especially mixed for him. I am not expert enough to know exactly in what manner that powder differed from the "black" powders of today. In Sir Sam's time manufacturers were already experimenting with improved powders; and, since they were not the modern "smokeless," they were all spoken of as "Black."

Aside from Sir Samuel's own gun, several such guns were turned out by Purdey of London. They may still be purchased as rather expensive curiosities in various parts of Africa.

AS TO my statement, "bullets weighing about a quarter of a pound": I have in my possession a spherical ball of this exact weight. That would mead it was made for a four bore smooth-bore. I have not seen the gun myself, but accept the statement of its existence from Sir Samset Jang of Nepal, India, who a long time ago gave me the balls.

Incidentally, it will interest readers to know that Oriental elephant hunters used to use a huge thing that threw a ball of half a pound and had to be propped up on a forked stick, like an early arquebus. I have no means of guessing what the charge might have been. Such a weapon may be seen in the museum in Calcutta.

—GORDON MACCREAGH

Gordon MacCreagh offers us some information on the question we put to old Africanders at one of our recent meetings.

Huntington Beach, L.I.

HERE IS one of the coupla hundred replies you will doubt-less get to the "must" elephant query.

The word is really *musth*, a Sanskrit word meaning lustful, or sex crazy. It has been taken into Urdu and thence into Hin-dustani, from which it has been Anglicized into must.

It is applied by their mahouts to elephants in captivity when they, the males only, exhibit signs of sex urge during the breed-ing season. The symptoms are nervousness, irritability, loss of appetite, and an ill-smelling discharge from the pits between eye and ear.

By no means do all male elephants *go musth*. Some never do.

Some exhibit the symptoms every season. An alert mahout can always detect the signs before any damage is done. Upon noting the signs, precautions to be taken are, naturally, to see that the animal is very securely chained to its stake by the hind leg, to avoid exciting it, to keep clear, and to feed it various herbs which are supposed to be cooling and soothing.

Native mahouts have a weird list of things which are supposed to be efficacious; amongst them are chirretta twigs, saltpetre, and opium.

I don't know what veterinary practise has to say for or against any of these. I do know that, working a gang of teak elephants, I had an old chief mahout who talked the elephant language, who used to tell the lusty young males that women were no good anyway, and who would give them balls of opium as big as his fist wrapped up in rice flapjacks. The trouble symptoms would pass off in a couple of weeks, and the animal could then be worked again with perfect safety.

The main trouble with *musth* is that frequently a commercial concern, hating to lose a couple of weeks' work out of a beast that cost as much as fifty men to keep, hopes to continue work with an animal whose symptoms are not very pronounced; and then, something happens to irritate the beast and he goes right off the handle. And, having gone, it is up to his immense dignity to smash things up all around just to work off his temper.

Mahouts say that wild elephants never go *musth*, for the reason that they are not forcibly kept in unnatural sex conditions.

They are awfully human things, are elephants.

It would be right interesting to hear from someone who has had experience with the African elephants that the Belgian government has trained to work in the Congo country.

—GORDON MACCREAGH

A note from Gordon MacCreagh, of our writers' brigade, about the diet of condors:

Centerport, L.I.

HAS NOBODY written in as yet to say that condors regularly raid the Chincha Islands? These are the guano islands off the Peruvian coast that pollute so much of the southern atmosphere when the wind is right. The Peruvian government maintains a small staff of rifle sharpshooters on the islands for the, sole purpose of shooting off the condors, which they accuse of eating the eggs *and young* of the guano birds that nest there.

It seems that the inference would be, not that condors object to fresh meat, but that they are not equipped to pursue and capture live animals; at all events, no live animals that have any agility or speed.

I can't imagine that a dog just killed by anything else would taste any different than a dog just killed by a condor. All that would be necessary would be for the condor to be able to catch and kill his dog.

And if a fledgling in a nest tastes good to a condor, why not a grown up chicken—if he could catch it?

—GORDON MACCREAGH

THE MEN WHO MAKE THE ARGOSY

I CAN'T LIE about my age because it's in *Who's Who,* and it's older than I like to believe because I aim to go world tramping as soon as I can get money enough to leave my wife at home—if she'll let me. For the old days are gone—and wonder whether there might be eats and a camp cot wherever it might be that I would arrive.

That was the way I began. I was getting an education in a German university when I seconded a sap in a duel, and it turned out more serious than we had thought; so everybody concerned laid low for a while. Me, I had been writing to a man in Calcutta—where one shook the rupee trees and gathered wealth and glamour at the same time. This kind gentleman promised me a salary of 200 rupees per month if I would take a job in his barge business.

Well, barges were as good as anything else in the romantic East. I worked out as an under steward; and the kind gentleman gave me the job. But at the end of a month when I asked him for some rupees, he said, Oh, yes, he'd give me 200 of them per month—as soon as I had learned the barge business and was of some use to him.

So I had a fight with his son-in-law and got fired, and I took a train and went as far as it went That was Darjeeling. I became a tea coolie driver and collected those marvelous Himalayan beetles and butterflies for a museum collector And from that I graduated to collecting on my own. I got into bigger stuff. Live

animals for Jamrach, then the big Liv-
erpool dealer. I understand during the
war they ate them all up. I moved into
the Malay islands and sent in various
leopards and tigers and things. But my
specialty was big snakes and orang-
utans.

The war came along. I came home
and lost a lot of time in a Navy training station. In the Navy I met a god
called Discipline.

A couple of years sped. I sold my
outstanding worth to a scientific expedition that proposed to find new
end uncharted ways across South America, over ghastly Andean
passes and through the whole length of the Amazon valley,
which is quite a large and a wet place.

Then a spell of writing it all Up. Then a quite crazy dash to
Abyssinia—because nobody seemed to know anything much
about it.

But my fate had descended upon me by this time; and she
was crazy, too, and came along—and suffered for her temerity.

Thin tent walls out in the open bush and lion noises outside
rasped her nerves all up. And drove her crazier; so she came
again the next time.

That time took us further into the interiors of things. British
East Africa and Uganda borders. And we bought some mules
that bad been scientifically inoculated against tsetse fly so that
we wouldn't have to bother with the hideous porter safari
problem. And the tsetse flies killed off half the mules anyhow,
and we struggled on into bad country, and lions ate up the rest.
So we had our safari after all. And the safari was tsetse speckled and ran away in heaps. And we lost baggage and were sick
and the rainy season came along and caught us out in the woods;
and a good time was had by all. So we came home.

Third class on a French boat to Japan—and don't you ever try that—and on to Seattle. Then we bought a used—a very used—flivver and came across continent via the auto camp routes. And we took in Columbia River Highway and Yellowstone Park and Jackson's Hole and Shoshone Canyon and Dead wood and Cody and Custer and all the places where we found all the names of our youthful readings to be honest to God true places—Dead Man's Gulch and Two Mile Bend and Snake River and Massacre Rocks and Poison Springs. And we got an awful kick out of it all.

—GORDON MACCREAGH

www.ingramcontent.com/pod-product-compliance
Lightning Source LLC
Chambersburg PA
CBHW050125030726
47505CB00007B/2042